"Damn you, Lacy!"

"You can close your eyes and think of England," she whispered mischievously, because this was fun. It was really fun, taunting him. The idea of seducing Cole and making him enjoy it was the most delicious fun she'd had in eight long months. And if there was a little revenge mixed up in it, so what?

He muttered something under his breath, finished his cigarette, and slammed it into the fireplace. "Damn you!" he repeated.

She moved around in front of him, making him look at her. "Why did you come to me that night, if you didn't want me?"

"I did ... want you," he bit off.

"And now you don't? I'll come home, Cole. But on my terms."

Oh God, she was killing him by inches! His body felt like drawn cord. What she was demanding was impossible, but he couldn't let her carry out her threat. He did want her; terribly. "Your terms," he said curtly. "Blackmail, you mean."

LACY

Diana Palmer

IVY BOOKS • NEW YORK

Ivy Books
Published by Ballantine Books
Copyright © 1991 by Susan Kyle

Library of Congress Catalog Card Number: 91-92200.

ISBN 0-8041-0790-4

Printed in Canada

First Edition: December 1991

For my agent, Maureen Walters, of Curtis Brown, Ltd., with love and thanks.

══ Chapter One ══

THE PARTY WAS GETTING NOISIER BY THE MINUTE. Lacy Jarrett Whitehall watched it with an air of total withdrawal. All that wild jazz, the kicky dancing, the bathtub gin flowing like water as it was passed from sloshing glass to teacup. She wasn't really as much a participant as she was an onlooker. It made her feel alive to watch other people enjoying themselves. Lacy hadn't felt alive in a long time.

Many of the neighbors were elderly people, and she suffered a pang of conscience at what, to them, must have seemed like licentious behavior. The Charleston was considered a vulgar dance by the older generation. Jazz, they said, was decadent. Ladies smoked in public and swore—and some actually wore their stockings rolled to just below the kneecap. They wore galoshes, unfastened, so that they flapped when they walked— hence the name given to the new generation: flappers. Shocking behavior to a society that had only since the war come out of the Victorian Age. The war had changed everything. Even now, four years after the armistice, people were still recovering from the horror of it. Some had never recovered. Some never would.

In the other room, laughing couples were dancing merrily to "Yes, We Have No Bananas" blaring from

Lacy's new radio. It was like having an orchestra right in the room, and she marveled a little at the modern devices that were becoming so commonplace. Not that any of these gay souls were contemplating the scientific advances of the early twenties. They were too busy drinking Lacy's stealthily obtained, prohibition-special gin and eating the catered food. Money could almost buy absolution, she mused. The only thing it couldn't get her was the man she wanted most.

She fingered her teacup of gin with a long, slender finger, its pink nail perfectly rounded. The color matched the dropped-waist frock she was wearing with its skirt at her knees. It would have shocked Marion Whitehall and the local ladies around Spanish Flats, she thought. Like her friends, she wore her hair in the current bobbed fashion. It was thick and dark and straight, and it curved toward her delicate facial features like leaves lifting to the sun. Under impossibly thick lashes, her pale, bluish-gray eyes had a restlessness that was echoed in the soft, shifting movements of her tall, perfectly proportioned body. She was twenty-four, and looked twenty-one. Perhaps being away from Coleman had taken some of the age off her. She laughed bitterly as she coped with the thought. Her eyes closed on a wave of pain so sweeping that it counteracted the stiff taste of the gin. Coleman! Would she ever forget?

It had all been a joke, the whole thing. One of brother-in-law Ben's practical jokes had compromised Lacy, after she'd been locked in a line cabin all night with Cole. Nothing had happened, except that Cole had given her hell, blaming her for it. But it was what people thought happened that counted. In big cities, the new morals and wild living that had followed World War I was all the rage. But down in Spanish Flats, Texas, a two-hour drive from San Antonio, things were still very straitlaced. And the Whitehalls, while not wealthy, were well known and much respected in the community. Marion Whitehall had been in hysterics about the potential disgrace, so Cole had spared his mother's tender feelings by marrying Lacy. But not willingly.

Lacy had been taken in by Marion Whitehall eight years ago, after Lacy's own parents died on the *Lusitania* when it was torpedoed by the Germans. Lacy's mother and Cole's had been best friends. Lacy's one remaining relative, a wealthy great-aunt, had declared herself too elderly and set in her ways to take on a teenager. The Whitehalls' invitation had been a godsend. Lacy had agreed, but mostly because it allowed her to be near Cole. She'd worshipped him since her wealthy family had moved to Spanish Flats from Georgia when Lacy had been just thirteen to be near her great-aunt Lucy and great-uncle Horace Jacobsen, who had retired from business after making a fortune in the railroad industry. Great-uncle Horace had, in fact, founded the town of Spanish Flats and named it for the Whitehall ranch, which had sheltered him in a time of desperate need. He and Lacy's great-aunt had been a social force in San Antonio in those days, but it was Spanish Flats Ranch, not great-uncle Horace's towering Victorian mansion that had fascinated Lacy from the beginning—as did the tall cattleman on the ranch property. It had been love on first impact, even though Cole's first words to her had been scathing when she'd ridden too close to one of his prize bulls and had almost gotten gored. That hadn't put her off, though. If anything, his cold, quiet, authoritative manner had attracted her, challenged her, long before she knew who he was.

Coleman Whitehall was an enigma in so many ways.

A loner, like his old Comanche grandfather who'd taken him over in his youth and showed him a vanished way of life and thought. But he'd been kind to Lacy for all that, and there were times when she'd glimpsed a different man, watching him with the cowboys. The somber, serious Cole she thought she knew was missing in the lean rancher who got up very early one morning, caught a rattlesnake, defanged it, and put it in bed with a cowboy who'd played a nasty practical joke on him. The resulting pandemonium had left him almost collapsed with laughter, along with the other witnesses. It had shown her a side of Cole that she remembered now for its very elusiveness.

Despite his responsibilities at home, the lure of airplanes and battle had gotten to Cole. He'd learned to fly at a local barnstorming show, and had become fascinated with this new mode of transportation. The sinking of the *Lusitania* had brought his fighting blood up, and convinced him that America would inevitably be pulled into war. He'd kept up his practice at the airfield, even though his father's death had stopped him from joining the group of pilots in the French Escadrille Americaine, which became the exclusive Lafayette Escadrille.

When war did break out in 1917, a neighboring rancher had taken responsibility for the ranch and womenfolk in his absence, keeping the land grabbers away with financial expertise. Meanwhile Lacy and Katy and Ben and Marion had watched the newspapers with mounting horror, reading the posted casualty lists with stopped breath, with sinking fear. But Coleman seemed invincible. It wasn't until the year after the armistice, when he'd turned up back at the ranch after a few sparsely worded letters, an old flying buddy in tow, that they'd learned he'd been shot down by the Germans.

He'd only written that he'd been wounded, not how. But apparently it hadn't done him any lasting damage. He was the same taciturn, hard man he'd been before he'd gone to France.

Well, not quite the same. Lacy treasured the precious few memories she had of Cole's tenderness, his warmth. He hadn't always been cold—especially not the day he'd left to go to war. There had been times when he was so human, so caring. Now, there was a coldness that was alien, a toughness that perhaps the war had created. Not that the family had any real idea of what the war had been like for him on a personal basis; he never spoke of it.

Ben had been too young to fight. With Cole's return, he'd followed after his big brother with wide, dark eyes, all questions and pleas to hear about it. But Coleman wouldn't tell him a thing. So Ben hounded Jude Sheridan. Jude, whom Coleman called Turk, had been an ace pilot with twelve credited kills. He was an easygoing, too-handsome man with a quick temper and a physique that kept young Katy awake nights sighing over him. Turk had filled Ben's ears with bloodcurdling tales—until Coleman had gotten tired of it and stopped Turk from encouraging his young brother.

That was about the same time that he'd had to stop Katy from tagging along after the tall, blond flyer who'd become his ranch foreman. Turk was good with horses, and he had a shocking reputation with women. But that was something Katy wasn't going to find out, Cole had informed her coldly. Turk was his friend, not a potential conquest, and Katy had better remember it. Even now, Lacy could see the heartbreak on the slender, green-eyed girl's face as Cole blasted her dreams away. He'd even gone so far as to threaten her with firing Turk altogether. So Katy had withdrawn—from her brother, from her

family—and had gone wild with the new morality. She'd
bought outrageous clothes; she began to use makeup.
She went to parties in San Antonio and drank outlawed
bathtub gin. And the more Coleman threatened her, the
wilder she got.

About that time, Ben had turned his attention to Lacy.
It had been embarrassing, because she was twenty-three
and Ben only eighteen. Coleman teased him about it
when he got wind of it, which only added to the
frustration. One night, Ben lured Cole and Lacy to a line
cabin and locked them in. He went home to bed, and by
the time they were discovered the next morning, they
were hopelessly compromised. So Coleman did the
expected thing and married her. But he resented her,
ignored her, put a wall between them that all her efforts
hadn't dented. He refused to let her close enough to give
their marriage a chance.

There had been an attraction between them for a long
time—a purely physical one on his part—that had found
its first expression the day he'd left for the war. Despite
the promise of that long-ago embrace, he hadn't touched
Lacy since he'd been home again, not until after the
wedding. The tension between them had reached flash
point after an argument in the barn. Cole had backed her
up against the wall that rainy morning in the barn and had
kissed her until her mouth was swollen and her body
raging with unexpected passion. That night, he'd come
to her room and, in the darkness, had taken her. But it
had been quick, and painful, and she remembered the
strength in his lean hands as he'd held her wrists beside
her head, not even allowing her to touch him through the
brief intimacy while his hard mouth smothered her cries
of pain. He'd left her immediately, white-faced, while
she cried like a hurt child, and he hadn't touched her

again. The next morning, he'd acted as if nothing at all had happened. If anything, he was harder and colder than before. Lacy couldn't bear the thought of any more of his brutal passion and his indifference. She'd packed her bags and gone to San Antonio, to be a companion to her great-aunt Lucy, Great-uncle Horace's widow. Shortly thereafter, the gentle old lady had died. Now Lacy had the house and plenty of money that she hadn't even expected to inherit. But without Cole, she had nothing.

She still shuddered, thinking about the morning she'd left Spanish Flats. Marion had been hurt, Katy and Ben shocked. Coleman had been . . . Coleman. Revealing nothing. Eight months had passed without a word from him, without an apology. Lacy had hated him at first because of the pain he'd inflicted so coldly. But one of her married friends had explained intimacy to her, and now she understood a little. She'd been a virgin, so it wasn't unexpected that her first time had been difficult. Perhaps Cole just hadn't cared enough to be gentle with her. At any rate, if it happened again, it might be less traumatic, and she might get pregnant. She blushed softly, thinking of how wonderful it would be to have a child, even under these circumstances. She was so totally alone. She could never have Cole, but it would have been nice to have his child.

It was such a good thing that she had Great-aunt Lucy's inheritance. Added to the unexpectedly small inheritance her parents had left, it had made it possible for her to live in style and give extravagant parties. Coleman hated guests, and gaiety. Lacy could have done without them, too, if she'd had Coleman's love. Even his affection. But she had nothing, except the contempt that had burned from his dark eyes every time he looked at her. She had money, and he was losing more of his by the day. That had been a point of contention between them from the very beginning. Cole had never gotten over the fact of her wealth . . . and his lack of it. It was an unexpected prejudice in a man who didn't seem to have a bigoted bone in his lean body.

Lacy sipped her gin quietly, her eyes on the clock. Marion had written to say that Cole would be in San Antonio today, on business. She'd asked him to stop by and see Lacy while he was in town. Lovely Marion, always the matchmaker. But she didn't know the real situation. There was nothing more hopeless than the relationship the way it was now. Even if Lacy had thought about asking Coleman for a divorce, as old-fashioned and proper as he was, she knew Cole would never agree to that. It had been his own principles, added to his mother's horror of scandal, that had made him drag Lacy to the altar in the first place after the night in the line cabin, even though he hadn't touched her. Apparently he was content for things to go on as they were; for Lacy to live in San Antonio, while he contented himself with business-as-usual at Spanish Flats. She laughed bitterly. All her young dreams of marriage and children and a husband to love and cherish her, and this was what she had. Twenty-four years old, and she felt fifty.

Children had been another problem. She'd worked up enough nerve to approach Coleman shortly after their marriage and ask him if he wanted them. She'd thought in her innocence that a child might make their relationship easier. His face had gone a horrible pale shade, and he'd said things to her that she still had trouble accepting. No, he'd told her, he didn't want children. Not with a pampered little rich girl like Lacy. And after a few more insulting words, he'd stormed off in a black temper. She'd never had the nerve to ask him a second time. In her heart, she'd hoped that she might become pregnant after that uncomfortable night in his bed, but it hadn't happened. Maybe it was just as well, because Cole would let no one close to him. She'd tried everything except being herself. It was hard to be herself around Cole, because he inhibited her so much. She wanted to play with him and tease him and make him laugh. She wanted to make him young, because he'd never been that. He'd been a man ever since she'd known him, a solitary, lonely figure with steel in his makeup—even at the age of nineteen—which he'd been when Lacy came to live with the Whitehalls.

In the other room, the radio was giving out New Orleans jazz, and the new Charleston dance was being demonstrated by two visitors whom Lacy didn't know. There were a lot of people in the house that she didn't know. What did it matter? They filled the empty rooms.

Lacy walked down the hall, her knee-length gray dress clinging softly to the slender lines of her body, down her hose-clad legs, to her buckled high heels. She felt restless again, hungry. She remembered the hardness of Cole's mouth, the aching sweetness of his kiss that left her lips softly swollen. All that exquisite passion they'd shared the morning in the barn, and it had led to . . . that. She shivered. Surely women only allowed men such license with their bodies to get children.

Bess, one of her married friends, had told her that sex was the most exquisite experience of her life. "*Mahhh-hhvelous*," she'd said, laughing, her eyes full of the love she shared with her husband of five years. Lacy had been curious, despite her bad experience, to find out if intimacy could be pleasurable. But she wasn't quite curious enough to let George Simon have what he'd been lusting after for the past few weeks. George was a sweet man, a good friend. But the thought of his greedy hands on her body was somehow offensive. It was a kind of sacrilege to think of letting anyone but Cole touch her that way.

What utter rot, she thought, with a harsh laugh. Ridiculous to moon over a man who didn't love her. But worshipping him was such a habit. And she did. She loved everything about him, from the way he sat his horse to the arrogant tilt of his dark head, to the way his skin caught the light and burned like bronze. He wasn't terribly good to look at, except to Lacy, but he had a masculinity that set her teeth on edge, that made her body go hot and throbbing. Just to touch him could make her tremble.

She sighed shakily as her gray eyes swept the hall. Would he come? Her heart pounded beneath her bodice. Just to see him, she thought, just to lay eyes on him once more, would be heaven. But it was already eleven o'clock, and Cole was usually in bed by nine so that he could be up at the crack of dawn. She turned back toward the living room with a heart like lead. No, he wasn't coming tonight. It had been a foolish hope.

She went back to her guests, laughing, drinking more and more gin. The police made raids once in a while, but Lacy didn't care if they came and found the gin. She might go to jail, and Coleman might come and bail her out. Then he might bring her home, and be so inflamed by smoldering passion that he'd do to her what Rudolph Valentino, as the sheik, had done to Agnes Ayres in that wildly passionate film *The Sheik*. Her heart ran away. She'd gone wild over that movie two years ago and had learned to do the tango soon after Valentino's *Blood and Sand* film was released. But, of course, no one in her circle could do it like Valentino.

She took another sip of gin, lost in her thoughts. She jumped as a hand lightly touched her shoulder. She looked up, wide-spaced eyes huge in her face, and relaxed a little when she saw George Simon behind her.

"You startled me," she said in her calm, very Southern drawl.

"Sorry," he said, grinning. Well, his teeth were perfect, even if he was slightly balding and overweight. "I just thought you might like to know that you have a visitor."

She frowned. It was midnight, and despite the fact that the huge Victorian house was overrun with people, it was unusual for anyone to come calling so late. And then she remembered. Cole!

"Male or female?" she asked nervously.

"Definitely male," George said, without smiling. "He looks like the portrait over the living room mantel. That's where I left him, staring at it."

Lacy spilled the drink down the front of the stylishly wispy dress and mopped frantically at it with a handkerchief. "Oh, damn," she said curtly. "Well, I'll worry about that later. He's in the living room?"

"Say, kid . . . You're like flour in the face. What's wrong?"

"Nothing," she said. Everything, she thought as she turned and walked stiffly down the long hall, dimly lit by sconces, her wide-heeled shoes beating a dainty tatoo on the bare, polished wood floors as she walked.

She hesitated at the doorway, her eyes huge in her face, her hand poised on the doorknob. She knew already who was going to be waiting for her. She knew by George's description, but even more by that smell, that pungent smoke that teased her nose even as she opened the door and saw him.

Coleman Whitehall spun on his booted heel with the precision of an athlete. Which he was, of course; ranch work demanded that kind of muscle. His dark eyes narrowed as he looked at Lacy, blazing out of a face like leather under hair as dark as her own. His skin was bronzed, a legacy from the Comanche grandfather who'd instilled pure steel in his makeup and taught him that emotion was a plague to be avoided at all costs.

He was wearing work clothes. Jeans and boots, with wide, flaring leather chaps and a vest over his blue-patterned shirt, leather wristbands on the cuffs. A string hung out of the pocket, which would be the tobacco pouch he always carried, along with a small, flat packet of papers to roll cigarettes from. His forehead was oddly pale as he watched her, his wide-brimmed hat tossed carelessly onto an elegant Victorian wing chair. He lifted his square chin and stared at her with unblinking, unforgiving eyes, the very picture of a Texas cattleman with his weather-beaten face and unyielding pride and blatant arrogance.

She closed the door and moved forward. He didn't frighten her. He never had, really, although he towered over her like a lean, taciturn giant. He'd hardly smiled in the years she'd lived under his roof. She wondered if he ever had as a boy. She loved him. But love was something he didn't need. Love. And Lacy. He could do very well without either, and he'd proven it over the past eight lonely months.

"Hello, Cole," she said softly.

He lifted the smoking cigarette to thin, firm lips that held a faintly mocking smile. "Hello, yourself, kiddo. You look prosperous enough," he. mused, his eyes narrow on her short dark hair in its bob, her face with its outrageously dark lip rouge, her blue eyes quiet and abnormally bright as she stood before him, very trendy in her soft gray dress that clung to her slender figure and displayed her long, elegant legs with scandalous efficiency.

She didn't avoid his stare. Her eyes wandered over his face like loving hands, seeing the new lines, the rough edges. He was twenty-eight now, but he'd aged in these months they'd been apart. The war had aged him. Marriage hadn't seemed to help.

"I'm doing very well, thanks," she said, trying to keep her voice light. It was hard to handle this meeting, with the memory of her abrupt departure—and the reason for it—still between them. He seemed unperturbed by it, but her knees felt weak. "What brings you to San Antonio in the middle of the night?"

"I've been trying to sell cattle. Winter's coming on. Feed's getting hard to come by." He studied her blatantly, but there was no feeling in his dark eyes. There was nothing at all.

She moved closer, inhaling the masculine smell of him, the scents of tobacco and leather that had become so familiar. She touched his sleeve gently, loving the warmth of him under it, only to have him jerk away from her and walk back toward the fireplace.

Her hand felt odd, extended like that. She pulled it back to her side with a wistful, bitter little smile. He still didn't like her to touch him, after all this time. He never had. He took, but he never gave. Lacy wasn't sure that he knew how to give.

"How is your mother?" she asked.

"She's fine."

"And Katy and Bennett?"

"My sister and brother are fine, too."

She studied his long, lean back, watching him stare at

his likeness above the mantel. She'd had it painted soon after she'd left Spanish Flats, and it was his mirror image. Dark, brooding, with eyes that followed her everywhere she went. He was wearing work clothes in the portrait, with a red bandanna at his throat and a white Stetson atop his dark, straight hair. She loved the portrait. She loved the man.

"What's that in aid of?" he asked insolently, gesturing up at it. He turned, pinning her with his dark gaze. "For show? To let everyone know what a devoted little wife you are?"

She smiled sadly. "Are we going to have that argument again? I'm not suited to the ranch. You've been telling me that since the day I stepped on the place for the first time. I'm—how did you put it?—too genteel." That was a lie. She was well suited, and she loved it. Her eyes glared at him. "But we both know why I left Spanish Flats, Cole."

His eyes flashed, and a dark stain of color washed over his high cheekbones. He averted his eyes.

Oh, damn—Lacy thought miserably. My tongue will be the death of me. She laced her hands together. "Anyway, you never knew I was around," she said stiffly. "Your day-to-day indifference finally chased me away."

"What did you expect me to do?" he asked curtly, "Sit around and worship you? My ranch is in trouble, teetering on a precipice in this damned slow agricultural market. I'm too busy trying to support my family to dance attendance on a bored society girl." He stared at her with cold, dark eyes. "That lounge lizard who led me in here seems to think you're his private stock. Why?"

That sounded like jealousy, and her heart jumped, but

she kept her features calm. "George is my friend. He'd like to marry me."

"You've got a husband. Does he know?"

"No," she said carelessly. He was getting on her nerves now. She went to the decanter and poured herself a china cup of gin, lacing it with water. She turned back defiantly and sipped her gin, knowing he'd recognize the smell. He did; she saw it in his disapproving stare. She grinned at him impishly over the rim of the delicate china cup. "Why don't you go and tell him?"

"You should have already," he said, his voice deep and smooth.

"What for?" she asked innocently. "To make him jealous?"

She could see the control he was exercising, and it excited her. Pushing Cole had always excited her.

"Lead him on," he dared, "and I'll kill him."

Now that was pure possession, and it irritated her. He didn't want her, but he wasn't going to let anyone else have her. His flashing dark eyes were telling her so.

"You probably would, you wild man," she drew back, lifting her chin to glare up at him, unafraid. "Well, let me tell you something, Coleman Whitehall. It's a pleasant change to be admired and sought after by someone after being ignored by you!"

He stared at her with an odd expression. Almost amusement. "Where's that temper been all these years?" he taunted. "I've never seen it before."

"Oh, I've discovered lots of bad habits since I got away from you," she told him. "I've decided that I like being myself. Don't you like being disagreed with? God knows, everybody at the ranch is terrified of you!"

"Not you, I gather," he drawled, taking a last draw from his cigarette.

"Never me." She sipped some more gin, feeling reckless. "I'm doing great without you. I have a big, fancy house, and beautiful clothes, and lots of friends!"

He finished the cigarette and tossed it into the burning fireplace. The orange-and-yellow flames highlighted his bronzed skin, his sharp, well-defined features.

"The house and clothes don't suit you, and your friends stink," he said easily, standing erect with his hands on his slender hips. "You're getting as wild as Katy. I don't like it."

"Then do something about it," she challenged. "Make me stop, big man. You can do anything . . . Just ask Ben; he's your fan club."

He smiled ruefully. "Not since you left, he isn't. Even Taggart and Cherry stopped talking to me once you were gone."

"Nice of you to come right after me and take me home," she said sarcastically. "Eight months and not even a postcard."

"You're the one who wanted to go." His dark eyes searched her face quietly, and something flashed in them for an instant. "You're not happy, Lacy," he said quietly. "And that crowd in there isn't going to make you happy."

"What is, you?" she demanded. She felt like crying. She took another sip of gin and turned away from him, hurting like she never had. In the quiet, understated elegance of the enormous room, with its faint odor of lilacs, she felt as out of place as he looked. "Go away, Cole," she said heavily. "There was never any room for me in your life. You wouldn't even sleep with me—until that last night." She didn't see the expression that statement put on his face. "I decided to cut my losses and go back to the city, where I belonged. I thought you'd be pleased. After all, the marriage was forced on us.''

His face hardened. ''You might have talked to me before you left.'' He remembered how it had felt to watch her leave. She couldn't know that his pride had been shattered by that defection, even though it was justified. He'd done his best to drive her away, to make damned sure he didn't lose control again as he had that one night. The memory of the way he'd hurt her didn't sit well on his conscience.

He might not have loved her, but he'd missed her. The color had gone out of his world when she'd left it. He stared at her now with an expression he was careful not to let her see. She was so lovely. She deserved a man who'd be good to her, who'd take proper care of her and give her a houseful of children. . . . His eyes closed briefly and he turned away. ''But maybe it was just as well. We'd said it all already, hadn't we, honey?'' he asked quietly.

''Yes, we had,'' she agreed. ''I suppose we were just too different to make a successful marriage.'' She bit her lower lip and closed her eyes. That was a lie, too. But it would please him to have her admit what he already believed.

''Is he your lover?'' he asked suddenly, nodding toward the closed door. ''That limp-wristed lizard who showed me in here?''

''I don't have a lover, Cole,'' she said, lifting her eyes bravely to his. ''I've never had anyone . . . except you.''

He avoided her eyes, looking over at the mantel. Absently his fingers reached for the Bull Durham pouch. He pulled out a tissue-thin paper with deft, quick fingers and dabbed tobacco in a thin line in the middle of it,

rolling it and sealing it with a flick of his tongue. He
struck a match on the bricks of the fireplace and bent his
dark head to light the finished product. Deep, pungent
smoke filled the room.

She toyed with the dainty lace-and-cotton handkerchief in her hands. "Why did you come here?"

He shrugged, his broad chest rising and falling
heavily. He turned around and his dark eyes searched her
pale ones. He noticed her flushed face and the faint mist
in her eyes. His heavy brows came together. "Have you
been drinking all night?" he asked curtly.

"Of course," she said, without subterfuge, and
laughed defiantly. "Are you shocked? Or is it that you're
still back in the Dark Ages, when ladies didn't do that
sort of thing?"

"Decent women *don't* do that sort of thing," he told
her, his voice unusually deep as he glared at her. "Or
wear clothes like that," he added, nodding toward the
expanse of leg below the knee-deep hem of her skirt with
her rolled-down hose held up by lacy garters.

"Don't tell me you're shocked to see my legs, Cole,"
she taunted, lifting her chin as she smiled at him. "Of
course, you never have seen my body, have you?" He
looked frankly uncomfortable now, and she liked that.
She liked making him uncomfortable. Her hands moved
slowly down her body, and she watched his eyes follow
the movement with satisfaction. "You can't even talk
about sex, can you, Cole? It's something dark and
sinful—and decent people only do it in the dark with the
lights off—"

"Stop it!" he said shortly. He turned his back on her,
smoking quietly, one hand touching the soft curve of a
chair back. His breath seemed to come unsteadily. "Talking about . . . that . . . won't change what happened."

He almost sounded as if he regretted it. Perhaps he did. Perhaps he thought of it as a weakness. His upbringing had been rigid at best, and his Comanche grandfather had all but stolen him from his parents in those formative young years. He'd learned how to be a man years before age caught up with his conditioning, and tenderness hadn't been part of his education.

The music suddenly got louder, attracting his attention to the closed door. "Is this a regular thing now, these parties?"

"I suppose so," she confessed. "I can't stand my own company, Cole."

"I'm having some problems of my own." He sat down in the dainty wing chair, looking so out of place in it that Lacy almost smiled in spite of the gravity between them.

She perched on the edge of the velvet-covered blue sofa and folded her hands primly in her lap.

"The elegant Miss Jarrett," he murmured, studying her. "I had some exquisite dreams about you while I was in France."

That shocked her. He'd never talked about France. "Did you? I wrote you every day," she confessed shyly.

"And never mailed the letters," he said, with a faint smile. "Katy told me."

"I was afraid to. You were so reserved, and just because I was best friends with Katy and living in your house was no reason to think you'd welcome my letters. Even after the way we said good-bye," she added, with unfamiliar self-consciousness. "You never wrote just to me, after all."

He didn't tell her why. "I wouldn't have minded a letter or two. It got pretty bad over there," he said.

She glanced up and then down. "You were shot down, weren't you?"

"I got scratched up a little," he said curtly. "Listen, suppose you come back to Spanish Flats?"

Her heart leapt straight up. She stared at him, searched his dark eyes. He was a proud man. It must have taken a lot of soul-searching for him to come and ask that. "Why, Cole?"

"Mother . . . isn't well," he said after a minute. "Katy's being courted by some wild man from Chicago. Bennett's trying to run off to France to join Ernest Hemingway and that Lost Generation of writers." He ran a hand through his damp hair. "Lacy, they foreclosed on Johnson's place yesterday," he added, looking up with eyes as dark as his hair.

Her heart jumped. Spanish Flats was his life. "I still have the inheritance Great-aunt Lucy left me, and some from my parents," she said gently. "I could—"

"I don't want your damned money!" He got up, exploding in quiet rage. "I never did!"

"I know that, Cole," she said, trying to soothe him. She stood, too, standing close to his tall, lean body. She stared up at him. "But I'd give it to you, all the same."

There was a flicker of something in his dark eyes for just an instant. He reached out a lean hand, the one that wasn't holding the cigarette, and drew his hard knuckles lightly down her creamy cheek, making her tingle all over. "Skin like a rose petal," he murmured. "So lovely."

Her full bow of a mouth parted as she sighed. She searched his eyes while time seemed to stop around them. She was a girl again, all shy and weak-kneed, worshipping Cole. Wanting him.

He saw that look and abruptly moved away again. Just like old times, Cole, she thought bitterly. She bit her lower lip until it hurt, trying to banish the other rejections from her mind. He didn't want her to touch him. She'd have to get used to that.

"This was Mother's idea," he said tersely, smoking like a furnace. "She wants you to come home."

"Marion, not you." She nodded, sighing. "You don't want me, do you, Cole? You never have."

He stared up at the portrait without speaking. "You could come back with me on the train. Jack Henry is servicing my Ford, and Ben took Mother's runabout yesterday and vanished with it. I caught the train instead."

The music got louder again. Someone, probably someone tipsy, was playing with the radio knob.

"Why should I?" she asked, with what little pride she had left, shooting the question at him so sharply that it made him look at her. "What can Spanish Flats offer me that I can't have right here?"

"Peace," he said shortly, glaring at the music beyond the door. "These aren't your kind of people."

Her lips tugged into a smile. "No? What are my kind of people?"

He lifted an eyebrow at her. "Taggart and Cherry, of course," he said.

Taggart and Cherry were two of the oldest ranch hands. Taggart had ridden with the James gang, back in the late 1800s, and Cherry had driven cattle up the Chisolm Trail with the big Texas outfits. They could tell stories, all right, and if they'd bathed more often than twice a month, they'd have been welcome in the house. Cole was careful to see that they sat on the porch when they came visiting, and that he was upwind of them.

She couldn't help the grin. "It's winter. You won't have to worry about getting downwind."

He smiled gently, traces of the younger Cole in his

face for just a split second. Then he closed up again, like a clam. "Come home with me."

She searched his eyes, hoping to find secrets there, but they were like a closed book. "You still haven't told me what I'll get if I come," she repeated, the alcohol dimming her inhibitions, making her reckless for a change.

"What do you want?" he asked, with a mocking smile.

She gave it back. "Maybe I want you," she said blatantly, the gin giving her a little reckless courage.

He didn't say a word. His face hardened. His eyes went dark. "You hated it that night," he said curtly. "You cried."

"It hurt. It won't again," she said simply, airing her newly acquired knowledge. She lifted her chin stubbornly. "I'm twenty-four. This"—she gestured around her—"is what I have to look forward to in my old age. Loneliness and a few hangers-on, and some wild music and booze to dull the hurt. Well, if I'm going to grow old, I don't want to do it alone." She moved closer to him, her face quiet with pride. "I'll go back with you. I'll live with you. I'll even pretend that we're happy together, for appearances. But only if you stay in the same room with me, like a proper husband." She hated making it an ultimatum, but she wanted a child. She might have to trick him into giving her one, or blackmail him into it, but she was determined.

He actually trembled. "What?" He sounded as if she'd astonished him.

"I want the appearance of normality, and no giggling family making fun of me because you make it so damned obvious that you don't want me."

"Stop cursing—" he shot back at her.

"I'll curse if I feel like it," she told him. "Cassie was forever making horrible remarks about your insistence on separate rooms, and so were Ben and Katy. Everyone knew you weren't behaving like a husband. It was just one more humiliation to add to the humiliation of being treated like a stick of furniture! So, if I come back, those are my terms."

He swallowed. His dark eyes touched every line, every curve of her face. For an instant, she could see him wavering. And then he closed up, all at once.

"I can't be guided like a blind mule," he told her bluntly, his stance threatening. "If you want to come, all right. But no conditions. You'll have your old room, and you'll sleep in it alone."

"Would it be that hard for you to sleep with me?" she taunted. She slid her hands over her slender hips. "George wants to."

His chest expanded roughly. "George can damned well go hang!"

"If you won't, I'll let him," she threatened. Her eyes sparkled with the challenge. Let him sweat for a change. Let him wonder and worry. "I'll stay right here, and—"

"Damn you!" His dark eyebrows seemed to meet in the middle as he glared at her. "Damn you, Lacy!"

"You can close your eyes and think of England," she whispered mischievously, because this was fun. The idea of seducing Cole and making him enjoy it was the most delicious fun she'd had in eight long months. And if there was a little revenge mixed up in it, so what? The thought of luring him into her bed, of tempting and tantalizing him, was delightful, especially now that she knew it was unlikely to be painful a second time. Untold pleasures lay in store for both of them, if she could bluff him.

He muttered something under his breath, finished his cigarette, and slammed it into the fireplace. "Damn you!" he repeated.

She moved around in front of him, making him look at her. "Why did you come to me that night if you didn't want me?"

"I did . . . want you," he bit off.

"And now you don't?"

Oh, God. She was killing him by inches! His body felt like drawn cord. What she was demanding was impossible, but he couldn't let her carry out her threat. The thought of Lacy with any other man cut his heart. He drew a deep breath. He couldn't show weakness, not now.

Attack was the best defense. He lifted his face and glared down at her. "Sex is a weapon women use," he said coldly. "My grandfather taught me to live without it."

"Your grandfather almost succeeded in making a slab of stone out of you!" she shot back.

"Caring is a weakness," he said shortly. "It's a disease. I won't be owned by any damned woman—much less a society girl from Georgia with a fat wallet!"

Her face blanched. Her fists clenched at her sides. So it was going to be war. All right. He was asking for it.

"Nevertheless," she said tautly, "if you want me to come back, you'll have to share a room with me. I'm not going to have the family laughing at me a second time. You don't even have to touch me, Cole," she conceded, hoping proximity might accomplish what blackmail couldn't. "But you are going to have to share my room. If you want me back . . ." she added calculatingly. "And I think you need me—at least to help you cope with Katy. Don't you?"

"Haven't you any pride, woman?"

"No. I gave it up the day I married you," she told him. "My pride, my self-respect, and my hopes of a rosy future. If you want me back, I'll come. But on my terms."

His eyes were fierce, black as coal. He drew in a slow, deep breath. "Your terms," he said curtly. "Blackmail, you mean."

He looked so formidable that she almost backed down. Then she remembered how she'd learned to treat George when he got out of hand. She wondered absently if it might work on stone?

She moved a little closer, coquettishly, and deliberately batted her long eyelashes at him. "Kiss me, you fool!" she said vampishly, lifting her face and parting her red lips.

He stared down at her through narrowed eyes and hoped like hell she wouldn't notice the sudden thunder of his heartbeat at that innocent teasing. "Stop that," he said irritably, giving nothing away. "All right," he said, with a rough sigh, "we'll share a room."

"Finally, a chink in the stone!" She sighed, smiling wickedly, and he actually seemed to soften a little. Miracle of miracles! Had she accidentally hit on a way to get to him?

He scowled at her for another few seconds, half-irritated, half-intrigued by this new Lacy. He pursed his lips and almost smiled down at the picture she made. "I'll pick you up in the morning at seven." He glanced toward the hall. "You'd better send that pack of coyotes home."

She curtsied. "Yes, Your Worship!"

"Lacy . . ." he said warningly.

"You're so handsome when you're mad," she sighed.

The scowl got worse. He actually seemed to vibrate, and she felt a fever of pleasure that she could knock him off-balance. If he were vulnerable, there might be a little hope. Eight months, wasted; years wasted—and now she'd discovered the way to reach him!

"Good night," he said firmly.

She gave him an impish little grin. "Wouldn't you like to stay the night?"

"I would not," he said shortly.

"Then enjoy your last night alone," she said, with a gleam in her blue eyes. She turned and walked away, on legs that could hardly hold her. And she was laughing when she reached the room where the party was still in full swing.

But the man letting himself out the front door wasn't laughing. He never should have agreed to her terms. He should have told her to take them and go to hell. Only he was so hungry for the sight of her that his mind had stopped working. It was probably all bluff on her part, about sleeping with that tall clown. But how could he risk it? By God, he'd beat the man to death if he so much as touched her!

The violence of his feelings disturbed him. She was just a woman, just Lacy, who'd been around so long she was like the flowers his mother always put on the hall table. But things had been different since that night with her. He hadn't meant to touch her. The marriage had been forced; he'd been determined to find some way to drive her from the ranch without ever consummating it. And then he'd started kissing her, and one thing had led to another. He wasn't sorry, except for hurting her. It had been magic. But it was too big a risk to repeat. How in hell was he going to share a room with her and keep his secret? In that intimacy, which he'd avoided for years

even with his men, how could he keep her from finding
out?

He'd lose her when she knew, he thought. That hadn't
bothered him at first, but he'd had too much time to
think. He'd missed her. He'd wanted her. Avoiding her
hadn't worked. He'd tried that, eight months' worth, and
tonight was the first time he'd felt alive since she'd left
him. He sighed. Well, he'd take it one day at a time.
That was what Turk always said: Stop gulping life down
in a swallow. So maybe he'd try that. As he left the
house, the look in his eyes was as grim as rain, as
hopeless as dead flowers on a grave.

══ Chapter Two ══

LACY SAT DOWN HEAVILY IN THE WING CHAIR, STILL reeling from her demands and Cole's reluctant agreement to them. She'd been bluffing, but fortunately he didn't know that. Imagine, she thought, shy little Lacy Jarrett actually winning one over Coleman Whitehall. The gin had helped, of course. She still wasn't used to it, and it had gone to her head. Also, she mused, to her tongue.

Back in the old days, she would have been too shy to even speak to him. Her eyes closed and she drifted back to those first, nerve-wracking days at Spanish Flats following the death of her parents.

Katy had been welcoming, like Marion and Ben. But Cole had been formal, distant, and almost hostile to her. She'd made a habit of keeping out of his way, so quiet when he was at the table for meals that she seemed invisible. It didn't help that she started falling in love with him almost at once.

There had been rare times when he was less antagonistic. Once, he'd helped her save a kitten from a stray dog. He'd placed the tiny thing in her hands and his eyes had held hers for so long that she'd blushed furiously and was only able to stammer her thanks. When she'd gotten sick from being out in the sun without her bonnet, it was

Cole who'd carried her inside to her bed, who'd hovered despite Marion and Katy's ministrations until he was certain that she was all right. Occasionally he'd been home when Lacy went for the quiet walks she enjoyed so much, and he'd fallen into step beside her, pointing out crops and explaining the cattle business to her. Eventually she lost much of her fear of him, but he disturbed her so much when he came close that she couldn't quite hide it.

Her reactions seemed to make him irritable, as if he didn't understand that it was physical attraction and not fear that caused them. Cole didn't go to parties, and Lacy had never known him to keep company with a woman. He worked from dawn until well after dark, overseeing every phase of ranch operation, even keeping the books and handling the mounting paperwork. He had a good business head, but he also had all the responsibility. It didn't leave much time for recreation.

The blow came when war broke out in Europe. Everyone was sure that America would eventually become involved, and Lacy found herself worrying constantly that Cole would have to go. He was young and strong and patriotic. Even if he weren't called up, it was inevitable that he would volunteer. His conversation about the news items in the papers told her that.

Aviation, the new science, was one of his consuming interests. He talked about airplanes as some boys talked about girls. He read everything he could find on the subject. Lacy was his only willing audience, soaking up the information he imparted enthusiastically—even while she prayed that the flying fever wouldn't take him over to France, where American boys were flocking to join the Lafayette Escadrille.

But America's entry into the war in April, 1917,

smashed Lacy's dreams. Cole enlisted and requested service with the fledgling Army Air Service. He'd wanted to volunteer for the famous Lafayette Escadrille a year earlier, along with other American pilots attached to the French Flying Corps. But the death of his father and the weight of responsibility for his mother and sister and brother—not to mention Lacy—put paid to that idea. However, when President Wilson announced American participation in the war, Cole immediately signed up. He found neighbors willing to handle ranch chores for him while his mother and Lacy assumed the duty of keeping the books, and Cole packed to leave for France.

He and Lacy had begun to enjoy a closer relationship, even if it was still tense and tentative. But the knowledge that he was going to war and might never come back had a devastating effect on Lacy's pride. She burst into tears and was inconsolable. Even Cole, who'd misinterpreted her nervousness before, finally realized what her feelings for him were.

She passed by his room the morning he was dressing to leave—and was shocked when he dragged her inside and closed the door.

His shirt was completely unbuttoned down the front, hanging loose over his elegant dress slacks. He seemed taller, bigger, in disarray, and Lacy eyes went shyly over the expanse of tanned muscular chest with its thick, dark covering of body hair.

"You cried," he said, without preamble, and his dark eyes held hers mercilessly.

There was little use in denying it. He saw too deeply. "I suppose you have to go?" she asked miserably.

"This is my country, Lacy," he said simply. "It would be the essence of cowardice to refuse to fight for it." His strong, brown hands held her upper arms firmly.

"Haven't you heard anything I've said about air power, about the edge it would give us on the Hun if we could assist the French Lafayette Escadrille in developing it?"

"Why the French?" she asked absently. The scent of him, the closeness of him, made her dizzy with pleasure. She only wanted to prolong it.

"Because the American air corps has no planes of its own," he said simply. "We'll be flying Nieuports and Sopwiths."

"Flying is dangerous . . ." she began.

"Life is dangerous, Lacy," he replied quietly. He looked at her soft mouth with its dark lip rouge. Absently he reached up and smudged it with his thumb, smiling as the bloodred color transferred itself from her lower lip to his skin. "Like being branded," he teased. "I could use this war paint on my cattle."

"It washes off," Lacy pointed out.

"Does it?" He reached in his pocket for his handkerchief and, holding her firmly by the nape of her neck with his free hand, proceeded to wipe off every trace of it.

"Cole, don't!" she protested, trying to turn her head.

"I'm not wearing that stain to the train station," he replied, his mind on what he was doing, not what he was saying.

But Lacy went quite still, her wide eyes unblinking on his hard, dark face. "W—what?"

He smiled with faint indulgence as he finished his task and tossed the handkerchief onto his dresser. "You heard me." His gaze went over her soft oval face, from her short dark hair to her big blue eyes and down her straight little nose to the bow mouth he'd wiped clean. "This might have been unthinkable before. But I don't know when I'll come back again. Isn't it permissible for a patriotic lad to be sent off with a kiss?"

Her fingers plucked nervously at the buttons of his shirt, tingling as they felt the warmth of his bare torso under them. "Of course," she said, almost strangling.

His lean hands framed her face with an odd hesitancy and he moved closer, towering over her.

She could barely breathe. She'd dreamed of this moment for years, lived for it, hoped for it. Now it was happening, and she was self-conscious and shy and scared to death that she wouldn't live up to his expectations.

"I . . . know nothing of kissing," she confessed quickly.

She felt more than heard his breath catch, but the only sign he gave of having heard her was the jerky pressure of his hands increasing as he bent toward her.

"Practice makes perfect, don't they say, Lacy?" he asked in an oddly husky tone, and his rough, coffee-scented mouth ground into hers without preamble or apology.

She gave in without a protest, yielding to his superior strength, to his growing hunger. She knew nothing, but he taught her, his mouth invading hers in the silence of the big, high-ceilinged room, his arms slowly enveloping her against the taut fitness of his tall body.

He lifted his head just briefly, to draw breath, and his dark, narrow eyes met hers. She was dazed, weak, clinging to him while her parted, swollen lips invited again the madness he was teaching her.

"Don't stop," she whispered shamelessly.

"I'm not sure I could, in any case," he whispered back. His head lowered again and this time his mouth was gentle, teasing, exploring hers with tenderness and lazy hunger that grew to anguished passion in no time at all.

She felt the wall at her back, cold and hard, and Cole's heated body pressing her into it, in an intimacy that she'd never even dreamed. The contours of his flat stomach had changed quite suddenly; his mouth was hurting hers.

Frightened, her hands pressed frantically against the hair-roughened strength of his chest.

Cole drew back at once, his own eyes as shocked as hers at the barriers of decency he'd overstepped in his mindless desire. He stepped away from her, dark color overlaying his high cheekbones.

Lacy's swollen lips were parted as she struggled for breath and composure, staring up at him with embarrassed comprehension. He shuddered just slightly, and, Lacy's eyes encountered with sudden and startled starkness the visible evidence of his loss of control. She blushed red and averted her eyes even as Cole turned away from her.

She didn't know what to say, what to do. Her body felt oddly swollen and hot, and there was a tightness in her lower stomach that she'd never experienced. Her bodice felt far too tight. She tugged at the lace of her white midi blouse and searched for the right words.

"I beg your pardon, Lacy," Cole said in a taut, all-too-formal tone, although he didn't look at her. "I never meant that to happen."

"It's all right," she replied huskily. "I—I should have protested."

"You did. Too late," he added, with faint dryness, as he turned toward her, back in command of his senses once more. His dark hair was disheveled, lying over his broad forehead, and there was still that faint color on his high cheekbones. His deep brown eyes held a light that was puzzling as they swept with new boldness over

Lacy's slender body and back up to her own vivid blue
eyes.

"I—I should go," she faltered.

"Yes, you should," he agreed. "You'll be compromised if any of the family find us alone like this in my
bedroom."

But she didn't move. Neither did he.

His chest rose and fell deeply. "Come here," he said
softly, and opened his arms.

She went into them gracefully, and lay her hot cheek
against his cool, damp chest, the thick hair tickling her
skin. His heartbeat was deep and quick, like his breathing, but he held her with utter decorum, his arms
protective rather than passionate.

"Wait for me," he whispered into her ear.

"All my life," she replied brokenly.

His arms contracted then, and he shivered with feeling.
But after a few seconds, he put her away from him,
searching her eyes with banked-down hunger.

"I love you," she said unsteadily, damning pride and
self-respect.

"Yes," he said, his voice deep and quiet, his face
giving nothing away. "Try to help Mother with Katy and
Ben while I'm away. Stay close to the house. Don't go
out alone, ever."

"I won't."

He drew in a slow breath. "The war won't last
forever. And I'm not suicidal. No more tears."

She managed a shaky smile. "Not until you leave, at
least," she promised.

His fingers traced her cheek tenderly. "I thought you
were afraid of me, all these years. But it wasn't fear, was
it?" he asked, his jaw tightening as he looked at her.
"You've loved me for a long time, and I never saw it."

She nodded slowly. "I never meant you to know."

"It's just as well that I do, now," he replied. He bent and brushed a slow, tender kiss over her lips. "Write to me," he whispered. "I'll come home, Lacy."

"I'll pray every night for you," she replied. "Oh, Cole. . . ."

"No more tears," he said sternly when her eyes began to sparkle with them. "I can't bear to see you cry."

"Sorry." She drew back from him, her heart in her face. "I'd better go, hadn't I?"

"I'm afraid so." His eyes swept over her one last time. "We'll say our proper good-byes when I leave."

"Our proper good-byes," she agreed.

It had been the last time she'd seen him alone. He said a very formal good-bye to the family before a neighbor drove him to the train station. Lacy watched the Model T Ford drive away and she cried piteously, along with Marion and Katy, for the rest of the day.

Cole did write, but not to Lacy. He wrote to the family, and because there was no mention at all of what they'd shared in his bedroom, she didn't write to him, either. Apparently he was eager to forget the intimacy. It was never referred to. His letters were full of airplanes and the beauty of France. He never spoke of the dogfights he participated in, but his name drifted back home to Texas in newspaper accounts of the air war, and along with several other Americans, he became known as an *ace*.

Katy grew wildly infatuated with the aces she read about—and especially with one they called Turk Sheridan, a blond Montana boy with nerves of steel who was considered the most daring of the fliers.

Late in 1918, as life droned on at the ranch, they received word that Cole had been wounded. Lacy almost went mad before they finally found out that he wasn't critically ill, and that he would live. The letter came from Turk Sheridan, who added that he might come back with Cole to Texas after the war as the two men had become fast friends and Turk himself was a rancher.

Katy was over the moon about their prospective new lodger, but Lacy was worried about Cole. When his letters came again, they were in a different handwriting, and the tone of them was stiff and distant.

Cole came home soon after the armistice in 1919, with the big blond Turk in tow. Lacy went running to Cole, despite all her stubborn determination not to. When he put out his hands and almost pushed her away, his rejection total and all too public, Lacy felt something die inside her. There was no expression on Cole's hard face, and nothing in his eyes. He was a different man.

He threw himself into the business of trying to get the ranch back on its feet, while Katy began a long and determined pursuit of Turk Sheridan, whose real name was Jude. Soon after the war, a wealthy great-aunt of Lacy's died and left her an inheritance of monumental proportions. Lacy was grateful because it gave her some measure of independence, but it seemed to set her even further apart from Cole, who was foundering in hard financial times following the war.

They planted crops to supplement the cattle they raised, and Turk got his hands on an old biplane and used it to dust the crops with pesticides. It amazed everyone that not only did Cole refuse to go near it, he didn't even care to discuss airplanes anymore. That shocked Lacy, who one day made the mistake of asking him why he'd lost his fascination with flying. His scalding reply had hurt her pride and her feelings, and she'd walked wide around him afterward.

About that time, young Ben developed a huge crush on Lacy. It was disturbing, because he was nineteen to her twenty-three and Lacy's heart had always belonged to Cole, even if he didn't want it. She let Ben down as gently as she could, but in revenge, he coaxed Lacy and Cole to a line cabin and locked them in, having had the foresight to also nail the shutters closed so that they couldn't be forced from the inside.

Cole mistakenly thought Lacy had put Ben up to it, knowing how she felt about him, and Lacy shivered remembering the harsh, furious accusations he'd thrown at her all through the long night until some of the ranch hands rescued them the next morning. Lacy was compromised, and Cole was forced to marry her—not only to spare her reputation, but to save the family's good name.

He'd been glad enough when she'd left. If that was so, then why, she wondered, did he want her to come back now? She didn't dare think about it too much. With any luck, it wasn't purely because of his family. There was a small possibility that he'd actually missed her.

She'd bluffed him into agreeing to her terms, to sharing a room. But remembering that night he'd stayed in her bed, she had faint misgivings about the wisdom of her actions. Despite her longing for a child and the depth of her love for him, she dreaded its physical expression. Well, she thought, that was a bridge she'd cross when she had to. Meanwhile, going home had a delight all its own. She was getting a little tired of the high life.

═══ Chapter Three ═══

K ATY WHITEHALL OPENED HER EYES TO A BLINDING whiteness. She groaned and turned over, shielding her eyelids from the sunlight coming in through the white curtains.

Her long dark hair lay in tangles around a white face, and huge green eyes opened, wincing. She tried to lift her head, groaned again, and fell back onto the pillows with a resigned sigh.

The door opened and Cassie came in, shaking her gray head, glowering down at the young woman as she put a cup of hot tea on the bedside table.

"Told you, I did," she said in her deepest drawl, her black eyes accusing. "Told you that firewater would give you the devil's own headache. Shameful, that's what it is, coming in here in the wee hours of the morning. Mr. Cole would horsewhip you, was he here to see!"

"Well, he isn't. He's in San Antonio, selling cattle." Katy dragged her slender body into a sitting position, her small breasts outlined under the pale fabric of her gown. She pushed back the weight of her hair and reached for the tea.

"Maybe he's gone to see Miss Lacy as well," Cassie ventured, her hands on her broad hips.

Katy eyed her carefully. "Think so?"

"Well, miracles happen, don't they?"

Katy forced a smile as she sipped the sweet tea. "So they say. Ben shouldn't have done that to them," she murmured.

"One joke too many," Cassie agreed. "Left alone, they might have come to marriage all by themselves, for the right reasons." Her dark face puckered as she pursed her lips. "He used to watch her, when she first came to live here," she reminded Katy. "My man Jack Henry said he'd be mechanicing and he'd see Mr. Cole watching her like a chicken hawk, them dark eyes just fiery and full of longing."

"You read too many of those outrageous novels," Katy chided, giggling as the old woman shifted uncomfortably and averted her eyes. "You know very well that Cole's immune to women. If he wasn't, he'd have married long ago. He never was around girls very much. It was always business."

"Had to be, didn't it?" Cassie defended him. "After Mr. Bart died, weren't nobody else to take care of his place. Ben were too young, and Miss Marion never had no business head."

"Thank God Cole did, or we'd all be out looking for work." Katy stretched, shuddering as the movement hurt her head. "I never should have had that third drink," she moaned, holding her forehead in both hands.

"Mr. Turk had words with that young man who brung you home last night," Cassie volunteered suddenly.

Katy's heart jumped, but she didn't look up immediately. Her big green eyes widened. "Turk did?"

Cassie smiled. Katy was only twenty-one; every single emotion showed on her face. Cassie had always known how she felt about Turk, but it wouldn't do to encourage her. Cole wouldn't stand for it. He'd already made that clear.

"Mr. Cole told him to watch out for you," the old woman said.

Katy glowered up at her. "I don't need watching."

"Yes, ma'am, you do," came the hot reply. "Carousing all hours, drinking in public, cussing like a sailor . . . You're shaming us all! Your poor mama won't even go to her bridge club because she's so afraid somebody will say something about you to her!"

The younger woman sat up straighter. "Well, Danny Marlone doesn't think I shame him," she replied, hiding her sudden vulnerability to her mother's pride in blustering.

"He's a gangster!" Cassie was off and running now, her eyes huge in her face. "Yes, he is— One of them Chicago mobsters, right down to that striped suit he wears and them fancy cigars he smokes and that big fedora! He's not the man for you! He's leading you off into hell!"

Katy sighed wearily. "Danny's a nice man. He's just a northerner, and that's why you don't like him. I like him a lot. He's good to me. He buys me things," she added, touching the diamond necklace he'd given her just last night. She smiled. "He's very generous."

Cassie's eyes narrowed. "And what you giving him in return, girl?"

Katy actually blushed. "Not . . . that!" she burst out, sitting straighter and then groaning when it hurt her head. "I'm not sleeping with him!"

"Maybe he'll expect you to, what with presents like that," Cassie replied gruffly. She turned and went to the door. "Miss Marion has rode into Floresville with Mrs. Harrison to get her hair fixed, on account of Mr. Ben ain't brought her runabout home yet. She say she be back about noon. Which it nearly is.''

She closed the door with a bang, and Katy glared at it. Danny was not a gangster. Not really. He might have done a few shady things, and he did run a speakeasy in the Windy City. But he was slick and Italian and handsome, and she liked being seen with him. She especially liked having Turk see her with him. Because she knew the foreman didn't like it, and that made her blood sing.

Damn Turk! she thought, dashing aside the covers, headache and all, to get to her feet. Damn him! Letting Cole order him around, heeding that warning to keep his hands off the boss's sister! She'd gone right through the roof when Ben had told her that. He'd overheard a hot argument between Turk and Cole, with Cole coming out on top, as usual. Turk had added that he liked women, not little girls, and that he didn't have any interest in young Katy in the first place! Oh, how that had cut. It had cut her young heart to shreds. She'd been avoiding Turk ever since, and when she'd gone to that party in San Antonio and met Danny Marlone, she'd encouraged him like crazy. For the first time, she'd used her femininity to attract a man. It didn't help that she began to wonder if it might even work on Turk. It was too late now. Cole had seen to that.

Sometimes she hated her big brother's tyranny. Cole had been like this as long as Katy could remember. Always in charge, always throwing out orders. Ben had worshipped him for a long time, although her baby brother was beginning to lose that enchantment as he aged. But Lacy . . . Oh, poor Lacy. The older woman would wear her poor heart out on Cole's utter indifference, and Katy could have cried for her friend. Cole had been quieter since Lacy'd left. Almost lonely, if the iron man ever got lonely. At any rate, he was working himself to death. And when Marion had asked him to stop and see Lacy, he didn't even protest. Maybe he missed her. Katy grinned impishly. That would be something—to have her indomitable older brother actually fall in love. Cassie could be right; he might feel something. But he had a lot of practice at hiding his emotions. Especially since the war.

She tugged on a blue polka-dotted little frock with a swingy skirt and puffy sleeves that gave her a baby-doll look. She left her hair long and tied it back with a bright blue ribbon. Not bad, she told her reflection in the mirror. Not bad at all. She lifted her hair. Maybe she'd have it cut, like Lacy's. She liked Lacy's hair. She liked Lacy.

Her thin brows drew together as she thought about her best friend in San Antonio. She'd visited Lacy once or twice in the past month, once to go to a party. Odd, it didn't seem like Lacy to have a houseful of people and all that booze. Katy had always been the flashier of the two girls, always out for adventure and excitement, the wilder the better. It had been Lacy who was quiet and dry-witted, bubbly only with people who knew her well. That Lacy wouldn't have liked wild parties. But Cole had changed her. His constant indifference and neglect had done something terrible to her friend. It had aged her. Ben and his stupid plotting! If only he'd stopped to think what he was doing. Locking them in a boarded-up line cabin that not even Cole's fabulous strength could break them out of. She shook her head. Ben should have realized that Lacy wasn't for him. And there was little Faye Cameron, who worshipped him from afar, hanging on his every word. But Ben had no time for that tomboyish child with her soft blond hair and big blue

eyes, despite the fact that most of the boys on the ranch
adored her. Ben thought her young and frivolous and not
nearly sophisticated enough for a fledgling famous writer
such as himself.

Well, poor little Faye would have to fight for her own
ground; Katy didn't have time. She was expecting Danny
later in the day, and she knew he was going to ask her to
go back to Chicago with him. She wasn't sure what she
was going to say. He had to leave the following morning.
His business in San Antonio was over, and it hadn't
included an impromptu meeting with a young Texas lady
at a local party that had led to a week of frantic dating.

What would Turk say if she agreed to go with Danny?
The question intrigued her. She knew very well what her
brother would say and do. And it would be prudent to
leave before he returned from San Antonio if she wanted
to go through with it. But first she wanted to see Turk.
She wanted to see his face when she told him.

He was down at the corral, tossing out orders to a few
cowhands on horseback. Katy's green eyes adored his
tall, muscular body as he stood with his back to her, his
deep voice faintly raised as he spoke. His hair was
blondish-brown, sun-bleached and thick and straight.
His face was handsome enough, with strong lines and a
mouth she'd dreamed of kissing. He had big, rough-
looking hands and equally big feet, and her heart went
crazy just looking at him.

The cowboys turned their mounts and rode off. Turk
stared after them, his wide-brimmed straw hat pushed to
the back of his head, his jeans close-fitting, sensuously
clinging to his long, powerful legs above booted feet.

"Hi, cowboy," Katy drawled. At least her head hurt
less, but her heart didn't. It got bruised every time she
looked at him.

He turned, one corner of his chiseled mouth tugging up at the sight of her in the revealing fabric of her dress. "Hello, tidbit. Going somewhere?"

"Just waiting for Danny." She shrugged. "He's taking me for a drive in his Alfa Romeo."

The gray eyes darkened. He didn't say anything, but the rigidity of his face spoke volumes. "Cole won't like it."

"Cole isn't here," she replied haughtily.

"For God's sake, Katy! What's gotten into you lately?" he demanded. "You've gone hog-wild, and at the worst possible time. Cole's got enough worries, with foreclosures all over the place and your mother's health failing."

That was true. Despite her vivacity, her trips to the hairdresser, her forced cheeriness, Marion was growing thinner and weaker by the day. Katy didn't like being reminded of it, and her chin lifted.

"Nothing I do will help Mother," she told him. "She's not been the same since Cole ran Lacy off."

"He didn't run her off," he said curtly. "She left."

"What was there to stay here for?" she demanded, exasperated. "When he wasn't ignoring her, he was treating her like a rug. They didn't even share a room! Cole never wanted to marry her; Ben forced him to."

"Little Ben has a bad case of exalted ego," Turk said, his eyes cold. "Someone needs to show him how to be less self-centered."

"Faye's trying," she said mischievously. "Maybe if she chases him long enough, she'll catch him."

"They're worlds apart," he replied, his gaze wistful, as if he were talking about someone else. "Nothing in common except their birthplace. He's a city boy, despite the fact that he grew up here. She's a country girl."

"Two worlds can merge." She looked at her feet. "You were a city boy," she said. It was blatant fishing, because she didn't know that. She knew nothing about Turk except his real name and his war record.

"No," he replied. "I was born in Montana. I grew up on a ranch down on the Yellowstone."

"You didn't go back there after the war," she murmured.

His eyes darkened as they studied her averted face. She was fishing. Always fishing, always wondering about him. He wondered about her, too, but it wouldn't do to let it show. Cole had said hands-off, and he owed Cole too much to argue. Besides, he told himself, Katy was just a kid. She'd get over him.

"There was nothing to go back to," he said. His eyes grew dull and sad as the memories came back. "Nothing at all."

"Don't you have family anywhere?" she asked curiously.

That shouldn't have set him off, but it did. Sometimes Katy irritated him with her constant probing into his life. He didn't like it. He didn't want her any closer than she was right now. In that, he and Cole were almost too much alike. Okay. If she wanted the truth, she could have it. He stared harshly down at her. "I had a wife. She died one winter, while I was away selling cattle. She froze to death sitting up in a chair. She'd gotten sick and couldn't build a fire. She was pregnant."

Katy felt her body go rigid with the words. She looked up into a face like stone . . . and suddenly understood so much. A wounded man. A badly wounded man, heart dead, and he wanted no more of love or commitment. And now it all made sense. The way he'd avoided her, the way he went through women as if they were no more than toys with which to amuse himself. Of course. There was safety in numbers. If he had a lot of women, he didn't have to worry about the risk of involvement.

Her face went white. She stared at him helplessly, all her dreams dying slowly in the green eyes that went quietly dead in her face.

He saw that, and his conscience stung. "Yes," he said curtly. "Yes, I thought so. Bringing that Northern hoodlum down here, running wild, all of that was because of me, wasn't it? Because I wasn't dancing attendance on you!"

It hurt to hear it put into words. It stung her eyes and made them water.

He saw the tears and felt vaguely guilty. She was just a kid, after all. And even if he wanted her as much as she wanted him, there was no way it could work. He wasn't sure he had anything to give. Like Cole said, Katy was too vulnerable for a quick affair.

"Katy, I'm sorry if that hurts. But, girl, I've got nothing left to give," he said softly. "I don't want your young heart, Katy. I can't give you mine. I lost mine when I lost Lorene. If it weren't for Cole, I wouldn't even be alive. Don't you understand? I loved her," he said roughly. "I can't ever love anyone else!"

"I haven't asked you to love me! I don't feel like that . . ." she burst out, hurt pride and frustrated passion making her wild.

"I'm not blind!" he tossed back, his gray eyes stormy. "You've followed me around, sighed over me, made love to me with your eyes for the past few months! You've done everything to make me notice you except strip naked!"

She drew back her hand and slapped him across the cheek as hard as she could. Her face was wet, and she didn't even realize that it was soaking with spilled tears. She sobbed as she looked at the redness her fingers had made. "Damn you! Damn you! I don't care about you. I never could!"

"Oh, for God's sake," he growled. It was all getting out of hand. He started to reach for her, to try and explain.

But she shrugged off his hands and ran, blind, uncertain of the direction she was taking. She ran past the corral where the remuda was kept, through the spread of mesquite trees with their feathery, thorned fronds blowing softly in the wind, down the trail into the hay barn. Sobbing, she fought her way through the bales to a dark, quiet corner and lay in the yellow, sweet-smelling hay, her body shaking from the force of her pain.

Her heart had fed for years on the hope of someday having Turk for her very own. She went to sleep dreaming of how it would be if he kissed her, if he loved her. She planned a future that was based on loving him, that included marriage and children. And now, none of it would ever happen. He had nothing to give. She didn't know how she was going to stay alive. . . .

Footsteps sounded behind her, but she wouldn't look up. She knew she was in disgrace. Shame washed her in blushes. She couldn't face him.

"You little fool," Turk muttered. He knelt beside her, forcing her onto her back with hands that had no gentleness. He glared down at her, feeling impotent, hating the indignity of her behavior for both of them. "This won't help, Katy."

"Leave me alone," she whispered, shaking. She rubbed her eyes with the backs of her hands. "Go away and let me be by myself."

He caught her wrists and pulled her up, holding her in

front of him, his gray eyes fierce as they held her tear-soaked green ones. "Listen to me, young lady. I came out of the war alive—when more than any damned thing, I wanted to die. Your brother forced me to go on; he got me off the bottle and gave me a job and I owe him for that. He said hands-off where you're concerned, and by God, hands-off it's going to be. Do you understand me?"

"You don't need that for an excuse," she shot back. "We both know you don't want me!"

"Do we?" he asked under his breath.

The way she looked was tearing him apart. Loyalty to Cole stopped him only for a second. He'd watched her, too, although he hated admitting it. He'd watched her and wanted her for a long time, and only his conscience had kept him from running screaming to her room in the darkness. He wanted her. God, he did! And she wanted him, too. He could see it, almost taste it. Would it be so wrong, just one time, just once to hold her and touch her and end the exquisite torment of desire she aroused in him? Afterward, would she hate him? He tried to think of afterward, but the scent of her—the vulnerable tenderness in those big green eyes—made him reckless. Oh, to hell with it! She was going to give in to somebody, maybe that lousy gangster. So why should he hold back? At least, he wouldn't hurt her. . . .

His hands went out to her hips. In his kneeling position, he drew her roughly to his body and pressed her belly into his. He watched the shock in her eyes dilate the pupils until they were black, and he laughed bitterly as he felt her body stiffen in the blatantly intimate embrace.

"Do you feel that, Katy? Has your Chicago gangster taught you what it means?" he asked suggestively, dragging her hips slowly against the hard thrust of his to let her feel graphically the tangible proof of his desire.

Her nails bit into the hard round muscles of his arms through his brown-patterned shirt and she trembled. Her eyes were on his mouth now, because what he was showing her embarrassed her.

"I've seen you in your room at night," he said his lips against her forehead, his voice husky and rough, "standing in front of the curtains to undress, your arms lifted, your breasts straining against those thin gowns you wear. And I've gone running into town to have a woman, to forget, to get rid of what you've done to me."

"I didn't . . . know," she whispered, her voice as unsteady as his. She could feel her breasts swelling against him, even through the two thin layers of fabric. His chest was warm and hard, and she felt the cushy springiness of hair that must cover it.

"Does he make love to you, that slick gangster?" he whispered.

"Not—not yet."

"Are you going to let him, Katy?" he asked under his breath.

"Yes!" she said recklessly. "Yes, because you won't!"

"Oh, but I will, tidbit," he breathed, bending. His hands slid down her hips to her waist, then up still further to her unbound breasts. He cupped their small softness, taking their warm weight, his thumbs teasing the nipples hard. She bit back a cry, and he slid his mouth down to hers to take it into the warm darkness past his lips.

It was the first kiss, the very first one she'd ever shared with him. Her eyes closed, her head went back to give him full access. Her mouth opened hungrily, eagerly, letting his tongue probe inside, letting it tangle with her own in the hot, still darkness of the barn.

His fingers had a faint tremor now. She felt them on the buttons of her dress. She stiffened, but she didn't stop him. This was all she'd have of him when she left with Danny. Because she was going. After this, after what she'd told him, after what she was going to do with him in this dark barn, she'd have to leave.

"You know what this is going to lead to?" he asked, his mouth poised just above her own as he found the last button at her waist.

"Yes," she said, shaking. "I'll be . . . leaving with Danny," she told him. She would, she'd have to, because of what was going to happen now. She'd have to ask Danny to take her away, today. He would, she knew. She couldn't tell him why, but he'd do what she asked. Meanwhile, she wanted this man obsessively. And these few minutes with him, even without his love, would last all her life. "You don't have to love me. Just be my lover. I'll live on it . . . all my life!" Her voice broke. "Because I lied. I do love you. I always have, always will. I love you, Turk!" Her voice broke as his hands moved.

"You little fool! You're not old enough to know what love is. This is just sex," he whispered angrily. But it didn't feel like just sex as he pulled the fabric slowly away from her pretty pink breasts and peeled it down to her waist, his darkening eyes sensuous on the creamy flesh with its dark pink tips gone hard with desire. "And speaking of little . . ." he murmured, reaching out to touch the tips with warm, slow fingers, watching her body tauten and tremble, her breath indrawn sharply.

She let him lay her down, let him remove the dress and the chemise and the garter belt and hose and shoes, until she was nude under the dark warmth of his eyes and the scent of her own body filled her nostrils.

"Cole and I used to talk about women when we were overseas," he whispered, kneeling over her as he stripped off his shirt. "He said that your grandfather was a full-blooded Comanche, and that the old man used to say that Indians could smell a woman. Now I know what he meant." He tossed his shirt aside and reach for his belt, smiling sensually as she watched him. "Don't turn your face away, Katy," he said gently as he began to lower the tight jeans and shorts he wore under them. "You let me see you. Now I'm going to let you see me."

Her eyes widened as the jeans slid away from his body . . . and she saw for herself the wild difference between man and woman, between male and female.

"My God, what an expression!" He laughed softly as he moved away long enough to remove the rest of his clothing.

"I've never seen a man . . . like that," she whispered as he stretched alongside her.

"Not even the Chicago hood?" he taunted.

"Oh . . . no," she said, her voice faltering, her eyes widening as he loomed above her.

"Don't worry. I won't hurt you too much," he said softly, Cole's warnings and his own misgivings drowning in a passion too-long denied. His hand smoothed down her body, feeling the softness of her breasts, brushing over her belly and down to the exquisite softness below it. He touched her with blatant intimacy, and she flinched and caught at his hand.

"Shh," he whispered. He opened his mouth on hers, tasting its soft trembling, and ignored the dainty little hand tugging halfheartedly at his fingers as he found a moist opening and began to play around it.

Her body arched and her voice broke on a faint little cry.

His lips lifted until they were just brushing hers. "I don't have anything to use," he whispered. "And I'm just not confident enough to try rolling away from you in time. So we're going to make love this way. I'm going to be your first man, but not technically. Do you understand? I'm going to fulfill you without the risk of pregnancy, and then I'm going to show you how to do it to me."

"But . . ." she protested as his fingers moved again. She cried out, gasping, as he found more sensitive tissue and began to stroke it.

"Look at me," he whispered as he increased the pressure and the rhythm, holding her shocked eyes. "Let me watch you."

Her face went bloodred as he stroked and tormented. She began to writhe helplessly, and his dark eyes were all over her, watching her breasts swell and tauten even more, watching the restless movements of her long, elegant legs, hearing sweet, whimpering sounds that aroused him unbearably.

He was hurting. Worse. Dying. He grasped one of her hands and pushed it against his swollen flesh, wrapping it around him, holding it there when she would have jerked it away.

"God, I hurt," he whispered, his voice tormented even as his hand grew more bold where it touched her. "Like this . . . Help me!"

He taught her the movement, whispered explicit, embarrassing instructions that she was too aroused to protest. She touched him, stroked him, closed around him, and felt him throb. Her eyes looked up into his, and he saw her pupils beginning to dilate.

"Turk!" She cried out, her voice frantic, rasping.

His free hand was behind her neck, holding her still,

his other hand feverish, his eyes shockingly thorough as he held her wild gaze. "Now," he whispered roughly. "Feel it, Katy. Feel it. Feel it, and let me watch!"

Spasms of hot lightning shot through her virginal body. She arched up against that tormenting hand and cried out, forcing him to fulfill her. Her body went into convulsions, and he watched, feeling them as his hand probed gently past the maidenhead. He shook all over, and in that moment of feverish arousal, forgot caution.

"To hell with this!" he groaned. He forced her back into the hay with the hot pressure of his open mouth. His body rolled onto hers and he thrust her legs apart with his hand. He went into her with a rough, piercing motion, burying himself, and she was so involved in her own culmination that she didn't even feel pain. She welcomed him, arching up to his hard, hot body, her hands finding his hips, her nails digging in.

He rocked furiously above her, his breath dragging out in gasps, his thighs shuddering as he arched down again and again, his eyes on her, his jaw clenched with the most exquisite pleasure he'd ever had.

"Take me inside," he whispered, his voice strained, deep with mingled arousal and passion. "Take me, Katy!"

It happened for her again. The whispered words, the rough motion of his body, the feverish rhythm with which he drove into her made it happen again.

She closed her eyes and arched her head back with a peculiar little cry, her nipples hard and pointing. One of his hands swallowed one of them roughly. His mouth forced hers open and penetrated it in the same motion, with the same rhythm, as his body. She heard the noise of the sliding hay under them, smelled the hot, pungent smell of their union, heard his heart slamming in his

chest, felt the wiry roughness of his body hair against her
soft skin. And then he cried out, with such achingly wild
pleasure, that her eyes opened and she looked up, seeing
him arched above her, his neck corded with muscle, his
face violently red, his eyes closed, his teeth clenched. He
convulsed again and again with rippling muscle, and she
looked down to where they were locked together and
watched as he suddenly drew back and covered her body
with his. She felt a wetness on her belly after his body
shuddered and then collapsed on top of her, gasping for
breath. "Oh, God," he breathed unsteadily. "I hope it
was in time! I couldn't stop . . . !"

Her hands touched him with wonder. He'd said that he
wouldn't and then he had, suddenly, as if he hadn't been
able to hold back. Her eyes closed as she drifted in the
soft aftermath, a little sad because she knew that this
would be the last time, the only time. Because she loved
him, and would lose him. He had no heart to give her,
only a body that knew no emotion past fulfillment; any
woman would have done.

"Are you all right, Katy?" he asked, lifting his
sweaty head to look at her with soft concern.

"Yes, I'm all right," she replied, with the shreds of
her pride. She even managed a smile, but she couldn't
quite look at him.

"And this is why I wouldn't touch you before," he
said gently, watching her move slowly away and start
putting her clothes on again. "Because afterward comes
shame . . . and then guilt."

He was being tender, and she hated it. Hated what was
only pity mingled with conscience. She drew her under-
pants back on and her garter belt over them. There was
no self-consciousness left, at least. Danny would like
that. He didn't know she was a virgin. He'd even said

that he wouldn't want one. So all her problems were solved at once. She'd given her virginity to the only man she'd ever love—to pave the way for the only man who loved her.

"Say something," he said quietly, watching her, vaguely ashamed of his own loss of control. He hadn't meant to let it happen. His big body still trembled softly with the force of his fulfillment. Was it because she'd been a virgin that it had been so intense? he wondered dazedly. He'd never felt it like that.

"I'm all right!" she said roughly. Would the shame never stop? She knew he didn't love her, but she'd thought the experience with him would be profound, reverent. And it had only been sex. Very pleasurable, very nice. But without his love, it was only physical. She wondered if she'd always remember it with the same degree of bitterness.

She pulled the chemise over her head and then pulled on her dress. Behind her, she heard him putting his own clothes back on and tried not to remember the beauty of his body without them. Hard muscles covered with dark blond hair, strength and beauty in every sinew. She'd never forget this. He would, of course. There would be other women. Her eyes closed; she didn't want to know about them. She was only one in a line, and that's all she would ever be. Now she wouldn't even have the dignity of being the one that got away. And when it was too late, she finally understood why he'd kept his distance. He'd wanted her to keep her illusions. Now she had none left.

With her hand on the last button, she stepped into her wide-heeled shoes and turned to face him with her chin proudly lifted.

"Thanks for the lesson," she said quietly.

He actually winced. "No," he said under his breath, searching her dark, wounded green eyes. "No, don't make it into something cheap. It wasn't."

Her lower lip trembled, threatening to leave her defenseless. She forced herself to smile. "Okay."

He moved forward, catching her arms as she tried to get away, to run.

"Don't go," he said. "Don't let that man make you into a plaything. He'll use you and throw you out."

She looked up, loving him with her eyes. "So long, cowboy." She smiled faintly, sadly. "I loved you, Turk," she whispered. She touched his hard face, feeling the muscles harden. "I always will, until I die. I may have other men, but I'll never give all of myself again."

"He'll hurt you!" he ground out, hating this, hating the pain. He hadn't expected that it would hurt when she left, that he wouldn't be able to take her in his stride and walk away.

She touched her fingers to his firm mouth. "No. You've seen to that," she said, her voice exquisitely tender. "No one could possibly have made it as perfect as you did. He won't hurt me." Her eyes searched his one last time, sad and resigned. "I'll love you until I die, Turk."

She turned and moved quickly away, so that he wouldn't see the tears. It was good-bye. They both knew it.

Long after she'd left, Turk sat on the steps of the barn loft, smoking a cigarette, his eyes blank and sad. After Lorene, he'd never wanted anyone else, not permanently. He'd wanted to have Katy; he couldn't deny that. He'd only kept his distance so long because he'd promised Cole. But now . . .

His body ached. Despite the feverish fulfillment he'd had with her, a completion he'd never known with another woman, ever, he was hungry all over again. He remembered her small, taut breasts under his chest, the nipples arousing him as they rubbed against his muscles. . . .

He got up abruptly and took the cigarette outside to grind it out under the heel of his boot. His face set into harsh lines, he went back toward the house. He owed Cole so much, but there had to be a way out of this. Maybe he could talk to her, maybe they could work something out.

It had only been thirty minutes or so since she'd left the barn, long enough to smoke three cigarettes. So it came as a shock when he got to the house and found it empty.

Cassie came back into the kitchen from the pantry to find him staring toward the staircase.

"If you looking for Miss Katy," she said shortly, "she ain't here. She done gone, luggage and all, with that Chicago gangster."

He felt his heart sinking. He turned, his eyes dark, quiet. "When?"

"Not five minutes ago." She sighed. "Mr. Cole going to be like a wild man. And how is I going to tell Miss Marion?" Her tired, lined eyes misted. "My baby, gone off with that—that man! How come you let her go, Mr. Turk?" she demanded.

"She's of age," he said harshly, when all his fighting instincts were screaming for him to go after the man and kill him. But what could he offer her? He didn't want to get married. And after what had happened, it would be impossible all the way around if she stayed here. His friendship with Cole would be at risk; Katy would grow to hate him. And that Chicago man did seem sincere enough, explaining patiently to Turk the night before that their late arrival had been innocent. He cared about Katy, he'd told Turk. He wouldn't do anything to hurt her. Perhaps he'd marry her . . .

Why should that hurt so much? He turned on his heels and stalked out of the house. Cassie was crying softly as he went out the door.

The shock was almost too much for Marion Whitehall. She came home to a tearful Cassie and was hit with the news just as she put her purse down on the hall table.

Her elegant features contorted; her dark eyes filled with tears under their frame of curling, silvery hair. "Gone?" she exclaimed. "My Katy, gone? To—to live with a man? Why didn't someone stop her?"

"Mr. Turk got here too late, and Mr. Cole ain't come home yet, that's why," Cassie moaned. "And I was out in the garden. Nobody was here to stop her. Mr. Turk said she was of age—and he just stomped off somewhere in a temper. Mr. Cole going to be so mad!"

Marion sat down. She felt sick all the way to her shoes. Katy. Her baby. How could she do this? "Has Ben come home?" she asked.

"I doesn't think so," Cassie said, sobbing. "He didn't come down for breakfast, so I looks in his room, and he ain't been in it. So I reckon he ain't here. Oh, Lord! What a terrible day this is! What a terrible homecoming for Mr. Cole!"

Marion felt the tears running down her cheeks. "Did she leave a message? A note? Anything?"

"I'll go look," Cassie said, ambling toward the staircase.

Just then, the front door flew open, and Ben Whitehall came rushing through it, his dark eyes wild, his dark hair disheveled like his once-immaculate gray suit. "I got it!" he burst out, "I got it! I got it! He hired me!"

He grabbed Cassie and spun her around in an impromptu dance, too exuberant to notice that nobody was smiling. "I'm going to work for a brand spanking new San Antonio newspaper." He laughed. "They hired me to write news. I've been out with the owner and his daughter, and I have to go back—" He stopped, frowning as the somber faces of his mother and housekeeper penetrated his enthusiasm. He let go of Cassie. "What is it? What's wrong?"

"Your sister just left for Chicago," Marion said miserably, her face a study in desperation and shame. "To live with the owner of a speakeasy!"

═══ Chapter Four ═══

BEN'S FACE FROZE. HE STRAIGHTENED, RUNNING AN idle hand through his thick, dark hair. He stared at his mother. "She left with that gangster?" he asked, as if he could hardly believe what he'd heard. "Why didn't somebody stop her?"

"Turk apparently didn't get here in time," Marion said quietly, her eyes wet with tears. "My little girl . . . in that terrible place! Oh, Ben! What will become of her?"

"Now, Mama," Ben said awkwardly. He knelt before her, rubbing her hands in his. "Mama, she's a big girl. Are you sure they aren't getting married?"

"I don't know," she said. "Cassie's looking for a note or something. Why did she do it?" she asked, lifting eyes as dark as his own to question him. "She's been so wild lately, but I never expected her to do anything like this. Ben"—she leaned forward urgently— "Coleman will kill him."

"Yes, I know," he said. It was the truth, too. Cole had a hell of a temper, and he doted on Katy. He wouldn't put it past his big brother to get on the first train North with a pistol on his hip.

"How are we going to tell him?" she persisted, gnawing on her lower lip.

Ben forced a smile. Just his luck, he thought miserably. Here he'd came home with the best news of his budding career, and there was nobody to listen. Sister Katy had stolen his thunder.

"Here," Cassie called from the hall, waving a piece of paper. "She did leave us a note!"

Marion took it from her with trembling hands and read it. "Mama and all," Katy had scribbled. "Danny and I are engaged. We are going to Chicago today to meet his parents. We'll invite you all to the wedding! Wish us luck. Love, Katy."

Ben met his mother's dark eyes. "Do you believe it?"

She shook her head. "But it's important that we make Coleman believe it . . . Do you understand me, Ben, Cassie?"

They both nodded. Cole's temper wasn't something to arouse unnecessarily. It was frankly dangerous.

Meanwhile Katy was sitting jauntily beside Danny in the spiffy Alfa Romeo, forcing herself to laugh gaily and pretend wild enthusiasm for the long trip North.

Beside her, Danny Marlone was grinning from ear to ear, his complexion even darker against his perfect white teeth. He gave his companion a warm glance and began to whistle.

"You'll love the Windy City, babe," he said. "I'll show you all the best places. There's a beach . . . You'll love that. I've got this big house, all stone, on a hill overlooking the lake, chock-full of servants. You'll have everything you want. Everything!"

"Darling, I did tell this one itty-bitty white lie," she said, wanting everything aboveboard.

He caught her hand and pressed the palm to his lips. "What itty-bitty white lie?"

She swallowed, trying not to think about Turk and how it had been . . . "Well, so that my brother wouldn't kill you, I said we were getting married."

"Darling! But this is so sudden!" He chuckled, grinning at her.

She just stared, taken aback.

"It sounds great, doesn't it? Mr. and Mrs. Danny Marlone," he said, clasping her fingers closer. He laid her open palm on his thigh. "Yeah, I like that. We'll go whole hog, too. Announcements in all the papers, only the best people at the wedding. Your family can come. Your big brother can give you away. Oh, it'll be great, honey!"

Her breath lodged in her chest. She couldn't believe what she was hearing! "But I thought you just—just wanted to have an affair!" she burst out, turning to face him.

"I want you," he said, and the look in his eyes made her feel oddly humble. That wasn't lust. That was love, pure and simple, and even while she marveled at being the recipient of it, she ached to have that look from Turk. She never would, now. Never.

"For keeps?" she whispered.

He nodded. He pulled the car to the side of the road and let the engine idle while he stared at her. "For keeps. Let's get married."

"I'm not a virgin," she said straight-out, without going into detail.

"Neither am I. So what?" he asked bluntly.

Her cheeks went rosy. She smiled, feeling really shy. "Well . . ."

He bent and put his mouth over hers. It wasn't unpleasant, letting him kiss her. He ran his hands slowly over her shoulders, down over her breasts, and that wasn't unpleasant, either.

He laughed. "You're not that experienced, either, chick," he whispered as she flushed again. He winked at her as he moved back under the wheel and put it in gear. "We'll get along okay. Now sit back and watch this baby run!" He hit the accelerator, and the car shot forward with a surge of pure power.

Katy, sitting beside him, suddenly felt as if she'd won a lottery. So there wouldn't be any disgrace. She'd be a respectable married lady, and Cole wouldn't come and kill Danny. She closed her eyes and smiled. She wondered what Turk would say when he found out. He'd probably be relieved to hear that she was out of his hair once and for all, she thought bitterly. She comforted herself with the hope that she wouldn't be pregnant. Turk had tried to spare her that shame. It was one thing to go to Danny without her chastity, quite another to present him with another man's child. She had too much character for that kind of dirty trick. But . . . what if Turk's actions had been too late?

Far away, on the northern end of San Antonio, Lacy was clutching her husband's sleeve as he helped her on board the morning train that ran down through Floresville and stopped on a siding near Spanish Flats.

He was deadly quiet this morning, all business. Still in his work clothes, he drew feminine eyes nevertheless. But he never returned those sly glances, or even acknowledged them. He helped Lacy into a seat and slid lazily down beside her. Deceptive, that slow movement of his lean, hard body. She'd seen him in a hurry once or twice, and he was as quick as greased lightning and twice as dangerous.

"Katy will be glad of some young company," he remarked as the train pulled slowly out of the station, lurching with the first movements.

"What's he like, this Chicago man she's seeing?" Lacy asked.

He shrugged. "Italian. Dark, well mannered, a little shady. Turk doesn't like him."

"Turk doesn't like anybody around Katy, and you know it," she murmured dryly, glancing up at his hard face.

Dark, angry eyes cut down into hers. "Turk is the best friend I have in the world. But even he isn't permitted that kind of familiarity. Katy isn't going to become one of Turk's castoffs."

"Oh, no," Lacy said demurely, folding her hands over the lap of her dark skirt. "But she's perfect for a gangster?"

"It isn't that kind of relationship. She's young. She's just having a fling," he said.

She watched him cross his long legs and roll a cigarette. He was so capable, she thought. Always in perfect command, taking charge, making everything all right. She'd felt secure with him, even in their early days together. She'd never been afraid when Cole was anywhere around.

"Why won't you let Turk near her?" she asked bluntly.

He turned in the seat, with his arm draped carelessly over the back, and studied her. "Because he seduces everything in skirts," he said matter-of-factly. "Katy would be easy prey. Then it would be impossible. He'd be embarrassed and guilty about it, and she'd be compromised or worse. I'd have to do something about it, and that wouldn't help anybody. No. It's better this way."

"You don't think he could settle down, maybe get married?" she persisted gently.

"He was married," he said. "She died. He's never wanted anyone else like that. I'm not sure he can. He likes his own company now."

"Like you," she said, smiling faintly.

His broad shoulders lifted and fell. "I'm used to it. It takes too much time and effort, letting people get close. More often than not, they find a weakness and exploit it. If you keep them at arm's length, that can't happen."

"It's a pretty lonely life," she reminded him, gray eyes soft and searching.

"Loneliness and independence are different words for the same thing. Freedom. I like mine. I don't think I could survive being hog-tied and smothered."

"I never tried to smother you," she said, defending herself. "I just hated being ignored constantly."

"And the one time I didn't ignore you," he replied quietly, watching her blush, "you cried all night long. I heard you, even through the wall."

She turned her face away, but he caught her chin and jerked it back around to search it, his eyes dark and fierce.

"You walked away," she said unsteadily, glancing around. There was no one near enough to hear them; the train was remarkably uncrowded for that time of day. She looked back at him. "You knew you'd hurt me, and you couldn't get out fast enough. Of course I cried."

"What could I have said or done then?" he asked, eyes narrow and dark. "I thought you wanted me. You seemed to, that morning."

Her lips parted at the memory of it: his mouth warm and searching, his body hard and hungry against her own. It had been so sweet, so heady. "Yes, I wanted you," she whispered. "I thought it would be the way it was that morning. But afterward, it was like being . . .

used," she said falteringly. "You wouldn't even let me touch you."

His jaw clenched as he stared down at her, his chest rising and falling unevenly. He did want, so desperately, to tell her why he'd hurt her. But he wondered if she'd believe him even if he could make his pride bend that far. "That's past history, anyway, Lacy," he said curtly. He lifted the cigarette to his parted lips and took a long draw. "We'll have to make the best of things, if we can."

She looked out the window, to the low horizon and acres of flat, unfenced land outside it. "I don't suppose it's occurred to you that we could get a divorce?"

"No. So it looks as if you're stuck, doesn't it, kiddo?" he asked, with a cold smile.

"Or you are," she replied sweetly, and smiled back.

He glanced down at the neat dark suit she was wearing and the pretty little hat on her dark head. "I'm glad you aren't wearing any of those outrageous new dresses like what you had on last night," he commented. "I have a hell of a time keeping my cowhands working as it is, without you women driving them crazy. They've been hanging around the house for weeks now, trying to get a glimpse of Katy's legs. I finally burned two of her more revealing dresses."

"Just your style, cattle king," she taunted. "If you can't reason with people, run over them. You were always like that, even when you were younger."

"Don't expect me to change, Lacy. I'm too old."

She shook her head, staring at the rugged features, the straight nose and chiseled, wide mouth, the square jaw. It wasn't the nicest face she'd ever seen on a man, but it suited him, and she loved every hard line of it. Bronzed skin, deep-set dark eyes, heavy brows, thick straight hair that fell into an unruly heap on his broad forehead. He was sensuous. Yes, he really was, she thought suddenly, even in the way he moved. But it was only an illusion, because he was more repressed than any man she'd ever known and he hated the very idea of sex. She'd wondered a time or two how many women he'd had in his life. Oddly, enough, she sometimes thought there had hardly been any.

"You're staring, honey," he chided, watching her intense scrutiny.

"You're a very sensuous man," she said quietly, watching the impact of that statement freeze his hard features.

He turned his face away from her and leaned back to smoke his cigarette in a frigid silence.

"I'm sorry if I offended you," she said after a minute, settling down into her own comfortable seat as the train gathered speed.

"No. It wasn't that," he replied, his voice even, quiet.

Well, whatever it was, he didn't volunteer anything more. He sat with his hat down over his eyes, the cigarette smoking between his lean, dark fingers, and he didn't say another word.

Still, her eyes continued to study him, running like hands down his long, lean body with its rippling play of muscle as he shifted.

"Why do they call Jude Turk?" she asked unexpectedly.

His thin lips actually smiled, but he didn't open his eyes. "Because there aren't any fiercer fighters than the Turks. He's a force to behold when he's mad, kiddo. A mean man."

"As mean as you?" she teased softly, her blue eyes twinkling in their frame of soft, forward-curving hair.

He glanced down at her with one eye. "About half," he said. That eye went down to her full breasts and lingered, then went back up again to catch her blush. "Embarrassed?"

"You're the one who won't talk about sex," she reminded him.

He looked as if he wanted to say something, but he shrugged and closed his eyes again.

If only he could talk to her, she thought miserably. If only they could just communicate. She sometimes thought that there was a loving, giving man locked up in those suppressed emotions. That Cole was a keg of dynamite, waiting for a match—that as a lover he'd be everything she could want. If she could only find the spark to ignite him. But he seemed not to care about that side of his nature. And only occasionally, like just now, did any hint of it come out. He was the most complex and puzzling man she'd ever known. Perhaps that was why, after all the years she'd known him, he still fascinated her.

Ben was waiting for them at the siding, dressed in a beige city suit with a derby on his head, hands in his pockets as he leaned back against the building. The aging but jaunty black runabout was parked nearby, its top down.

Lacy couldn't help but grin at the picture of gay youth he presented. "The future famous writer," she murmured. "Do you think he'll make it, Cole?"

"I suppose he'll keep trying until he dies, at least," he said. "Don't encourage him," he added unexpectedly.

She glared at him as he got up to let her out of the seat. "I never did."

"He's still got a wild crush on you," he said. His dark eyes narrowed. "This time, if he makes one move toward you, brother or no brother, I'll beat him to his knees."

"Cole!" she gasped, shocked by the hard look in his eyes.

"You remember what I said," he told her, and took her arm firmly in his hand as he retrieved the carpetbag with her clothes in it and walked off the train with Lacy in tow.

"Lacy, darling!" Ben said in his most sophisticated tone, spreading open his arms. "How are you?"

"She's fine," Cole said, with a cutting edge in his deep voice as he dared Ben to come one step closer. "How's Mother?"

"Upset . . ." Ben started, obviously nonplussed by his brother's sudden possessiveness. "Katy's gone."

Standing next to him, Lacy actually felt the tension grow in Cole's lean, powerful body. "She's what?" he demanded.

"It's okay; she's not going to live in sin or anything," Ben said quickly. "She's going to marry that Danny Marlone. He's taking her to his mother's until the wedding."

"It's too quick," Cole said shortly. "They've only known each other for a few weeks. And where the hell was Turk while this was going on?"

"At the ranch. He said she was of age. Besides," he added ruefully, "she was long gone before he knew about it."

"He could have gone after her!" Cole shot at him. "So could've you!"

"And done what, for God's sake?" Ben demanded coldly. "She's over twenty-one!"

Cole glared at him until he actually moved backward a step.

"He's right," Lacy interrupted gently. She touched his arm, noticing with a faint hope that he didn't jerk away this time. "She's a grown woman. You can't force her to come back. And knowing Katy, she'd never go off with a man she didn't love."

"You don't know her lately," he replied quietly. "She's changed. Gone wild."

"It's just the new age." Ben laughed. "Times are changing, for the better. Everything's looser, less rigid. Girls are getting liberated, that's all."

"They're getting loose, that's all," Cole returned curtly. "Short skirts, cussing, drinking, running wild with men . . . The younger generation's going to hell!"

"Well, yours sure did the world a lot of good, didn't it?" Ben shot back. "The war to end all wars . . . isn't that what they called it? How many men did you kill, big brother?"

Cole hit him. The movement of the taller man's fist was so fast, Ben didn't even see it coming. And Lacy didn't say a single word. If anything, she moved even closer to Cole, her accusing blue eyes on Ben's bruised face as he got slowly to his feet, rubbing his chin.

"Okay, I was out of line," he muttered, glaring at his brother. "But so were you. The world's changing. If you can't change with it, you'll be left behind. Car's over here."

He went ahead of them, looking so ruffled and trying so hard to be dignified that Lacy had to fight back a smile.

"No censure?" Cole chided, glancing at her. "I thought you'd jump to his defense."

She shook her head. "I'm sorry you didn't hit him harder," she replied calmly.

He stopped walking and looked down at her, finding

the same wild spirit in her eyes that he'd seen and liked when she was still in her teens. It would have matched his own—in another time, another place. What a hell of a pity, the way it was between them. Perhaps he should have told her in the very beginning how little he had to offer. He should have told her the truth.

His fingers touched her hair. It was soft and cool, and he wondered why she was so rigid, hardly breathing.

"Does that frighten you?" he asked, searching her eyes. "You've stopped breathing."

"I don't want you to stop," she confessed in a whisper, returning the soft scrutiny. "I was afraid that if I moved, you'd think I didn't want you to touch me."

His fingers actually trembled. "Lacy—"

"Are you two coming with me or not?" Ben called belligerently from the car.

Cole couldn't help laughing. "Young rooster," he muttered. "Okay, son. We're on our way."

Lacy sighed softly as Cole moved ahead. Thanks, Ben, she thought viciously. Someday I'll do *you* a favor!

Just as they reached the car, a small blond whirlwind erupted from a horse and ran pell-mell toward Ben.

"Hi!" Faye Cameron burst out, jumping on to the running board to plant an airy kiss on Ben's cheek. "I didn't know you were back from the big city! How are you? Hi, Lacy. Good to see you again. Cole, you're looking good."

"What do you want?" Ben muttered, glaring at her. "I told you—I don't have time to come calling right now. I'm busy."

"But it's my birthday party," Faye told him, her big blue eyes wide and hopeful. "I'll be eighteen. Oh, Ben . . . You promised you'd come. It's tonight!"

Ben shifted his hat on his head and looked and felt

uncomfortable. That was the trouble with women, he thought irritably. You took them to bed once or twice and they tried to own you. Still, he thought, watching her, she was a hot little thing in bed, all soft little breasts and hot skin—and she'd do anything in the world to please him. If it hadn't been for her father, he'd have been over to see her before this. But the old man didn't like him, and Ben wasn't sure what Ira Cameron might do if he found out Ben had seduced his only child.

"Gee, honey, I'm sorry," Ben said soothingly, tweaking her hair gently. "But I've just got myself a nice job in San Antonio, writing for a newspaper."

"Ben, how great!" she burst out, all smiles.

Well, at least he had one person to share his triumphs with. He grinned. "I'll be the only reporter on the staff, too. Mr. Bradley said I was so good that he wouldn't need anybody except me! I get a pretty good salary and my own office, and I've even been invited to visit the Bradleys at their home."

"That's swell, Ben," Faye said. She frowned. "But doesn't a big city newspaper need more than just one reporter?"

Ben had wondered about that himself, but he glossed it over. "I'm good, I tell you. And even people in San Antonio know about the ranch and that we're solid citizens. Mr. Bradley said that was good for business. I'll come over in a week or two and tell you all about it, okay? But just now I've promised to meet my employer and his daughter at their home for dinner," he added, and Faye seemed to understand. "I'll make it up to you."

"Sure," Faye said, but it was with a pale smile. So the boss had a daughter. And her Ben was so ambitious . . . She moved back from the car, all her bright laughter gone, her beauty diminished. "Sure. Well, nice seeing you. 'Bye!"

She ran for her horse, but not before Lacy had seen the pain and tears in her eyes. Poor little thing, she thought bitterly. Ben was so thoughtless!

Cole didn't say a word. Perhaps he thought Ben was justified. Men!

They got into the car, and Ben cranked the engine. Behind them, Faye Cameron sat tall in the saddle, her young breasts thrusting against the fabric of her yellow shirt, her well-rounded hips emphasized by the jeans. The sun made a halo of her blond curls, made silver tracks of the wash of tears on her pale cheeks. As she watched them drive away, she dashed an angry hand over her wet face.

"I'll make you care someday, Ben Whitehall," she whispered brokenly. "Someday, somehow, I'll make you care!"

She wished she knew more about men. She'd tried to be everything he'd wanted in bed. She'd let him do the most incredible things to her young body without a single protest, when she wondered if it was quite normal. He'd even kissed the inside of her thighs!

Of course, Ben was experienced. He'd told her once about one of his women, describing in detail exactly what he'd done to her. Faye had turned red and gasped at the brazen conversation, but she'd listened all the same. And when he'd finished, and Ben saw the look on her face, he'd thrown her down on the bed and taken her, standing up, her thighs in his strong hands as he looked down at her body on the bed; then he'd laughed as he shuddered with completion. The memory made her hot all over. She shifted uncomfortably in the saddle, her lips parted, her breasts gone hard with desire. She wanted him to follow her home and make love to her. But he wasn't going to do that. She'd have to wait until he could fit her into his busy life.

She turned the horse slowly, hurting as she never had before. If only she could read and write, if only she were intelligent and educated. Ben only wanted her in bed because she wasn't smart enough to associate with him in public. But maybe if she got pregnant, he'd want her. Her lips pursed. Yes. Maybe that was the only way she'd ever get him. And Cole would make him marry her. She smiled. It would be poetic justice, even, since it was Ben who'd forced Cole to marry Lacy. She sat up straighter as she urged her mount into a canter. It was a beautiful day after all. It felt good to be eighteen and already a woman.

Behind her, the roadster lurched into motion as Ben pushed down the accelerator. He wondered if Faye was going to be difficult. She was a sweet kid, but that Jessica Bradley was some chick! He couldn't think of anything he'd like better than doing to the sleek brunette what he'd been doing to little Faye. Only more of it. He began to whistle as the car went racing madly down the long dirt road toward Spanish Flats.

Chapter Five

BEN HAD THE TOP DOWN, AND THE OLD 1914 runabout was filled with choking dust. It was a good thing his mother had stopped him from putting that Lizzie label on it, Lacy thought wryly, or people would have done some staring. GIRLS, WATCH YOUR STEP-INS painted on the side would have drawn a few eyes! That fad had really caught on with the young people, even in Spanish Flats.

The runabout was a tight fit for the three of them. It was as old as Cole's big Ford touring car, but few local people could afford new cars anyway. Just to be able to own a Tin Lizzie was quite a feat following the war, given the problems of depending on agriculture for a living. Lacy felt her lungs filling with dust, but she held her tongue. Cole was used to dust; he lived with it day in and day out. He'd only think less of her for acting like the tenderfoot she sometimes was.

Sitting close beside her, his long arm over the back of the seat, Cole stared straight ahead, his body as taut as drawn cord. Lacy felt that tension and was puzzled by it. Surely the argument with Ben hadn't caused it, and she was certain it wasn't proximity to her. Perhaps it was the memories young Ben had unwittingly aroused. Or maybe, she grinned to herself, it was that Ben was driving. Odd that Cole hadn't protested, but he sometimes indulged his younger brother. And it was obvious how much Ben enjoyed driving. Cole tended to be more at home on horseback. Once he'd driven his big car through a haystack, and the guffawing cowboys who saw him do it were saved from certain death only by divine intervention. It had started raining just as Cole went for the first man. Cole hadn't driven a lot since then.

"How was the big city?" Ben yelled at Lacy above the road and engine noise.

"Lonely," she said, without thinking.

"That isn't what Katy said after she went to that last party!" Ben chuckled.

Lacy stared at her hands in her lap. "No, I guess not." She remembered the party. It had been like all the others she gave. Wild and bright and long. And the only person who hadn't enjoyed it was Lacy herself. She enjoyed nothing without Cole.

His fingers touched her neck, lightly brushing it, as if by accident. Her pulse increased, her breath decreased. She looked up into dark, searching eyes and felt her whole body go rigid with mingled desire and pleasure.

His eyes dropped to her mouth, lingering there for so long that her lips involuntarily parted. She wondered what he would do if Ben weren't sitting beside them, and thought in her heart she knew. She would have given anything at that moment to have Ben leap out of the car and vanish, so that she could be totally alone with her husband.

Ben didn't vanish, of course, and Cole was distracted by a herd of cattle being moved in the distance. His eyes narrowed, watching, and Lacy smiled at that intense scrutiny. Just like a cattleman to be fascinated by anything on four legs.

It took only a few minutes to get to Spanish Flats, and Marion came rushing out to meet them. She didn't hug Cole—that was forbidden, and everyone in the family knew and respected his dislike of physical contact. But she hugged Lacy, warmly and for a long time. Marion did look thinner, older.

"I'm so glad you're here to help me cope, darling," Marion said brokenly. "My baby's run off with a gangster, Lacy!"

Lacy patted her on the back awkwardly. "Now, Marion. She's a big girl, all grown up."

"And if she isn't now, she soon will be," Cole said shortly. "Is it true—about the marriage?"

"Why, yes, of course." Marion lied glibly, not believing it would really happen. She even smiled. "We'll all be invited to the wedding."

"You can go for all of us," Cole said, his smile as icy as his tone. "If I went, I'd kill the—" He almost said it, remembered Lacy and his mother in the nick of time, and walked off without another word.

"Whew, that was close," Ben said, with a shudder. "I opened my mouth out of turn and set him off at the siding. He's still mad."

"Why did you do that to him, Ben?" Lacy asked softly, her eyes quiet and accusing. "You know he won't talk about the war."

"Maybe that's why," Ben muttered. "He's hiding something. He's been hiding it ever since he came back, and Turk helps him. Neither one of them will tell the truth . . ."

"What happened is their business," Marion said, touching her son's arm lightly. "It's none of ours."

Ben sighed roughly. "Well, maybe so. I'll put up the car and bring your bags in, Lacy."

Lacy followed Marion inside, to be grabbed and soundly smothered by Cassie, who cried all over her and enthused about her coming home—and then rushed off to get hot tea to serve.

"You look well, at least," Marion said later as they sat alone in the elegant living room sipping sweet tea from the dainty china cups Marion had brought here from her girlhood home in Houston.

"I wish I could say that I felt it," Lacy confided. "I've been dead for eight months. It's been horrible without him."

Marion put her cup down gently on the carved oak coffee table. "He hasn't been the picture of joy, either. He's been even more quiet than úsual, working until all hours. You know, I didn't even have to twist his arm to get him to go see you. He almost volunteered."

"Maybe he wanted to see how many lovers I had." Lacy laughed bitterly.

"He knows better than that," the older woman scoffed. "So do I. I used to watch you, watching him. So much love, all wasted on him. He and Turk are much alike, Lacy. They wrapped themselves in steel after they came back from the war, and now they're trying to live without ties of any kind. I don't know what happened, of course, but I'm almost certain that Katy didn't go to Chicago for love of that smooth-talking gangster she's been dating."

"You think Turk said something to her?" Lacy asked, studying the wrinkled face.

"I'm certain that he did. Perhaps he told her that there was no hope, or said something cruel to her. But Katy wouldn't have gone like that without a reason. And she didn't seem in love to me. At least not with Danny Marlone!"

Katy was her friend, but Lacy wondered if anyone really knew her heart. Lacy never had, although she loved the younger girl like a sister. If there was one man in the world Katy would die for, though, it was Turk. Just the least notice from him could put the younger woman into dreams of ecstasy for hours. It was almost pitiful, the way she watched him and found excuses to be with him. Turk, on the other hand, was, as Marion had said, a lot like Cole. His face gave away nothing, and he seemed to hide his own vulnerabilities in humor. If he had vulnerabilities. Perhaps personal tragedy had damaged him, too. Cole had said that Turk's wife died. That would be shattering, especially to a man who was so much a man. It would be like an indictment of his masculinity that he'd failed to save her.

"You're very quiet," Marion murmured.

"I'm worried about Katy, too," she confessed. "Is he a nice man, this Danny? Will he be good to her?"

"I suppose so, darling. But it's his business that bothers me. He owns a speakeasy, and I don't think he's above making dishonest deals. It bothers me. Still, what can we do? She's a grown woman now. I was married and had Coleman when I was just her age. My hands are tied." She took another sip of tea. "At least Coleman believed me. He won't go rushing up there with his pistol."

"Believed you?" Lacy probed.

"Darling, I don't believe a word of the note Katy left me," came the quiet reply. "I don't think that man has any intention of marrying her."

"Oh." Lacy felt shattered by that statement. She loved Katy. Katy had always been a good girl, despite her coquettishness. And now, for her to go and—and live with a man! Oh, Katy, how could you? she thought miserably. How could you let Turk cause you to do something like that?

Then she remembered her own threat to Cole if he didn't share her room. About George. Well, she comforted herself, the ends justified the means, didn't they? But until tonight, she wouldn't know. And remembering the last time, she wondered if she was going to have enough courage to go through with this. She did love Cole. But would her love for him be enough to save their marriage?

Ben borrowed the car for his dinner date, careful to reassure his mother that he was leaving in plenty of time for the long drive—and that he wouldn't wreck her pretty little black runabout.

Mothers, he thought to himself as he gunned the engine going down the long, winding dirt road. The sky was cloudy, but perhaps it wouldn't rain. Anyway, there was a top—if he could remember how to put it up!

He was still bothered about the new atmosphere between himself and Cole. In all the arguments they'd ever had, Cole had never lifted a hand to him before. That was out of character, even if the display of temper wasn't. He'd certainly hit a nerve. He knew that his big brother was hiding something; he just couldn't figure out what it was. Marion had said it was none of his business, but he wondered all the same. Cole was so secretive about his private life. And especially about Lacy.

Ben grimaced, remembering how he'd brought about that disastrous marriage. He hadn't meant to force them into a corner; it had all been a big joke. But it wasn't funny the next morning when they were let out. Lacy had been white as a sheet and crying, something the spunky girl had never done in front of him before. Of course, the look on Cole's face had been enough to reduce a strong man to tears—utterly ferocious. Ben had gone to visit an aunt in Houston the same day, to get out of Cole's way while he cooled off. And by the time he came back, Cole and Lacy were married.

He'd wanted Lacy for himself. She was so lovely, so cultured. While Coleman had been away during the war, Ben had been Lacy's shadow Then when Coleman had come home again, the older man had been so cold and remote that no one could approach him except Turk. He'd actually backed away from Lacy when she'd gone running, with her heart in her eyes, to welcome him home from France after armistice was declared. He knew he'd never forget the way Lacy had looked, or how she'd reacted to Cole's distance during the months and years that followed. She'd been talking of leaving the ranch, for the first time, when Ben had hit on his practical joke. He'd asked Lacy to marry him, in desperation, and she'd refused with such gentleness.

It had almost killed him to know, finally, that she'd only felt affection for him, and that had rankled. Like Katy, Ben was used to getting his own way, especially with women. He sighed, thinking about the girls he'd been out with in San Antonio. He sometimes felt certain that he knew more about women even than Cole did. Cole seemed remarkably repressed; he always walked off when Ben and Turk started talking about their conquests. Especially since the war.

Turk was a rounder, he thought. The ace pilot had been his hero for a long time. Cole was too hard an act to follow. Turk was more human. Ben admired his success with women, his cool, easy manner. Turk was high-tempered, too, like Cole, but he was a little more forgiving and less rigid in his attitudes. Ben wondered how Cole got along with Lacy when the lights went out.

He thought that might have been why Lacy left him in the first place. They'd had separate rooms, and Ben suspected, as did the others in the family, that the marriage had never been consummated. That would hurt a woman like Lacy, to have everyone think her own husband considered her undesirable. She'd stayed in San Antonio eight months, and there had been a man hanging around her, from what Katy said. But for Lacy to come home with Cole, the man must not have meant much to her. Lacy probably still loved Cole, despite everything. Looking back, he couldn't remember a time when Lacy hadn't looked at the older man with her heart in her sad eyes. But Ben hadn't noticed—not until he'd played his infamous practical joke and forced Lacy into the anguish of a loveless marriage. He sometimes felt very guilty about that.

His mind went back to meeting them at the siding, to little Faye Cameron's sudden appearance. She was a cute thing, that blond tomboy, but hardly the kind of woman he needed. Writers, he decided, were loners. They couldn't be restricted to just one woman. They needed lots of women.

Of course, there was Jessica Bradley, the daughter of the new periodical's publisher. She was a dish. Very dark, with creamy skin, and a very kissable mouth, and a body he was aching to get his hands on. Now *there* was a sophisticated little doll. He began to whistle as he thought about her and increased his speed. Poor little Faye would just have to set her sights a little lower. A rancher's daughter needed a cattleman, anyway, not a famous writer.

The Bradleys were waiting for him when he got to the elegant residence near the Alamo. Randolph Bradley was tall and silver-haired, with a neatly clipped mustache and very blue eyes. His daughter apparently took after her mother, whose portrait hung above the elegant mantle in the Victorian living room.

"Mama is in Europe, of course," Jessica informed him as they sipped champagne cocktails before being served dinner in the spacious dining room. She moved closer to him, drowning him in exquisite scent. "She detests the frontier. It's nothing like New York. But Papa insisted that we come here to take over this territorial publication."

"Papa knows a good business venture when he sees one," Bradley said haughtily. He looked down his nose at her and made a face. "This little publication is going to become a force in Western journalism, you wait and see, daughter. Now, Whitehall, tell me about yourself. Your people are in cattle ranching, I understand."

Ben felt uncomfortable. "Why, yes," he replied, with a faint smile, trying to sound as confident and urbane as his host. "My brother handles that end of it, of course. I'm more into the—uh . . . financial side of things." Thank God Cole wasn't here to hear him or he'd be into something else—like Cole's fist!

"Good man. Nasty things, cattle," the older man said, lifting his glass. "We're going to make you into the reporter of the century. Scandal, crime, tragedy— We'll make a fortune! Here's to profit, son."

Ben lifted his own glass. Waterford crystal, he recognized. Very nice. The bit about scandal, crime, and tragedy had gone right over his head. "Here's to profit!"

It was a wonderful evening. Old man Bradley went out of his way to be courteous, and Jessica's dark eyes made Ben into a nervous wreck with their frank sensuality. He was never aware of what he ate, but he was thankful for his mother's insistence on proper table manners. At least he didn't embarrass himself by not knowing which fork to use.

"Well," Bradley said when they'd finished dessert and were sipping glasses of brandy in the living room, "I must get my rest. Bed at eight every evening, you know, son. It keeps the body fit."

"Yes, of course," Ben said falteringly, rising to his feet awkwardly. "I must be getting back home . . ."

"That long drive at this time of night? Don't be absurd!" Bradley scoffed. "You'll stay with us. Can't have my star reporter on the road in the middle of the night. I need you, my boy. Your connections in San Antonio will be invaluable to me . . . to us! Advertising counts, you know, and a locally known name sells ads. Good business. Sleep well, my boy. Good night, my dear," he told Jessica, bending to kiss her cheek warmly.

"Good night, Daddy," Jessica said demurely. "I'll show our guest to his room. An early night won't hurt any of us."

"My thoughts exactly." Bradley chuckled as he climbed the winding staircase.

"Come along, Bennett," Jessica told Ben. She put her glass down and took his hand in hers.

She was wearing a filmy blue creation, very lacy and clinging, and Ben's heart actually hurt him with its wild pounding. She was the most sophisticated woman he'd ever known. His age exactly, but she was much more worldly than he was. And so sexy!

As she opened the door to a room in the wing across from where her father had vanished, he expected her to bid him good night. But she came in with him . . . and locked the door behind her.

"Now," she whispered huskily, "I can do what I've waited all night for.

"And what is that?" he asked, drinking in the scent of her.

"This," she murmured, drawing his head down to hers.

God, could she kiss! He felt his toes curling at the first impact of her soft, moist lips. Her tongue went quickly into his mouth, thrusting, teasing. He reached for her, all restraint gone at the intimacy of her hips pushing urgently against his. She was no virgin. Not this little number!

Seconds later, she led him to the bed, but she moved back when he reached for her.

"Not yet, little Ben." She laughed softly. She backed away, smoothing the dress down her body, her dark eyes sultry and triumphant as she saw the desire in his.

She peeled the buttons from their buttonholes with slender, deft fingers, and let him watch as she peeled the bodice down and stepped out of the dress, standing only in her pale lilac chemise and hose. Holding his eyes, she toyed with the thin straps, easing them slowly down her arms, her lips parted, her tongue touching her teeth.

Ben sat rigidly on the white coverlet, astonished at her lack of embarrassment. She tugged the chemise away from her small, taut breasts and let it fall. Standing in her knickers and garter belt and hose, she kicked the chemise across the polished wood floor and lifted her arms to remove the hairpins and loosen her long, dark hair.

Her back arched as she moved toward him. "How do you like me, little Ben?" she whispered. "Hmm?"

"God, you're . . . lovely!" he choked.

"Then don't sit there, lovey dove . . . Show Jessica you like her," she whispered, lifting his hands.

She put them on her firm breasts, his palms hard against the taut, dark nipples, and watched with glittery, excited eyes as he caressed them.

"Come on, honey. Don't be slow," she teased, drawing his hands down to her knickers and garter belt.

He removed them with trembling hands, his heart pounding as he eased them off and peeled down her silky hose. She laughed a little wildly, sliding back onto the coverlet, glorious in her pink nudity, moving sensuously on the bed under his intense stare.

"Are you just going to stand there looking?" she challenged.

"Oh." He blinked. "No, of course not!" He felt as if it were the first time. His hands were all thumbs as he got rid of the gray suit and most everything under it.

He had a good body, thank God. Smooth and not too pale, and fairly muscular.

He removed his shorts and turned, watching her eyes go down to the explicit masculinity of him.

"Well, my goodness. You're not *little* Ben after all, are you, honey?" She laughed softly, holding out her arms. "Come here, you adorable savage, and love me to death!"

This, at least, was familiar territory. He might not be the world's greatest reporter, but he knew what to do with a woman. As she learned, quickly and with some measure of astonishment.

He laughed to himself at her shocked eagerness when she felt his tongue on the soft, warm inside of her thighs. She was noisy, all right, he thought as he moved up to her soft breasts and felt her go rigid and whimper when he caught a dusky, fragrant nipple delicately in his teeth and nibbled it. Yes, she was going to make a lot of noise. He hoped no one was close enough to hear her.

While Ben was enjoying his evening, Lacy was cursing her own—along with the impulsive threat that had forced Cole into the intimacy of sharing her room. She was alone, pacing the floor, dressed in a soft pink cotton gown and flowing robe, And the fact that they were married didn't make her feel any less like a vamp. It had started out to be fun, but now she was nervous. She'd felt something new and delicate in her relationship with Cole all day. A warmth that had been lacking before, a tender beginning. She didn't want to jeopardize it. But she was so inexperienced. She knew nothing of men, except what little she'd learned that unpleasant night with Cole.

She clasped her hands together as she paced the wooden floor in her bare feet. She hadn't seen Cole since that afternoon. She'd spent most of it with Marion, talking mostly about Katy. And Cole hadn't come in for supper. There'd been a sick bull, and he and the veterinarian had spent the evening worrying over it out in the barn.

Perhaps he'd just been looking for an excuse to avoid her, she thought miserably. And perhaps he'd go on finding them, every night . . .

She spun around as someone quietly opened the door. She froze in place, staring, as Cole, covered with dust and looking as if he'd just been brawling with a mob of cattle out on his range walked wearily into the room.

"How's your bull?" she asked softly.

His dark eyebrows lifted. He even managed a tired smile as he tugged off his wide-brimmed hat and sailed it across the room onto a chair. "That wasn't the question I expected, Mrs. Whitehall," he replied as he stood before her, tall and overpowering in his lean masculinity.

"Wasn't it?" she asked, with a demure, shy smile.

"I need a bath," he said. "And a lot of sleep." He cocked his head down at her. "Unless . . . ?" he probed,

taking the attack into the enemy camp. He wanted to see
if she was bluffing. And he almost smiled when her face
went bloodred and she couldn't look at him to save her life.
He was right. She was putting on an act. She wasn't half
as confident as she made out, and that pleased him. It gave
him some badly needed confidence of his own.

He moved closer, smelling of dust and cattle, and she
looked up to find a strange, soft expression—or what
passed for one—in those very dark eyes.

"Instead of getting things on a physical level right at
the outset, Lacy," he began, his voice deep and soft,
"suppose you and I get to know each other? That's the
one thing we've never done. Not even in the beginning,
when you came to live here."

She relaxed visibly. He saw that, and relaxed himself.
He'd been pushing himself all day, finding excuses,
giving his men hell because it was staring him in the face
and he didn't know how to tell her—

"Yes," she interrupted his thoughts. "I'd like that."
She ventured a glance up at him. "I didn't mean to make
it sound so blatant in San Antonio. I'd been drinking."

"I know." He hesitated, seeming as shy as she felt.
"Lacy, about sharing the room . . ."

"Please don't shame me, Cole," she whispered,
averting her eyes.

"I was going to say that I . . . don't mind it," he said
hesitantly.

She looked up, delightfully surprised. Her face brightened; her warm blue eyes smiled at him. She tingled with
pleasure, and it showed. "Thank you," she whispered.

"Okay, kiddo," he said, regaining a little of his old
confidence. He touched her chin with his knuckles,
smiling faintly at her. "I guess we can keep from kicking
each other out of bed."

She beamed, her face gloriously beautiful. She glanced up and then down again. "I hope you don't snore, cowboy," she murmured.

"Not me, lady. How about you?" he added as he started into the bathroom.

She picked up a cushion from the chair to toss at him, and he retreated into the bathroom with a laugh. Minutes later she heard water running.

She found a magazine and curled up with it. How odd this felt, to share a room with a man. Even the sounds of bathing were intimate. She wondered what Cole looked like without his clothing. She'd never seen him that way. The one night they'd been intimate, he'd never turned on the light. In fact, looking back, she was almost certain that he hadn't even undressed completely. Since he'd come home from France, she'd never seen his shirt open, or off, and most of the cowhands went bare-chested from time to time, especially in summer. But not Cole. Not ever these days.

Involuntarily her mind went back to the day he'd left to join his unit for overseas duty. His shirt had been off then, and he'd kissed her and kissed her. She remembered tugging hungrily on the thick hair that covered his broad chest, how it had felt to be close to him, to let him kiss her. She'd thought it was a beginning, but it hadn't been. He hadn't even written just to her alone once he was gone. And when he came back, he couldn't bear to let her touch him at all. Not until that morning in the barn, before he'd come to her room that one night after they'd married. But that was a sad, shaming memory. He'd hurt her badly, and she'd cried. They hadn't talked about it until he'd come to see her in San Antonio. It was still hard to discuss it.

Thinking back made her sad. She shook her head as if

to clear it. Then an article in the magazine caught her eye and she became engrossed in it.

He came out of the bathroom much later, clad in pajamas and a flowing robe. It was his room, after all; he had clothing in the closets, too, next to the ones she'd put there on her arrival. She looked up, forcing a smile.

"You look a few shades lighter," she remarked dryly.

He chuckled, pausing at the vanity mirror to sweep back his straight, thick hair with a comb. It was wet, almost black with dampness, and although he was completely covered in the navy pajamas and robe, it was so intimate to see him in nightclothes.

He saw her expression in the mirror and half smiled. "You're the one who wanted to share a room, honey," he reminded her. "Too late for embarrassment now."

"I suppose so," she murmured. She studied him, thinking how attractive he was, how masculine. "You never told me how your bull was?"

"The vet said he'll live." He turned, studying the brass bed with its huge, spacious mattress. "Which side do you want?"

"I like the one I'm on, if you don't mind," she said, putting aside the magazine.

"As it happens, that's the side I *don't* sleep on," he answered. He sat down on his side of the bed, yawned, and fell back onto the pillows. "God, I'm tired. The days get longer, or I get older."

"Twenty-eight isn't old," she remarked. She studied his lean, dark face. He'd shaved, and his smooth brown cheek tempted her lips, but she liked the idea of making haste slowly. "Sleep well."

"You, too, honey." He rolled onto his side, studying her with those dark, probing eyes. "You look pretty in a nightgown, Mrs. Whitehall," he added, with a smile.

She lowered her eyes to his thin mouth. "I'm glad you think so." She wished she were more experienced, that she knew what to do next. If she moved closer, would he interpret it as a plea to be made love to? Would he like that . . . or would it put another wall between them?

Beside her, Cole was just as uncertain. He didn't want to rush her. She'd only just come back. And he meant it, about wanting something more than a physical relationship. He almost laughed at the irony of that thought. He'd fought this intimacy of being together; he was also too uncertain of what she'd do if she should find out. She was a tenderhearted woman, but he didn't want her pity. He wanted . . . more than that. He remembered, too, that she'd fought him at the last, the one time they'd been in bed together, and that she'd cried piteously. It didn't help his pride or his self-confidence to realize that the experience must have been as unsatisfying for her as it had been for him.

"Do you suppose you might kiss me good night?" Lacy asked hesitantly. "Just that. I'm not asking you to . . ."

"As if you could, after the last time," he said quietly. "We're married, Lacy," he said gently. "And I don't find kissing you any kind of penance. Come here."

She moved closer. The darkness was intimate, even with the little bedlight burning above them on the brass rail. She looked straight into his eyes as his mouth moved just over hers, poised there for a second, and then covered her lips warmly, briefly.

"You taste of coffee," he whispered.

"You taste of tobacco," she whispered back.

He kissed her again, liking the soft, trembling warmth of her mouth under the slow, easy movement of his. He felt himself going rigid. Odd, how quickly it happened with her. His eyes closed and one lean hand went to her neck, tilting her face to give him better access to her mouth.

"Lacy," he whispered unsteadily, "open your mouth a little . . ."

She did, in shocked pleasure, a tiny gasp at the unexpectedly ardent command escaping into her mouth.

"Yes . . ." he breathed, and she felt his tongue slowly probing past her lips, into the dark recesses of her mouth, finding and teasing her own tongue in a silence hot and heavy with rustling breath and moist contacts.

Her fingers went up to his lean cheek, touching it lightly, moving down to feel his mouth locked with hers. Feeling that soft joining between them excited her, and she moaned.

His mouth lifted suddenly. "Hell, I can't take much of that," he said unsteadily.

"It's so exciting to kiss," she whispered back, searching his dark, fiery eyes.

"Yes, and it leads to something you and I aren't too good at, doesn't it?" he asked, his voice faintly cutting.

She swallowed. "It hurt," she agreed. "One of my married girlfriends said it usually does . . . at first."

His heart skipped. He'd never talked about it. He couldn't discuss intimacy, except maybe with Turk. But, then, Turk was a man.

"You're downplaying it," he said huskily. "It was bad, Lacy. Really bad. I had nightmares about it weeks later."

"Oh, Cole," she whispered softly. "It wasn't your fault. I never blamed you." She leaned forward and pressed her lips softly to his closed eyelids with a tenderness she felt to the depths of her soul.

He trembled at that soft contact, his body aching to

satisfy itself in hers. But the memory of how he'd hurt her stopped him. Besides, if he started to make love to her tonight—and then didn't remove his clothes—it would lead to questions he didn't want to answer yet. Better to ache than to risk that. God, he wanted her! Wanted her beyond all reason. When her warm, soft hands touched his face, she made him feel as if he were flying. He wondered how they might feel against his chest, on his belly, his hips and thighs, and he groaned aloud, because that was something he could never allow her to do.

He moved away from her, onto his back. "It's late. We need some sleep," he said in a voice more tender than any he'd ever used with her before.

"Yes. You, too."

She curled up under the sheet, facing him, sighing softly as the fever burned in her unsatisfied body. She wished she could ask him to hold her, but she'd felt the rigidity in his arms and hands and she already knew that men could easily be aroused beyond reason. She didn't want to do that to him. The past was going to take some forgetting, for both of them. As he'd said, they needed time to really get to know each other. Intimacy could come later.

She closed her eyes, drinking in the scent of his soap, and smiled as she drifted off to sleep, secure in the delicious comfort of his body next to hers.

═══ Chapter Six ═══

JESSICA STRETCHED WITH A SATED SMILE ON HER face, glancing lazily at the man lying on his side next to her.

"You are a surprising gentleman, Ben Whitehall." She laughed. "A very surprising gentleman, indeed."

"I may be young, but I'm not innocent." He grinned, pleased with himself, and with her. She was a wildcat in bed, her appetites as hot and uninhibited as his own. He'd done things to her and with her that he'd never done with anyone else. She was unique in the women of his acquaintance. "Are you sure your father's really asleep?" he asked.

"Of course. Are you trying to run me off?" she asked.

He let his dark eyes slide down the length of her supple young body. He felt himself stirring again, and watched her amused gaze drop to find the evidence of it.

"I don't think I can let you out of my sight, to tell the truth," he said dryly, looming over her.

She lifted her arms around his neck and surged upward as his warm, hard weight settled exactly over her own eager body. "I was hoping you might say that," she whispered into his approaching mouth. She reached out and touched him, stroked him, her eyes as wild and passionate as his own. "Let me show you something

94

different . . ." she whispered, and laughed delightedly as he grimaced and clenched his teeth.

He felt himself losing control. His eyes closed as her fingers worked magic on him. And just before she arched her hips and swallowed him up, he remembered thinking that she was much more addictive than any alcohol he'd ever had. . . .

Morning was breaking over Chicago, leaving the city in a warm golden glow. Katy Whitehall stretched at the window, her eyes searching southward wistfully. She wondered if Turk had even missed her. She missed him more every minute. But she'd get over him. Somehow, she'd get over him.

There was a knock on her door. She turned as Danny's mother, Mrs. Bella Marlone, came in with a cup of coffee.

"Here, is good coffee, I make," the very-rounded elderly lady murmured, her hair in a bun, silvery wisps escaping it, a beige dress neatly belted around her ample middle. She smiled at Katy, dark eyes flashing. "So nice, that you and my Danny gonna get married," she said warmly. "I like this, having a nice young girl around to talk to me. You don't mind, that you and Danny live with me?" she added, worriedly. "In Italy, you know, not the same as here. Family *molto importante* . . . very important."

"I understand that," Katy replied. "My family is very close."

Mrs. Marlone nodded. She sat down in a chair by the bed, watching Katy perch on the edge of the coverlet and sip her coffee. "Danny say the ceremony be Monday," she said out of the blue.

Katy's hand trembled, but she kept it steady. *So quickly!* But that might be best. She wouldn't have time for second thoughts, for rushing back to Spanish Flats. As if there were any reason to rush back. After all, Turk didn't want her—not for keeps. He never would.

"Monday. That will be nice." Katy agreed warmly. "I'll take care of him," she added slowly.

"We both take care of him," Mama Marlone said firmly. "I cook for him, clean, look after the bambinos when they come. You have plenty of time to stay pretty for my boy."

So that was how it would be, Katy thought wistfully. A live-in mother-in-law with a domineering personality—who lived only to provide the best for her son. She sighed. This was going to be a problem.

She told Danny so later, and he frowned.

"Now, look, babe," he said slowly, pulling her into his arms, "I'm all Mama's got in this country. If you don't like it, I'm sorry. But I can't throw her out in the street. She's made a lot of sacrifices for me."

"I didn't mean it like that," Katy said, trying to pacify him. She looped her arms around him with a forced smile. "I'll help you look after her," she said, making her first peace offering.

"That's my girl." He bent, smiling, and kissed her. This was pleasant, she thought. Very nice, very different from Turk's possessive, feverish kisses. She closed her eyes more tightly, trying to forget.

Danny was trembling when he let her go, his face flushed, his hands hot on her breasts under her loose-fitting blouse. "I want you," he whispered roughly.

"Monday," she whispered back, smiling.

"I'll die," he groaned.

"Not likely." She laughed. Her eyes searched his and she sobered. "Danny, does it matter to you that I'm not a virgin?"

"Hell, no," he said honestly. "I'm glad, if you want the truth. It will be good for us, even the first time together. I'll treat you right, honey. Now come on downstairs. I want you to meet a couple of my buddies."

His *buddies* looked like dyed-in-the-wool mobsters. Grange was tall and big and dark and didn't volunteer a single word. Sammy was short and lean and had eyes that bulged just a little. Katy nodded as they were introduced.

Grange nodded back. Sammy grinned crookedly.

"Grange is my driver," Danny told her, puffing on a cigar. "And Sammy here, he runs errands. Anybody does me dirt, Sammy takes care of them. Know what I mean?"

He couldn't mean . . . ? Of course not, she told herself firmly. She'd read too many books. She pushed back her long hair and grinned.

"I'll feel safe with you two around," she told them.

"You'll be safe," Grange said, his voice dull and deep. "Me and Sammy won't let nothing hurt the boss's moll."

"You bet." Sammy chuckled. He patted his inside jacket pocket softly. "We'll protect you from hoods and such, Miss."

The *and such* sounded ominous. She glanced up at Danny worriedly.

"Don't go getting hysterical," he said gently. "I make a few enemies along the way, but it ain't nothing to worry about. Grange and Sammy can handle it."

"Well, if you're sure . . ."

"Sure I am!" He chuckled. "Come on. I'm going to buy you the damndest wedding gown. Say, kid. You want your family to come to the wedding?"

She did, but she could imagine Cole or Turk showing

up and her blood froze. "No," she said quietly. "I'd really rather have a very quiet, private ceremony."

"Yeah. Me, too. And a quick one," he added, with such a tormented expression that she laughed.

The word reached the ranch Monday evening that Katy and her Chicago boyfriend were officially married.

Cole read the telegram to Marion and Lacy and left it with them as he went out to find Turk and give him the news. He wasn't looking forward to it. He'd noticed a change in his friend since Katy's abrupt departure. He was disturbed by what had happened, and he wondered if he hadn't somehow caused it all by refusing to let Turk near Katy. If Katy'd felt that way about the ex-flyer, how had he felt about her? And now it was too late for both of them, and Cole felt responsible.

Turk was saddling a horse when Cole found him in the stables.

"Hello, boss." The younger man grinned, pushing his wide-brimmed hat back on his head as he tightened the cinch. "Looks like a nice, cool day."

Cole nodded absently. He rolled a cigarette and lit it before he said anything else. He leaned back against a stable wall, his dark eyes quiet and steady.

"I thought you'd rather hear this from me. Katy's married."

Turk's eyelids flinched. Just that. Nothing more. He turned back to the horse, jerking the cinch so that the animal shifted restlessly and had to be calmed. "To that Chicago gangster?" came the terse question.

"That's the boy," Cole answered. He took a draw from the cigarette. "They're going to live with his mother."

"What a hell of a great start for a marriage." Turk laughed, but the grayness of his eyes darkened as he turned back to give the saddled animal to one of the cowboys. The man had sprained his wrist, and Turk had to help him into the saddle, but the diehard wouldn't stay in bed like the doctor had told him. Turk made some offhand remark about his stubbornness, and Cole watched, not fooled by the casual conversation. Turk was cut up inside. Cole knew it without a word being spoken.

When the cowboy left, Cole took a draw from his cigarette and resumed the conversation. "Katy couldn't manage enough grit to tell me herself. She sent a telegram."

"How's your mother taking it?" Turk asked as he fixed a bridle that didn't need fixing.

"Very well. I was surprised. Lacy looks a bit disturbed. She hadn't met the man, you know, and Katy's half her heart. They've lived in each other's pockets for years."

Turk turned, studying the taciturn man against the wall. "What do you think?"

"I'd like to kill the son of a bitch," Cole said calmly.

"Yeah. So would I." Turk moved away from the horse, leaving him hitched to the stall, and held out his hand for the makings. Cole tossed them to him, watching him roll a cigarette with remarkably steady fingers. That had been one of the act pilot's trademarks during the war, that cool nerve. Nothing ever seemed to rattle him. It was something he had in common with Cole.

"For God's sake, say something," Cole shot at him. "This is me, remember? I know you like a brother, so stop pretending you don't give a damn."

Turk looked up, his gray eyes quiet and dull. "What can I say? You're the one who told me to keep my hands off her."

"I thought she'd be one in a line," Cole said matter-of-factly. "You don't have a hell of a great record with women. You collect scalps, son."

"After I lost my wife, there didn't seem to be much reason not to," he answered shortly. "I didn't think I had anything to offer."

"And now?"

The big shoulders shrugged. He stared down at his worn, dusty boots. "I think about Katy all the time," he confessed, his voice hesitant. "I took all that damned hero worship for granted. Now I'd give anything to have her look at me that way." His eyes closed on a wave of unexpected pain. "Oh, God, it makes me sick. I ran her off, Cole. It's my doing. My fault. I told her I had nothing to give, that she'd wear her heart out on me. I suppose it was the last straw for her." He drew in a breath of smoke and let it out. "She left minutes later." He didn't add what had happened, really happened, in that barn. Cole was still the only friend he had. If Cole knew the truth, he didn't know how he might react.

"I can take part of the blame," Cole said patiently. "Maybe if I hadn't said anything to you about her . . ."

Turk smiled ruefully. "You were only trying to protect her. I'm a rounder; we both know how much I love the ladies. But it was never like that with Katy, Cole. I couldn't take her in my stride and treat her like some cheap conquest. She was always special."

"Maybe he'll be good to her," the taller man said hesitantly.

"Maybe ducks will win elections," Turk said, scoffing. He stared at the tip of his cigarette. "Hell, it makes me sick to my stomach to think of her with that slick-talking gangster!"

"Gas up the plane," Cole said, only half jokingly. "We'll fly up to Chicago and strafe him."

Turk managed a smile that he didn't really feel. He searched his friend's dark, steady eyes. "There's too much Indian in you, sometimes. You have a taste for vengeance that may do you in one of these days."

Cole's thin mouth tugged up. "I'm emotional."

"It never shows." Turk pursed his lips. "Why don't you tell Lacy the truth?"

The smile faded. "Watch out," Cole warned gently. "There's a line even you can't cross with me."

"Go ahead, punch me," Turk said. "But I'll say it anyway. You're wrong about Lacy. She's tough. And if you don't watch it, you could lose her again."

"Not if I can help it," the older man said involuntarily.

"Then stop playing your cards so close to your chest. You're worse than I am about hiding what you feel." He lifted the cigarette to his mouth again, and a cloud of smoke separated them. "She has to feel something for you, or she wouldn't have come back, Cole. Think about that."

"I've thought about it," he ground out. He sighed heavily, his eyes searching the horizon. "I've made a hell of a mess of it. I hurt her . . ." He actually reddened, averting his eyes.

Turk studied him carefully. It could be dangerous to push him too far, but he didn't want to see the man hurt anymore. He chose his words before he spoke. "Sometimes it's difficult for a woman the first time. Women aren't like us; they have to get worked up to it."

Cole literally gaped at him. "They *what*?"

Turk stuck his hands in his pockets. "They have to be

aroused. It hurts them if they're not, even if it isn't the first time.'' He studied the quiet, still features. ''You didn't know.''

Cole sighed heavily. He smoked a cigarette, his eyes still on the horizon. ''My God, no wonder . . .'' he breathed. ''No,'' he said harshly. ''I didn't know.'' He glared at the blond man. ''Go ahead. Laugh!''

Turk shook his head. ''Not at you. Never at you. I understand better than anyone. After all, I know the whole story,'' he said quietly. ''It's nothing to be embarrassed about.''

''Isn't it?'' He stared down at the ground, a faint reddish flush on his lean cheeks. ''I'd rather die than let her know.''

''She doesn't have to, if you're careful,'' Turk said. His narrowed eyes met the older man's. ''You can make her want you.''

Cole's teeth ground together. It was killing his pride, but what he felt for Lacy was even stronger. Well, hell; Turk was his friend, wasn't he? The one person in the world who knew why he was like he was. ''How?'' he asked shortly.

''Make her tell you what she likes you to do,'' Turk said gently, his voice not condescending or amused. ''That sounds damned sophisticated; it turns women wild. Act confidently. Watch her reactions and pretend you know what you're doing, even if you don't. It takes stealth,'' he added, with a faint smile. ''It's like planning a campaign, old son. You get the objective in sight and work your way to it by inches.''

''How can I tell when she's ready?'' he asked quietly.

Turk told him, without embarrassment, the subtle signs of a woman's arousal. ''There's one other thing,'' he added. ''When a woman is enjoying it, don't look for her to smile. She'll look as if she'd being torn apart. She may cry or whimper or bite and scratch you. Don't be afraid that you're hurting her. She'll tell you if you are. Pleasure and pain are sometimes twins in appearance. It's in your favor that she doesn't know any more about it than you do," he added dryly. "You don't know what an advantage that is!"

"Hell of a thing," Cole said, with a sigh, studying his cigarette. "To get to my age and be so damned stupid. But before the war, I had the responsibility of supporting the family after Dad died. Afterward . . ." His face lifted, his eyes darkly tormented. "Afterward, I didn't have the guts to try. Lacy will never know the hell it was to find myself forced into marriage with her. I've always wanted her, Turk. But I can't stomach pity. I couldn't know how she'd react unless I let her see . . ." His eyes closed briefly and he looked away. He lifted the cigarette to his thin lips again. "Fighting Germans was one thing. Facing Lacy with . . . that . . . is another thing entirely."

"Still sorry I took that pistol away from you, aren't you, cowboy?" Turk taunted. "Well, I'm not sorry. And one day, you won't be sorry, either. Lacy is one of those rare women. You'll find that out. And if you'll go slow with her, and do what I told you, you may find yourself blessed in ways you never suspected."

"How the hell did you learn so much about women?" Cole asked curiously.

"They always seemed to fall into my arms," Turk said, chuckling. "And marriage is a great teacher. It's exciting to go on journeys of discovery with your woman, to find all the ways you can please her and be pleased by her." He searched the older man's eyes. "That's more exciting than a full-scale battle."

"Experience helps a little." Cole sighed.

"Getting it is better. More fun," Turk said, grinning.

Cole finished his cigarette. "It would be easier if I had a little more time with her. But right now, things are rough. Getting rougher, too," he added, with a meaningful glance toward the cattle over the fence. "Look at the poor bastards. I can't get enough feed—can't afford enough feed—to get them through the winter. Without them, I'll never meet the notes at the bank. And old Henry sure as hell wants this ranch. He foreclosed on Johnson, and Johnson owed less than I do."

"You've got friends," Turk reminded him. "Your neighbors have known you all your life, and all theirs. You've done a lot for them. They won't forget. If it comes down to a fight, they'll stand behind you."

"What can they do? The economy's killing us all. They keep talking about damned prosperity, but look around you. Farmers are going bust everywhere. Maybe it's great on Wall Street, but we're a long way from New York. I think we're heading for disaster. It's too good to be true, that financial upswing. It's not natural."

"The war inflated everything," Turk said. "Now that it's over, a lot of people are out of work. And it's worse for farmers and ranchers than it is for business people. I wish to God Coolidge would do something."

"Give him time," Cole replied. "He's only just got into office. Maybe he will."

"Maybe." Turk tossed his cigarette into the dirt and ground it out under his heel. "I guess I'll go ride the fence line. I'm depressed enough to dig postholes today."

"Don't let it get to you, about Katy," Cole said as the younger man mounted his gelding. "She's a Whitehall. She'll manage."

"Sure." Turk lifted his hat over his eyes. "It's for the best. What could I offer her?"

"Maybe more than you realize," the older man replied. "At any rate, I'm sorry I fixed things for you. Katy's special to me, too."

Turk managed a smile. "See you."

Cole watched him ride off with mixed emotions. He seemed to be fouling everything up lately. It was his marriage, of course. It was what he felt for Lacy turning him inside out. He wanted her. More than anything, he wanted a good marriage. But he knew so little about women, and he had deep emotional scars and a secret he could hardly bear to share with anyone. Especially with a woman.

Lacy. His mind went back a few nights, to that warm, slow kiss he'd exchanged with her, to the conversation they'd had. She seemed as eager as he to make their marriage work. She'd trembled when he'd kissed her. He wished he'd felt a little more confident, so that he could have assessed the exact extent of her involvement. Now that he knew the signs, perhaps he could grow bolder with her. He hadn't touched her again, not even to kiss her. They'd talked, and once he'd taken her walking down the path to the cold little stream running between the barren trees. But he hadn't tried to make love to her, even though he'd shared the bed with her. That hadn't been easy, sleeping with the scent and warmth of her beside him in the darkness. He'd had to force himself to work later and later, so that she was usually asleep when he came in at night. But he had the oddest feeling that she wanted him to make love to her. Only how could he do that, make love to her, fully dressed, and not have her ask why?

He groaned aloud as he finished his cigarette. Perhaps as time went by, as he learned to trust her, he might get over his apprehension. God, he wanted to! He wanted to strip that soft, warm body and see it, in the light, and touch it. He wanted to make her cry out; he wanted to see her face contorted with longing for him. He went hot all over just thinking about it.

With a rough word, he stalked off to saddle his own horse. He had work to do, cattle to worry about. He could worry about other things in his spare time.

He looked out over the horizon, his gaze steady and level. He wondered how Katy and Ben were managing. Young Ben had decided to stay in San Antonio to begin that new job he was so excited about. Cole smiled faintly. Ben was so young, so emotional. He loved the boy, although it had needled him that Ben asked so many damned questions about the war. Cole didn't like remembering it, much less talking about it. Perhaps if he could have admitted that to Ben, explained it to him, there wouldn't be so much friction between them. He shook his head ruefully. Someday, his own obsession with personal privacy was going to be his undoing. But for now, there was no way he could change that.

Back in San Antonio, young Ben was managing very well. His mother had agreed to let him keep the runabout for a while, and he was doing rather well at his new job.

He'd moved into a boardinghouse, and he'd been sneaking out with Jessica every night since that first night they'd spent together. He was on fire for her, all the time. Finding places to be together was getting harder, but it was exciting, too. One night, he'd sneaked out one of his landlady's sheets, neatly folded under his jacket, and he and Jessica had spread it on the front seat of the runabout and made wild, uninhibited love in the cold evening air sitting straight up under an oak tree. Their bodies had been feverish enough that they didn't even notice the cold. They'd been totally nude together, and the danger of discovery had made it all the more exciting. Afterward she'd laid in his lap, still undressed, and she'd let him do things to her in the moonlight that could arouse him even in memory.

The only drawback about his new life was the journalism itself, even though it had originally been the most exciting part. Ben didn't really care for sex and scandal in print, but that was what Mr. Bradley demanded for his tabloid. The local newspaper had done their best to compete, but Bradley's tabloid was outselling them all. And it was because of Ben's talent with words. He could turn the most ordinary police news into delicious scandal. There had been threatened lawsuits, and once a victim's brother had even punched him in the nose while he sat at his desk. But still, the tabloid's sales excelled. The addition of a crossword puzzle page had boosted them still more, taking advantage of the nation's growing infatuation with crosswords.

One day, Bradley had instructed Ben to come up with a hoax, since there was no real news to parlay into sales that week. So Ben had obligingly taken a tall tale of Turk's and expanded it into front-page news.

It seemed, he wrote, that there was a big-footed wild creature, as big as a grizzly bear, roaming around area ranches. It walked like a man, and had fur that was more like human hair. A local rancher had actually found some of it tangled in his barbed wire, near the horribly mutilated bodies of two of his cows. Ben even had a photograph of some of the ''fur''—which was actually a tuft of Ben's own hair that Jessica had clipped with her scissors. It had been planted on a string of barbed wire, where the paper's photographer snapped it. The story caught on, and sales went up again. And every week, Ben added to it.

He and Jessica were getting thicker by the minute. His writing in the tabloid was attracting national attention, carefully nurtured by Jessica's father. And Jessica, seeing opportunity knocking, began to make subtle and not-so-subtle hints about marriage.

Ben obligingly proposed. And then Jessica announced that she and her father wanted to meet Ben's family. Ben almost had apoplexy at the thought of taking them down to Spanish Flats. Oh, the house was elegant enough; it had been built originally by a Spanish grandee. But Cole was a wild man, unpredictable at best, and so was Turk. Ben worried about what his big brother might do or say when confronted with his young brother's "large financial and business interest in the ranch." Ben didn't want to have his chin smashed in front of his intended. So he kept putting Jessica off with tales of the family traveling widely in Europe, off to visit the Hemingways in France, and then on to Spain for the bullfights. . . .

It worked. He settled down to his job, and put off his worried mother with the occasional phone call. Katy's marriage to a Chicago businessman had come as a shock, and he was careful not to mention the circumstances to his employer and his fiancée. He didn't want them to know about Katy's racketeer husband, either. His family seemed to be doing its best to disgrace him, he thought angrily.

Far away, in Chicago, Katy was getting used to the new routine of her life with mingled amusement and apprehension. Danny noticed that she was around occasionally, but his main interest was in his speakeasy and courting local politicians and making money.

Most of the people who came to visit were fascinating. There were public figures and well-known gangsters, and Katy got an education that her family wouldn't have approved of. It began with the expensive clothing Danny insisted on buying for her. Then there were jewels and furs and race cars. All the glitter inevitably led to the parties, where gin flowed like limitless streams. And Katy learned how to drink like a fish.

She drank more and more as Danny's neglect grew. In bed, he was always in a hurry. Even that first night, he'd been quick and silent, taking her without preliminaries, unless those hard, rough kisses had been planned to arouse her. They hadn't. In a way, she was glad that her husband was quickly satisfied. That way, she wasn't tempted to compare his loving with the long, slow, sweet initiation she'd been given by Turk Sheridan. She closed her eyes, sighing at the memory of how exquisite her first time had been. No man could have satisfied her now. Danny liked to have her, but he seemed more interested in making money than making love.

After the first few weeks, when he was always ready to go to bed with her, he didn't even seem to care if she went to bed first. He never woke her, either. And the more he neglected her, the more she drank. She wasn't in love with him, but it hurt her pride that he'd turned from her to business so quickly. And then, to top it all, there was Mama Marlone.

Mama Marlone was condescending—when she wasn't indifferent to Katy's presence. Everything she did was for Danny. She cooked, she cleaned, she fussed over him, she ironed his clothes. There was no maid, no housekeeper; Mama took care of her boy. Katy was in

the way. Katy didn't do enough for him; Katy should
have been at the club with him, making sure he was
looked after while he worked, made to eat properly. Katy
should have done everything . . . except marry him.
That became Mama's primary lecture as time went by.
And the more Danny neglected her, and the more Mama
complained about her, the more she drank.

Then came the worst thing of all. Danny decided that
he didn't have enough influence with a neighborhood
boss to ask him to make a deal with Danny to merge their
bootleg booze operation. So he was going to promise the
gang boss that he could have a special treat if he
agreed—he could have Katy.

Chapter Seven

LACY WAS BEGINNING TO WONDER IF ANYTHING SHE did would be enough to catch Cole's attention these days. Increasingly, the small amount of ground she'd captured with her arrival had been lost. She'd seen that he was worried about the ranch, that financial problems were besetting him. And now they were beginning to interfere with the delicate thread of their marriage. For the past week, she'd hardly seen him. He came to bed after she was asleep, and was awake and gone before she opened her eyes.

Katy's marriage had unsettled him. Apparently it had unsettled Turk, too, because the blond cattleman spent more time out on the range away from the house.

It was a warm day for November—unseasonably warm—and Lacy went walking in her shirtsleeves, wearing only a silky, beige knee-length dress and her comfortable walking shoes. She and Marion had spent the morning addressing envelopes for a party Marion had decided to give for Bennett and his fiancée. Oddly enough, Ben hadn't wanted her to give the party, but Marion had burst into tears and accused him of being ashamed of her. And Ben had given in. So there was to be a party, and all the neighbors were invited. And, because of the expense involved, Marion had been too

111

nervous to approach Cole about it—so Lacy was deputized to go find him and ask.

She almost welcomed the opportunity to see him without the prying eyes of Cassie and Marion and the cowboys. He was alone at the corral, the small one separate from the stables, exercising a new colt. There wasn't another soul around. Nearby, a huge oak still had a few leaves that hadn't dropped off, and those that had fallen made a colorful carpet on the ground.

Lacy loved November. She loved autumn. With a sigh, she sat down to wait until he finished what he was doing, her eyes glancing nervously at the darkening sky. It looked like rain, and she hadn't a parasol with her.

Out in the corral, Cole was working the young horse. It was an Appaloosa by the look of it, just beginning to show its spots. The breed was foaled snow white. The spots only appeared later, and Lacy loved their conformation. She didn't know a lot about horses, but she loved the Apps.

Cole's wide-brimmed hat covered his eyes, shading them from the sunlight that had fast vanished behind the clouds. He was wearing denims today, tight jeans, and an equally tight chambray shirt that clung to every muscle of his body. He was so masculine, Lacy thought, sitting with her knees drawn up, her arms clasped around them. She loved to look at him. She adored his tallness, his muscular deftness as he ran the young mare around the corral on the leading rein. He could do anything with animals. With them, he had a tenderness that she'd never experienced from him.

He didn't really care for people, she thought sometimes. Perhaps he'd been hurt too much over the years. She recalled Katy saying once that Cole had been laughed at as a boy because of his big feet and lanky body and his awkwardness with girls. And as if that weren't enough, his grandfather's unorthodox teachings had added to it. He was taught how to hunt and stalk and live off the land. He was taught to shun emotion and distrust other people, because that's how his grandfather was—with everyone except Cole's grandmother, at least. But Cole hadn't been encouraged by anyone to learn tenderness. And at school, it wasn't until he learned to use his fists that the other boys accepted him. The girls never had. He'd been shunned by them—not because he was unattractive, but because his taciturn, cold manner intimidated them.

It had never intimidated Lacy. Although she'd been shy, she'd always talked to him, listened to him. Sometimes, rarely, she'd teased him. That had amused him, or seemed to, back in their early lives. He was only four years her senior, but now she felt as if he were much older. He made her feel girlish and inhibited. And she was determined to change those feelings. If she wanted a marriage at all, she was going to find some way to get through to him.

Cole had spotted her, although he didn't show that he had. He kept on working the horse, wondering why she'd come. After his interesting talk with Turk, he'd been oddly nervous around her, uncertain of himself. And that had angered him, so he'd kept his distance. Perhaps it had bothered her that he was avoiding her. He stopped in the middle of the corral, removed the leading rein from the mare, patted her neck gently, and took off the bridle, allowing her to run free. He had to see if Lacy looked bothered.

He climbed over the fence fluidly, rather than take time to release the gate, and walked toward her slowly, with the rein and bridle in one lean, powerful hand.

"Hello, city girl," he taunted, with a faint smile. "What brings you out here?"

She glanced up at him impishly, forcing herself not to retreat. It was only a mask, she told herself. He was hiding behind it so that she couldn't get close enough to wound him. He'd almost admitted as much once.

"Oh, I thought if I came out here in one of my shocking dresses, you might throw me down in the leaves and make wild, passionate love to me," she murmured demurely, and her heart slammed against her ribs at her own shocking boldness.

Cole's own heart went wild at the blatant admission. Was she teasing, or did she mean it? He stared down at her darkly, his eyes intense, searching her averted face. "You've been seeing too many of those Valentino movies," he said, with a laugh.

"I guess so." So he wouldn't play. All right, she'd try something else. "The mare's pretty," she said.

He pulled the makings from his pocket and settled down beside her. "Yes, she is. She's going to make good breeding stock when she's old enough."

"Going into the horse-raising business?" she asked, with a grin.

"I have a few horses to keep me happy," he replied as he licked the paper to close the cigarette, then struck a match to light it. "Besides my quarter horses, I mean."

"Those are the ones you work the cattle with, aren't they?" she murmured casually, staring at the corral.

"What cattle I have left," he agreed, with a sigh. "It's going to be a damned long winter."

"Can't you get some hay from the neighbors?" she asked.

"Honey, the neighbors are as bad off as I am. I even tried selling off some of the cattle, but the prices are so low that I'd come out even worse than if I keep them and pray for higher prices come spring." He stared at the tip of his cigarette. "We may be in for some hard times, city girl. You might do well to pack up and go home."

She turned toward him, her big, grayish-blue eyes steady and quiet in her creamy-complexioned face, her dark hair curving softly toward the red mouth and pert straight nose. "Home is where you are, cowboy," she said quietly. "I'll take my chances here, if you don't mind."

Why should that unsettle him so, the way she said it? He had to grit his teeth to keep from making a grab for her. She was a thoroughbred, all right. Class, from her dark hair to her dainty feet. His eyes went down her body, lingering on her breasts straining against the silky, thin fabric of her dress. He stared at them until he saw hard peaks clearly outlined, and something Turk had told him came flashing into his mind without warning.

Apparently Lacy knew what it meant, too, because she abruptly drew her knees up again to hide it. "Uh . . . Marion asked me to come and talk to you," she said abruptly.

"Did she? Why?" But he wasn't really listening. She was aroused by him, and he knew it, and was touched by it.

"Ben's engaged, you know."

"So I heard."

"She wants to give an engagement party."

His face hardened. That got through. "Where does she plan to get the money? Rob a damned bank?"

"Now, Cole . . ." she began, and laid a gentle hand on his arm, feeling the hard muscles contract with a feeling of wonder. For an instant she forgot what she was going to say. Then she got a grip on herself. "I told her that I had plenty of silver and china that I could have brought down here from San Antonio to use for the party, and that we could butcher a steer and a pig, and use some of the canned vegetables that Cassie has in the pantry for an informal buffet. It doesn't have to be an elegant sit-down dinner. Just something for the neighbors, mainly.''

He looked thunderous with his sharp features turned away from her, his bronzed skin drawn taut over his cheekbones, smoking his cigarette without a reply.

''Don't,'' she said, her voice soft and quiet. ''Don't be like this. I can't help the inheritance, and we are married . . .''

''Are we?'' he asked.

She gnawed on her lower lip. He sounded so bitter. ''Ben deserves something from us, doesn't he?'' She changed tactics. ''He's a Whitehall, too—and this job is important to his future. He hasn't had any attention at all from us since he started it, because of the way things have been here. Cole, can't we do just this for him? And can't you let your pride go just for once and let me help?''

''Lacy . . .'' he began curtly, glancing down at her.

''For Ben,'' she coaxed.

He sighed half angrily. Once, he'd have walked away from her in fierce protest. She weakened him with her own vulnerability.

He stared at her. ''You women. You get suffrage, and now you think you're men, don't you?''

''Not quite,'' she murmured, with a demure little smile. ''Your boots wouldn't fit me, bigfoot.''

He couldn't believe he'd heard that. He lifted an eyebrow, the smoking cigarette forgotten in his hand, and studied his feet.

''Well, they are big,'' she said, defending herself.

He actually laughed. Not a lot, more a sound than an outright guffaw, but it relaxed his hard features a little. He glanced ruefully at the size of his dusty, scuffed, brown leather boots. "Big enough, I guess," he agreed. He pulled at the cigarette. "Okay. Tell Mother she can have the damned party if you foot the bill."

"We're married," she repeated once more. "Pride shouldn't be involved."

"Pride is my one biggest fault, Lacy," he said. He watched the filly prance with narrowed eyes. "I got a double dose when I was born. It's damned hard to take money from a woman."

"Do you think it would be a bit easier for me to take it from you, Coleman Albert Whitehall?" she demanded sharply.

He glanced at her, half amused by the flash of temper and pride. Yes, she was just as proud as he was, in her way. "Point taken, Alexandra Nicole."

She smiled with delight. She'd never told him her middle name. There was only one way he could have known it. "I didn't know you'd ever looked at our marriage license."

His shoulders rose and fell. "It hung on the wall for several weeks, until the sight of it began to get to me." He finished the cigarette and ground it out carefully on a bare spot so that it didn't catch the dry leaves on fire. "Pride again, Lacy. I couldn't even apologize for what happened that night."

It amazed her that he'd even thought he needed to. Surely that was a small crack in the stone that surrounded him. She stared at his lean, dark hands as they clasped one raised knee before she lifted her eyes. "I knew you didn't mean to hurt me," she said softly.

His dark eyes held hers, and the silence around them

grew suddenly tense and warm. "What we did together that morning made my blood sing," he said huskily. "I thought about it all day, dreamed about it, tasted it. By nightfall, I was burning up." He reached out, touched her parted lips, feeling the softness of flesh under the dark red lip gloss, feeling them tremble at his touch. She looked so vulnerable. She touched something deep inside him, and the words came out without conscious volition. "Lacy . . . I didn't know," he said hesitantly, because the words came hard, "that women had to be aroused first."

Her heart stopped beating. It actually stopped. She stared at him in amazement as the meaning of the words penetrated her mind.

Dark, ruddy color ran along his high cheekbones, but he didn't blink as he looked at her. "That's right, Lacy. It was my first time, too."

She could barely speak at all, "But . . . why?"

"You must remember how things were when you first came to Spanish Flats," he reminded her. His eyes lingered on her mouth. "I had too much responsibility. Then, the war came. There was so damned much horror." He sighed heavily. "Afterward," he said, averting his eyes, "I didn't care about women." He picked up a stick and twirled its roughness in his hands while he felt her eyes on his profile. "I wouldn't have hurt you deliberately, Lacy. I just didn't know much."

Tears stung her eyes. She lowered them to his long-fingered hands so that he wouldn't see. She could only imagine how much courage it took for him to admit that to her, with his black pride.

"I'm glad," she whispered fiercely, startling him. Her eyes lifted to his still face, her voice gentle but a little unsteady. She managed a watery smile. "If you'd told me that eight months ago, I'd never have left you!"

He scowled, searching her wide, misty eyes. "I thought you went because I'd hurt you, made you afraid of me."

She shook her head. "It was because I thought you'd only used me. I couldn't believe it was because you hadn't been with anyone else. Men these days . . . well, they're mostly sophisticated, like Turk."

He relaxed. The ridicule he'd dreaded wasn't forthcoming. He could hardly believe that she didn't mind his inexperience. He felt lighter than air as he looked at her. "I never had the chance to get sophisticated," he said simply. "My father's death was untimely. Besides all that, you know how I was around women."

"Yes," she murmured, with a dry smile. "Devastating!"

"Don't be cute," he said curtly.

"I'm not. I worshipped you from afar, but you were so aloof and unmoved by me that I thought I fell short of your expectations."

"Well, I'll be damned," he said half under his breath.

"I did everything but wear a sign around my neck," she whispered. It was hard to be honest like this. She couldn't look at him then; she was too embarrassed. "I thought you were the most wonderful thing since indoor plumbing."

He actually laughed. "You ran a mile to get out of my way!"

"I was afraid you'd see what a flaming crush I had on you."

"If I had, you'd have been in a hell of a lot of trouble," he said teasingly. "I thought you were a dish, Mrs. Whitehall. Long, elegant legs—"

"Coleman!"

"Excuse me. Limbs."

She gave him a hard glare, her face bloodred, and he just smiled.

He studied her slender body openly, his eyes dark and appreciative. Turk had said to act confident, to pretend he knew what he was doing. It seemed to work, too; it actually intimidated her, made her more feminine.

"Shy, aren't you?" he said softly, liking her reactions. He took off his hat and tossed it to one side, sprawling back to lean against the trunk of the big tree and stare at her with a purely masculine smile.

She felt her face going hot. This was getting entirely out of hand. She'd been the one doing the chasing back in San Antonio, and now she seemed to be the quarry. If he was that inexperienced, how did he know so much?

"Getting cold feet?" he taunted. "I thought you were the one who couldn't wait to share my bed."

"Cole . . ."

"What a red face." He chuckled. "The only delicious prospect about the whole thing is that you know even less than I do."

"If it's such a nice prospect, why have you been spending the past few nights with your cattle instead of me?" she said, puzzled.

"You didn't seem to mind," he shot back.

Her head turned, blue eyes sparkling with temper. "No, I don't mind," she said shortly. "Sleep in the bunkhouse, for all I care!"

So she did care where he spent his nights. His thin lips drew into a slow smile. God, she was pretty in a temper. He felt his body going hot and taut, and he shifted so that she wouldn't notice. Talking about it was one thing. Being blatant was another. He didn't want to embarrass

Lacy. For all her honesty, she was almost as reticent and reserved as he was.

She started to get to her feet. He reached out, one of those lightning movements she'd seen a few times, and caught her by the arm. He jerked her down into his hard arms and turned her so that she was lying on her back. He slid his hands into hers, pinning them above her head, and his darkened eyes went down to her breasts. Yes, there were the hard little peaks Turk had told him about, betraying her own arousal, and he thought he'd never felt quite as whole, quite as masculine, as he did then. His blood throbbed in his veins; his chest swelled with pride.

Her eyes widened, looking up into his hard, dark face, and she felt her body tingle with excitement. This was what she'd wanted all along, what she'd dreamed about. There was desire in his face, and she wasn't so afraid now that she knew how inexperienced he was. Intimacy was something they would learn together.

His fingers linked into hers in slow, exquisite movements, and all the time he stared down into her eyes. "You aren't afraid, are you?" he asked quietly.

"Not now," she whispered. Her lips parted on excited little breaths. The wind rustled the leaves above them, and the oak smell of the ground under her back was as pleasant as the tobacco-and-leather fragrance of Cole's taut, hard-muscled body.

His hands contracted gently where they held hers and his attention diverted to her soft mouth. He bent slowly, opening his lips as they poised over hers. As he watched, her own lips began to part. He moved down, fitting his mouth slowly to hers, tasting its warm moistness, feeling the very texture of her lips as he increased the pressure.

He felt dizzy as his tongue pushed into her mouth and felt the soft, shy response of her own. He groaned softly, aching for the warm nakedness of her body, aching to touch her in the most intimate ways. Would she let him? he wondered. And if he lost his head, would she wonder why he wouldn't let her touch him, or undress him?

The questions distracted him. He lifted his head, feeling her excited breath on his moist lips, and looked down at her. Her blue eyes were narrow, lazy with pleasure, her lips slightly swollen.

"Don't stop," she whispered huskily.

He searched her face. "Don't touch me," he whispered back. He let go of her hands, waiting to see what she did.

She lay quietly, her hands beside her head, her eyes steady on his dark face. She had suspicions about this side of him, too—about why he didn't want her to touch him or look at his unclothed body. But for now, she had to teach Cole to trust her.

He poised above her for a long minute, long enough to realize that she was obeying him without protest. His jaw tautened. "No questions?" he asked.

"No questions," she whispered. Her soft eyes searched over his face, adoring it. "Are you going to make love to me?"

His body tensed at the query. His lips parted and he looked down at her taut breasts. "Would you let me, in broad daylight?" he asked tersely.

"Yes."

He felt a fine tremor go through his aching body. God, he wanted to. He wanted to bury himself in her. This time, he wanted to make her cry and bite him as he gave her pleasure. He wanted her to feel what he was feeling, to give as well as take.

"You've never looked at my body," she said in a stranger's husky voice, challenging him. She was on fire for him now; she wanted everything with him. "You've touched it, but you've never seen it. Don't you want to?"

He shuddered. "My God, of course I want to!" he bit off. "But, Lacy, it's broad daylight—and my men do occasionally use the barn!"

If she'd been less dazed from his kisses, she might have laughed at the almost desperate note in his deep voice.

Even so, his reason was getting lost in the stormy urgency of his own body. He slid his fingers very slowly past her collarbone, watching how still she lay as he began to trace the soft slope of her breast. He felt her tremble, heard her breath catch. He slid his hand a little further, until the tips of his fingers touched the hard tip of her breast. She made a sound. It was staggering to watch him touch her so intimately. She had to fight not to protest, even now.

She was softer than he'd dreamed. He'd been too nervous and hungry to do much of this that night they'd spent together. Turk was right; it was better when she was vulnerable and submissive. It gave him pleasure that he could do this to Lacy. He looked into her shocked eyes. "I like that," he whispered roughly. "I like the sound you just made."

He rubbed his fingertips over the hardness, and she whimpered, biting her lower lip. If she died right now, it would be all right. It was so unbelievable to lie with Cole in the sunlight and feel his hands taking possession of her body, arousing her, enjoying her. And he *was* enjoying her. She saw his face, saw the pleasure there, and glowed all over with pride.

With a harsh breath, he pushed his palm gently against the hard nipple and swallowed her breast. Her lips parted and she arched, moaning, too far gone to care that he was seeing her blatant vulnerability to his caresses.

God, she was lovely! He'd never seen a woman's bare breasts before, except in pictures. He hadn't been able to see Lacy at all the night he'd spent with her. But he wanted to see Lacy like that, to open her dress and look at her. But he had to keep his head. Someone could walk by at any time.

Lacy watched him through slitted eyelids. She thought that there had never been anything as sweet as his hand on her body. She arched it a little, pulsing with delight. It was all of heaven, this tender loving. And she hadn't thought him capable of tenderness.

"You . . . hardly touched me that night," she said jerkily.

"There wasn't time," he replied. His eyes fell to her soft, firm breast. His fingertips rubbed slowly at the nipple. "Lacy, what does it feel like when I touch you like this?"

"It makes me weak all over," she whispered, her voice husky. "It makes me . . . shaky."

His nose nuzzled against hers. She could feel his breath on her lips, quick and rough. His thumb and forefinger gently contracted, and she shivered.

"Did I do it too hard?" he asked softly, lifting to search her eyes as his hand stilled. "Did it hurt?"

"Oh, no," she whispered. She swallowed. "Cole . . . you—you could do it under my dress, on my skin."

He felt his body going even more taut and his eyes flashed. "Lacy, do you remember where we are?" he asked through his teeth.

"On the moon?" she whispered dizzily, reaching up toward his mouth.

"Don't I wish," he moaned against her mouth as his settled on it. His hand flattened over her bodice, slow and warm. It was like that day before he'd left for the army, when she couldn't get enough of his mouth. She melted in his arms, her nails biting into the nape of his neck as she tried to make him come closer still.

"Cole!" she whimpered, and tears misted her eyes.

He lifted his head, fighting for control. She looked like a virgin sacrifice lying there so submissive, and his body had begun to hurt. "I want more, too, little one," he said roughly. "More than you realize. But we have to stop now, while we can."

It was so similar to what he'd said years ago when he'd left her. The words echoed in her mind. Her eyes opened and she looked up at him with possession.

"It was like this before you went away to fight the Hun," she whispered. "Remember, Cole? You pulled me into your room and closed the door. We kissed and kissed, and you made me leave, because we were both trembling."

"I remember," he said. "Oh, God, I do! I lived on that memory the whole time I was away. It kept me going when I wanted to give up—" He stopped short.

She touched his mouth hesitantly. "But you wouldn't let me near you when you came home," she said sadly. "You pushed me away."

He drew in a slow breath and sat up, running a rough hand through his dark hair while he tried to breathe normally. "There were reasons."

She was just beginning to realize what they might be. Bits and pieces of conversation filtered through her mind while she lay there and looked up at him.

"Will you ever tell me why?" she asked softly.

He glanced down at her, his dark eyes kindling all over again. He looked away to the horizon. "Perhaps. One day."

"When?" she asked daringly, searching his dark eyes.

His teeth ground together. He stared down at her, hesitating. He wanted her mouth again. He wanted to touch her, to lie with her. He almost groaned aloud. "Don't rush me."

She forced herself to calm down, to smile up at him. "All right," she said, without arguing. "Don't growl at me."

"You get me so damned hot that I don't know what I'm doing or saying!" He laughed, bending to crush a hot, hungry kiss onto her smiling lips. "I happen to want you like hell, Mrs. Whitehall. But we've got to make haste slowly."

"Whatever you say, boss," she murmured dryly.

She watched him pull away from her again, his dark eyes intent on her body for a long moment before he got to his feet and busied himself rolling a cigarette; she dusted off her skirt and stood up, too.

"Cole?" she asked when she was beside him.

He turned, smoking cigarette in hand. "What, honey?"

"Do you think I'm . . . wanton?" she asked, with a frown, and seemed to be genuinely worried about it.

He smiled, his dark eyes warm and oddly affectionate. "No, I don't think you're wanton. But you're all woman."

She flushed a little and folded her hands neatly in front of her as she walked alongside him toward the house. He had a long, elegant stride that made almost two of hers. He walked like an outdoorsman. What he'd said so casually made her glow with pride. "You're pretty exciting yourself, barnstormer," she said huskily.

She heard him laugh softly as her blue eyes scanned the long horizon, the familiar lines of the house in the distance. Texas was so big, she thought. Big and sprawling and still reminiscent of the old frontier.

"Taggart said that the Mexican Army came through here on the way to the Alamo," she said out of the blue.

"It did," he replied. "They camped just out there." He gestured toward a long space between clumps of mesquite trees.

"So long ago," she sighed.

"Not even a hundred years ago," he taunted. "Just yesterday, in fact."

She laughed up at him, her face radiant. "Which one of your grandfathers was Comanche?" she asked curiously.

"Dad's father," he said, smiling. "The old man wouldn't live on a reservation when they came along. He hightailed it up into the mountains after he got shot in a fight and came upon a lone white woman, a widow, with two small sons. As the story goes, she nursed him back to health and hid him from the cavalry, but she used up her meager store of weapons and the snows came. She and the boys were starving. My grandfather had left, but he came back to check on them and found them starving. He took it on himself to provide for her, and them, despite her objections. Eventually he married her. My father was one of the children she bore him. They died within five months of each other. Devoted to the very damned end."

"He must have been a special man," she remarked.

"He was a renegade," he said. "He loved to invite my father's college friends over and serve them dog and

snake and any other damned shocking thing he could find
for my grandmother to cook. He never truly accepted the
white man's ways, and when I came along, he practically
kidnapped me and brought me up like a Comanche. He
and my father fought constantly about who I belonged
to."

She searched his hard face. "You never talk about
your father, Cole."

His shoulders lifted and fell. "He was a hard man.
Much harder than my grandfather, in his way. He gave
Mother hell all his life. She was never strong, but what
spirit she had, he crushed."

She stopped walking. "Did she love him?"

"She couldn't have loved him. Not the way he treated
her," he said, his eyes dark and fierce with memory.
"He was the coldest human being I ever knew. He
touched and was touched by no one. Not even his own
children. He wanted me for no other reason than to keep
me away from my grandfather."

"Perhaps he cared about you and just didn't know
how to show it, Cole," she said.

He looked down at her. "I don't show things, do I,
Lacy?" he asked quietly. "I can talk about my father's
coldness with such ease, but I've inherited it."

She shook her head slowly. "Not in many ways," she
said. "You're a passionate man." Her face flamed and
she looked away.

"I've always hated that side of my nature," he said,
his voice deep and cutting. He moved closer to her, so
close that she could feel the heat of his body, smell the
tobacco scent of his shirt. "I hated you, at first, because
you aroused it."

"Do you still?" she asked demurely.

He touched her waist with his lean fingers, drawing

her slowly to him. "I feel light-headed when I make love to you," he said under his breath. "Young and uninhibited and full of ginger. Today I gave in to it for the first time in my life, and I'm still floating. Does that answer your question, Mrs. Whitehall?"

Her eyes searched his. "I love you, Cole," she said softly.

He breathed slowly, deliberately. "Do you?' he whispered unsteadily. It made him feel light-headed, hearing her say that. Did she mean it, or was it a residue from the passion he'd stirred in her? If only he could be sure!

"Cole, what are you keeping from me?" Her voice was soft, tender, her eyes steady and warm.

His pulse jumped. She saw too much. His fingers traced over her cheek. "Dark secrets, Lacy," he said bitterly. "Things I don't want to remember. Things I don't want to face."

"They won't matter," she said.

He drew in a slow, sad breath. "They will," he replied flatly. "Perhaps all too much."

"Tell me, Cole."

He stared down at her mouth. "Not now."

She wondered what they were. Perhaps something he'd done in the war had made him withdrawn and ashamed. Or perhaps it had something to do with his reluctance to undress in front of her . . . Maybe he was deformed in some way.

None of that would matter, she thought miserably, watching him. She loved him.

He saw that adoring look and it was the only hope he had. He couldn't go on without telling her. He should have told her at the very beginning, before they'd married. He hadn't expected that things would develop like this between them. He'd been shocked by his own desire for her, as well as by hers for him. But what kind of future could he offer her? His eyes darkened with torment.

"Trust comes very hard to you, doesn't it?" she asked gently.

"Harder than you know," he replied. "Trusting people . . . letting them get close. I've always been a loner, all my life. But if it's any consolation, nobody's ever been as close to me as you are."

Her heart swelled with that reluctant admission. "Isn't it strange the way things have worked out?" she asked. "I went to San Antonio feeling that it was all over. And now . . ."

"Have you ever considered that what you feel for me might be infatuation?" he asked, frowning. "You're remarkably innocent yourself."

"I had George Simon hanging around all the time," she said, with a faint smile. "I couldn't even let him touch me. And," she added wryly, "even after what you'd done to me I still preferred being hurt by you to being pleasured by any other man."

He ground his teeth together. "And you didn't even know that I hadn't hurt you deliberately."

"Oh, I knew you hadn't done that," she said, repeating what she'd already told him. "I know you very well, Cole. I've seen you nurse a bird with a broken wing back to health. I've seen you bandage coyotes—the songdogs that some legends say would stay with a wounded man and protect him from predators until help came. Other people kill them, but not you. A man who can feel that kind of compassion even for a wild animal isn't likely to deliberately hurt anyone."

He turned away. My God, she knew him! She saw

right through him, and that was vaguely disconcerting. No one ever had, until now.

"Other people don't see you that way. You frighten the men and intimidate the women," she said dryly, beginning to walk again. "But I've loved you for a long time. I see you in a different light."

"I've never loved anyone," he said slowly. "My family, of course, but it isn't the same, is it?" He glanced down at her. "So many things are new with you. Touching. Holding. Wanting."

"For a rank beginner, you're not bad," she said in a husky, vampish tone, batting her long eyelashes at him.

Instead of being offended, he laughed. "You damned tease," he muttered. "Look out, or I'll throw you down in the dirt and take you right there."

Her face went red and her breath rustled softly in her pale throat. "Why, you mountebank!" she accused. "And you said *I'd* been seeing too many Valentino movies!"

He lifted his chin arrogantly. "I sneaked into a theater when none of the boys were looking and saw that movie—the one about the sheik," he confided dryly. "I can't imagine how the moviemakers got away with it. Shocking!"

"I bet they'll make a fortune. The way he backs her up against the wall of the tent, and that look in his eyes . . ." She shivered. Her blue eyes darted up to his face. "Reminds me of you."

"Does it?" he tossed the cigarette down and caught her up in his arms, lifting her clear off the ground. "If things were different, I'd have made love to you back there." He jerked his head toward the tree where they'd lain.

Her arms linked around his neck hesitantly, so that she

didn't disturb him. "Cole, does it have something to do with—with why you don't want me to see your body, or touch it?" she asked daringly.

He actually trembled. His eyelids flinched. He started to speak, his lips were actually moving, when the sudden sound of approaching hoofbeats interrupted the subtle spell.

His head turned as Turk came galloping up, looking oddly amused when he saw the boss with his wife in his arms.

"Excuse me. I didn't know you two were going to be spooning in the middle of the trail," Turk drawled, tugging his hat over his eyes.

Lacy leaned back in Cole's hard arms and glared up at him. "You're not the only lady's man around, Mr. Sheridan." She grinned. "And you don't have the advantage of dark, smoldering Latin eyes."

Cole actually laughed. Despite the gravity of the situation, and the horror he expected to see on her face once she knew his secret, he laughed.

"Valentino in the flesh." Turk grinned. "Yes, I do see the resemblance."

"Do you want a job?" Cole asked his friend. "The stables need mucking out—"

"Don't let me interrupt you," Turk said quickly. "It's just that old man Cameron is coming up the road hell-for-leather; he's been drinking, and his face is bloodred. I think you're in trouble."

"I wonder what in hell little Faye has told her Daddy?" Cole sighed bitterly. He put Lacy down. "I knew there was going to be trouble when Ben told her he was going to miss her birthday party."

"I don't think it's that," the blond man said, with a quick glance at Lacy.

"I do know the facts of life," she told the ex-flyer. "I won't turn into a lily pad if you mention the word sex in front of me."

Turk burst out laughing, and Cole's face broke up.

"Ben's probably seduced her. Isn't that what you're trying so hard to insinuate?" Lacy asked Turk.

"The very thing," he replied easily. He crossed his hands over his pommel. "Ben sneaked out two nights in a row to go and see her before he left for San Antonio. One night I followed. He went to the Cameron place."

"And?" Cole prodded.

"She was waiting for him at the front door. Nobody else was home. Her dad's car was missing."

Cole made a hissing sound. "Oh, sh—" He remembered Lacy and bit off the rest of the word. His upbringing wouldn't allow range language in front of a lady. No decent man swore around women, although his father certainly hadn't spared his mother.

Lacy threw up her hands. "I give up. What has suffrage gotten us, anyway? Equality only on paper and in the cities." She put her hands on her lean hips and glared at the two of them. She enunciated the word quite clearly and gave him a triumphant smile. "Isn't that what you were—Cole!"

He'd aimed a sharp slap at her backside and connected, inclining his head with a jerk when she jumped and turned red. "Say it again in front of me and see where it gets you . . . and equality be damned!"

Turk was trying to hide a grin. Lacy stomped her foot, turned, and stormed off toward the house.

"What a hell of a woman," Cole said, with obvious admiration, watching her. "Oh, God. I'll die if she walks out a second time."

"She won't," Turk said quietly. "Not that lady."

"She doesn't know," Cole said, watching the black Model T Ford come crawling up the long drive.

"It won't matter to her. Haven't you noticed the way she looks at you, you idiot?"

"Infatuation wears off," Cole replied. "And she's not like some women. She isn't going to be happy without—"

"What if it was her?" the other man demanded hotly. "Think about it. What if it was her instead of you? Would you walk away?"

"I don't know," he said bitterly, averting his eyes. "God, I don't know! It would take a hell of a lot of love to accept what I am."

"She's *got* a hell of a lot." He hit the other man on the shoulder with rough affection. "Unbend a little. You'll break. And speaking of breaks, here comes your next outburst of bad temper. I'm leaving before I get caught in the crossfire."

"I ought to give him Ben," Cole grumbled.

"I'll help you catch the boy," Turk promised. "He could use a little trouble. You've paved his way all his life."

"Who else was there?"

"Point taken. Okay, I'm gone. Domestic squabbles are not my first love."

Cole just kept his eyes on the black car as it chugged up just in front of him and stopped.

Ira Cameron dragged his black-suited bulk out of the car and straightened meticulously. He needed a shave. His jowls hung down almost to the stained white collar of his shirt, and his hair looked as if it had recently been stuck to the inside of a cereal bowl. His hammy hands both met on the door as he closed it, and he stared at Cole blankly until his small dark eyes could focus.

"There you are, Coleman," he mumbled. He leaned on the hood, glaring at the younger man. "I been looking for you. What's this about your baby brother ruining my baby girl?"

"Women don't get ruined, they get laid," Cole said imperturbably. "And Ben wouldn't need to rape one."

"That's a lie!"

"Oh, hell, Ira. You know she worships him," Cole muttered as he pulled out the makings and began to roll a cigarette. "She's run after him for months. What do you want me to do? Drag him back from San Antonio and force him to marry her?"

The heavyset man shifted restlessly. "It would save her good name." He nodded slowly.

"It would ruin her life," Cole shot back. "Living with a man who was forced to marry her . . . She'd hate him. And go ahead, Ira. Ask me how I know."

Ira cleared his throat. "Heard that young Ben played one joke too many. Still, he wouldn't be a bad son-in-law."

"He's engaged. To some fancy city woman. Rich, too."

Ira sighed. "Well, that's that, then," he muttered. He ran a hand through his sweaty salt-and-pepper hair. "Hell, now what do I do?"

"Send Faye over and let Lacy talk to her," Cole replied, knowing that his feisty wife would know exactly what to say, even if he didn't. He smiled a little. "She's got a way with people. She isn't even afraid of me."

"That makes her a minority, all right. But Ben oughtn't have seduced her."

"I'll agree with that," Cole said. "And he'll hear about it when he comes down here."

Ira nodded. Cole was as good as his word. "You tell him I think he's a scoundrel. And if he sets foot on my place again, I'll blow off his leg."

That was drunken bravado and frustrated pride, and Cole recognized it as such. He only nodded back, letting the older man get away with it.

Ira straightened. Well, he wasn't such a weakling after all; he'd even stood up to Coleman Whitehall. "I'll say good day, then."

"Be careful in that thing," Cole said. "You're a little shaky on your feet, old fella."

"I'll be fine, you know. Just sampling my own product." He grinned. "Chicago ain't the only place that can produce bathtub gin. And times is hard, Cole."

"So I've noticed."

"I can let you have a bottle."

"I don't drink," came the quiet reply.

"Oh. Well. Too bad. I'd hate like hell to have to face the day sober." He lifted his hand and got back into his car. He almost ran it through two fences getting it turned, but he finally made it down the road.

Cole watched him go, sighing bitterly. So Ben had jumped another fence. Poor little Faye. Ben should've known better. And Cole was going to give him hell when he came down here. He owed Faye that much. Poor little kid. Wearing her heart out on a man who didn't want her. He cocked his head toward the house. Was he doing that to Lacy? Was that how she'd felt when he'd let her run off to San Antonio and hadn't gone after her?

He grimaced. He felt almost as sorry for himself as he felt for Faye. He knew that Lacy was aroused by him, that she cared for him. But his own feelings frightened him. He was going to have to trust her with all his dark secrets, and that might mean losing her forever.

He didn't know how he was going to go on living if he laid his pride at her feet and she turned away from him.

He lifted his cigarette to his mouth, took a draw, and ground it out underfoot. Well, there was only one way to find out. If she truly cared about him, perhaps it would all come right in the end. And if not . . . He turned back toward the corral. It might be just as well not to think about that right now.

═══ Chapter Eight ═══

IRA MANAGED TO STOP THE CAR JUST IN FRONT OF THE steps—no mean feat when he could barely find the brake. He staggered out, weaving for a moment on the wide running board before he went around the car and sat down heavily on the wooden steps.

"Papa, what did he say?" Faye asked nervously from the doorway. She was wringing her hands with frustration and unease. Telling her father about Ben's seduction of her had been a last-ditch stand, but even as she wailed, she'd known it wasn't going to work. She couldn't possibly compete with the San Antonio woman Ben had mentioned. She'd lost him. Her father's face told her own story, and she felt as if her heart had withered inside her frail body.

"Ben wasn't there. Coleman said he'd talk to young Ben," Ira said. "Won't do any good, though . . . What with him just getting engaged and all."

Faye thought her heart would stop beating. "En—gaged?"

"That's what Cole said. To some woman in San Antonio." He grimaced at her expression. "Faye, don't cry. There's a honey. I'm sorry, girl."

"Oh, Papa!" Faye ran back into the house in tears. How could Ben be so callous? He'd never said he loved her, but surely he realized that she was a good girl? She'd never even kissed anyone except Ben, and here he was about to marry that socialite!

She threw herself across the bed and wailed until her throat was sore and her eyes were red. She wasn't pregnant. She'd wanted to be, but the three times Ben had made love to her had been rushed—and he hadn't even been quite sober any of them. There wasn't going to be a baby. Ben didn't know that, though. She brightened a little at the thought of Coleman telling Ben. It might bring him back to her. Even if he didn't love her now, she could make him love her. She'd treat him so good he'd *have* to love her. All she had to do was hold on and she might win him yet, despite his fancy woman. . . .

A few minutes later, Marion Whitehall sought out Lacy, unaware of the reason for Ira's abrupt departure out front.

"You look worried," Lacy said as they had coffee together in the kitchen.

"I am," Marion replied. She sat down heavily; she didn't look well. She was pale. There were new lines in her face, more gray in her once-dark hair. "It's Benjamin's party. However shall we—"

"There's nothing to worry about," Lacy interrupted, smiling. "I talked Cole into letting me take care of the expenses."

Marion all but gasped. "You did? But how?"

That was something Lacy wasn't willing to admit. She creamed and sugared her coffee, avoiding Marion's sharp eyes. "I appealed to his logic," she replied. "Anyway, he'll allow me to do as I think best, Ben will have his party."

"But will he come to it?" Marion said miserably. "Lacy, he's so reluctant. It's almost as if he's—well,

ashamed of us. Those San Antonio folk he's staying with
are monied people. Perhaps he doesn't want his future
father-in-law to see how we live here.''

"How we live!" Lacy put down her coffee cup.
"Marion, we're quite civilized. We have indoor plumbing, electricity, even a telephone!" She stopped short of
mentioning that she could compete quite comfortably
with Ben's city friends with her own inheritance. She
didn't say it because she didn't want to make Marion feel
worse.

"But we're not wealthy, dear. And these newspaper
people would see that. I do not like to think of how
Coleman would react to snobbery."

Neither did Lacy. "I'm sure they have manners," she
said, but she didn't sound or feel convincing.

"Ira was here about Faye, wasn't he?" Marion
continued. "I suppose Benjamin's done something scandalous to that poor girl?"

"We're not suppose to know," came the dry response.
"We're the weaker sex. We must be protected from such
things, lest we suffer the vapors." She made a fainting
gesture with her arm across her eyes.

"We have the vote, dear. We no longer have the
vapors," Marion reminded her, with a smile, her mood
lightening a little. "All the same, I worry, Lacy," she
added. "Faye is a delicate child, all eyes and thin lines.
She seems so ill at times, as if she can barely get around
at all."

"She's a sweet little thing. But Ben is very young
still—and in love with the idea of being a famous
journalist. He *is* talented, you know . . . and marriage to
a newspaper heiress can't hurt his career."

"Is his profession more important than his family?"

"Give him time," Lacy said gently. "He's a Whitehall. He'll remember it one of these days. He's feeling his wings for the first time. Let him fly.''

Marion leaned back against her straight-backed chair. "I shall pray that he doesn't land himself in a cactus plant.''

"You do that." Lacy laughed.

"It's just that—Oh, my!" Marion sat very still and her eyes widened. Her hand went to her chest. "Such . . . pressure! Lacy, how odd . . .''

She pitched headfirst toward the floor; only Lacy's quick intercession saving her a bad fall. But Marion was unconscious, and Lacy was scared to death. She didn't know what to do, so she ran for the back door and yelled for Cole. Please God, let him be in the barn and not out on the ranch somewhere!

As if in answer to a prayer. Cole came out of the dark barn at once. "What is it?" he called.

"It's Marion! Do hurry! I'm afraid it's her heart!"

He broke into a run and made it through the kitchen door just as Lacy was holding a bottle of ammonia under Marion's nose in an attempt to bring her around.

After a minute, the older woman began to stir, coughing. Lacy helped her into a sitting position with Cole's help.

"I feel so sick," Marion said, swallowing. She was deathly pale and her skin felt clammy.

"I'm sorry, but we'll have to drive you in to Dr. Simon, Mother," Cole said quietly. "No arguments," he added when she hesitated. "This isn't the first spell you've had. It's time to let a doctor tell us what's wrong.''

Marion subsided. "Very well," she said weakly. "But I shall be sick all the way.''

"We can carry a basin and a damp cloth with us," Lacy suggested, and went to fetch them.

Together they got Marion into the runabout, and Cole
drove them to town.

Lacy had been hoping for a miracle. None was
forthcoming. Dr. Simon diagnosed Marion's condition
as heart dropsy. It was a death sentence, as they all
knew. Weeks, months, maybe a year, but Marion's fate
was sealed just that quickly, just that finally.

Cole was silent all the way home, and Lacy and
Marion talked halfheartedly about the weather. Dr.
Simon had prescribed some pills for Marion, to help the
pain, and bed rest as long as her weakness and nausea
persisted.

"We'll have to cancel Ben's party—" Lacy began.

"We shall not," Marion replied firmly. "It may be
the last . . ." Her voice broke and she had to stop and try
again. "It might be the last party I see at Spanish Flats.
We shall not cancel it. Go right ahead with the prepara-
tions, Lacy—and I shall do everything I can to help
you."

"It's out of the question," Cole said curtly. It was the
first time he'd spoken, and despite the paleness of his
face, he was determined.

"Don't argue with me, please, Coleman," Marion
said gently. "I have the right to decide how I spend the
time I have left."

"Simon should never have told you!"

"Yes, he should. You know that I dislike lies. It was
only what I suspected, at any rate. I think I knew, even
before he told me," she said quietly, her eyes lackluster
but resigned. "I'm a Whitehall, you know," she added,
with a forced smile. "We're a very strong breed."

Cole's dark eyes slid over her face that showed faint
terror, and then to Lacy's equally grim one. Somehow,
the fear in Lacy's eyes made him strong. He smiled at her

gently, reassuringly, and saw her relax a little. They'd manage, he told her without words.

"All right," he said finally. "Have your damned party, if you must."

"It will give Bennett something to remember," she agreed. "A fine send-off for his engagement and his job."

"As long as his city friends don't come down here with their noses in the air," Cole replied. "I won't tolerate snobbery—not even for my brother's sake."

"I'm sure they're not snobs, dear," Marion said, but she didn't look all that certain.

"No?" Cole turned onto the ranch road, sending a cloud of dust behind them as he accelerated. "I've heard some gossip about the girl he's getting engaged to. She sounds pretty fast to me."

"It's Ben's life," Lacy reminded him.

"So it is."

"Coleman, please slow down. You'll snap the bands again," Marion said, with a weak sigh.

"I carry plenty of spares," he replied patiently.

"Tires, too, I hope," Lacy murmured. "We had two punctures the last time I took my great-aunt Lucy to town to shop."

"Did you change them yourself?" he asked, with a teasing smile.

She beamed at the comradery. "No. Fortunately some of great-aunt Lucy's gentlemen friends drove us, both times. San Antonio has so much traffic that I would find it terrifying to drive there. If I could drive," she confessed.

"Never learn, dear," Marion advised. "What you learn, you may be forced to use one day. Better to remain ignorant and untaxed."

"The voice of wisdom." Cole chuckled. But inwardly

he was worrying about how to tell Katy and Ben about their mother. He hated the thought of admitting they were going to lose her. It hurt him as nothing else ever had. At least he had Lacy, he thought, thanking God and his mother for arranging that meeting in San Antonio. It wouldn't be as hard with Lacy beside him through the ordeal.

Lacy was thinking the same thing, and wondering how Cole was going to tell the others. She was glad it wouldn't be on her shoulders. But, then, Cole's shoulders were very broad, and he never shirked responsibility. Just being with him gave her a sense of confidence and optimism, although certainly there was very little to be optimistic about at the moment. She slid her fingers into Marion's and held on tight. This woman had been both mother and father to her for eight years. It was going to be terribly painful to lose her. But perhaps with plenty of rest and care, Marion could live a little longer. Lacy would certainly do her part, she thought, to stretch however much time she had left.

Back at Spanish Flats, Marion was coaxed into lying down and resting after she'd had one of the pills Dr. Simon had prescribed. Lacy stayed with her until she fell asleep and then she went to join a somber Cole in the kitchen, where he was drinking a cup of coffee.

He looked up as she walked into the room, his face pale and drawn, his eyes bitter and sad.

Lacy, impulsive as always, went straight to him and gently drew his cheek to her breasts, holding him there with her own cheek on his dark hair.

She felt his quick, indrawn breath, and thought ruefully that she'd probably done the wrong thing again. But his arms suddenly clasped her trim waist and he groaned as he held her.

"I love her, too," she said gently, her eyes closing. "But we'll manage, somehow."

"We'll have to," he said stiffly. His heart felt as if it had nails in it. Ten penny nails, at that. Lacy smelled of light cologne and her breasts were soft against his lean cheek. She had a big heart, he thought proudly, and let himself relax. It was the first time in adulthood that he'd accepted comfort from anyone, but today he needed it.

"You'll tell Ben and Katy?" she asked.

"Yes. I can telephone Katy I suppose," he muttered, disapproval in his tone. "Ben can wait until his party to hear about it. That will give him a little more time to live in blissful ignorance. Perhaps I'll wait until then to tell Katy, too."

Putting it off until the last minute, Lacy thought, but she didn't say it.

Finally Cole spanned her waist with his big, lean hands and moved her away from him. He put her into the chair next to his and handed her his handkerchief while he filled a white mug full of steaming black coffee for her.

She dabbed at the tears. "Thank you."

He shrugged. "I don't feel any less miserable than you do, if it helps. I didn't mind so much giving up my father. He was a hard, cold man, Lacy . . . With selfish ways and a savage streak. But Mother is—well, Mother."

"I know." She handed him back the handkerchief and sipped her coffee, her blue eyes meeting his over the rim of the mug. "I won't let her tire herself with this party, but it would be more of a strain on her if we tried to cancel it. She's got her heart set on giving Ben a royal send-off for his wedding and his new job."

"Spare her as much as you can, then. I'll have the men

butcher a steer for you, and a pig, too, if you want it. We can have Taggart and Cherry cook it.''

She managed a wobbly smile. ''So long as they don't have to serve it,'' she said.

He smiled. ''Yes, I understand. We'll keep them downwind of everyone while they cook it.''

''I can get some of the wives to help me prepare the rest of the food and serve it. Cole . . . I don't suppose it would be wise to invite little Faye?''

''No. We can't do that to Ben.''

''She's so fragile. I feel quite sorry for her.''

''So do I, Lacy. But people can't love to order.''

Her blue eyes searched over his hard, dark face. ''No, they can't,'' she said softly.

He met that telling look and his jaw tightened. ''One of these days you'll look at me like that and I'll jump the fence.''

She caught her breath. ''I don't understand.''

''Don't you?'' He moved suddenly, catching her by the nape of her neck with one big hand and pulling her mouth up to meet the hard descent of his.

He kissed her hungrily for the space of several seconds. Just when she relaxed and gave in, he let her go.

''You'd give me anything I wanted,'' he said huskily, his eyes glittering into hers at point-blank range. ''Do you have any idea how it makes me feel to know that?''

''No, because you keep pulling back,'' she whispered unsteadily.

His thumb moved slowly under her lower lip, taking away the dark traces of smudged lip rouge. ''I can't make love to you in the light, Lacy,'' he said roughly. ''I'll never be able to.''

She didn't want to speak, to break the spell. He'd never been so frank with her. "It won't matter," she said fiercely. "Don't you understand, Cole? I love you!"

"Love may not be enough," he said wearily. He got to his feet half angrily. "I have to get back to work."

Lacy got up, too, and retrieved the handkerchief she'd borrowed from beside his plate. "Just a minute. My lip rouge doesn't look that good on you."

He stopped, standing very still while she wiped his thin lips and removed the traces of dark red from them.

He watched her face hungrily. After a minute, he took the stained cloth away and, holding her head in one hand, removed the rouge from her own mouth.

"Why . . . ?" she exclaimed.

He tossed the handkerchief onto the table and bent to lift her off the floor in his bearish embrace. "Kiss me," he breathed against her lips.

She tingled all over with excitement. She smiled as she gave in to him, her arms around his neck. He was very strong and warm, and she loved the strength as well as the familiar scent of him. Her mouth opened involuntarily and she clung closer as his arms contracted while the long kiss went on and on.

When he let her back down, her body brushed against his, and its changed contours made her step back quickly, blushing.

"We're married," he said quietly, dark color staining his own cheeks as he tried not to appear as embarrassed as he was. "We'll both have to get used to it, I guess."

She swallowed. "Sorry. It's the age of permissiveness, after all. But I suppose I'm still back in the Victorian Age."

"So am I, if it's any consolation." He touched her

cheek gently, his eyes soft and quiet on her face. "Do you want to know what happened in France, Lacy? Are you sure you want to know?"

"Yes."

"I'll tell you tonight, then," he said grimly. "We might as well have everything out in the open. Then you can decide whether or not you want to stay. When you know the truth, San Antonio may appeal to you very strongly."

He turned and left her there, his spurs making musical noises as he strode out the back door and onto the porch.

He didn't want to tell her. But she had the right to know. If she loved him enough, it would be all right. He hoped she did. He'd never hoped anything as much. With his mother's terminal condition, he didn't know if he could cope alone. He'd never needed anyone before, but he needed Lacy. God willing, she wouldn't run out on him now.

Lacy watched him go with mixed emotions. Finally he was willing to tell her the truth. She knew it had something to do with what had happened overseas, but she didn't know what. When he told her, perhaps they could settle down to a new understanding and build a lasting relationship. She took the used cups to the sink and began to run water to wash them.

It was late when Cole came back. He'd been helping two of the men build a bigger calving barn, and they were just now through with the frame. The tin was going on the next day. It was hard work, but the hay-filled stalls were handy for two-year-old heifers who were giving birth for the first time, and for cows who had a hard time. The old barn was getting rickety. Cole's father had always maintained that it was far easier to build a new structure than to repair an old one.

Lacy was sewing a new dress, so Cole told her to keep on with what she was doing. He went to the kitchen and lifted the white linen cloth that covered the leftover food from the evening meal. He filled himself a plate of cold ham and rolls and canned peas. Then he opened the small icebox and, with the ice pick, chipped off some ice to fill a tall glass. He didn't want to have to ask Lacy to make coffee for him, and he was hot despite the chill because he'd been working. He poured sweetened brewed tea from the ceramic pitcher on the table into his glass. Then he put everything on a tray and went to his mother's room to sit with her while he ate.

Marion was propped up in bed nibbling on a piece of coconut cake, looking worn and pale. But she smiled at him all the same.

"How are you feeling?" Cole asked as he put his tray on her bedside table and tossed his hat onto a nearby chair.

"A little better, I think. Thank you, dear. You look tired."

"We got the calving shed framed in," he said wearily. "Tomorrow, we'll roof it with tin. Thank God we live in an area with a relatively warm winter. Turk's told me horror stories about calving in a Montana winter, with five feet of snow on the ground."

Marion nodded. "That's why the cattle industry does so well here in south Texas. Or so your father always said."

He took a bite of ham and studied her narrowly. "Did you love my father?"

She started, her eyes wide and round. "Why, of course!"

"How could you when he was so cruel to you?" he asked quietly. "He treated you like a stick of furniture when he wasn't berating you for some reason or other."

Marion smiled gently. "You saw the temper. I saw the boy I fell in love with trying too hard to cope with life." She lay back against the mound of pillows, her eyes misting in memory. "He was eighteen and I was sixteen when we married. We took Daddy's buggy and drove to Reverend Johnson's house late one afternoon with our marriage license. He married us and his wife gave us supper. I was so happy, Coleman. Those first years were bliss."

"And then?"

She put down the thin white saucer with the cake on it. "And then we bought this ranch. Your father was never cut out to be a rancher. He was a city boy, with big ideas. He would have made a fine businessman. He never was able to cope with cattle."

"That isn't how I remember him," he muttered.

"Oh, he learned," Marion said, correcting him. "But he hated the cattle industry, the dust and dirt and carnage of it. A man who is forced to do something he finds abhorrent can be turned cruel."

"Perhaps," he said noncommittally.

"You don't believe me. You love what you do; you enjoy working out of doors. I think you even like the challenge. Someday, Coleman," she continued, her eyes soft, "you won't have to live like this anymore. You'll have something better."

"I don't need frills," he protested gently. "I suppose Lacy wouldn't mind them, though."

Marion's eyes twinkled. "Do I dare ask if things are better for the two of you?"

"They're much better," he said, but his eyes were sad. "For the present."

The elderly woman studied him without speaking for a

long moment. "Lacy loves you very much," she said. "You're like your father in some ways, Coleman—afraid to trust, to open yourself to others because people who can come close enough can hurt you. Lacy never would."

"People can hurt without intending to," he said, and abruptly changed the subject. Not even to his mother could he talk about his deep fears, his insecurity, his scars. He didn't want to tell Lacy, but if their marriage was to have a chance, he'd have to.

When he got up to go, Marion reached out and gently touched his hand as it held the tray of empty dishes.

"You will take care of Ben and Katy . . . when the time comes?" she asked worriedly.

His face went hard as he looked down at her, seeing his life flash before him, all the memories of her loving care, her tenderness. "Haven't I always?" he asked quietly. "Now stop that. God was here first. He made doctors."

Marion smiled. "Yes, He did, didn't he?"

"You remember that." He bent and kissed her forehead gently. He wasn't an affectionate man, but he did love his mother. She touched his hair gently, remembering the tiny, black-headed baby she'd cradled in her arms, held against her heart, twenty-eight long years before. Many a dark night she'd rocked him in the cane-bottom rocker near her bedroom window, watching him nurse while her husband slept soundly in the bed nearby. Tears stung her eyes hotly, but she hid them. A mother's memories were precious, and private, something she rarely shared even with the children who provided them.

"Will you take my saucer back to the kitchen with you?" she asked, managing to sound almost normal.

"Certainly." He added it to the tray and smiled at her. "Try to sleep."

"I'll do that. Pull out the top light as you go, will you, dear?"

"Sleep well."

He reached up to the metal string attached to the socket of the lone, stark bulb suspended from the high ceiling and tugged. The light went out promptly. Cole shook his head at the modern miracle. The family had gone to bed by kerosene lantern until two years ago. Electricity was still a luxury, like the telephone, but Marion had said that cattle prices went up while Cole was in France recuperating in the hospital after the war. So many new things graced the old house on his return. He did know how war seemed to boost the economy, so he'd never questioned it. His mother had so enjoyed those luxuries that he didn't have the heart to chide her about the money that could have gone into an improved breeding program. With the neighbors' help, and Taggart and Cherry overseeing his cattle, at least the ranch had done okay while he was off fighting. That was one big blessing. Now if he could just manage to pay off the mortgage before he lost the whole business, that would be his best one—next to keeping Marion alive as long as possible, he added silently, and with an absent prayer.

But at the moment, he had another worry on his mind. How to tell Lacy, as he'd promised he would tonight, that her dreams of a family could never come true.

Chapter Nine

B Y THE TIME COLE FINISHED HIS BATH AND DRESSED in clean clothes, Lacy was sitting in front of the small fireplace in their bedroom, having laid a fire in it. She was hemming the dress she'd made, her face glowing softly in the firelight. The high-ceilinged rooms were quite cool in November, despite the fact that it was south Texas. The fire felt good.

Cole paused beside her chair. "I put the dishes in the sink," he remarked quietly. "They'll keep until morning."

She smiled up at him. "Thank you. How is Marion?"

"I pulled off the light. She said she was going to try to sleep." He sat down in the straight-backed chair beside hers and ran a restless hand through his hair, damp from the tub. "I promised you an explanation."

She slid her needle through the fabric of her dress and her hands stilled. Her blue eyes held his. "Yes."

"It's going to be hard."

"I told you before . . . nothing will matter, Cole," she told him.

"Won't it?" he asked, with veiled sarcasm. He leaned back in the chair precariously and began to roll a cigarette. "You knew that I was wounded in France, and that it took a long time for me to heal. What you don't

153

know is how it happened.'' He put the finished cigarette in his mouth and reached over to get one of the big kitchen matches that were used to light fires. He stuck it in the stone hearth and lit the cigarette, tossing the used match into the fire. ''I was flying back from a raid on the German lines. There were several of us, in formation. We were surprised by a German circus that was on its way back to camp after raiding our front.''

''Circus?'' she asked, curious.

''It was what we called a formation of fliers,'' he explained. ''The name of the squad's lead pilot determined its name, Richthofen's Circus was headed by the Red Baron himself.''

''I see.''

''It was a madhouse. You can't imagine the complexity of trying to balance a wire-rigged flying machine in the air and rain bullets at an enemy at the same time. My outfit was a biplane, a Nieuport, and just as I leveled off on the enemy's tail, I was hit by gunfire from above. I went down with the engine in flames.''

Lacy hadn't moved. She hoped she was still breathing. ''You crashed in flames?''

''Not quite that. The planes were made of wood and wire and dope-covered fabric, so they burned quite easily. But I got lucky, because there was a flat plain close by. I was able to land the plane. But my foot was caught and I couldn't get out. And just after I was on the ground, it burst into flames.'' He glanced at Lacy's horrified face. ''Turk had seen me go down. He landed almost simultaneously and ran toward me. I was on fire when he pulled me out of the plane.'' He shivered with the memory of the heat and agonizing pain. ''He smothered the flames and sat with me until the medics came. I spent months in the hospital. At first they thought I might die, but I kept improving. Turk sat with me. Talked to me. Encouraged me. He pulled me back from the edge.'' He didn't look at her now. ''When I was well enough, the doctors told me what had happened, what I could expect. After they left, I made a grab for my service revolver. Turk took it away from me.''

Lacy let out her breath. ''Oh, Cole,'' she said, horrified.

He laughed coldly, staring into the flames, wincing at the dancing heat. ''My back and legs were pretty bad, even my stomach. I healed, but there are some terrible scars. That's not even the worst of it.'' He lifted the cigarette to his lips and took a long draw. ''They said I might not be able to father a child.''

She was out of her chair and on her knees in front of him even as he finished speaking, her arms sliding around him, her face against his chest. She held on tight, not even speaking.

His hands rested lightly on her hair as he tried to assimilate what her actions meant. Was it comfort or pity?

Even as he tried to decide, there was a perfunctory knock on the door and Ben flew into the room. He looked dusty and disheveled, and his eyes were wide with worry.

''Cole, I've got to talk to you!'' he said urgently. ''Sorry, Lacy. But this won't wait. Cole, please, now!''

Lacy got up, her face hidden, letting Cole rise. He glanced at her, but she wouldn't meet his eyes. He went out with Ben, closing the door behind them.

''Well, what is it?'' Cole asked. He knew it couldn't be about Marion, because he hadn't told the boy yet.

''Faye called me,'' Ben muttered. ''She tracked me down in San Antonio and swears she's pregnant and it's mine. My God, Cole. I'm engaged to be married! I haven't got time for this mess!''

"You had time to sleep with Faye and get her pregnant,'' Cole accused coldly. "You dishonored her. Shamed her. Ira came to see me today, talking wild.''

"I never meant to let things go so far,'' Ben groaned. "I was drinking, and she was so willing, so sweet. I couldn't stop. I've stayed away since then. It's been over three months since I was with her. And I know it can't be mine—if she's even pregnant.''

"How do you know?'' Cole asked curtly.

"Because I wanted her, really bad, a few days later, and she said she couldn't because it was the wrong time of the month,'' Ben told him. "So it can't be mine.''

Cole had worked with cattle breeding more than long enough to know about cycles, menstruation, and ovulation. He nodded. There were exceptions, of course, but it was unlikely that Faye would be pregnant if she was telling Ben the truth months ago.

"What am I going to do? I can't let Jessica find out about her,'' Ben wailed. "She might break the engagement, and then where would I be? Her father would probably fire me!''

"You aren't marrying the girl because of your job?'' Cole asked warily.

"I'm marrying her because she's good in bed, rich, and has all the right connections,'' Ben said shortly. "Why not? I'm tired of being poor!''

Cole was disgusted, and it showed. "Money won't buy you everything, and living off a woman is shoddy.''

"You ought to know.'' Ben shot back, irritated by Cole's disapproval.

"What do you mean?'' the older man demanded.

"You've been living off Lacy for years. Or didn't you

know that all these modern conveniences are things she paid for?" Ben scoffed. "She even paid off the second mortgage on the ranch so it wouldn't be repossessed while you were in France. Things got hard; Lacy saved us."

"Why wasn't I told?" Cole asked, his face white.

"You didn't ask," Ben said uneasily. He didn't like the way his big brother looked. "Why isn't Mother still up?"

Cole had never felt so cruel in his life. Lacy had supported him, and he hadn't known. Damn Ben for making him feel like a fool!

"Mother has heart dropsy," he told Ben, putting the knife in without a scrap of conscience. "The doctor says she's dying."

Cole turned and left Ben standing there, his eyes bulging in a white face, while he went back into the bedroom and closed the door—and he wasn't sorry. Damn Ben! He wasn't sorry at all that he'd done it!

Lacy was sitting by the fire, her face drawn and quiet. She looked up expectantly. "Cole—" she began softly.

"You've been pouring money into the house and the ranch," he accused coldly. "Why keep it from me?"

Her face gave away her guilt. "Because I knew you'd be furious," she said simply. "I had it, the ranch needed it . . ."

"You'll get it back," he said shortly. "Every penny."

"Do we have to talk about that tonight?"

"No." He went to the wardrobe and pulled out his pajamas and robe. He turned back to her with cold eyes in a hard face. "I'm going to sleep in the guest room from now on. If you don't like it, go back to San Antonio. Go to hell for all I care."

Lacy couldn't believe what he was saying. She stood

up. "Cole, please don't do this; don't be like this. Times were so hard here during the war. You were away . . . There were bills due, and threatened foreclosure . . . I had the money, and more. You couldn't have expected me to let you lose Spanish Flats!"

"I won't take money from a woman," he said, with furious pride.

"Cole, please listen!" she pleaded.

"Good night, Lacy." He went out, slamming the door behind him

Lacy sank down into her chair, a dull throb at her temples. She might have guessed that his icy pride would defeat her once he found out about her financial support of his family. She'd hit him in his most vulnerable spot. He wouldn't forget or forgive. Now they were right back where they'd began, and if Cole's expression had been any indication, they were going to stay there for a long time. She'd wanted to tell him that she was sorry they couldn't have a child together, but that it didn't matter. His scars didn't matter. She loved him; she wanted to live with him, no matter what. But he was in no listening mood. She closed her eyes and leaned back in the rocker. Should she go back to San Antonio? She remembered all too well what it had been like just after she and Cole had married. He'd frozen her with every glance, every word. She knew she couldn't bear that indifference and anger anymore. But how could she leave Marion?

She couldn't, she decided finally, she'd have to stick it out—at least until after they gave Ben his engagement party. She'd make decisions as she had to. Right now, she just wanted to go to bed. This had been one of the worst days of her life. First Marion, now Cole. Ben had told him, of course. Her eyes flashed. No matter what it took, little Bennett was going to get his ears burned

tomorrow. She could have cheerfully taken a buggy whip
to the spoiled little boy.

She didn't know that Ben was already being taken to
task for his indiscretion. He'd gone to bed in his old
room, and tears had filled his eyes when there was no one
to see. He'd never imagined that his mother could die.
Cole had no right to throw it at him like that. He hadn't
meant to spill the beans about Lacy's financial support. It
was just that Cole's old-fashioned righteousness rubbed
him raw sometimes. He was old enough to marry and
live as he pleased, and Cole could like it or lump it.

He felt sick as he thought about losing his mother.
Now Faye was even threatening his future, phoning him,
crying about being pregnant. He'd have to sort her out
before he left again, that was for sure. She couldn't be
allowed to go around telling lies about him. Suddenly
life was just too complex for words, he thought miserably!

In Chicago, Katy had settled into a dismal routine of
sorts, being Danny's wife in public and his own whipping
boy in private. His mother complained and nagged all
day long, and when Danny was home, he took over.
Nothing Katy did was right. He didn't even want her in
bed anymore, and they'd only been married a few weeks.

"You're not the girl I thought I was bringing home,"
he said, with faint contempt, one evening as they arrived
at a local speakeasy where Danny was to have a business
meeting with local gang lord Blake Wardell. "You don't
smile, you don't bubble. You just sit and glower.
Mama's disappointed."

"So am I," Katy said dully. "I should have stayed in
Texas."

"You'll have your uses, baby doll," he said mysteriously. "Never let it be said that I wasted an opportunity." His eyes approved of the tasseled gown she was wearing; but then he looked at the feathered headband around her upswept dark hair. "You ought to cut that hair. You look odd."

Everyone else seemed to have the popular bob, but Katy didn't like it. She enjoyed long hair. If it defied convention, so much the better. Life with Danny was hell. Even pining over Turk back at Spanish Flats seemed better than this walking death. She was property—like one of Danny's cars—and she wondered now if he'd even cared about her in the beginning. If he had, Mama Marlone had certainly put paid to that. She did everything she could to turn Danny against Katy. He wouldn't have brought her here tonight if he hadn't wanted to put up a good front for a prospective business partner.

Blake Wardell was a big, dark man with eyes that were kind despite his reputation as one of the biggest gangsters in Chicago. He was a gambler by trade, and he ran casinos all over the country. Danny wanted to get in on the action.

Katy was drawn to the big man. Something about him reminded her of Turk. Perhaps it was his size, or the way he smiled, or the soft darkness of his eyes when he looked at her. Katy could look at him and remember, so well, that last day with Turk. She had no regrets at all about what had happened, not one. She knew, was almost certain, that she was pregnant. She knew, too, that the child was Turk's and not Danny's. A baby would give her one sweet part of Turk to treasure during her hellish marriage, and Danny wouldn't know.

But she did want, so desperately, to tell Turk. He was her life, but he didn't want her. He'd said so. He'd let her go—without a single attempt to stop her, to ask her to stay. He didn't want her, and she was just going to have to accept that. Her life was here now, in a world she'd never known existed until she came to Chicago.

The mobsters fascinated her. They didn't have two heads or carry guns in their teeth at all. They were ordinary men, nothing spectacular. They just made their living outside the law, and seemed to think nothing of talking about the way they did it. Katy had heard some hair-raising stories of gang killings and extortion. Danny had friends who had actually murdered people. Katy took it all in with fearful awe, even as she wondered what her poor mother and Lacy would think if they could see her now. Thank God Cole couldn't, she affirmed silently, or he'd have been on the next train with a gun packed in his valise. His only communication with her since her marriage had been a terse letter of congratulation. She knew he disapproved of Danny. He didn't know about what had happened between Turk and herself, and she could at least spare him the destruction of his friendship with Turk. It didn't matter, when she and Turk would probably never even see each other again as long as they lived. If only it wasn't so difficult living with Danny. Just lately, his behavior had begun to change. He was frequently wild and violent, and Katy was becoming very afraid of him. He'd already hit her once. . . .

"You're very solemn, Mrs. Marlone," Blake Wardell said quietly, smoke wafting from a big cigar in his left hand. There was a ruby ring on his little finger, but he wore no other jewelry.

Katy looked at him with subdued interest. He had thick eyebrows and a big, imposing nose. Under it was a wide, hard-lipped mouth and a square jaw. Chiseled granite would have been a perfect description of the contours of his broad face. But his deep-set eyes were its saving grace. They were dark and alive, eyes that could say more than words. He smiled at her and they warmed, like dark flames.

"Katy doesn't say much these days," Danny said sarcastically. "She doesn't do much, either. She's kind of like a figurehead. She decorates the place."

"Danny, please," Katy said, wincing.

"She certainly is decorative," Blake replied, with gallantry. "How can you risk showing her off to other men?" he asked Danny.

The question stopped Danny's cold glare short. He eyed Blake with sudden interest.

Danny wanted a cut of Wardell's operation and he didn't have enough capital to buy it. But Wardell certainly seemed fascinated by Katy. His expression told Danny that he found Katy not only attractive, but desirable. Well, well. Danny knew what a cold little fish she was, but Wardell didn't. This unexpected development might work to his advantage.

"Why don't you dance with Blake, Katy?" Danny suggested. "She's a good dancer," he told the older man.

The music playing was a Charleston, and Katy hesitated. Rebellion was one thing, but she felt suddenly conspicuous.

"I don't know if I should . . ." Katy began.

Danny's whole expression became threatening, and Katy noticed it with subdued fear. "Don't be such a goose," Danny muttered. "Go on, Katy. Dance with the nice man."

That was a threat. She didn't protest again.

Wardell laughed softly, thinking she was embarrassed at being asked to do the dance in public. The Charleston was actually considered quite decadent by a certain segment of the population who thought it signaled the rot of society. The same people had tried to ban jazz as a detriment to morality.

"If you don't like the music, Mrs. Marlone, I can fix that," Wardell said. He signaled to the waiter, handed him a bill, whispered something to him, and nodded toward the band. The waiter grinned, nodded, and went to speak to the bandleader. Seconds later, the wild music faded, to be replaced by a slow, sweet melody that Katy recognized instantly.

"Better?" Wardell teased, standing.

Katy blushed, because the band was playing "A Pretty Girl is Like a Melody," a song that became popular the year after the war ended.

"You *are* pretty," he said when she was loosely held in his arms, moving briskly in a fox-trot to the sweet tune. "Doesn't your husband tell you?"

Katy made a gesture with one shoulder. "Not really."

"What a pity." His eyes went over her hair in its loose bun at the nape of her neck, down the length of her dress that reached just below her knees and was held up by diamanté straps. The sparkle of the rhinestones did something exquisite to her milky smooth skin, and he wondered how she'd look naked in a diamond necklace. The thought aroused him and he laughed, deep in his throat.

She looked up, confused by the laughter. "Why are you laughing?"

"I don't know you well enough to tell you," he said. "But that will change."

Katy cleared her throat. The scent of him was very masculine, spicy, and clean. Danny didn't bathe often and always seemed to smell of sweat. Katy actually found him repulsive. She would probably have found him really repulsive if he wanted sex.

But Blake Wardell smelled nice, as Turk always had, and his cologne was familiar. Probably it was the same that Turk used, and that might explain her mixed feelings about this big, dark man. He seemed to find her attractive, and in turn, he actually attracted her. That was disturbing. Suppose she was one of those women she read about who enjoyed a variety of men? She felt horrified. She hadn't been raised to be a loose woman, but she was intensely drawn to Blake Wardell. She was, too, almost certainly pregnant. . . .

"What's wrong?" he asked, his big hand closing gently around her cold fingers.

She looked up; her face was as open as a book.

He smiled very gently. "It's all right," he said softly. "I feel it, too."

"I'm . . . married," she stammered.

"That doesn't matter."

"But . . . !"

He bent, his mouth whispering against hers so briefly that she could hardly believe it had happened. "I said it doesn't matter. Come here." He drew her close, and she shivered at the feel of his body so intimately against her own. Turk, she thought, her eyes closing as she remembered the day she'd left Spanish Flats. Oh, Turk! she moaned silently, actually feeling as if she'd betrayed him—when it was Danny she should have felt guilty about betraying.

Danny watched Katy dance with Wardell with no feeling of jealousy or anger. He smiled. Good. Good. Wardell wanted her. Plans were forming in his mind like clouds. Katy might become the wedge he used to get in on Wardell's action. At least, he thought, she'd finally do him some good. God knew, it was like taking a statue to bed. She hated sex. He supposed most women of her sort were like that. He preferred experienced women who knew what to do. His eyes cut around to a cute little blonde who was giving him the eye from the next table. He glanced at Katy and Wardell and thought, Why not? He gestured toward the blond, left a tip on the table, had a waiter tell Katy he'd had to leave, and walked out with the blonde on his arm.

It was the beginning of a new chapter in Katy's life. From that night on, Blake Wardell seemed always to be around when she and Danny went out on the town. She welcomed his company, because Danny didn't mistreat her then. But Blake was potent, and his presence was having a violent effect on her emotions.

It all came to a head when Danny ran her out of their bedroom with his verbal abuse during one of his tantrums. Mama Marlone wasn't home to witness it, having gone to visit a relative that night. Danny caught up with her and hit her. She fell down the stairs, and Danny actually left her lying there and went out.

It was Blake Wardell who found her, half-conscious, bleeding, moaning in pain. She knew almost certainly that she'd lost the baby. He called an ambulance and went with her to the hospital, holding her hand while she cried her heart out.

When she came to, he was sitting by the bed, holding her hand again.

"You had a miscarriage." he said quietly. "I'm sorry."

Tears ran down her cheeks. "I know," she sobbed.

"You poor kid! Where's Danny? I'll call him," he offered.

"No! He . . . made me fall," she said tersely. "He hit me."

Her eyes closed, and Blake groaned. "He didn't know about the kid? You hadn't told him?"

She let the tears flow. "It wasn't his," she whispered secretly. "It was Turk's baby."

His face hardened. "Turk who?"

"Turk Sheridan. He was my brother's foreman—*is* my brother's foreman, back home,' she said, faltering. "I loved him, but he was still mourning his late wife and he didn't want me."

"Still carrying a torch for him?" he asked quietly.

"I told you he didn't want me." She cried all the harder.

With a long sigh, he gathered her up close and held her, his dark face against her hair. "Don't cry, Katy," he said softly. "I'll take care of you. I want you. I'll always want you."

Her arms clung to him. He was warm and strong and protective. He was everything Danny wasn't. Except that he wasn't Turk.

"Danny's always throwing us together," she said when the tears began to slow. She wiped at them carelessly. "You watch him, Blake," she added, lifting her red-rimmed eyes. "He's a bad man."

"I know that." He touched her mouth. "I can take care of myself. You, too, if you'll leave him."

She wanted to. But she was afraid of what Danny might do. She shivered and touched her bruised face. "I can't."

"Listen," he said angrily, "I won't let him hurt you. Danny's a smalltime operator. I'm not. I've got leverage and I can use it. Give me the right and I'll send him back to Italy in a syrup can!"

If she hadn't cared about him, she might have agreed. But Danny was devious—and his behavior grew wilder every day. She was afraid of what he might do, not only to Wardell but to her family back in Texas. He had contacts everywhere.

"No," she said after a minute. "No. I don't want you hurt."

His face changed. Half his age seemed to drop away and he looked at her with wonder. "You . . . don't want *me* hurt?" he echoed blankly.

His expression touched her. She smiled wanly and lifted her hand to his broad face. "You look shocked."

"I am. Nobody ever gave a damn about me before," he said shortly. "My mother walked the streets for a living. I don't even know who my father was. I grew up rough and hard and in trouble with the law. I've never had anything that I didn't have to take."

She felt a stark compassion for him. He wasn't altogether bad. She'd seen him go out of his way to help people down on their luck, and he was here now when she had nobody else to look after her.

Impulsively she drew his face down to hers and put her soft mouth over his hard one.

He stiffened, and she started to draw away, but his big hand slid behind her head and his mouth opened on hers.

He was at least as experienced as Turk, if not more, she thought dizzily. She liked the way he teased her mouth with his lips and teeth before he penetrated it deeply with his tongue and made her gasp with the sudden heat of desire.

He heard the soft sound and lifted his head. Dark, knowing eyes narrowed as they met hers. "You feel guilty. Don't. You can't help it any more than I can."

She swallowed, her eyes troubled.

"I know," he said quietly. "You love your foreman. It's his memory you think you're being disloyal to—not your husband's—isn't it?"

She nodded helplessly.

He smoothed back her damp, disheveled hair. "Well, for what it's worth, I feel a little guilty myself. You're married. I haven't got many scruples, but cutting a shine with a married woman is something I've never done before."

His dry tone lifted her mood. "I won't tell if you won't tell," she whispered, with a rare glimpse of her old spirit.

He caught his breath at the difference in her, at the sparkle of her green eyes, the radiance in her face. He had a fleeting look at what she'd have been like in love, and he cursed her brother's stupid foreman for throwing her love away. He realized suddenly that he'd have given anything for it.

"I wish it had been me instead of Danny," he said shortly. "Or, especially, me instead of the man back home." He drew back reluctantly. "But I guess you'd have been worse off with me. I'm a gambler. I make my living on the weakness of other men. Besides that," he added, turning his face away, "I'm sterile. I had mumps late in life. I can't ever make a woman pregnant."

Tears stung her eyes at the way he said it, as if it devastated him. She touched his hand and curled hers into it. "I'm sorry."

He looked down at her. "If Danny hits you again, I'll kill him," he said matter-of-factly.

She flushed. "Blake . . ."

"You won't talk me out of it. How would you like to go to the theater when they let you out of here? We'll find something to cheer you up."

She smiled up at him gratefully. "I'd like that."

His eyes narrowed. Finally he smiled back. His gaze went down her body and back up. "I'm sorry about the kid."

"So am I," she replied. "But it's for the best, I guess. He wouldn't have wanted it . . ." She broke down helplessly.

He bent and kissed the fresh tears away. "Stop that," he whispered at her lips. He nibbled them tenderly and then caught the soft lower one in his teeth. "Go to bed with me, Katy."

She caught her breath. Her eyes widened.

"Don't panic. I don't mean now." He kissed her again. "I've never had it with a woman I've cared about," he said, with blurred hunger, "a woman I could respect. I think I love you, baby."

She stared at him. "Do you, really?"

He nodded. He moved close to her mouth again and brushed it tenderly with his. "I'm big," he said. "A lot bigger than Danny."

She blushed at the blatant statement. It was something even Danny had never talked about, much less Turk.

He smiled at her color. "Best you know it before you decide. I've had prostitutes run from me."

Her heart stopped in her chest. She searched his eyes. "But you wouldn't hurt me," she said then, certain of it. "I don't like it with Danny. I never did."

His eyes narrowed. "And the foreman?"

She averted her face. "I—I loved him," she stammered.

He sighed. "Well, I can't be somebody else in bed. But I'll be good to you, Katy." He drew her head to his lips. "It might not be too bad with a man who loves you more than his own life."

Her eyes closed. He wasn't Turk. But he was certainly the next best thing. "Blake . . ."

"You weren't raised to commit adultery, I know. But think about it. I want you so desperately," he said huskily. "God, Katy. I want you more than I want to live!"

She clung to him. He wasn't half as bad as he seemed to think he was. There was good in him. If it hadn't been for Danny's violence, she might have gone to Blake. But it was a risk she couldn't take. She was well and truly trapped. The only thing she didn't understand was why Danny kept pushing her at Wardell.

Chapter Ten

BEN WENT TO SEE FAYE EARLY THE NEXT MORNING. Fortunately her father, had gone to town, and she was alone at the house.

She stiffened when she found him on the doorstep, her blond hair disheveled, around her face in a mass of curls, an old toweling robe wrapped loosely around the cotton gown that hung loosely over her too-thin body.

"So it's you," she said petulantly, "Come to tell me about your fancy lady in San Antonio, have you?"

"You aren't pregnant," Ben said shortly, glaring at her. "Why did you tell that lie?"

"It wasn't a lie," she said evasively. "I could have been." She looked up, her full lower lip trembling. "You know I could have been! You were the first one, the only one!"

Ben felt uncomfortable. She looked small and helpless, and her big eyes were brimming over with tears. "Look here, Faye," he said, without anger. "You don't understand how it is. I don't want to spend the rest of my life knee-deep in cattle. I want more than that. Jessica can give it to me. She's wealthy and socially secure. It's more a business arrangement than a marriage."

"What will she get out of it?" Faye demanded.

171

He smiled insolently. "You know what she'll get out of it."

Faye went scarlet and looked away.

That shamed him. She loved him. She'd given herself trustingly, and he'd made light of the gift. "I'm sorry," he said, taking her gently by the shoulders. "Really, I am." He frowned, remembering. He'd taken a long time with Jessica, because she was experienced and demanding. But the times he'd been with Faye, he was tipsy and in a hurry. "Faye, you didn't enjoy it, did you?" he asked suddenly.

She averted her face. He turned it up to his, and something in him flinched at her expression. She looked . . . anguished.

"Are you pregnant?" he asked very gently.

The tears spilled over. "No!" she choked. "I wanted to be. I prayed to be. But you don't love me, do you? . . . So it would have been awful for you. Oh, Ben, I'm sorry!" she whispered brokenly. She covered her face with her hands and she was trembling terribly. "I'm sorry! I loved you so much, I thought you just *had* to care a little about me, but you don't. You never did. I was just easy and I gave in like a woman of the streets!"

He pulled her close, groaning. She was so damned fragile. Why did she have to be like this, so sweet and vulnerable? He couldn't afford to involve himself with her again, not when he was engaged! He was sitting on top of the world, and all he had to do was sacrifice little Faye to have everything he'd ever wanted.

"I love you so," she sobbed into his shirtfront.

He drew in an anguished breath, his hand absently smoothing her hair. "Don't cry," he whispered. He closed his eyes. "Faye, my mother's dying," he blurted out.

She drew away a little, wiping at her tears. "Your mother? Oh, Ben, no!"

"Her heart." He moved her hair back from her face, his eyes sad, his face contorted by sorrow. "I didn't know. I'm going to lose her, and what will I do then? My brother and sister and I have never been close, but Mother and I always were—perhaps because I'm the youngest. She's going to die!"

"She's a good woman," Faye said gently. Her hand reached up to his face, her eyes filled with compassion. "She'll make the sweetest angel, Ben . . ."

Her voice broke. He clasped her close, shivering with grief. She held him, soothed him, whispered soft nothings that comforted him. Little Faye, with her big, generous heart.

"It's all right, Ben," she whispered. She rubbed her cheek gently against his. "You'll get through it. Doctors can make mistakes, you know. She might have years left!"

She made him feel whole again, as if he could conquer the world. He took a deep, slow breath and lifted his head, not at all embarrassed to let her see the traces of tears on his thick lashes. Faye had been a part of his life since they were children. He was her first man. He felt protective about her, safe when he was with her. But he'd taken her for granted. Even now, he had no right to be with her. It wasn't honorable.

"You're sweet," he said softly. He smiled and bent to touch her mouth with his. But at the instant of contact, he knew his mistake. It was like fire against dry wood. Despite Jessica's skill and variety of techniques, Faye aroused him until he was mindless—just by touching him.

He groaned, reached to pull her hips against his.

She gasped at the quickness of his need for her, at the hot pressure of him against her belly.

"Faye!" he whispered, shivering.

He ground her mouth open under his and guided her backward to the long, worn sofa. Oblivious to where they were, who they were, even to the fact that her father could come back any minute, he lowered her down. His hands slid gently over her, feeling her small breasts go taut in his hands, her body shiver responsively.

Seconds later, he divested her of robe and gown and looked down at her body. He'd never really seen it until now. The times he'd made love to her, he'd been less than sober and it had been dark. But now he looked at her, and she was white-skinned and exquisite, even with her thinness. Her nipples were mauve and hard, rising as if they begged for his mouth, blushing with the same color that touched her cheeks.

"Pretty little thing," he whispered. He lowered his mouth to her breasts and began to suckle them. She cried out her ecstasy. It was all he needed to send him right over the edge. He pleasured her with his mouth and his hands in the way he'd first pleasured Jessica, except that Faye was inexperienced and totally abandoned in her reception to his caresses. She made him feel like the most male man who'd ever lived, moaning and trembling and sobbing as he kindled the flames in her body. She'd never been aroused to this point before, probably because he'd been too selfish to care. But now he did. He lifted his head long enough to look at her, and pride blazed in his eyes as he saw the blatant need in her face, the helpless writhing of her body, the trembling of her long legs.

He couldn't wait long enough to undress. He unfastened his trousers, lowered himself over her body with a minimum of movement.

"Easy," he whispered when she tried to pull him down. He hesitated, poised so that he was just barely touching her.

She cried out again, a sound he'd never heard echoed from a woman's throat.

It aroused him feverishly, but still he kept control. "Lie still," he said huskily. He rested his forearms beside her head and watched her face while he moved slowly down. She shuddered at the first taste of penetration. He held there, smiling hungrily. "More?" he whispered.

"P—please!"

He moved again, his eyes glittering. "This much?" he asked, feeling her body tremble violently. "Or this much?" And he pushed down, hard.

She felt him fill her all at once and she convulsed. It was vaguely terrifying, the hot, black oblivion of fulfillment. She'd never known it until now, and she was afraid of it. She tried to struggle, but she couldn't even see. Her body throbbed with each strangled cry as ecstasy threw her rhythmically against his hips.

Ben watched her, awed by her face, her body. Odd that Jessica had never looked like that. Of course, Jessica had been with other men. Faye hadn't. Faye hadn't had anyone except him . . .

The thought worked its way down his backbone until it expanded, throbbed, and suddenly burst into splinters of the most delicious pleasure he'd ever experienced.

His face blazed red with it, his body arched, and he gasped as it rolled over him, shuddering, exploding like rainbows of fire.

Faye came back to consciousness just as she felt him burst, her eyes wide and fascinated as she watched him above her. She'd never seen him like this, either. She looked down and she saw him as she hadn't dreamed of seeing him. Seconds later, he pulled back, and she couldn't drag her eyes from him.

"Ben!" she gasped. "Ben, my gosh!"

He collapsed beside her, his body shivering in the aftermath, his heartbeat audible, his breathing strained.

His eyes were closed—then he groaned as he realized what he'd done. Damn his hormones, and damn Faye's beauty!

She looked down at him, her heart in her eyes. "You . . . didn't have to . . . do that," she said, faltering as his eyes opened. "You . . . I mean, you didn't have to make it—make it good for me, too."

"No, I didn't," he said flatly.

"Then, why?"

He looked at her breasts, relaxed now, pretty and soft, and he felt himself going hard again. He couldn't believe it. He couldn't!

He lifted her over him, fitting her to his body with abrupt ease, holding her there. "Again," he said huskily. "I'll give you that again."

"But, you're . . . engaged, Ben," she whimpered.

"She can't give me this," he ground out. "Oh, God, Faye. Nobody can give me this but you!"

He held back just long enough to satisfy her before he gave himself to her one last time and felt the sun explode in his veins. It was the most incredible ecstasy. Why couldn't he feel it with the woman he was pledged to marry?

Later, he rearranged his clothing while Faye slowly pulled on her things. He didn't look at her. He was too ashamed.

She went to the door, opening it. She didn't lift her eyes. "Good-bye, Ben," she whispered, her voice wobbly. "Thank you," she added hesitantly, "for show-ing me how it could have been. It was so beautiful."

Her control broke on the last word, but she bit her lip, hanging on tight to her pride.

Ben paused at the door. He'd never felt quite so low. Faye had comforted him, and he'd given her nothing except the risk of a child. He felt suddenly shocked at the thought of Faye carrying his baby. Shocked and uncertain.

"I'm sorry, Faye," he said inadequately.

She shook her head. "I wanted to. It's all right, I won't tell anyone. I shouldn't have let Papa go to see Coleman. He won't know about this, I promise."

He tilted her face up to his haunted eyes. "If I gave you a baby, I want to know."

Her heart stopped. "I couldn't do that, Ben," she said. "You'll be married. It wouldn't be right."

"What in God's name *will* you do?"

"I'll get rid of it," she whispered, strangling on the words. "It will be all right."

"Get rid of it?" he burst out, enraged.

The sudden sound of a car in the distance alerted him to the possibility of her father's arrival home. He groaned inwardly at his stupidity. He was getting worse by the day. He looked at Faye and tried to find words. Surely she wouldn't risk killing herself in one of those filthy clinics!

"I probably won't, anyway," Faye said, with savaged pride. "I didn't before."

He hadn't been that thorough before, he wanted to add. But she was right. Perhaps fate would be kind once more. Anyway, he had to think of his future. Jessica could give him everything he wanted.

"Good-bye, Faye," he said stiffly.

She looked up, her eyes adoring him sadly. "Do you love her?"

He shifted. "She's very well-to-do."

"I see."

The two words enraged him. "At least she's got more pride than to give her body to an engaged man!"

Faye didn't look up again. She looked . . . crushed.

He cursed roundly and went back to the car, cranking it viciously. He refused to think about anything except his marriage. Faye was truly in the past—starting now.

Faye watched him drive away with a long sigh. So long, pal, she thought with bitter humor. I hope you get all the money you want. But it won't be enough. It never is. She turned and went back inside.

Ben pulled up at the front door of Spanish Flats with anger smoldering inside him. He'd hurt Faye, his mother was dying, Cole and Lacy weren't even speaking today, and somehow he felt responsible for the cares of the whole world. Perhaps he was growing up, he thought bitterly.

He got out of the runabout and walked up onto the porch with a step slower than his usual one. Lacy was in the living room, but she came into the hall when she heard him. She looked as Victorian as Cole this afternoon, dressed in a very correct, high-necked, gray and white dress, not one of her short and fashionable ones. Her eyes were as icy cold as Cole's had ever been.

"Thank you very much for destroying my marriage— what there was of it," she said to him. "Cole was never meant to know. You promised you'd never tell him!"

He winced at the whip of her words. He'd always loved Lacy, even if she couldn't see him for dust. She could hurt him more than anyone else in the world.

"I'm sorry," he said quietly. "He accused me of marrying for money and said that only a weasel would live on a woman's wealth. I lost my temper and hit back."

Lacy felt faint. After that, to tell Cole that he'd been living on Lacy's money had been a cruelty beyond words. Her eyes closed and her face paled. "I see."

"He got even," he said huskily. "He told me about Mother with no preamble at all."

Lacy stared at him. "Do you care?" she asked. "You've cut Faye up like a Sunday chicken, you've ruined my marriage, you've decided that wealth and position are worth more than your family's pride or your self-respect. I can't imagine that you feel anything these days, Bennett."

"You're wrong," he said. "You're so wrong."

"Your mother is giving you an engagement party," she continued, unabashed. "It may be the last party she ever gives. You are coming to it, with your fiancée, if I have to have Cole and Turk drive up to San Antonio and bring you here roped and laid over a saddle. Do you understand me, Bennett? You are going to do this one thing for your mother. And there had better be no snide remarks about the way we live from your intended."

Ben went rigid with wounded pride. "Threats, Lacy?"

"Promises," she corrected. "Your fiancée isn't the only wealthy person in San Antonio." She smiled with cold intent. "In point of fact, I have twice her wealth and ten times her contacts among the right people." Her blue eyes narrowed with venomous fury, something that Ben had never been on the receiving end of before. "One word from me in the right ears, and your precious newspaper will lose enough advertisers to go under. Do I make myself perfectly clear?"

His breath drew in quickly. "You wouldn't."

"I would do anything for Marion and Cole," she replied.

"Not for me?" he asked, wounded.

"I'll tell you something, Bennett," she said quietly. "My youngest isn't going to be a spoiled brat whose selfishness extends to every single facet of his life. You exist for one person's pleasure—your own. You won't even give a thought to the lives you damage, the hurt you inflict, so long as you have what you want."

Ben colored. "That isn't true!"

"You cold-bloodedly seduced little Faye and then refused to have anything to do with her, after you'd ruined her reputation," she said. "You threw a family secret at Cole that destroyed what little happiness I'd managed to find here. You hesitated so long about answering Marion's letter concerning your engagement party that she convinced herself you were too ashamed of her to let your society fiancée set foot here."

His face stiffened as the words hit home. "I'm not ashamed of my mother," he choked.

"She thinks you are," Lacy replied. "That's why you're coming to the party."

"Cole won't let you pay for it—and he can't afford it," Ben muttered quietly.

"He agreed before you came along and hurt his pride. He won't go back on his word, even if he wants to. I'll finance the social event, and try to make sure that the house lives up to your expectations," she added, with cold sarcasm that stiffened him. "After that, I'm going back to San Antonio to live unless your mother is too frail for me to leave."

"What about Cole?" he asked.

"What about him?" she said, lifting her head proudly. "It's a pity you don't know what happened to him. If you had an ounce of compassion in your entire body, you'd probably drown yourself for the things you've said to him about the war over the years."

She turned on her heel and went back into the living room. This time, she closed the door behind her.

Ben went to his mother's room, feeling as if he'd been kicked. He went in and sat by the bed.

"Hello, dear," Marion said. "I didn't know you were here until noon. I slept, I suppose."

"It's good for you to rest," he said evasively.

"Coleman told you?" she asked.

He nodded, drawing in a wretched breath. "Oh, Mama," he groaned.

She held out her arms and drew him to her, rocking him gently, cooing above his head as she had when he was an infant. Her youngest. Her very favorite. Although she made sure the others didn't know, Bennett was her whole heart. It was going to hurt him much more than Cole and Katy when the time came. But meanwhile, at least she could comfort him. Her poor baby.

Later, when he was calm, she mentioned the party very hesitantly.

He felt guilty at what he'd said and thought as he saw the apprehension in her tired eyes.

"It's very kind of you to give us a party," he said. "We'll be very happy to come. I'm sure you'll like Jessica."

She smiled radiantly, and he was glad he'd agreed. But inwardly he was dreading it. Jessica wasn't all that likable, except to a man in bed. She was a snob and she had a cutting tongue. She could very easily savage his gentle mother, and if she found the house and furnishings shoddy, she wouldn't hesitate to say so.

That could have terrible repercussions. Cole wouldn't tolerate rudeness, and Lacy had made a threat that unsettled Ben greatly. She was, indeed, more well-to-do than Jessica and her father, and a newspaper ran on goodwill and the generosity of its advertisers. Advertising kept the doors open. If Lacy influenced people to stop those ads—and give them to a rival paper—it wouldn't take long for Ben's journalistic career to become a thing of the past.

He'd have to cross that bridge when he came to it. Meanwhile it would be politic to get back to San Antonio before Cole came home. After the anguish he'd caused, it would be safer out of reach of Cole's tongue and Lacy's icy formality. Not to mention out of reach of Faye's soft arms. He felt terrible guilt about his seduction of her. She loved him, and he'd used her. Today had made it all worse, somehow. Making love to her had kindled something incredible inside him, something that Jessica couldn't give him in a hundred years. Jessica was hard and cold and mercenary, even as she was sexually exciting. Faye was vulnerable and gentle and loving, and what she gave him in bed made him spin from dizzy pleasure. But Jessica was rich and Faye wasn't. He had to keep that in mind. The problem was remembering it, and not Faye's voice whispering that she loved him more than her own life.

Cole came in very late. Marion was asleep, and Lacy was clearing away the dishes.

"Where's my brother?" he asked, having whipped himself into a furious temper. He'd come home with the express purpose of thrashing Ben to a bloody pulp.

"In San Antonio, I imagine," Lacy said coolly. "He borrowed the runabout. Marion said it was all right."

"She would. He's her favorite," Cole replied.

"You aren't supposed to know." She put the butter in the icebox and folded the linen cloth on the table. "Have you written Katy about Marion?"

"Yes."

She didn't ask anything else. He was obviously in no mood for conversation. Neither was she.

He watched her work, his eyes sad and irritated. She'd given him so much. He'd given her very little over the years, save his indifference and his lust and, reluctantly, his name. She'd saved the ranch from ruin, and he'd cursed her for it. But it was hard on his pride to work as fiercely as he did and still fall short of her wealth.

"I'll be leaving after the party, if Marion doesn't need me," Lacy said quietly.

His heart stopped beating. He didn't want that. God, he didn't want that! It would tear him apart to have to lose her twice.

"Unless Katy comes home, which is doubtful, there won't be anyone else to look after Mother," he said.

Lacy didn't flatter herself that he wanted her here. She was simply a convenience. "Very well. I'll stay . . . as long as I'm needed."

He hesitated. She knew everything there was to know about him now. It made him feel vulnerable, raw. "What I told you . . ."

She turned, her eyes cool, her body poised. "Will go no further," she said instantly, misunderstanding his hesitant beginning. "I should have thought you'd know without asking."

His face went hard. "It wasn't a question. I owed you the truth, I suppose."

"Only the truth," she said angrily. "If you prefer to, why not think of the money as a gift to Katy and Marion and Ben? They were my family all those years since my own were lost at sea."

"Them, and not me?" he asked, trying not to show how painful it was that she didn't include him.

"You never wanted me around," she said, with dignity. "I was an embarrassment when I was trailing around after you, an encumbrance when you left for war, and an unwanted burden as a wife. I never was able to think of you as family, now more than ever."

His jaw tautened. "You wanted me."

She swallowed. "I loved you," she said, correcting him. "But love eventually dies . . . like a flower that has no place in the sun to warm itself." She lowered her eyes.

"Then you don't"—he hesitated—"love me?"

Her eyes went to the window. "I don't want to love you," she said, correcting him. "I imagine if I work at it quite hard, I'll accomplish it one day."

His eyes closed. "Lacy," he whispered huskily. "God, how did it ever come to this?"

She lifted her face and saw his tormented expression. "You'll only be getting what you wanted all along," she said tautly. "To be rid of me!" she cried, and turned to run out of the room.

"No!"

He caught her, whipping her into his arms, bent over her with anguished eyes in a face that was paper-white. "No!" he groaned, dragging in a harsh breath as he rocked her against him. "I—don't want to be rid of you," he managed unsteadily.

She felt as if time stopped all around them, spinning a web of sudden silence and hesitation. She became aware of Cole's breathing, quick and labored, of his hard pulse against her breasts. He smelled of leather and hemp and honest sweat, and at least he felt something for her. Or was it because of Marion that he was giving the impression that he did?

══ Chapter Eleven ══

COLE FELT LACY TREMBLING AND HE FELT BAD, HE
seemed to never get on the right foot with her. He'd
hurt her again. He didn't know what to do, what to say,
to make things right.

"I won't leave Marion," Lacy said shakily. "This
. . . isn't necessary. You don't have to pretend that you
mind if I leave."

He lifted his head, looking down at her with hard,
glittery eyes. "But I do mind. I always did."

"You didn't even write."

"What could I have said?" he asked quietly. "That
I felt like some kind of animal after I'd finished with
you, and you cried and . . . bled . . ." He let her go
abruptly and moved away, anguish in every line of his
body.

Lacy was startled by the action. "It was my first
time," she said, hesitant to talk about something so
intimate even with her own husband. "I had a married
girlfriend in San Antonio, who . . . explained it to me.
It's unpleasant for some women. I was simply unlucky."

"In more ways than one. If I'd been more experienced,
it might have been easier for you." He leaned his
shoulder against the wall, unable to look directly at her.

186

"I couldn't take that again," he said heavily. "I didn't go after you because I thought you'd never want me to touch you, and I still wanted to."

"You didn't say that."

His broad shoulders rose and fell. "How could I? You didn't know what I was, what the war had made me. You didn't know that I wasn't a whole man anymore."

"That isn't true," she said huskily. "You're more man than I've ever known in my life, and I loved you! If you'd been missing both your legs, it wouldn't have mattered—and even then you would have been a whole man!"

He risked a glance toward her, recognizing the truth in her eyes. He drew in a slow, unsteady breath. In his posture, in his working clothes, he looked like an old-time cowboy, right down to the battered Stetson and the stained leather chaps.

"There could only be the two of us," he began finally. "No children, ever. And in bed . . ." He turned his attention back out the darkened window, to the faint silhouette of the flat horizon. "In bed, it would still be uncomfortable and embarrassing."

"Why?"

"Because I don't know how," he said shortly, glaring at her. "Don't you remember?"

"Most people don't know how at first. They learn."

"Do they?" he scoffed. "If you ever saw me in the light, you'd run screaming for San Antonio," he said harshly. "You'd hate yourself for ever letting me touch you in the first place!"

"Rubbish!" she shot back, furious with him. "You're scarred. So what? You can walk and work and your brain is still in good order. As for a child . . ." She swallowed, because it hurt that there wouldn't be one. "It's very possible that I'm barren, did you consider that? Some women never conceive. I might have been one of them."

Hope, like a tiny candle in the darkness, was beginning to kindle deep inside him. He leaned back against the wall, his knee bending as he propped back on the high, slanted heel of one boot, the spur jingling faintly.

"It was good the other afternoon at the corral—when you came to ask me about Ben's party," he admitted.

She blushed. "Very good," she said huskily.

He hesitated. "It would always be in the dark," he said slowly. "And I don't know if I could bear having you touch me where I was burned, either."

"It hurts you?" she asked, concerned.

"No. It . . . the skin is different. Thinner, very smooth in patches." He almost choked on the words. "I'm damaged."

Her heart almost broke at the look on his face, at the odd, rare vulnerability. She breathed very slowly. "If I were burned like that, would you not want to touch me?"

His eyebrows lifted. "What?"

"If I were . . . damaged as you are, would you find me repulsive?"

"Of course not," he replied.

She smiled. She didn't say anything. She simply stood and looked at him, until the message got through and he realized what she was saying.

He let out a ragged breath. "I see."

"No, I don't think you do—not just yet," she replied. "But given time, you might. I do very much like the idea of getting to know each other before we become intimate again," she continued.

"So do I." He began to smile. "And for the time

being, I'll stay in the guest room. We can share the
bathroom between . . . although not at the same time,''
he added when she blushed.

She nodded. Her eyes searched his. ''I know it hurts
your pride that I paid for things while you were away.
You might remember that your parents took me in and
supported me when my own died, so it was more a
repayment of a debt.'' His face went hard, and she
added, ''But if you like, I'll let you pay me back when
the ranch is solvent again. As it will be,'' she added,
with conviction. ''I've never for a minute doubted that
you'll make a go of it. Even Turk says you've got few
equals when it comes to breeding superior bloodlines.''

He smiled at her with his eyes. ''He should know. He
had a hell of a good ranch up in Montana.'' He sighed.
''He misses Katy. He hasn't been the same since she left.
I thought I was doing the right thing for her, keeping
them apart. Now, I'm not so certain.''

''Perhaps he didn't know how he felt about Katy until
it was too late,'' she ventured.

Cole was watching her hungrily. He nodded, his eyes
narrow and thoughtful. ''Perhaps not. Sometimes a
woman comes up on a man's blind side. He can't see her
until she's gone.''

She moved a little closer to him, and looked up at his
face. ''Did you . . . miss me?''

''Oh, yes,'' he said, searching her eyes. ''In France,
you were all I thought about. After I crashed, I had
nightmares about coming home and having you scream
when you saw me.'' His face hardened. ''That was why
I took the pistol—''

''I don't care what you look like!'' she burst out. ''All
I wanted was for you to come home alive, Cole. In any
condition at all!''

He swallowed. She made him feel humble.

"That was why you didn't want to marry me," she said, suddenly certain as she looked up at him. "You thought I wouldn't want you."

"I lacked the confidence to risk it," he replied. "Ben forced us into it, and I was terrified. I tried to keep intimacy out of it, even then, but we started kissing each other out in the barn . . . and my own need of you defeated me. By the time I got home that night, a loaded gun wouldn't have slowed me down." He touched her cheek. "It was . . . so good," he said roughly. "So good! I didn't know a damned thing about women except what I'd heard in the Air Service. I thought you were enjoying it, too. Then it was over, and you cried. When I saw why, I wanted to blow my brains out." He drew her forehead to his chest and held her loosely, his cheek on her dark hair.

"It won't ever be that bad again," she said gently.

He framed her face in his big hands. "You might be happier with someone else," he said, still unconvinced.

"I'd have to learn how to stop loving you first," she said simply.

He smiled. It made him warm inside when she said that. He'd never really been able to let himself love anyone except his mother and siblings. Love was a risk, because it made one vulnerable. But he could love Lacy. Oh, yes, he thought as he bent his head toward her, he could love her!

His mouth touched hers softly, and then not so softly. He felt her soft lips part under his, moist and sweet and warm, and he lifted her close while the kiss burned into his mind, his heart. He groaned against her mouth and felt her gasp at the telltale sound that heralded his pleasure.

The slamming of a door startled them, bringing them quickly apart, both looking guilty as Marion came slowly into the kitchen.

She laughed delightedly at the looks on their faces, at the embrace they were obviously just breaking. "And I thought you weren't speaking," she teased.

They both laughed, breaking the tension. Marion beamed as they drew her into conversation. They weren't fooling her. At least here was a marriage that had a chance. It gave her some comfort to know that Cole, at least, wouldn't be alone when she was gone. But what of Ben and Katy? Cole had told Ben, but what about Katy? She wanted to ask, but the lightness of the moment was too precious to be disturbed by stark reality. Later, she promised herself, she'd ask Lacy.

In Chicago, the letter from home lay all alone on the dark hall table. Katy had seen it, and Mama Marlone had told her it was there, but she hadn't opened it. She'd avoided it for days, until Mama Marlone began to chide her about it. Then she took it and placed it on her dresser, in the small cedar jewelry box that Blake Wardell had bought her earlier in the week. She didn't want to open it. That heavy scrawl was Cole's handwriting, and she knew he was angry with her. The past week had been very trying as Danny pushed her into Blake Wardell's company almost every night. Blake wanted her, and he was working some dark magic on her, because she wanted him, too. In her confused state of mind, nothing really made much sense. She was learning how to be gay. That included jolts of bathtub gin that were beginning to make her life bearable.

She finally opened the letter and read it, then burst

into tears. Danny was never home. She couldn't depend
on him for comfort. But that night she told Blake
Wardell, and he pulled her into his arms and held her
while she cried. It was the one bright moment since
she'd come to Chicago, and when he handed her a glass
of gin, she drained it. For a while, it numbed the hurt.
She couldn't bear to think she was going to lose her
mother.

Later, she begged Danny to let her go home. He flatly
refused. He didn't tell her why it was so imperative that
she remain in Chicago, but Blake Wardell was just
beginning to weaken, to give in to Danny's proposition
of a business partnership. He couldn't afford to let Katy
go home. Wardell's ardor might lessen in her absence,
and Danny could lose his edge.

"Your mother will live for years," Danny said curtly
when she cried. "My uncle had dropsy. The docs told
him he'd kick off in a month. He lived five years, for
God's sake. I can't let you go back home. You're my
wife."

"Five years?" Katy asked, brightening.

"Sure," he said. "Write your mama a letter and say
you'll be there as soon as you can—that I'm too busy to
bring you and that you can't leave here without me.
You'll think up something convincing to write. And stop
worrying, for God's sake. Nobody lives forever."

He could afford to say that, she thought. He had a
living mother who doted on him. If the situations were
reversed, he'd have been on the next train like a shot.
She tried again.

"I could just visit for a day or so," she said.

He whirled on his heel and struck her so hard across the
mouth that her lip bled. She cried out and backed away.
It was like the night she lost the baby. He hadn't apolo-

gized for that, or said one world about her miscarriage. He wasn't really sober enough lately to notice anything much.

"I said no," he told her, his eyes glittering as if he'd enjoyed what he'd done. He moved toward her, and she backed away. He chuckled, his eyes dilated. He'd been off dope for several weeks when he met Katy, but the withdrawal had been too hard, so he'd gone back to his old habit. It grew daily, just like old times. It was one reason he needed Wardell as a partner, because Wardell made money. Lots of it. He'd shot up only that morning and he was feeling it good. He liked having Katy afraid of him. It made him feel even better.

"Scared, kid?" he taunted. "You cold little piece of ice. I must have been crazy to marry you!"

"Danny, don't!" she cried

He pulled off his belt. "You'll like it," he said huskily, aroused by her fear as he never had been by her body. "They all like it. You'll see."

When he finished with her, she lay bruised and sick on the satin coverlet of the bed. Danny had dressed and gone out, whistling. Katy barely made it to the bathroom in time. She was bleeding from what he'd done to her, bruised and humiliated by the perverted pleasure he'd taken in her revulsion. She shuddered, wondering how she was going to survive her marriage.

"You'll do what I say from now on," he'd told her when he'd finished. "You got that, kiddo? You'll do just what I say, or I'll bring in the boys and let them watch next time." His eyes had brightened maniacally as she shrank from him. "I like to watch. Maybe I'll give you to somebody so I can. Wardell wants you. When he makes a move, you go along, you get it? I've got plans for Wardell, and you're my ticket, toots. He already knows I don't mind."

She could hardly speak through her bruised mouth. "You'd let him . . . ?" she sobbed.

"Why not? You were no virgin," he said insolently. "A slut like you shouldn't care. You're nothing in bed, but maybe he won't mind if he wants you enough. Just don't cross me, babe, or what happened just now will look like heaven next time."

Katy bathed, wincing as the water touched her body. She sobbed bitterly. She'd brought this on herself, with her rebellion, her desperation to get away from a dead-end relationship with Turk. But she still loved Turk, even now, and that was an even worse punishment than what Danny had done to her. She closed her eyes, almost choking on fear and unhappiness. He resented the fact that she hadn't been a virgin, despite what he'd said before they'd married. He thought she'd had plenty of men, and he didn't respect her.

Danny was going to give her to Blake. She cared about Blake, but what Danny proposed doing was monstrous, like selling her into prostitution. She was more afraid of him by the day. He'd killed a man. He'd do that to her if she didn't go along. She was frightened, and she didn't dare go to the police. He had several of them in his pocket, and she didn't know which ones she could trust. Mama Marlone wouldn't help. She could write to Cole, but it might get him killed. This was her problem. She was going to have to bear it, somehow.

Later, she sat down at the desk and wrote to her mother and to Cole, making up lies about why she couldn't come home. It took a long time, because she didn't want her tears to soak the paper. . . .

Cole made no remark at all about his letter, but Marion showed hers to Lacy with tears in her eyes.

"Doesn't she care?" Marion asked piteously. "Doesn't she understand what Cole told her?"

Lacy hugged her close. "You know Katy loves you," she said soothingly. But she was worried. She knew Katy as well as Marion did. Katy loved her mother, and she wasn't selfish or uncaring. Something was wrong; she could feel it. Katy was hurt or in trouble and wouldn't tell anyone. Lacy only wished she could do something, at least find out what the trouble was. But she knew, as Katy probably did, that Cole would be on the way to Chicago at the first hint of trouble in Katy's life. She didn't want him hurt, and Lacy certainly didn't. Mobsters were dangerous, and they killed without compunction. Lacy didn't want her husband to be another victim of the gang wars.

But as the weeks went by, Katy's life worsened. She hadn't actually seen him use it, but she'd overheard his men talking about his increased drug habit. She was on the receiving end of a kind of cruelty she'd never even read about. She was afraid that one night Danny might go too far and kill her. Her only compensation was that he hit her where it didn't show, so that Blake Wardell didn't get suspicious. She couldn't forget what Blake had threatened to do to Danny if he hit her again. She didn't want him to know. She couldn't bear to see Blake hurt.

Blake had become a fixture in her life, to Danny's delight. He took her to the theater, to the ballet. He squired her around town and took her to the best restaurants, the best parties. He taught her to fit in and treated her royally. He bought her presents. She grew drunk on his kindness, because Danny was never kind.

She grew drunk on gin, too. It was the only thing that kept her going, made life bearable since the miscarriage.

She forced her mind not to dwell on it. No one at the ranch would know, anyway. She couldn't go home to see her dying mother without risking death herself. Perhaps if she drank enough, she could kill herself. That would end the anguish of living. But it would hurt so many people. She ground her teeth together. There was just no escape.

Blake had taken her to a particularly good nightclub, and she was pretty high when they left.

"You drink too much these days," he said as they drove away in his chauffeured limousine. "It isn't good for you."

"Nothing is," Katy said drowsily. She leaned her head back. "I hate my life. I hate it all."

Blake pulled her close, his very size comforting as her cheek pressed against his broad chest. "Leave him," he said abruptly. "I'm no prize, but I love you. At least I wouldn't hurt you."

She nuzzled closer. "I know that."

He hesitated. "Katy, Danny put a girl in the hospital a few months ago. When he's on dope, he's a different man. He went back to it just after he married you." His eyes narrowed at her sudden stiffness. "He doesn't leave bruises where they can be seen, but I bet you've got marks all over you."

She looked up at him, pleading. "'You mustn't do anything," she said huskily. "You know how crazy he is! He might kill you!"

"That isn't likely."

"He wants something from you, doesn't he?" she asked, because Danny had mentioned it in a lucid moment.

"A cut of my business," he agreed.

"And I'm the collateral."

He cocked an eyebrow. "How long have you known?"

"Danny told me himself." She laughed unsteadily. "He told me to play ball or else."

One eye narrowed. "Do you want to . . . play ball?"

She sighed, laying her head against his hard arm while she studied him. He was very much a man, and she *did* want him. She wanted to let him love her one time. To have a man be kind to her would be a real novelty. Danny would know because she'd tell him, and maybe he wouldn't beat her again. Beyond that, it would repay Blake for all his kindnesses to her. She was so busy giving herself reasons to allow it that she pushed the real one to the back of her mind—that she wanted him, too, because there was a very special tenderness in their relationship that she'd never experienced, even with Turk. Of course, Turk hadn't loved her. Not as Blake did.

"It wouldn't be any hardship for me to sleep with you, Blake," she said softly. "I think you've known that all along. You're very special to me."

"That poor blind fool back in Texas," he said softly, his cheeks flushing with feverish desire. He drew her up against him and kissed her, his mouth exquisitely loving.

She'd always enjoyed kissing Blake. Every time it was different. Mostly his kisses were comforting or affectionate. But this one was more. This one, besides being warm and respectful, was deeply arousing.

The gin made her ever more receptive than she would normally have been to his tenderness. She put her arms around his neck and didn't even protest when he got a little rough. He wouldn't be cruel to her. He couldn't be. He loved her too much.

He had the driver take her home. The house was dark, because Mama Marlone was spending the weekend with her sister in New Jersey. Danny was out, she supposed.

Blake told the chauffeur to go home and he went inside with Katy.

"Danny might come home . . ." she began worriedly.

He took off his coat and helped her out of hers, then he swung her up easily in his arms and started up the stairs. "Danny wouldn't interrupt us," he said simply.

He was probably right. She didn't care anyway. She was feeling the gin. Her head was floating. Blake was strong and warm and he loved her. She felt cloud high.

She let Blake undress her, enjoyed feeling like a desirable woman again. He whispered how lovely he found her, touched her white body as if he'd never seen a woman undressed. His mouth was reverent on her swollen breasts, his hands warm and expertly arousing. She trembled with need long before he pulled away from her to undress. But when he started to take off his own clothes, she averted her face.

"Still shy?" He chuckled. "You're one in a million."

She was staring at the closet, there was something odd about the slant of the door, but before she could decide what it was, Blake was in bed beside her, the white sheet just covering his hips as he turned toward her.

He was bigger close up, more threatening without his clothes. He was hairy and dark-skinned, not flabby at all. Katy touched his wide shoulders and met his eyes, fascinated by the tenderness in them. Turk had been tender. Turk! Oh, Turk, she thought guiltily, and put her mouth hungrily against Blake's to blot out the guilt.

Her ardor threw Blake off-balance, but he recovered after a few seconds. He'd wanted her for a long time. He adored her. He wasn't going to rush through such a delectable interlude.

He took his time, kissing her softly for several minutes before he felt her relax and curl into his body. Then he began to touch her, caress her. He pulled the sheet away and looked at her again, pleased with the soft contours of her body, with the soft thrust of her pretty pink breasts. He smiled as he bent to excite them with his mouth, his teeth, his tongue. She liked it. She began to writhe, and then his mouth went quickly down her body. With his lips, he found her where no other man, not even Turk, ever had, and made her gasp.

"No!" she protested as the sensations ran over her like fire.

"Yes," he replied, and kept on.

She cried out with the throbbing pleasure. When he felt her helpless arching, he moved between her legs and pushed himself into her. She opened her eyes and gasped at the size of him.

"Shh," he whispered. He was still, very still, giving her time to adjust to him, to relax again.

"Oh, my . . . God!" she cried brokenly. "I won't . . . be able to . . ."

"Yes, you will, sweetheart. Easy, now. Don't be afraid of me. I won't hurt you. I love you, Katy. I love you so much!" He brushed his lips softly against hers, his hand moving down her soft breast to her hip, her thigh, and then in between their bodies. He kissed her. At the same time, he began to touch her, bringing back the hot excitement that the shock of intimacy with him had made cold.

Seconds later, her taut muscles began to give, and he let her absorb him until she took as much as she could. No woman had ever been able to take all of him.

She looked into his eyes, staggered.

"Don't worry," he said softly. "I'd never hurt you.

Let me satisfy the urgency, then I'll satisfy you. All right? That's it. Just settle into the mattress and try not to panic. I know how badly I could hurt you if I'm not careful. But I will be. That's it, Katy,'' he whispered softly as he felt her relax. ''You're so lovely. I've never wanted anyone as much.''

He smiled as she lay looking at him. His big body shifted very gently, so that he was barely rocking against her. He bent and kissed her warmly, a groan tearing out of his throat as he felt the pleasure beginning at the very base of his spine. He loved her. Nothing had ever been so sweet!

His face darkened, distorted as the gentle rhythm spurred him to sudden, harsh completion. He ground his teeth together and shuddered, a sobbing cry passing his lips as he let go. She was every dream he'd ever imagined! He repeated her name, shivering with pleasure that never seemed to lose its keen edge.

Katy felt him throbbing deep in her body. She held him close, her breath catching as the helpless shudders tossed him in her arms. ''Oh, Blake,'' she whispered when he finally lifted his head and she saw his eyes.

''Are you shocked?'' he asked, shaken. ''Haven't you ever watched?''

''No,'' she whispered. She touched his damp, flushed face, his disheveled hair. ''Oh, I never dreamed a man could be so gentle!'' she said huskily.

''How could I be anything else with you?'' he asked unsteadily. His dark eyes smiled at her. He bent, brushing his lips over her taut face. ''It takes a long time for you, doesn't it?'' he asked, his voice husky with satiation, his face damp with sweat. ''You gave me completion. Now I'll give it to you. I want you to feel what I just did, to know the glory of being loved down to your soul.''

She closed her eyes and held him closer. Turk had never loved her, he'd had sex with her. But Blake *did* love her. She could love him back. She could, for this one night. "Blake—" she began.

"Don't talk." He shifted so that he could find her breasts with his mouth. He was very skillful, thorough and generous in a way Katy, with her inexperience, had never known. But it wasn't his skill that made her tremble with desire, it was the knowledge that he loved her, that her pleasure was everything to him right now. She lay back and gave in to him completely, enjoying the feverish pleasure he was giving her fluid body. She was very attracted to him, and she did genuinely care about him. She *could* love him!

He kindled her body into savage excitement so unexpectedly that she cried out in fear as he went into her. The shock of his possession was so overwhelming that she convulsed with hot pleasure, her cries like music to the man above her. His jaw tautened and he laughed deep in his throat as he watched her shudder and convulse, her wild eyes meeting his as she surrendered to the ecstasy he was giving her. He almost went over the edge, but he managed to pull himself back in the nick of time.

She pleaded with him not to stop, her voice breaking as she clutched at him, coaxing him back into her arms. She felt insatiable, drunk on fulfillment, and he couldn't resist her. He took her, shivering, from one silver peak to another, from one plane of ecstasy to an even longer one. She wept and clung to him, her eyes closed and nothing in her mind except Blake's delicious sorcery as she felt the shudders lifting her, illuminating her, satiating her in

physical joy. She arched up into his taut body and
screamed. Blake said something, his body giving way
finally to its own anguished need. She felt him shaking
above her, but she was so exhausted that she barely heard
his hoarse cries.

Someone was watching her. She felt it even in the
exhausted lethargy of pleasure that consumed her. Her
eyes opened as the last shudders began to die away and
she saw Danny, standing just outside the closet, watching. His face was sweaty, his eyes glazed. She stiffened,
horrified.

Blake was still shaking. He felt her move and scowled,
lifting his head to ask if he was hurting her. He saw her
expression, then followed her stare and cursed viciously
as he fought to get his breath back. "You sick little
pervert!" he said accusingly.

He dragged himself away from Katy and went after
Danny, who managed to get into the next room before
Blake caught up with him. Obscenities passed back and
forth wildly as their voices raised. The sound of a
struggle reached Katy, and then a gun discharged once,
twice.

Katy jumped out of bed and ran into the next room in
time to see Danny lying on the rug in a pool of his own
blood. It flowed from a tiny wound in his forehead, from
his chest. His eyes were open, but they didn't see her.
They didn't see anything. Blake was standing over him,
fiery-eyed, the smoking pistol in his hand and a robe
draped carelessly around him.

"The crazy fool," he spat. "The crazy fool! He tried
to kill me! Weasly little pervert— He had it coming for
what he did to you! Katy?" He moved toward her.
"Katy, it's all right, girl! He'll never beat you again.
Katy?"

Katy screamed, then felt the world go black around her as the sordid scene impeded on her shaky consciousness. She crumpled in pain and terror, unconscious before an anguished, cursing Blake Wardell caught her.

Chapter Twelve

LACY HAD NOTICED A NEW ATTITUDE IN MARION FOR the past few weeks. Ben phoned home frequently now, and he'd agreed without protest to let her give him a party. The older woman was brighter, more alive. She rested and took good care of herself. There were no more sick spells lately. It had to be an omen.

There was a cold silence between Cole and Ben since their confrontation. But Lacy and Cole were getting along better than ever. They talked, went places together. He'd even taken her with him to a cattlemens' association meeting in San Antonio, which had culminated in a banquet supper. He'd had to work hard today to make up for the lost time, but he didn't seem to regret his night off. Things were looking up. The party for Ben was tomorrow night, and Cole hadn't even muttered about having the men butcher a steer for food. Lacy had baked for days getting ready, and Marion had done as much as she could. The cowboys' wives had cleaned up the house and were going to help hang Japanese lanterns and decorate with fall flowers the next afternoon. Everything was under control.

It was Friday night, and Lacy was having a bath. The water was warm and bubbly. She'd added powdered soap to it, lightly scented. She felt absolutely decadent with the water just up to her waist, her pretty breasts bare. The air on them was curiously arousing. She felt free, all woman. She stretched lazily, her eyes closing with a drowsy smile as she savored the warm water on her skin.

The door opened suddenly . . . and she met Cole's shocked eyes as he froze inside the room.

"I didn't know you were in here," he said, but he didn't move. His eyes were on the stark beauty of her alabaster breasts with their small red crowns dark and hard. He'd never seen a woman like this. Even if he had, nobody could have compared with Lacy. She was beautiful.

Lacy couldn't speak. The impact of his eyes took her breath away. She'd imagined having him see her this way, but imagining hadn't prepared her for the way her skin tingled or the softly wanton impulses that throbbed in time with her heartbeat.

He hesitated at the door, color running along his cheekbones. "I'd better go," he said harshly.

"You're my husband, Cole," she reminded him huskily. "It's all right. You can look at me if you want to."

He did. His face colored even more, but he couldn't have averted his eyes to save his life.

"I wanted to wash my hands," he said, trying to sound normal.

"Go ahead, then," she invited.

He had to force himself to walk to the sink, to wash away the grime and horsehair. When he'd dried his hands, he turned back to Lacy, his gaze going helplessly to her breasts.

She tingled as he looked at her. Involuntarily her body arched.

"Lacy," he whispered in anguish.

"Oh, come here," she pleaded softly, holding out her arms.

He was in work clothes, as he usually was these days. He knelt beside the tub, his chaps making a creaking sound, his spurs jingling. She was so beautiful, and she belonged to him.

He bent to kiss her soft mouth, and while he kissed her, one lean hand went to her breast, cupping it. Her skin was cool and silky, and he groaned.

The gasp she made went into his mouth.

He lifted his head, breathless. His eyes were dark and intent, and his hand didn't move. "Is it all right if I touch you like this?" he asked.

"Yes." She ran her fingers over his hand, holding it there.

His body tensed with pleasure. He smiled gently, looking down to where his hand rested, so dark against her marble skin. He cupped her, his thumb sliding with sensual abrasion against the nipple. She gasped, and he liked that, so he did it again. She moaned this time.

He was feeling his way, literally, but he was beginning to discover what she liked. He shifted her a little and moved so that he could take her breast into his mouth. He suckled at it, hearing her whimper and he increased the pressure.

"You taste sweet," he whispered. "Like warm silk in my mouth." His tongue rubbed the nipple. She clutched at his shoulders. "Tell me if it hurts," he said, swallowing her up again.

It didn't hurt. It was heavenly sweet. She clung to him, inviting his mouth to the twin of the place he was tormenting, adoring the feel of his hands gliding down her body while he nuzzled her.

When he lifted her clear of the tub, she didn't say a word. He put her down on her feet, gently, and reached for a towel. He dried her in a soft, tense silence. She stood before him trembling—while he learned all of her with his hands and his eyes until she was dry at last.

"You look like a fairy," he breathed. "All white and pink."

"You can't imagine how I feel inside," she said shakily. She pressed close against him, feeling his arousal. She was wild for him, but she didn't know how to say it.

Tentatively her hands went to the buttons of his shirt. She looked up, waiting.

His jaw tightened. "I don't think I can let you do that in the light," he began.

"Just the front," she whispered. "I want to feel your chest against mine."

His cheeks went ruddy. "All right. Just that."

It was a milestone. Her fingers fumbled buttons while her heart threatened to burst. She pulled the fabric aside. There were white streaks mixed in with thick, dark hair and muscle, but it was the size and strength of his chest that fascinated her. She slid against him, closing her eyes as she felt skin against skin, the soft abrasion of body hair teasing her nipples into even harder peaks.

She moaned, moving softly against him.

His hands slid up her back, pulling her to him, and above her his face was rigid with desire. He looked down at where they touched, at her breasts lying on his chest.

"You're lovely," he said, his voice deep in the stillness. "You're the loveliest sight I'll ever see."

"I'm glad." She lay her hands flat on his chest and tugged gently at the thick hair. "I love the way this feels," she whispered. "It's so soft against my skin."

He smiled. It wasn't as difficult as he'd thought. His chest, at least, wasn't bad. Not like his back. He ran the knuckle of his forefinger down her breast until it was stopped by the junction of her nipple with his chest.

"Move back enough so that I can touch you," he whispered.

She laughed nervously as she complied. "I thought you didn't know much about women."

"I know enough to get by, I suppose." He took the nipple between his forefinger and thumb, and she gasped. "It's sensitive, isn't it?"

"Very."

He let go and slid both his hands down her sides to her hips, feeling the silkiness of her body with awe. He drew her up and pressed her against the hardness of him.

She stiffened involuntarily at the stark heat of him.

"Don't be afraid," he said gently. "I won't hurt you."

"I know." She swallowed. "We're taught all our lives not to let men touch us in certain places, in certain ways. Then we marry, and poof, anything goes. It takes a little time to adjust."

"For me, too. I've never seen a woman without her clothes. It intimidates me. I didn't realize how pretty you were going to be like this."

She smiled shyly and buried her face in his warm chest. "I'm glad you think I'm pretty."

He drew in a sharp breath at the feel of her lips on his skin. "Lacy . . ."

Her hands slid up his chest and down again while she pressed her lips a little clumsily to his throat. His heart was beating very quickly, and there was the faintest tremor in his legs.

"Marion's asleep," she whispered. "No one else is in the house."

He held her arms tightly and tried to think. "I need a bath," he said gruffly.

"Then take one," she said. "I'll keep for a few minutes."

He looked down at her with heated impatience, his face as tight as his body, his inhibitions plain on his face.

She reached up and brushed her mouth softly over his. "I'll put out the lights."

His eyes winced. "Lacy, you deserve so much more than I can give you," he said.

"I love you," she replied, her eyes adoring him. "You're all I want."

He wondered if any man had ever been as blessed as he was right now. He touched his lips to hers in a whisper of sensuality. "All right," he said. "I'll come to you when I finish in here."

"I'll wait."

She tugged out of his arms and slid into the toweling robe hanging on the door. She glanced at him with teasing eyes and left him there.

It was barely fifteen minutes later when he came out of the bathroom. She could see little more than his silhouette in the unlighted room, and there was no moon.

He slid under the covers and pulled her to him, delighted to find her as nude as he was. He smiled to himself as he molded her body to his, shivering at the ecstatic contact of her flesh with his.

"You're warm," he whispered.

"You're not, but you will be." She moved closer, careful to keep her hands at his chest and nowhere else. Her legs brushed his and she sighed as she laid her face against his hot throat.

The gentle submission made him guilty. He'd given her nothing last time, but she was as trusting as if he'd taken her to heaven. He tried to remember every single thing Turk had told him. Tonight, he was going to make her glad she'd married him if it took until dawn!

He kissed her slowly, ignoring his own needs while he set himself to kindle hers. His hands learned her, touching secret places, listening for the sounds that would tell him what pleased her.

He took his time, delighting in her eager responses, working his way over her breasts with little soft kisses that eventually led to hungrier ones and made her writhe.

The cover was hot. He threw it off, confident that she couldn't see him. The reverse was also true, and he spared himself a moment's regret. But he could feel her, smell her, taste her as he drew her small breasts into his mouth and made them firm and hard-tipped. He touched her, as Turk had instructed, to make sure she was ready for him. Then he eased over her, his mouth covering hers, and lowered himself between her soft thighs.

She stiffened helplessly, remembering.

"It's all right, little one," he whispered. "It won't hurt. I promise you it won't . . . not this time."

"I'm sorry . . ."

"Shh." He nibbled at her mouth while he positioned himself, one lean hand easing under her. "I know how bad it was the last time. But your body knows how to fit itself to mine now. It will be easy. No, don't stiffen like that, it will hurt."

"I'm trying!" She gasped.

He felt her body trying to reject him, and he stilled his body over hers. His mouth brushed hers, gently. His hand slid between them, smoothing over her flat stomach, her thighs, gently caressing, reassuring.

"You're part of me," he whispered. "Your body is especially designed to allow the invasion of mine. I want to feel you around me, as you were that night. I want to know the soft, moist wonder of your femininity enveloping me."

She shivered. The words were evocative, arousing. She felt herself sinking into the mattress as she gave in, finally. His hips moved, just slightly, and all at once it was happening.

It didn't hurt. Her mind registered that even while it was assimilating the shock of penetration, the raw intimacy of what they were doing.

"It's so intimate!" she blurted out.

"Yes." His mouth found her eyes, kissing them closed. His hips began a soft, slow rhythm that shocked her with the sharp pleasure every thrust produced.

She clung to his arms, tiny sounds escaping her throat as the springs creaked under them, and she was grateful that Marion's room was far enough away that she wouldn't hear them. Because now Lacy was starting to move with him, making the noise even louder. He was making her hungry. She lifted, fell, lifted with him, clinging, straining with jerky breaths as the pleasure came close and then darted away.

She chased it with him, her hips searching for the pressure and rhythm that would bring it back.

He felt her helpless movements, heard her breathing suddenly change. She began to go rigid, and he knew now exactly what to do.

He did it, with a skill he hadn't known he possessed. She went into convulsions and cried out. If Turk hadn't told him what to expect, the way she reacted would have frightened him out of his wits. But he knew that it was the culmination of her pleasure, and through his own violent excitement, he gloried in the knowledge that he'd given her a taste of heaven.

Seconds after she began to relax again, he stiffened over her and groaned harshly as ecstasy rippled down his spine and exploded in his body. He collapsed on her, his heartbeat audible in the heated stillness.

He heard soft weeping, but this time he smiled. It wasn't pain that had caused her emotions to spin out of control. No, this time it wasn't pain.

He rolled away from her and gathered her up close against his side. "And they say we can't fly without airplanes," he murmured drowsily.

"Oh, Cole," she breathed into his shoulder. "Cole!"

"Was it enough!" he asked gently.

"Yes." She shivered. "Yes, it was enough."

His hand smoothed her hair and he lay holding her for a long time without speaking, drinking in the peace and pleasure of being with her. Finally he turned toward her, his lips finding hers with tender pressure.

He felt her mouth tremble under his, heard her breathing jerk softly. He moved to find her breasts with his lips and caressed them until she was shivering.

"I want to make love again," he whispered into her mouth. "Do you?"

"Yes!"

He smiled against her lips until the heat and passion of her response made him too hungry. It was hours before they finally slept.

When Lacy woke, Cole was dressed and gone. She looked beside her, but the only evidence of his occupancy was a dent in the feather pillow. She stretched, wincing at the soreness of her muscles, and then she blushed, remembering.

She got up and went to make breakfast, smiling to herself. For the first time, she felt married.

Cole had strutted into the barn just after daylight, looking so smug that Turk forgot his misery and laughed.

"No smart remarks," Cole said challengingly as he started to saddle a horse.

"I didn't say a word."

Turk smiled as he saddled his own mount. "My wife and I knocked the slats out of the bed so many times the first week we were married that we finally put the mattress on the floor and slept there instead."

Cole flushed. He and Lacy hadn't knocked the slats out, but he knew the mattress springs were damned near sprung!

"Don't look so ruffled," Turk said. "Sex is a beautiful part of a relationship. It isn't something dirty and unnatural that needs to be hidden and glossed over. A passionate woman is worth her weight in gold."

"I'm still in the learning stages about passion."

"You'll get the hang of it." He pulled the cinch tight. "Heard from Katy?"

"Yes," Cole replied. "Some song and dance about having to stay with her husband."

Turk's hands stilled. He looked at the older man curiously. "Are we talking about the same Katy who hitchhiked to San Antonio to see Lacy when you refused to drive her?"

"Yes. I'm concerned. I don't like that dude she married. There's something vaguely sinister about him," Cole said flatly. "I wish I could get her down here long enough to find out what's going on. The letter she wrote to Mother wasn't much more coherent than the one I got. Something's wrong."

Turk felt the old guilt again. He'd wished a hundred times that he'd stopped Katy from leaving. He knew he could have, with a single word.

"Maybe she's pregnant," he said through stiff lips, and wondered even then if she could be, by him. That would sure as hell complicate everyone's life.

"Surely she'd have said so," Cole said.

"I guess she would've," he replied dully, but he wasn't convinced. The possibility existed.

"We have to dress up tonight for that party of Lacy's. Ben's bringing his fancy woman."

"I can hardly wait," Turk drawled. "Suppose we let Taggart and Cherry in the house so they can dance with her in honor of the occasion?"

"If we let those two in the house, there won't be an occasion."

"Just a thought, boss. Let's get to work, shall we?" He glanced at Cole musingly. "If you can sit comfortably, that is."

"Damn you!" Cole burst out laughing.

Turk rode on ahead, glad that at least *Cole* seemed happy. He didn't dare think about Katy or he'd go mad.

Dawn came cold and unwelcome in Chicago. Katy was lying, wide-eyed, in a white hospital bed, but she didn't seem to hear or understand anything that was said to her. She was out of shock now, but her mind seemed to be affected.

Danny had been taken away by the coroner, with Mama Marlone screaming and then yelling obscenities at Blake Wardell who'd, cold-bloodedly, killed her little boy. For Katy she hadn't even spared a thought, or for the big, dark man who was taken away by the police before he could try to talk to Katy, to apologize. The two morgue attendants had taken Danny away, snickering at the obvious ménage à trois that had ended in tragedy. "Some high livers, these mobsters," they'd said. "Plain degenerate. And this moll of Marlone's must have been pretty hot stuff." She'd been in a strange condition when they'd arrived, lying on a bed with her eyes wide open, but without moving or seeming aware of her surroundings. Must be the shock, they'd thought.

The doctors agreed it *was* the shock. She wasn't aware of anything. Danny's treatment of her—and the circumstances of his death—had snapped her mind. She'd most likely have to be committed, they agreed, but first her family had to be told. That caused a real stir, because nobody knew where or who they were, and the victim's mother had to be sedated. She wasn't able to tell anyone anything. That left Blake Wardell, who was in jail for murder. Well, someone could be dispatched to the city jail to question him. Surely he knew where the girl's people lived.

All that took time. It would be hours before they knew anything.

Meanwhile, at Spanish Flats, Lacy and Marion were dressing for a gala party to which all the neighbors were invited.

=== Chapter Thirteen ===

SPANISH FLATS RANCH HAD NEVER LOOKED SO ELE-gant, Lacy thought proudly as she surveyed her handiwork. Colorful Japanese lanterns adorned the wide, long porch and even the living room. The long buffet table in the dining room was decorated with fall foliage, its linen tablecloth pristine, set with food in silver trays. Lacy's best china was set out, along with a silver-and-crystal punch bowl and dainty crystal cups. Considering the number of friends and neighbors she'd invited, a buffet was the only possible way to serve. She hadn't enough tables and chairs to accommodate a sit-down affair.

The gramophone was set up in the living room and the rugs had been moved so that people could dance. It promised to be a gala evening. The house might be old, but it had class. Perhaps Ben's city friends wouldn't look down their noses. She prayed they wouldn't. Not that she was cowardly, but a scene would be terrible.

Lacy was wearing a Paris original silk dress with a soft V neckline. It draped seductively over her slender curves and fell in soft layers to her ankles—its length a concession to rural convention. Her gray shoes buckled, and she was wearing her aunt's diamond necklace and bracelet. She looked not only lovely, but expensive. That was deliberate—just in case Ben's intended thought she could look down her nose at the locals.

Marion's dress was dove gray. The older woman's silver hair was pulled into a soft chignon, and she smiled as she spoke to the ranchers' wives who made up the serving line.

Even Cole was smartly dressed. Lacy's loving eyes clearly approved of his dark suit and string tie and pristine white shirt. He looked very elegant and quite sexy. She wondered if she dared tell him that.

Beside him, Turk was glowering at the need for "dressing up," even if he did look smart and handsome in his dark gray suit and conventional tie. His blond good looks were a foil for Cole's darkness.

"Just in case any gentleman guest looks too hard at you, Mrs. Whitehall, you might mention that I've just cleaned my pistol," Cole said dryly as she joined them.

She blushed; she hadn't seen him until now. He'd gone straight out to work before she awoke, and she was in the kitchen already dressed for the evening when he came home to scrub up.

Cole grinned at her expression. He felt a little embarrassed himself, but it wouldn't do to show it. Remembering the feel of Lacy in his arms the night before made him ripple with pleasure.

She smiled back, glancing at Turk. "You both look very nice," she murmured.

"We're not a patch on you, sugarplum," Cole said softly. "Maybe I'd better display that pistol . . ."

She moved close to him and tucked herself neatly under his shoulder with a confidence she'd never felt in their turbulent relationship until now. "Just keep me right here and you won't need to," she whispered, nuzzling her cheek against his chest.

His heart jumped. "I think I'll do that," he said.

Turk knew when he was superfluous. "I'll go out and check on the side of beef on the spit," he volunteered. He hesitated. "I don't suppose Katy and her husband will be coming?"

"I thought it best not to invite them," Cole replied quietly. "Let me rephrase that," he added curtly. "Ben was disturbed that his fiancée and her father might think he was in the habit of associating with Chicago's criminal element."

Turk's face hardened. "I see. The fact that Katy's his sister made no difference?"

"Ben's very young," Lacy said, defending him gently. "He has yet to learn that wealth and position aren't everything."

She looked up at Cole as she spoke, and his eyes kindled with dark fires. Turk left, and they didn't even notice.

Cole's tall, fit body was reacting violently to Lacy's nearness. He almost choked on desire for her. His eyes went to the bodice of her dress and he remembered vividly what was under it, how her skin smelled, how it tasted.

"Oh, don't," she pleaded shyly, blushing. "I'll swoon if you keep looking at me that way, and what will people think?"

"That Valentino's got nothing on me," he whispered, laughing at her scarlet flush. "Do I embarrass you?"

"Only a little." She closed her eyes. "I love you so much," she said huskily. "So much that I'd die if I lost you again!"

He shivered. His arm clenched, crushing her against him. "Come here."

He drew her into the deserted hall and maneuvered her

back against the wall before he bent and kissed her until her mouth was swollen and red and she could barely breathe.

"Take me to bed," she whispered shakily against his lips.

"I hear a car," he whispered back, his breathing as unsteady as her own. "We have guests arriving."

"I have a headache," she said. "It's terrible. You have to put cold cloths on my forehead."

"Nice try," he said admiringly. "But they'd want to come up and check on you, and that could be embarrassing. We very nearly knocked the slats out this morning. As it is, the bedsprings are very explicit."

"Cole!" she gasped, drawing back, her eyes horrified. "Did someone hear?"

He grimaced. "No. But I shouldn't have mentioned it, should I? Now you'll go all nervous worrying that they will."

"It's . . . private," she said uncertainly.

"Very, very private," he whispered, rubbing the tip of his nose against hers. "I'll pull the mattress off on the floor tonight."

"Will you?" she asked, still shy with him and showing it.

His teeth nibbled gently at her lower lip. "Yes. I never dreamed of so much happiness," he said deeply.

"Neither did I."

He framed her face in his big hands and kissed her tenderly. "I'm sorry that I can't give you a baby," he whispered sadly.

"I'm sorry, too," she said. "But I won't be unhappy, Cole. I told you that nothing mattered more to me than being your wife. The scars don't matter. Infertility doesn't matter." She smiled softly. "I have no pride at all. I'd follow you crawling on my knees, over broken glass, all the way to the ends of the earth.''

His face stiffened. "I don't deserve this," he said unsteadily. "Nothing I've done in my life merits having you.''

She reached up and kissed him. "The angels love you, my dearest," she breathed. "So do I. Kiss me back. I like it when you kiss me very hard!''

He had her up in his arms, kissing the life and breath out of her, when Marion coughed audibly.

Cole put her down abruptly, and they both flushed at the lift of Marion's eyebrows and her smile.

"Ben and his fiancée are here," she told them demurely. "You had best wipe the lip rouge off before you come in, Lacy," she added, with a laugh.

"Oh, it's . . . smeared, isn't it?" Lacy said falteringly, digging for a handkerchief and her pocket mirror from her small purse.

"Not yours, dear," Marion teased, glancing at her tall, flustered son.

Lacy looked at Cole and grinned wickedly. He was covered in dark red smudges around his firm mouth. She grinned as she reached up to wipe away the stains. He grinned, too, as the absurdity got through to him.

They all went in together to find a nervous Ben and a rather bored-looking brunette, along with a white-haired gentleman, waiting impatiently.

"Here they are," Marion said, introducing Lacy and Cole.

Jessica nodded at Lacy, but she went right up to Cole and studied him with flirtatious interest. "So, you're Ben's older brother," she murmured. "How *lovely* to meet you.''

"Same here," Cole said, but he didn't smile or show

any particular interest. "Lacy and I have looked forward to being introduced," he added, pulling Lacy close to him. "This is your father?" he continued, glancing toward the older man.

"Randolph Bradley." The other man nodded, extending his hand to shake Cole's. His mustache twitched. "Sorry my wife couldn't come, but she's in Europe just now."

"She detests life in the raw," Jessica murmured. "How provincial it is out here in the sticks with all these foul-smelling cows," she added, enjoying her feeling of utter superiority in this run-down hovel. Ben's people were obviously hicks, and she was going to make sure that she didn't have to suffer them too often. She and her father had desperately needed Ben's journalistic talent, and she loved him in bed. But this was trying, this provincial mingling.

Cole bristled at the insult, but Lacy punched him in the ribs to keep him quiet and smiled sweetly. "I believe you publish what's called a tabloid, Mr. Bradley."

"That's right," he said, smiling at her. "I publish a newspaper. It's small, but we'll grow. Especially with talent like your brother on staff."

"How many reporters do you have?" Lacy asked.

"Only young Ben, as yet," Bradley confessed. "He's a marvelous writer. Just what we needed."

You needed his name and heritage, Lacy thought cynically, to open doors for you. But she didn't say it. Cole was spoiling for a fight. For Marion's sake, and Ben's, she had to prevent him from starting one. Ben was beaming, the insults Jessica had uttered going right over his head. He was all but strutting in his fashionable clothing, with his elegant fiancée at his side. Two neighbors arrived, and Ben turned with Cole to greet them, introducing Randolph Bradley to the newcomers.

Lacy, left alone with Jessica, smiled politely. "I like your dress, Miss Bradley." In fact, she did. It was long and black, with lace insets, and she wore pearls with it. She was a little overdressed, but perhaps that was intentional. It was more than obvious that Miss Bradley was bent on showing the locals what high society looked like. Inwardly Lacy was chuckling.

The compliment caught the other woman off-guard. "Thank you," Jessica replied, with a haughty smile. "I found it at one of the exclusive shops in New York." Her eyes ran over Lacy. "You must sew," she added; although the fabric looked something like silk, it couldn't be, she told herself. Silk on a rancher's wife was ridiculous.

Lacy didn't twitch a muscle at the sweet insult. "Yes," she said with a poised smile. "I make a great many of my own clothes."

"That's not a bad effort," Jessica said critically. "There's just one thing, dear—if you don't mind a little advice. Those rhinestones are a bit ostentatious. I know costume jewelry is all the rage, but that's overdone. Real diamonds like that would be worth a king's ransom. If you don't want anyone to know they're not real, it's best to wear just a few stones at a time."

Lacy had to stop herself from falling on the floor laughing. Her great-aunt's necklace *was* worth a king's ransom, like the accompanying bracelet and earrings that went with it. Her dress was a Paris original. Jessica obviously didn't expect to find elegance on a ranch, and who was Lacy to disabuse her? The fact that her great-uncle had been the richest railroad tycoon in south Texas was a secret she was going to keep until she needed to make it known. Bragging about her monied background was something she never did. For one thing, it would embarrass Cole.

"How kind of you to point it out," Lacy said, with a vacant smile.

"Well, you are rather living in the outback here." Jessica shrugged. "One doesn't expect countrywomen to know very much about fashion."

"You're so right," Lacy agreed pleasantly.

Other guests began to arrive. Lacy and Jessica joined the others to greet them, but Jessica was doing her best lady-of-the-manor impression. Her double-edged comments about the house festered until Cole was rigid from wounded pride. Lacy pushed him into the kitchen while Marion engaged the Bradleys in conversation. Ben hadn't seemed to notice Jessica's manner. He was beaming as neighbors enthused over his job and his fiancée, not knowing that most of them were simply being polite because the Whitehalls were a respected family in Spanish Flats.

Lacy tactfully pushed the kitchen door shut and turned to Cole. "It will be all right," she told him, pushing back a stray lock of dark hair from his forehead. "Don't scowl so; you'll frighten people."

"Am I scowling? That icy little brunette is about as welcome here as sin on a Sunday," he muttered. "Ben's making the mistake of his life."

"Indeed he is," Lacy said. "But it is his life, and you can't make decisions for him any more than you could make them for Katy."

He searched her blue eyes and relaxed a little. "My God, I got lucky," he said unexpectedly.

"Lucky?" she asked, puzzled.

He touched her throat lightly, watching her color at even the light contact. "Getting you back," he said simply. "I'm good with horses and cattle." He shrugged and smiled good-naturedly. "Never had much use for women, or much luck with them."

"You did with me."

"But I didn't know it, did I?" he asked, with a quiet sigh. "Not until the day I left to go to war and you let me kiss you. A revelation, that was—and I didn't have time to follow up on it. I had to leave you."

"I cried for days," she said. "Then I read the papers and cringed, praying that I wouldn't see your name among the missing or dead. When the letter came, saying that you were wounded but alive and recovering, I thanked God for a solid hour for taking care of you for me." She smiled. "I guess you hardly thought of me those long, hard years."

He hesitated for just a second. "I never showed you this, did I?"

He tugged on the gold chain dripping from his vest watch pocket, took out his worn pocket watch with the gold finish and the train embossing worn almost illegible by years of being handled. He opened the back, and there was a small black-and-white snapshot of Lacy's face and a tiny lock of her dark, fine hair.

She looked at it in disbelief. "How did you . . . ?"

"I had Mother get it for me," he said softly, "when you were asleep. I swore her to secrecy. I wanted something of you to take with me."

Tears welled in her eyes as she looked at him. "Why did you pull back that day?" She asked brokenly. "If we'd been intimate, I might have had your child!"

He took a ragged breath. "Don't you think I know that? That I haven't tormented myself knowing it?" He closed the watch and put it away as he struggled to compose himself. "But we weren't married, and there was no time to get that way. How could I leave you here in such a sordid mess—with the whole community gossiping about you, with your honor in the dirt?''

"It wouldn't have been sordid," she said quietly.

"Yes, it would've." He traced her lips with an unsteady forefinger. "Honor and duty and responsibility were drilled into me from my youth. To have compromised you, even for such reasons, would have destroyed something priceless. You are my wife," he whispered. "My most precious wife. You came to me in purity, without a whisper of gossip or a stain of conjecture on your character. These wild times will leave a trail of grief for the people who forgo morality for the lure of pleasure. The taint of promiscuity will follow them until they die." He smiled at her. "Our memories will be bright ones, worth remembering. I'll sit with you in my lap in the rocking chair one day long from now, and we'll think back on our lives with delight, not regret."

It was a long speech for Cole, who could sometimes sit for an hour without saying a word. She hadn't realized how he felt, that it was more than desire. But the watch told its own story, and it touched her deeply.

She smiled at him, her eyes drowsy with pleasure and happiness. "I hope we have a long time together, Cole," she said.

"So do I." He brushed his lips over her forehead. "I'd like to kiss you, but that war paint comes off pretty easily."

She laughed and stepped back, her blue eyes twinkling. "I'll not wear it from now on if you'll kiss me a lot," she promised, peeking up at him.

He didn't smile. His face went rigid.

Her uncertainty lay vulnerable in her eyes as the smile faded. She was sure she'd put her foot in her mouth.

"You set me on fire," he breathed, and his eyes glittered strangely.

Her lips parted softly on the held breath she expelled. "I thought I'd embarrassed you. You looked very uncomfortable."

He raised an eyebrow. "We're married. Why don't you look down and see for yourself why I'm uncomfortable?"

She did it before she realized what he was inviting her to see, and she averted her eyes with a gasp.

"Short skirts," he said with black humor. "Charleston music, lip rouge . . . I thought you were sophisticated."

"Not with you." She laughed at her own embarrassment. "We're married, but I still feel like a girl with you."

"Lacy, I hope you always do." He pushed back her hair. It was wavy from the curling iron and had a lovely black sheen. "I shouldn't tease you. I simply can't resist it."

"As long as it's only me that you tease . . . like that," she replied demurely.

"That's a safe assumption. I'm not comfortable with other women. I never have been." He linked her fingers with his and sighed. "Shall we go back out and brave the lions?" he invited. "I think I've recovered enough not to draw unwanted attention."

She didn't look this time, but she flushed. "Honestly, Cole," she murmured.

His fingers caressed hers. "It's all part of marriage," he assured her.

"Don't let Jessica unsettle you," she cautioned. "If worse comes to worse, I have an ace in the hole that she doesn't know about."

"Do you, indeed?" he asked. "What is it?"

She whispered to him, and he chuckled. "You won't mind, if I have to come out with it?" she added, worried.

"No," he said, surprising her. "But Ben will. So make it a last resort."

"Okay, boss," she said pertly.

"Tease me and I'll back you up against the wall again," he threatened. "And this time, I won't stop."

"In a houseful of people?" Her eyes kindled with humor. "You wouldn't dare."

"Yes, I would."

She didn't really believe him, but she moved quickly into the living room, just in case.

Marion was wringing her hands. It wasn't going well. Jessica was making her opinion of the ranch so obvious that people were beginning to murmur. Even Ben looked uncomfortable when Jessica began playing up to Turk and trying to get him to talk about the planes he'd shot down in the war.

Ben moved her to one side, nervous. "Don't do that, please," he asked, avoiding Turk's blazing eyes. "He and Cole never speak of France. You're asking for trouble. Turk isn't quite civilized even now, and my brother is a cougar when he's pushed."

"How exciting." She glanced toward the kitchen doorway, where Lacy and Cole were briefly silhouetted. Cole was quite something. Jessica found herself actually envying Lacy. That man would be more than enough for any woman, and he'd wear the pants, not his wife. Ben was easily managed, almost childish. Coleman White-hall would be his exact opposite, stubborn and masculine and very exciting.

"How long have they been married?" she asked, nodding toward Cole and Lacy.

"Almost a year."

"Really?" Jessica laughed, with faint envy. "My, my. They act like newlyweds, don't they? She's rather docile and backward. You'd think he'd prefer a different kind of woman."

Lacy was Ben's Achilles' heel. He didn't like having her described in those terms. He was getting nervous about the whole affair. He hadn't wanted to let Marion give him this party. Jessica tended to be abrasive, and she was every inch a snob. As much as Ben enjoyed her in bed, she was an embarrassment in public. If it weren't for the job, he wouldn't have let himself be coaxed into giving her that engagement ring at all.

His mind kept flying back to Faye, to poor little Faye who loved him, who would have died for him. So sweet, and so different from this cold-eyed woman who used her body like a weapon to extract what she wanted from men.

"Is Turk married?" Jessica was asking, her acquisitive eyes moving slowly over the blond ace as he stood alone at the punch table.

"No."

Jessica's pretty lips pursed. "What a waste. He has bedroom eyes. I'll bet he's built as well as you are, Ben."

He shifted uneasily. That wasn't the kind of thing a lady said. But, then, Jessica was no lady.

"Let's circulate," he said. "I see—"

He stopped dead and went pale as Faye Cameron came in the front door. She wasn't dressed for a party. She was wearing a simple gingham dress with a worn sweater over it. Her blond hair was disheveled and she'd been crying.

She went up to Ben, a scene he hadn't imagined in his worst nightmares, and stared at him.

"Well?" he asked, his eyes pleading with her not to

start anything. The neighbors all seemed to suspect why she was here, and some people, including Cole, were actually staring.

"Is this her?" Faye asked, staring at Jessica.

"This is my fiancée, Jessica," he said stiffly. "What do you want?"

Faye should have run at the tone—and the look that accompanied it—but she stood her ground. She was very pale and quiet. In fact, she was shaking. But she didn't back down an inch.

"I want to know if you still intend to marry her," Faye said quietly, "when I'm carrying your child?"

"That's a lie," Ben said easily.

"It was a few weeks ago," Faye agreed. "Now it isn't. You know why. And when."

His face went stark white. So that afternoon had paid dividends. But why now, for God's sake, when he was on top of the world? Why had she come here to destroy him in public, in front of his fiancée and his employer?

He started to speak, to ask her to go outside with him so they could talk. But Jessica beat him to the punch.

"Get rid of it, honey," Jessica told her—with cold insolence and a look that spoke volumes. "Girls like you know how, don't they? Ben can pay for it."

"What—what do you mean?" Faye stammered.

"Get an abortion." Jessica shrugged. "It's easy. Any madam can show you. But you won't get Ben, because I need him and he's marrying me. Shopworn little creatures like you can always get hicks. In a place like this, you'll strike paydirt," she added, with a meaningful glance around the crowded house.

The room had gone very quiet. Jessica didn't care. This creature had to be got rid of before she played on Ben's sympathies.

"Now get out," Jessica told the girl. "We don't want poor white trash like you in here—"

"Who the hell do you think you are, lady?" Cole's deep voice bit into her speech.

He resisted Lacy's frantic pull and went to tower over Jessica. "Faye, come here." He held out his arms, and Faye, frightened, ran to him. He pulled her close and looked at Jessica's shocked face with unrefined contempt. "This is my home," he told her. "I decide who goes and who stays. Faye Cameron is a sweet, nice girl who never did anything wrong in her life until she landed in the orbit of my licentious brother! If she's pregnant, the child will be a Whitehall, and will be provided for—not scraped out of her like some fungus! And if you open your mouth again in that venomous manner, you will regret it."

"You can't speak to my daughter like that," Randolph Bradley said haughtily.

"Oh, but he can," Lacy said. She moved forward, putting her arm around the other side of Faye to give her support. It had taken guts for Faye to come here. She wasn't going to let those people savage her, either.

"I hardly think a rancher has any right to treat people of our station in this manner," Jessica said sarcastically, getting her poise back. "Especially when we did Ben a favor just to come here. You're a nobody in San Antonio, Mr. Whitehall."

"The husband of the heir to the Jacobsen fortune?" Lacy replied. "You must be mad if you think Cole lacks social standing." She felt Cole's rage and saw Ben's anguish, but it was her turn now. She lifted her chin. "You didn't know that my great-uncle Horace Jacobsen founded Spanish Flats, I suppose?"

Randolph Bradley hesitated. "Horace Jacobsen? *The* Horace Jacobson, the railroad tycoon?"

"Why, yes," Lacy said pleasantly, aware of Cole's stiffness. She hated doing this to his pride, but it had become necessary to save Faye. "He left his fortune to my great-aunt, his wife, and it passed to me on her death." She fingered the diamonds. "These *rhinestones* were hers," she told Jessica. "Except that they are not costume jewelry. They once belonged to Mary Stuart, Queen of Scots, as legend goes. She was an ancestor of mine. And the dress I'm wearing, my dear isn't something I whipped up on my treadle machine." Her eyes glittered. "It's a Paris original; one which, I daresay, is quite beyond your pocket!"

Jessica was looking drawn. Ben tried to feel sorry for her, but it wasn't easy. Faye looked shattered, and he was going to catch hell from Cole; he could see it in the older man's furious expression. Lacy was just getting warmed up.

"There's just one more little piece of information I have to impart to you, Mr. Bradley," Lacy continued, with venomous politeness. "You number among your biggest advertisers two of my cousins who dote on me. One word from me, and I can close your newspaper down overnight!"

Randolph Bradley had never groveled in his life, but he came close to it then. Apologies for himself and his daughter flowed from his lips. Lacy wasn't listening. She was staring at Jessica with eyes that made vicious demands.

"You surely don't expect me to apologize," Jessica said icily. "That little slut isn't pregnant; she's just making it up to get Ben. But he belongs to me, now . . .

and I'm not sharing him. Take me home, Ben. And don't ever expect me to come back here again.''

"How could you?" Ben asked huskily, staring at Faye. "How could you do this to me, knowing what my career means? You vicious little liar!''

Faye leaned her tearful face against Cole's chest.

Cole's eyes flared at his brother. "You made her pregnant and cast her off, and you think *SHE's* vicious?'' he asked, his voice threatening. "You cold-blooded, mercenary opportunist!''

Marion came forward, white as a sheet. "Bennett, please don't spoil the party. All of you, please!''

She clutched her chest. Lacy quickly got her into a chair while people gathered around. Lacy ran for one of the pills the doctor had prescribed and came back to slip one under Marion's tongue. The pain seemed to subside fairly quickly, but she was still pale and sickly.

Cole looked at Ben over her head. "Take your streetwalker out of my house," he said, with icy fury. "If you come back, I'll beat you bloody. I swear to God I will!''

Ben hesitated, but only for a minute. He'd never seen Cole look at him like this before, as if he were a stinging insect. Even his mother's eyes were accusing, and Lacy and Faye wouldn't look at him. He was the wronged party here, so why did he feel so wretched and sick at heart? With a rough sigh, he took Jessica's arm, ignoring her affronted raging, and pulled her out of the house.

Randolph Bradley hovered uncertainly. "I apologize for my daughter . . .'' he began.

Lacy looked up at him. She was all but shaking with indignation because of Ben's treatment of Faye. This man had manipulated Ben and put them all in this shameful position. "I wouldn't count on being in San

Antonio too much longer, if I were you. In fact, I'd consider cutting my losses while I had the time.''

He swallowed. His new enterprise was going to end in ruin because of his spoiled daughter. He didn't know how he was going to cope. "Your brother-in-law will be out of a job." He used his last hole card.

"My brother-in-law deserves to be," she said curtly. "Please leave my home."

He did, rather hesitantly. The guests murmured among themselves. They'd take home enough gossip to carry them through the winter. Lacy grimaced.

Cole stood up. "Well, don't just stand there," he said, glaring at them. He pulled Faye to his side and smiled down at her. "I'm going to be an uncle. Sure as hell that's a reason for celebration! Put that music back on!"

The incredible statement saved the day. No one mentioned that the niece or nephew would be born out of wedlock, or that Faye was disgraced, or that the guest of honor had just been thrown out the door. The party began again, with pure revelry.

"Oh, Mr. Whitehall, can you ever forgive me?" Faye wailed. "I don't know why I did it!"

"Because you love him, of course," Cole said kindly. He handed her his handkerchief. "Mind the stains," he teased as she stared at the dark red smudges. "Lacy's lip rouge is potent."

"It must be, considering the amount of it you've removed tonight," Marion said, with a feeble attempt at humor that turned too soon to tears of grief and loss.

"Now, now," Lacy said, kissing her powdered cheek. "I'm going to send Mr. Bradley back to New York on a rail. Doesn't that make you feel better?"

"Ben will go with them!" she wailed.

"He'd better," Cole said, his eyes flashing. "I meant what I said. I won't have him in this house."

"He's your brother, Coleman," Marion choked. "My son!"

"He's a jackass," came the short reply. "And until he gets his priorities straight, he can stay away. How do you think Faye feels? He has no honor! He's put her in the family way and made out that it was all her fault. Then he stood and let that floozy call her a tramp in front of all her neighbors!"

"I'm going to have a kid and I'm not married," Faye said miserably. "I guess I *am* a tramp."

"You are not!" Cole's eyes looked threatening. "Don't you ever say that again. We'll help Ira with the expenses. That baby's going to be pampered. Spoiled rotten. That baby will be a Whitehall—and don't you forget it."

Faye brightened a little. "Gosh, you don't—you don't mind?"

He smiled at her. "No. I don't mind."

"People will talk." She sighed. "Everybody will know."

"It's better that way," Lacy assured her. "Secrets are dangerous. They make you vulnerable. If everyone knows all about you, you can never be blackmailed." She touched the bright blond hair. "There are always people who don't mind capitalizing on the pain of others. That's why you won't hide your baby, Faye. Everyone will know about it, and that's your protection. It will all be right out in the open, and you'll go to church with us every Sunday before it's born."

"Oh, no!" Faye gasped. "They wouldn't let me!"

Lacy drew her forward and turned off the gramophone, then held up her hand for silence.

"I need to ask something. Would any of you object if we bring Faye to church with us on Sunday, considering that she is an unwed mother?"

"Good heavens, no!" Mrs. Darlington gasped. "None of us are that perfect, my dear," she told Faye, and smiled at her.

The sentiment was echoed by any number of neighbors, and Lacy relaxed.

Cole pulled her into the circle of his arm, keeping a wary eye on Marion, who was looking brighter by the minute now that her medicine had taken effect.

"You handled that very well, Mrs. Whitehall," he said, smiling. "That was one terrific object lesson you gave Bradley."

"I'm sorry it came to that. Poor Ben."

"Poor Ben, the devil!" he returned. "Poor little Faye."

"She'll do," she told him. "She's tough. I'm glad we didn't try to cover it up. Faye would have been so miserable trying to hide her condition from the community, terrified that someone would find out. It's much better to have things aboveboard. We have no secrets from God, after all—even if people do hide them from one another."

"I suppose so. My mother has never been able to bear gossip. In her generation people died rather than disgrace the family."

"Can you imagine what some of our contemporaries will have to live down when they're grandparents?" she teased. Her eyes flirted with him. "Would you like to dance?"

"In lieu of kicking my brother and his woman back to San Antonio, sure."

"Ben will never forgive you for what you called her," Lacy said, her lips twitching.

"I'll never forgive her for what she said to Faye. Poor little kid . . . Look at her. She loves Ben so much that she'll ruin that child with loving when it's born. And he wants that city icicle."

"She may not be so receptive when my cousins get through with her father," Lacy said. "Ben wanted Jessica because of his career. She wanted Ben because her father needed him to write for the paper, knowing that he'd do it cheap because he was involved with Jessica. I expect there'll be a parting of the ways any day now."

"One can hope," Cole said. "But I meant it. Until— and unless—Ben apologizes, he can't come here."

"Not even to see Marion?" Lacy asked gently. "It will break her heart."

"He can see her in town," he said shortly, bending that much but no further. "I'll have Turk drive her."

"Poor Turk took off. Jessica was really giving him the eye."

"He isn't as much a lady's man as he was," Cole said thoughtfully. "Amazing, that. He's different lately."

"Since Katy left," Lacy agreed.

"Yes. Since Katy left." He sighed. "I wish I knew how she was. I'm sure something's wrong. I just feel it."

As if in answer to the statement, the telephone gave the ranch's three rings. Cole and Lacy exchanged long glances before he went quickly to answer it. Lacy held her breath, sensing disaster.

═══ Chapter Fourteen ═══

COLE DIDN'T RECOGNIZE THE VOICE ON THE OTHER end of the line. The operator had said it was a call from Chicago before she connected them.

"I want to speak to Mr. Whitehall," a strange male voice announced over crackling wires.

"This is Coleman Whitehall," Cole said shortly.

"I'm Lieutenant Higgins, of the Chicago police. I'm afraid I have some bad news. There's been a shooting," the caller replied, adding quickly, "Mrs. Marlone is . . . not wounded. Her husband, however, is dead. We have the culprit in custody. A Mr. Blake Wardell. He's a well-known local gambler with whom Mr. Marlone had dealings."

Cole sucked in his breath. Marlone, dead! That damned mobster! Cole couldn't find it in himself to feel sorry for the man, but he did feel sorry for Katy.

"Can I speak to my sister?" he asked, keeping his voice down so that Marion and Lacy wouldn't overhear. He wanted time to break it to them gently.

"That's the problem, you see. Until five minutes ago, we didn't know how to contact her family. Mr. Marlone's mother, regrettably, had to be sedated and couldn't tell us anything."

"Couldn't Katy have told you?" he shot back, fear knotting up his stomach.

"Mr. Whitehall . . ." Higgins hesitated. "Mrs. Marlone is . . . not able to speak. The attending physician feels that her mind has, forgive me, gone. He wants to speak with you about the possibility of having her transferred to a—to a sanitarium. He does not think that she will recover."

Cole felt the blood draining out of his face. He was utterly speechless for a space of seconds while the impact hit him. Katy's mind was gone. She was insane. Guilt, rage, murderous anger washed over him in turn.

"Where is she?" he choked, aware of an apprehensive Lacy and his mother watching him with wide eyes.

"In City General Hospital. Mr. Whitehall . . ."

"She witnessed the shooting?" Cole asked, with cold certainty.

"Yes."

"There's something more. What is it?" he added perceptively.

"When we arrived, two of the occupants of the room were . . . in a state of undress. Mr. Marlone, the deceased, was fully clothed and armed. I'm afraid the situation spoke for itself."

Cole wouldn't relay that message to the women, he decided instantly. But he felt furious anger at the dead man for putting Katy in such company.

"I'll be on the first train to Chicago," Cole said tightly. "Tell the doctor to do nothing until I arrive."

"Yes, sir. I'll have someone meet you at the station."

"Thank you." Cole hung up, barely aware of Lucy tugging at his sleeve, of Marion's worried face. He turned to them. "Katy's husband has been killed," he said gently. "She's all right, but Lacy and I will need to

go to Chicago and bring her home. She's . . . in shock,"
he said evasively.

"You're sure she's all right?" Marion asked huskily,
tears in her eyes. "Oh, Coleman. I can't bear much
more!"

"I do realize that." Cole put a supporting arm around
her and motioned to Faye. "Honey can you stay with
Mother tonight? Lacy and I have to go to Chicago to
fetch Katy home."

"I can stay," Faye said. "Papa's probably drunk by
now. He won't notice if I'm gone or not."

"If you have any trouble with Mother get Turk. He'll
handle things while I'm gone. Lacy, you'd better change.
I'll talk to Turk. He can drive us to the station."

Lacy didn't hesitate. She went immediately to their
room to put on her traveling suit and get a coat.

Hours later, tired and sleepy, they arrived at the train
station. As he'd promised, the police lieutenant had
dispatched someone to meet them—himself.

He was a tall, blue-eyed man with silvery hair and a
kind smile. "I'm Higgins. You're the Whitehalls, I
presume?" he asked, extending a hand to shake Cole's.
Cole hadn't changed his suit; he'd only added a black
Stetson and boots to the ensemble. He looked very
Western, something the older man seemed to find fascinating. "Never met a real rancher before," he told Cole
as they walked toward his car, "but we do a big business
in Texas beef down at the stockyards."

"So I hear," Cole said. "Has my sister said anything?"

"I'm afraid not. But I'm glad you came. I would have
hated seeing her sent to one of those places."

Lacy worried over that statement as they drove to the
hospital, Cole asking questions and the lieutenant field-

ing them. Cole had told her everything. Almost everything, she amended silently, certain that he was still holding something back. She only hoped that Katy wasn't as bad as they'd been led to believe. She noticed that Cole hadn't told Turk anything except that Katy's husband was dead and Katy wanted to come home. He said later that he had a few suspicions regarding how Turk felt about Katy, and he wanted to be there when the man was given the truth. Turk might go off the deep end, he said. Lacy wondered about that, too. The blond foreman hadn't been the same since Katy'd married.

Their arrival at the hospital diverted her thoughts to more immediate matters. They were shown to a ward of iron-railed beds. In one of them lay Katy, on sheets as white as her face. She was very still under the covers, her body pitifully thin, her brown hair disheveled, her green eyes dull. She looked at the ceiling, but she didn't see anything or hear anything.

Lacy bent over her, into her field of vision. "Katy?" she whispered.

There was no response. Not even the twitch of an eyelash. Cole left the ward with the doctor. When he came back in, he was somber and noticeably pale.

"Can you get her dressed?" he asked Lacy, his voice strained. "I'll wait outside."

"Y-yes," Lacy said falteringly. "Cole . . ."

"I know," he said huskily. He looked at Katy and winced, "God, I know. We'll cross one bridge at a time. Hurry. If we can, I'd like to make the next train out. We can sleep at home if you think you can manage."

"Of course I can," she said quickly.

He went out, alone with his thoughts. A nurse came in to help Lacy, pulling the curtain around the bed. While Lacy fought a limp Katy into her things, the nurse gave her instructions to follow when they got home—about a doctor's continued care, about simple nursing techniques like turning Katy every few hours so that she didn't get bedsores. Lacy was tired and sleepy, but she listened.

"Is there any chance that she'll recover?" Lacy asked Cole when he'd carried Katy down to the car. Lieutenant Higgins was still tagging along, concerned.

"Very little, the doctor said," Cole replied tersely.

"Miracles happen," the lieutenant insisted. "I've seen a few in my twenty years of police work."

"I hope you're right," Lacy said fervently. "Oh, poor Katy!"

"You realize that she's in no shape to testify?" Cole asked the police officer on the way to the train.

"Certainly. If her condition should change, however, we'd like to be notified."

"I hope I can oblige," Cole replied. "Maybe just being at home will do the trick."

"What about the man who did the shooting?" Lacy asked curiously.

"Ah, the crafty Mr. Wardell." He smiled. "Well, little lady, I expect to find him out on bail when the doors open in the morning. He's rich—and he has plenty of friends at city hall. He had no use for Marlone. Wardell may be a mobster, but he's an honorable mobster. He hates drugs."

Cole froze. "Drugs?"

"Didn't you know?" the lieutenant asked. He waited until Lacy got the message and went on ahead. Then he paused beside Cole. "Marlone was hooked on the stuff. He was into all sorts of perverted stuff with women. Wardell was in love with Mrs. Marlone here. Although he said himself that she'd had a few drinks and didn't really know what was happening, he was crazy for her.

He said Marlone had beaten her up bad a few days before. Last night, she was tipsy, and he lost control. Marlone didn't walk in on them so much as he sneaked in to watch.''

"Oh, my God," Cole ground out, sick at the sordidness of it. "Did Katy know?"

"Not until after. Neither of them did. Wardell jumped out of bed, yelling bloody murder. Marlone grabbed his gun and tried to shoot him, but Wardell was quicker." He looked Cole in the eye. "What happened was horrible, but she was the victim in all of it. She did what Marlone told her to do because she was scared stiff of him. He was so hopped up, he didn't mind killing people. She probably was afraid he'd kill one of you if she asked for help. Don't blame her."

"She's my sister," Cole replied, glancing down at her thin, vacant face. "I love her."

"Wardell will probably look for her," he said. "He's asked about her constantly. He feels responsible."

"A mobster with a conscience?" Cole scoffed.

"A man in love," Higgins said quietly. "I've known the guy a long time. I've never seen him like this. He's torn up. He tried to get her away from Marlone, but she was too afraid to go."

"You said Marlone's mother had to be sedated. Will she be all right?"

"She has family in Italy. I imagine she'll go back there, now. She never liked this country."

"It's unhealthy for some people," Cole said. His mind was reeling with what he'd learned.

They caught up with Lacy, who was frowning.

"You said Danny used drugs. Katy didn't take them, did she?" Lacy asked miserably.

"I'm sure she didn't, ma'am," the police officer replied gallantly. "There were no needle marks."

"Thank God," Lacy whispered, her eyes on Katy's vacant face. "My poor Katy!"

"I wish you well," the lieutenant said as he watched them board the train when it came, Cole cradling Katy as he carried her inside the compartment. "I'll be in touch."

"Thank you," Cole said, and meant it. "If you ever get down to Texas, you'll always have a place to stay."

The older man smiled. "Always fancied being a cowboy. I suppose it's nothing near as glamorous as Zane Grey says."

Cole smiled. "Not unless you like blood and sweat and getting kicked in the belly by mama cows."

"That's what I thought. Have a good trip." He paused. "About Wardell . . ."

Cole hesitated. He wanted to say to hell with the man. But he'd tried to help Katy when no one else had. And he knew himself how it hurt to love someone who seemed out of his reach. He sighed with reluctant resignation. "Tell him he can call. You have my number. But he's only to speak to me. You understand?"

"Very well," Higgins agreed. "Poor fish. He can't help himself. Too bad he didn't go respectable, with a brain like that. Good-bye."

Katy didn't stir all the way back to the siding at Spanish Flats. Lacy slept, curled up against Cole, while he dozed intermittently. She'd asked questions, but he'd kept from saying much. He didn't want her to know all of it yet.

His mind was cluttered with worries. His mother's health, the row with Ben, Faye's pregnancy, Katy's condition . . . On top of that, there was the financial situation, getting worse daily as cattle prices fell. He closed his eyes on a silent prayer. Nobody short of God could bail him out now.

Marion came out on the porch when she heard a car drive up. Cole and Lacy arrived with Katy. It was well after daylight, and they'd hitched a ride home with a neighbor who'd gone into town after his mail. Marion had hardly slept, despite little Faye's loving concern and care.

"Katy!" Marion exclaimed, shocked when she saw her daughter's face and blank stare. "Cole, what's happened to her!"

"Shock," Cole said instantly. "She needs plenty of rest and quiet, and she'll be all right. Let's get her to her room."

"I made up her bed," Marion said. "Oh, my poor baby!" She touched Katy's hair, but the girl didn't stir, not even when she was laid on the coverlet of her bed. Cole pulled a pillow under her head, and all three of them stood watching her, worrying.

"Where's Turk?" Cole asked.

"At the barn— No, I hear him," Marion said, smiling as the blond man approached down the hall. "He's been as excited about Katy coming home as I have. Not that we aren't sorry about Danny, of course," she added guilty. "Well she be going back for the funeral?"

That would be one for the books, Cole thought sadly.

Turk came into the room before Cole could speak, hat in hand, grinning. "So there you are, tidbit—" The grin faded; the light in his eyes went out as he saw Katy's face. He moved slowly to the bedside and looked down at her without speaking. "I thought you said she was all right," he said to Cole, his eyes flashing.

"She will be," Lacy said stubbornly. "She's had a shock, that's all."

"What kind of shock?" Turk asked. His face grew wild, like the thick blond hair his hand was worrying.

"Danny was killed in front of her," Cole said. He didn't add one word about the circumstances. Turk didn't need to know that. It would drive him mad.

"Tough," Turk said quietly. His eyes ran over her face with aching need. It had been so long since he'd seen her. He'd relived that afternoon with her every night, woke burning for her every morning, cursed himself for letting her leave with Marlone. Now she was back, but she wasn't. She was damaged. Thin and worn and older somehow, and her eyes didn't see anything. Surely, he thought fearfully, this was more than just shock at seeing her husband shot. He knew that look as well as Cole did. He'd seen it in the faces of airmen who couldn't get back on board their planes. He'd seen it on the faces of combat troops who couldn't get out of bed, their eyes mercifully vacant, their minds . . . gone!

He turned toward Cole's tormented face, and when he saw it, he knew. A look passed between them that the women didn't see. Turk felt his stomach caving in. There was something more. Something horrible. He looked at Katy and the light went out of the world as he realized that this was no minor case of shock.

If only he'd stopped her from leaving! There was an ominous stillness about her body that frightened him. Only her shallow breathing made her look alive at all.

"Where's Faye?" Lacy asked Marion.

"Out back. It's washday," Marion replied.

Lacy poked her head out the window and looked. There was Faye, and two of the ranch wives, doing the laundry. Faye held a long wooden battling stick; she was standing over a big black pot of boiling water where the white shirts were soaking. She stirred them, damp hair around her face. Nearby, two number two washtubs of cold water waited to rinse the soap and bleach out of the shirts. There was another washtub of soapy water with a wood and accordion-metal washboard, too, to scrub the work clothes on and loosen the ground-in dirt. Two long wire lines were attached to oak trees just behind the washtubs for hanging the wet laundry. Washing was an all-day job, and the ranch didn't boast a washing machine yet. It was the one luxury the women would have given their teeth for, but it was too expensive, Marion insisted, and dug her heels in when Lacy tried to buy her one. The telephone and indoor bathroom and electricity were already wearing on her conscience.

Faye looked happy, despite her chore. Lacy smiled. "Can we keep her, do you think?" she asked Cole. "Her father won't really miss her, and he's too drunk to look after her."

"I wouldn't mind," Cole said, agreeing, "but Ira wouldn't hear of it. He loves her, you know. Drunk or sober."

"I suppose you're right." She sighed.

"Besides, we've got Katy to take care of now," he added, his eyes troubled as he looked at his sister. "God knows what she's been through in the past few months. She's so thin."

"My poor baby," Marion said gently, tears in her eyes. "What a terrible night it's been for her."

"She'll get better," Lacy said, with conviction. "You wait and see."

"I do hope you're right," Marion said. But she looked worried all the same.

Turk hadn't said a word. He took one last look at Katy and left the room. He couldn't bear her silent stillness another minute without breaking down. Until he saw her in that condition, he didn't know that he loved her. Ironic, he thought, that he should know it now, when it was probably far too late.

In Chicago, Blake Wardell was stepping out into the street into early morning traffic. He needed a shave and his eyes were bloodshot. Beside him, his lawyer was talking, but he barely heard.

". . . clear case of self-defense," the attorney muttered. "Everyone knows Marlone was a dopey pervert. But if the woman recovers enough to testify—"

"No." Wardell stared down at him with blazing dark eyes. "You leave her out of it. I'll take the rap if I have to—I'll go up for murder one if I have to—but you leave her out of it, completely! Buy off anybody you have to, but keep her name out of the papers."

"We'll have to get Mama Marlone out of town," the lawyer said thoughtfully.

"Ship her home to Italy," he said. "Do it today. Then find the boys from the coroner's office and the cops who answered the call. Play on their sympathies, grease their palms. But cool them off. And have a private word with the publishers of those papers."

"You're taking a risk."

"I'd take poison for her," he said huskily. "Go on home. I want to see Higgins."

The lieutenant was in his office, and not at all surprised when Wardell came in the door, big and dark and oddly subdued.

"Here," Higgins said, handing the big man a slip of paper without being asked. "That's her brother's telephone number. He said you're welcome to call, but don't talk to anybody but him. He hasn't told the family all of it. He probably never will.''

"How was she?'' he asked quietly.

"Bad,'' Higgins said, pulling no punches. This man was well able to take anything life threw at him, even the loss of a woman he idolized. "Nobody knows if her mind's gone or not, but her brother won't let her be institutionalized.''

"Neither would I. Are her folks well fixed?''

"Beats me. They're ranching people. I imagine not.''

"Anything they need,'' he said. "Anything at all. Doctors, money, nurses . . . you name it.''

"Tell him. But don't expect help to be welcomed. He's got the devil's own pride.''

Wardell smiled faintly. That sounded familiar. "Okay. There are ways. I know bankers all over.''

"I'm not surprised.'' Higgins stood up. "If you do anything outside the law, make sure I don't know about it. You're in enough trouble.''

"Think so?''

Higgins shrugged. "Not really. Marlone was a dirty rat. He only got what was coming to him. No sane jury will convict you. I know several dames who'll dance on his coffin and make terrific character witnesses.''

Wardell looked at the slip of paper and almost caressed it. His only link with Katy. It was the most precious thing in his possession. He glanced at Higgins. "You told him, didn't you?''

He nodded.

"And he still gave me his telephone number.''

"A gentleman, is Mr. Whitehall,'' Higgins said. "A keen student of human nature, too, I imagine. You see, I told him how you feel about Mrs. Marlone.''

Wardell laughed hollowly. "For all the good it will do me. There's this guy, back home," he said, his eyes lackluster. "He was all she ever talked about. She was tipsy last night, and I took advantage of it. But she didn't even know me when she fainted . . ." His eyes closed and he turned away in agony.

"Wardell."

He paused, but he didn't look back. "Yeah?"

"Go legit," Higgins said. "You're wasted in the company you keep. A brain like yours, you could be governor."

"I thought you said go legit," came the dry reply. He went out, closing the door quietly behind him. Higgins smiled sadly and pulled out the file on the next case.

The drive to San Antonio was long and harrowing, and all the way, Jessica raged about the treatment she'd received.

"And you just stood there and let them wipe the floor with me!" she shrilled. "You're not even a man! I couldn't care less about you, Ben. I only kept you sweet because Daddy needed you!"

"Daddy doesn't need him anymore," Randolph said wearily from the backseat, his dead dreams leaving a bad taste in his mouth. "Ben's sister-in-law is going to put me out of business. She suggested that I cut my losses while I still had time. That's sound advice. I'm closing the paper and we're going back to New York. Sorry it worked out this way, Ben. I didn't know how much influence Mrs. Whitehall had."

"Neither did I," Ben replied quietly. Lacy had never mentioned her great-uncle around the ranch, or the fact that she inherited anything more than her great-aunt's house in San Antonio. To spare Cole's pride, he thought bitterly. Everything Lacy did was for Cole.

"What will you do?" Randolph asked.

"I'll go to Paris," he said abruptly, the sting of finding out what Jessica really felt for him little more than wounded pride. Maybe he even deserved what he was getting. He'd hurt Faye and his mother enough to deserve plenty more. He'd even hurt Lacy and Cole, despite the fact that they now seemed closer than ever.

"Joining the Lost Generation?" Jessica mocked. "What makes you think they'll have you?"

He glanced at her coldly. "Some people like me for myself."

"The little blonde? You could always go back to her."

Could he, really? Faye had loved him. He didn't imagine she could after the way he'd humiliated her tonight. Poor little thing. What if she was really pregnant?

"Watch where you're going, please, Ben. I don't want to have an accident on my way home," Jessica said haughtily.

He turned his attention to the road. He would go to Paris, he decided. He had some money saved. Cole wouldn't let him near the ranch, not even to see his dying mother. He groaned inwardly. Marion was dying, and he'd almost caused her to have a heart attack by taking these predators home to feed on her pride, at a party she'd risked her health to give him. He seemed to have fouled up everything he touched. Exile wasn't a bad idea. Nobody would miss him, he thought miserably. If he could find himself, maybe he could get his life back together.

He glanced at Jessica and was shocked to realize that

all he'd ever felt for her was physical excitement. They'd been using him. Lacy had seen it at once. Why hadn't he?

He could have screamed out loud. He'd made a fine mess of things. He wondered how he was ever going to make amends.

Chapter Fifteen

"**Y**OU HAVE TO TELL ME THE TRUTH," MARION told Cole, having followed him out to the front porch. "I have to know what's caused her to be like this."

He looked down at her with quiet anguish. "I can't."

Marion's eyes began to water. "Oh, Cole. Is it so terrible?"

"Yes." He glanced away from her, toward the stable where Turk had gone, and then back to his mother. She kept staring at him until, finally, he said, with great reluctance, "Mother, the doctors don't know how long it will take for her to recover. If she does," he added softly.

Marion caught her breath and clutched her chest.

"Oh, God!" he groaned. "Mother, I'm sorry." He picked her up and carried her back inside. "Mother, I'm sorry. I should never have told you!"

"Feels as if . . . a horse is sitting on my chest. Isn't that funny?" She could hardly breathe. "It's I who am sorry—to be adding . . . to your burden." Tears bled from her eyes.

"Don't be absurd. If anyone has the right to be upset, it's you. God knows, the past day has brought enough worry to fell any sane person.'' He lay her down and went to fetch her pills while Lacy was called to stay with her.

But the pill didn't work. Two pills didn't work. Lacy got up, and telephoned the hospital, and spoke to Marion's doctor.

"We have to take you to town, Mother," Lacy said gently. "Now, don't cry," she pleaded. "We can't leave you in pain like this. Cole, will you bring the car around?"

"Certainly."

He went to get the car, taking one precious minute to find Turk, who was leaning against the barn wall, his eyes unseeing in a face the color of rice paper.

Cole jerked the older man around by his heavy denim jacket and shook him, almost dislodging the black Stetson perched on the thick blond hair. "Come out of it. I need you," he said shortly. "I think Mother's having a heart attack. We're taking her to the hospital. Go and sit with Katy until I get back."

Turk's eyes were agonized. "She's gone," he said hoarsely. "She's a dead body breathing. My fault. All my fault. I could have stopped her with a single word . . . and I was too selfish to say it!"

Cole shook him again. "This isn't the time," he said sharply. "Come on."

He drew the other man out the door and propelled him toward the house. Turk went, his mind barely working.

Cole and Lacy loaded Marion into the car and shot off toward town.

Faye had come from the house to see what was going on. "Can I do anything?" she asked Turk, frowning at his wan expression.

"No. No, thanks. I'm going to sit with Katy. Just . . . do what you were doing, Faye."

"Sure."

She left, casting a doubtful look over her shoulder as he disappeared into the house.

Katy was in exactly the same position he'd last seen her, her eyes open and unseeing, her breathing very soft and quiet.

He sat down on the bed beside her and a big, callused hand went to her thin face, caressing it with shaky tenderness.

"What did he do to you?" he asked unsteadily, his heart in agony over the way she was. "I let you go, and look at you. I should have stopped you, Katy. I should have listened to my heart and not my head."

She didn't seem to hear him. Not a muscle of her body moved.

But he couldn't be quiet. He'd kept his silence too long already. He leaned closer, propping himself over her so that he could see her close up, so that his face filled her unseeing eyes.

"Listen," he whispered, "you can't do this to yourself. Marlone wasn't worth it. He was a crazy little maniac, and we both know that you only married him because of me. You never loved him. Don't destroy yourself over him."

A shudder ran over her thin body, and he caught his breath. She'd heard him! She must have heard him.

"Katy," he said softly. His big thumb smoothed over her mouth, gently disturbing its dry contours. "Look at me, sweetheart."

The endearment came quite naturally. He was hardly aware that he'd said it. But Katy's eyelids flickered and she stirred.

"That's it," he whispered. He looked into her eyes and saw, slowly, the first evidence of awareness in them.

She blinked. It all started to come back, and she moaned in anguish. "No!"

His thumb pressed down hard, stopping the words. "I'm here," he said. "I'm right here. Nothing and nobody is going to hurt you as long as there's one breath in my body. Do you hear me, little one?"

She swallowed. Her eyes were wide, terrified. "He—he was there," she managed hoarsely. "Watching." Her eyes closed. Tears washed down her cheeks. "Danny . . . all that blood." She began to sob. "Don't touch me. I'm dirty, dirty! I'm a tramp, like Danny said when he beat me. He said I was no virgin, I deserved everything I got!"

Turk shook with rage. He scooped her up in his arms and all but crushed her in his anguish. "You're not a tramp," he said into her ear, blaming himself all over again. He'd taken her virginity. Had Danny made her pay for that as well? "You're not dirty."

"I slept . . . with Wardell," she choked, feeling his body tense suddenly. "Danny told me to go out with him, threatened me if I didn't keep Wardell sweet for him. Danny beat me, hurt me. But Blake Wardell loved me, so much. So much! I was drunk. He wanted me, and it was so sweet to be loved, to forget what Danny had done to me. . . ." She shivered as if with a fever. Turk held her, his eyes unseeing as he struggled with jealous rage at what she was confessing. It was somehow so much worse that she'd slept with the mobster as well as Danny Marlone.

"Wardell took me to bed and afterward, Danny was

there; he'd . . . watched us! Blake was furious! He went
after him. Danny went for his pistol. There were
shots . . ." She shuddered helplessly with memory.
"Danny's dead. Danny was laying there in his own
blood, and his eyes were open, staring at me!" She
gasped for air. "I want to die! Let me die; I can't live
with it!" She fought his arms, her eyes unseeing again,
but with blind destruction this time.

This was something else Turk knew about. He'd had
to stop Cole from destroying himself in France when
he'd learned how terrible his injuries were. Katy would
try it. He knew without being told that she'd have to be
watched every minute from now on, until she could deal
with what had happened. With her upbringing, the
horror would be worse. But it didn't shock or disgust
Turk, who knew her so well. Not even the knowledge
that Danny had forced her into another's man's arms.
He'd deal with his jealousy somehow. If only he could
be sure that Katy hadn't fallen in love with Wardell.
God knew it could have happened. Danny had been
cruel to her; Wardell had loved her. Katy hadn't had
much kindness from men, starting with himself. He'd
hurt her. Danny had hurt her. How could he blame her
for turning toward the first man who showed her a little
compassion?

"I won't let you hurt yourself," he said firmly,
subduing her. "Lie still."

The tears came, horrible sobs that shook her body,
paled her cheeks, finally made her weak with their
violence.

"I'm sure Cole . . . knows," she choked. "They
must have told him. He'll be so ashamed of me.
Everybody will know. The scandal . . ."

He turned her face back to his and made her look at

him. "Nobody is going to throw you to the wolves. Stop it."

She bit her lower lip, averting her eyes. "I thought it was all so stupid, all the rules and straitlaced behavior and high principles. But now I understand why there are rules. They're all that keep us from becoming animals." She closed her eyes on a tiny whimper. "Turk, there's been so much terror. I just want . . . to sleep."

She was drained. On some level she'd probably been aware of everything that had happened. She hadn't wanted to come back, but Turk had brought her out of it. She accepted the fact that he could call her back from the grave. He was sorry for her, but he wouldn't want her now that he knew it all. She'd destroyed herself in his eyes forever. But what did it matter? He'd never wanted her, really.

"You won't tell Mother what I told you?" she pleaded suddenly.

"Of course not."

She blinked, looking around in confusion. "Where *is* Mother?"

"Having a checkup." Turk said, hedging.

"Is she all right?" she asked worriedly.

"Of course she's all right," he said, lying glibly. "They threw a big engagement party for Ben last night. She's overtired."

"That and me, too," she groaned. She lay back defeatedly. "And she's dying," she added dully. "It looks like I'm going to lose everything. I guess I deserve it, too."

"Don't talk like that," he said curtly.

Her eyes closed, locking out his cold stare. "Who's Ben marrying?" she asked after a minute.

"Nobody now. Lacy turned his snobbish city fiancée

every way but loose. Ben sent word this morning that
he's off to France for a while. I didn't have time to tell
anybody.''

"Poor Ben."

"Poor Marion," he corrected. "Ben's venomous
fiancée was making a hash of things, insulting everything
from the furniture to poor Faye.''

"Faye Cameron?" she murmured.

"She's . . . in the family way," he said finally.

Katy's eyes opened. "Whose baby is it?"

"Ben's."

"Worse and worse," she said miserably. "Poor Faye.
He probably thinks she isn't good enough for him, the
snob.''

"Cole and Lacy stood by her. She'll manage just fine
without Ben." He scowled, his face worried. "Katy . . .
are you . . . all right?"

Her gaze lifted to meet his and she flinched. "What do
you mean?''

A big, heavy hand moved gently to her flat stomach
and rested there, his eyes asking a question that his lips
couldn't form.

She averted her eyes.

His hand grew heavier, warm. "Katy," he said
quietly, "I want to know if you could be . . . in the
family way, by me.''

Her eyes closed. She couldn't tell him. She
couldn't . . .

"Please," he whispered, his face drawn. He turned
her face back, forced her to look at him. "Katy . . .''

She swallowed down her anguish. She hadn't wanted
him to know, but she couldn't lie anymore. She'd kept
it inside too long. "Danny knocked me down a flight

of stairs the first time he beat me.'' She had to force the words out of her throat, and she couldn't look at him as she added, "I lost the baby I was carrying."

He groaned harshly and got to his feet. He went to lean his hands on the windowsill, staring out through the distorted glass at the horizon. He'd made her pregnant. She'd lost the baby and gone through hell, all because he couldn't let her go untouched. She'd been a virgin, a sweet, innocent girl, and his mind could hardly deal with what he'd cost her. If he'd kept his head, she'd never have had to leave with Marlone in the first place. Damn Marlone! He'd beaten her, made her lose the baby. He cursed silently, his face rigid with grief and murderous rage. Damn Marlone! If ever a man deserved a bullet . . .

"It's all right, you know," she said dully. "It would just have been another complication. It was my fault, anyway—the way I ran after you and practically threw myself at you that last day. I never blamed you. I only got what was coming to me for being so easy and rebellious."

"I can't believe I'm hearing this," he said brokenly. "I took your chastity, tossed you into the clutches of that murderous maniac, got you involved in murder . . . gave you a baby. And you don't blame me?" He turned, his face hard with new lines, his eyes totally without emotion. "Well, I do, Katy. I blame myself for being blind and selfish and too yellow to go to Cole and tell him he had no right to dictate to me about you. He told me to keep my distance, and I did—out of loyalty to him. But he was wrong. Dead wrong. If it hadn't been for the strain of keeping totally away from you for so long, I wouldn't have been so eaten up with desire that I'd lose control and force myself on you like that.''

"You didn't . . . force me," she protested, blushing.

"Hell, yes, I did," he said. "You were just a girl, but I knew what could happen. I compromised you."

She turned her face sideways on the pillow with a tiny sigh. "It takes two to commit a sin, Jude," she said, unconsciously using his real name. "I thought giving in to you might make you care. But it didn't. You can't make people love you."

"Katy . . ." He moved closer to the bed, searching for the right words.

She looked up, reading his expression. "You love me?" she asked with a soft, cynical laugh. "Don't do that to me," she said defeatedly, closing her eyes on the shock in his face. "I don't need your pity, Turk. You needn't pretend you care now . . . when we both know you didn't before. Just let it be. I don't think I ever want a man to touch me again as long as I live, anyway. Just the thought of it makes me sick."

It did. That was no joke. The night before had been traumatic. She'd gone against all her principles to sleep with Wardell, partly out of fear of Danny, pity and desire for Wardell, alcoholic overindulgence, and the need to close her eyes and let herself be loved. The shock of finding Danny watching it all, and the subsequent violent way he'd died, had snapped something inside her. The thought of sex made her stomach churn.

"It's early days yet," Turk said after a minute, although his eyes were hooded. "You can't expect to get over something like this overnight."

"I suppose not." She put her hands over her eyes. "Poor Mama," she whispered. "So much scandal. Ben, and now me . . ."

"Your mother is human," Turk replied. "Cole spared her most of it. She only knows that Danny is dead. No more. Cole told nobody, not even me, what really happened."

She wiped her wet eyes and turned her face into the pillow. The disgrace would be total when the newspapers came out. Inevitably somebody from here would read about it. Everyone would know!

"Katy, don't," he said huskily. It hurt him to watch her like this. And the baby; if he thought about that for long, he'd go out of his mind!

"I've ruined my life," she whispered. "And my family's honor. I've destroyed everything."

"You're more a victim than anyone else," he said, pausing by the bed to look down at her. He winced as he remembered what she'd said about being beaten.

"Am I?" she said coldly. "I lived with a man who broke every law there was, committed adultery, drank like a lush. I've lived among mobsters, and I even know people who've committed murder. I'm not a very nice person."

He leaned over her, smoothing her dishevelled hair. "You're just Katy," he said softly.

Her eyes met his. "I'm nothing at all. I don't want your sympathy. I don't want anything from you."

His hand stilled. "That will change," he said, withdrawing his hand.

"No, it won't," she replied. "I've been bad. Now I have to atone for it."

"You're in shock," he said, refusing to listen to her. "You'll get over this. It will take a little time, that's all. How about something to eat?"

"Food would nauseate me," she replied. She closed her eyes again. "I only want some sleep. Please leave me alone."

"Only if you swear on the Bible that you won't do anything stupid."

She stared at him. "Like jumping out the window?"

He nodded. "That. Or anything else that's self-destructive." His eyes narrowed threateningly. "You might consider that your mother can't take much more right now."

"I know that," she agreed. She closed her eyes. "I won't put any more on her than I already have," she said wearily.

"Good girl." He moved to the doorway. "I won't be far away. Sing out if you need anything."

"With Cole gone, don't you have work to do?"

"He said to watch you."

"I see."

"No, you don't," he said through his teeth, infuriated by her tone, her stubborn refusal to believe he cared about her. "I'll be close by. Try to sleep."

"Sure." She folded her hands on her flat stomach and closed her eyes on tears she didn't want him to see. His baby had lain there, under her heart, and Danny had killed it when he knocked her down the stairs. He hadn't known she was pregnant until she lost the baby, and even then he'd thought it was his. He hadn't been particularly concerned. If it hadn't been for Wardell, she'd probably have died after the miscarriage. Afterward, she'd all but mourned herself to death. She'd started drinking then, out of anguish. Wardell's tenderness and sympathy had surprised her. It shouldn't have, she knew. He loved her. What a terrible irony. Wardell loved her. She loved Turk. And Turk loved . . . his dead wife, she supposed. Whatever his feelings, she didn't want the pity he was offering, or his pretended caring. All she wanted was sleep.

Turk sat quietly in the living room with his thoughts until Cole and Lacy came home. They were alone, looking grim.

"They kept her in the hospital," Cole told his friend. "Thank God she's not too bad, though. She may be able to come home by the end of the week if she improves. We'll have her home before Christmas, at least." He didn't add what they all knew; that Thanksgiving had been little more than a dinner, with no real celebration because of all the family turmoil. The family was coming apart at the seams.

"Good."

Turk looked odd. White and a little shaky. "Are you all right?" Cole asked him, concerned.

"Katy came around while you were gone," he replied dully.

"She's conscious?" Cole burst out, and Lacy's eyes grew wet with helpless tears. "Thank God!"

"Thank God," Lacy echoed, pressing into Cole's arms. "Let's go and talk to her!"

"She's asleep," Turk said, stopping them. "Give her time to rest. She'll be all right once she comes out of the depression."

"The doctors said she'd never be herself again," Cole said heavily. "I've prayed they were wrong!"

"So have we all," Lacy seconded. "Miracles still happen! Does Faye know?"

"No. She's still outside," Turk said. "You might tell her . . ."

"Yes, I might!" Lacy reached up to kiss Cole's cheek and went happily out the door. Cole knew then that something more was wrong, something Turk didn't want to say in front of Lacy.

"Okay. She's gone. Let's have it," Cole said quietly.

Turk averted his eyes. "She was pregnant," he said, his voice totally without emotion, as if everything in him had been drained out.

Cole cursed. "Damn the luck. She'll have a permanent reminder of that vicious, drug-popping weasel!"

"Drugs?" Turk asked.

"Danny was a doper. Not only that, he was perverted," Cole said flatly. "How does she feel about the child?"

"She lost it," Turk said. "He beat her, and she fell."

Cole's face went dark with angry color. He cursed steadily, his language deteriorating to the point that Turk was glad the women weren't within earshot.

"It gets worse," Turk said. He lifted his chin, his eyes full of self-hatred. He smiled insolently, hoping to make Cole mad enough to pop him. He wanted somebody to beat the living hell out of him. "The baby was mine."

But Cole didn't strike out. His dark eyes searched the other man's light ones. "Is that why she left?"

"No." Turk ran a rough hand over his jaw. "No, she left because she was wearing her heart out on me. I went over the edge. I'd wanted her so long, and she . . ." He couldn't bring himself to put any blame on her, to even intimate that her vulnerability and adoration had pushed him to his limits. "I just . . . lost it. I couldn't come to grips with what I felt for her in time, and when I came to my senses, it was too late. I thought she probably hated me, so I didn't try to stop her from leaving with Marlone."

There was a tense moment while Cole stared at the older man, finally realizing that nothing he could say would make any difference now. Turk had betrayed his trust, but from the look of the man, it hadn't been deliberate. Whatever Turk felt for Katy, it had to be something pretty powerful to make him as wretched as he looked now.

"Don't you want to throw a punch at me?" Turk asked curtly. "God knows you've every right."

Cole shook his head. "You haven't been the same since she left." Cole grimaced at the look on the other man's face. "I have to take some of the blame. You were a rounder, and I knew you'd never gotten over your wife. I didn't want Katy hurt." He laughed coldly. "Funny, isn't it? I tried to spare her, and caused her more grief."

"You did what you thought was best for her," Turk said quietly. "I couldn't blame you for that. You were probably right. But everything is different now, including the way I feel about Katy."

"You might tell her that," Cole said gently.

The pale eyes that met his were anguished. "I tried to tell her, in there. But she thinks it's just pity. She won't believe me."

Before Cole could react, a returning Lacy did. "I told Faye. She's going to be all right, isn't she?" she added worriedly.

"Of course she is," Turk said stubbornly. "She's still upset and blames herself for a lot of stupid reasons. But I think she'll be all right, in time." He grimaced. "God almighty, she won't have to go back and testify, will she?" he added, remembering the sordid circumstances under which her husband had met his fate.

"No," Cole said shortly. "I'll hide her out if I have to. It will be bad enough when the papers get hold of it. I'll bet Ben's newspaper friends will have him out here on our throats the second they get wind of it."

"Ben's gone to Paris," Turk said. "I didn't have time to tell you. He sent a message by a neighbor. 'Sorry for the trouble. I'm off to Paris.' That was all he said."

"Just as well," Cole said. "I told him he couldn't come back. He won't know about Katy unless he reads it in a paper."

"It will kill her soul to have it all come out," Turk said angrily.

"It won't do Mother's health much good, either," Cole replied. He took off his hat and sailed it onto the sofa. "What a hell of a mess."

"Amen."

Lacy took off her coat. "I'll fix some coffee and some lunch. Katy will probably sleep the clock around."

"I'll see if Faye is hungry."

They ate in a gloomy silence. Cole and Turk went out to work, but not before Turk warned them about Katy's confused mental condition. He cautioned them not to leave her alone for a minute, and made the women promise they wouldn't before he'd even leave the house. Faye and Lacy took turns sitting with Katy, but Katy still hadn't awakened when Cole came in after dark.

He was cleaning up when the telephone rang. Lacy answered it, but the operator asked for Cole.

She went to get him, wondering why he looked so worried.

"Whitehall," he said curtly, hoping he wasn't going to have to tell the police lieutenant that Katy was herself again. He couldn't let her go to Chicago and get embroiled with that bunch again.

"You don't know me," came the deep, gruff reply. "I just wanted to know how Katy is."

Cole knew instantly who it was. The mobster had grit—he'd have to give him that—to call here to ask about Katy under the circumstances. But he'd been kind to Katy, in his way, so Cole curbed his anger. "She said a few words to my foreman earlier. She's sleeping now."

"Thank God. Best thing for her, sleep. Damned sordid mess . . ."

"This is a party line," Cole cautioned curtly. "Wait a minute," he added, and listened to make sure nobody was eavesdropping. Fortunately that didn't happen often, and it was pretty obvious when somebody was. The line seemed secure for the moment. "All right, go ahead."

"I won't talk long. Listen, I took care of everything. Nobody's going to know anything. Not one word leaked out."

"How in hell . . . ?" Cole demanded.

"People love me. They keep quiet and I love them back," came the dry reply. "Don't ask. You tell Katy I said it's all over. My lawyer says he'll spring me without any trouble. Even your pal Higgins doesn't think I'll have to bribe a jury. So tell Katy not to worry about things. She's safe. I made sure of it. I won't have her name bandied about in sick gossip."

Cole hesitated. The man sounded pretty protective. "She can't testify," he said.

"Hell, man, I'd go to the chair before I'd ask her to!" he said huskily. "What do you think I am?"

His opinion of the mobster took a three-hundred-and-sixty-degree turn. If Wardell cared that much, he couldn't be all bad. "Thank you," he said finally.

"They said something about a sanitarium . . ." Wardell choked.

"There's no chance of that," he assured the man. "She's going to be fine. We'll take good care of her."

"You and the blond ace, right?" He laughed coolly. "I know about him. Katy cried all over me when she lost the kid. You know about the kid?"

"I know," he said uncomfortably.

"She loves that guy like I love her. Maybe he's got a little more sense now. If he doesn't, you knock some into him. He hurts her, he'll answer to me!"

"It isn't like that," Cole replied, almost smiling at the idea of a notorious mobster so concerned over a woman's happiness. "He'd never hurt her. He didn't know about the child. He's pretty torn up."

"He should have been better to her. Look, I've got to go. You need anything—money, nurses, anything—you let me know. Higgins knows how to get in touch with me."

Cole bristled. "We won't need any help."

"You and your damned black pride!" the deep voice raged. "I know you wouldn't even talk to me in the street, but this is for Katy! I feel responsible for what happened. You tell her I'm sorry, and she only has to let me know if she ever needs help. There won't be any strings, either. You got that?"

"I'll give her the message," Cole said stiffly.

"Don't do me any favors."

The sarcasm was potent. Cole calmed down. "I just put my mother in the hospital with a near heart attack," he said impatiently. "My brother's run off to Paris, leaving a pregnant girlfriend behind. Katy's half crazy, and the blond ace is eaten up with guilt—dodging me with half a bottle of illegal Russian vodka looking for his service revolver so he can blow his head off the minute I turn my back! I couldn't do you a favor if I wanted to!"

There was a pause. "Ever think about writing a dime novel?" came the dry reply.

Cole laughed in spite of himself. "Go rob a bank. I've got enough on my plate without adding a mob figure with a conscience to it."

"I'm not so bad," Wardell said. "I've never stolen anything from an honest man, and I don't usually kill people. You tell Katy she's in no danger from Danny's pals, either. I took care of that little complication."

"How about Danny's mother?"

"On her way back to Italy. See? No loose ends."

"You're tidy," Cole agreed.

"Pays to be, in my business. She's really okay? I knew he was roughing her up pretty bad. I tried to get her away, but she was too scared of him to come with me. I'm not sorry about what I did to him, either. He'd have killed her one night when he was hopped-up on dope."

"I didn't even know," Cole said heavily.

"She said you'd go gunning for him if she told you," he replied. "And that he'd probably catch you with your back turned and let his gangsters fill you full of lead." He hesitated. "I guess that flying ace would have done the same."

"In a second," Cole agreed. "He's not usually quite so stupid. But I complicated things by warning him off Katy in the first place."

"Interfering in peoples' lives is stupid."

"As you're certainly qualified to know," Cole shot back.

Cool laughter came over the line. "Yeah. Right. Too bad Katy couldn't love me back. I'd make a hell of a brother-in-law."

"I'd spend my life bailing you out of jail, so it's just as well," Cole muttered. He sighed heavily. "Don't worry about Katy. And thank you for keeping her name out of it." He paused. "Is your attorney certain about your chances?"

"This is Chicago," Wardell said, a shrug in his voice.

"If I don't have enough influence, I've got plenty of friends who have. Nobody liked Marlone."

"Katy will recover," Cole told him. "I'm sure of it. If worse comes to worse, she can give a deposition about what happened that night."

There was a stiff hesitation. "I'm the mug who got her into this mess, remember?"

"You're the mug who tried to get her out of Marlone's clutches, too," Cole said imperturbably. "I want to know the outcome of the coroner's inquest."

The silence lengthened. "Okay."

The receiver went down, and Cole hung up.

"Who was it?" Lacy asked gently, standing just in front of him with wide, curious eyes.

"Wardell."

"The gangster?" She gasped.

"He's not so bad. He loved Katy enough to keep her name out of the papers," he added.

"Oh, thank God," she breathed. "Thank God! But, what about him?"

"If I were a betting man," he said, moving closer to her, "I'd stake the ranch and everything else here on Wardell." He chuckled. "You smell sweet," he whispered, bending toward her mouth. "Kiss me."

"Cole!"' she protested at the very public living room. But his lips settled gently on hers, and then not gently at all, and she gave in at once.

They were feverish when the front door slammed; Turk cleared his throat audibly.

Cole let Lacy go and watched her flee, blushing, into the kitchen. He grinned at Turk.

"Better wire Valentino to hold on to his bedsheet," Turk said. He was a little unsteady on his feet.

Cole glared at him. "Get rid of that vodka."

"What vodka?"

"Don't play games." He moved closer. "You can stop worrying about Katy. She won't have to testify. Her name isn't even going to be connected with the case. Her mobster pal has covered it all up. He said he'd go to the chair before he'd ask her to go to bat for him, in fact."

Turk's face darkened. "He'd better stay in Chicago, if he knows what's good for him."

Dark eyebrows arched. "You sound pretty possessive for a man who's determined to die a bachelor."

Turk swayed a little more, feeling the effects of the alcohol. "He can't have Katy. You tell him I said so."

"Sit down before you fall down."

He resisted Cole's efforts to get him to a chair. "I won't. I have to see Katy."

Cole knew the set of his jaw and the fire in those pale eyes. It would take a free-for-all to get his friend out of the house. Much simpler to let him have his way.

"All right," he agreed. "But only for a minute. It's late, and we could all use a good night's sleep. Lacy and Faye are setting the table now for a late supper. I'll see about some black coffee to go with it," he added, with a meaningful stare, before he left Turk at Katy's door.

══ Chapter Sixteen ══

T URK KNOCKED AT KATY'S DOOR, HARDLY WAITING for the murmured reply before he walked in. A small lamp with a lacy cover thrown over it burned softly by the bed; Katy lay under a thick quilt in a lace-trimmed, yellow flannel gown that covered her arms.

Her long hair, which had obviously been washed, was spread on the pillow and she was still very pale, but there was more life in her than there had been when Turk left her earlier in the day.

"How are you?" he asked, his voice faintly slurred.

"I'm all right." Katy, who'd seen her share of intoxicated men, sighed. She stared at him, her eyes lingering on his towering physique, from long, powerful legs to narrow hips and broad shoulders. He had the athletic build of a working cowboy, without an ounce of fat on his tall frame. He still delighted her eyes, even after what she'd been through. But right now, he was more disheveled than usual, the top buttons of his shirt undone over a chest thick with dark brown hair, his thick blond hair drooping onto his forehead. It didn't need much thought to know he'd been at the bottle, even without his pale, bloodshot eyes to tell her, or his unsteady gait. "Oh, Turk! You've been drinking, haven't you?" she asked quietly.

He shrugged. "Plenty of reason."

"It won't help."

"That's what you think." He moved closer, but instead of sitting in the chair beside the bed, he sat down on it, his hip against her thigh.

"Don't!" she whispered, glancing past him at the closed door.

"Why not? Is it too intimate?" he asked, with a mocking smile. "I made you pregnant. Cole knows. He isn't going to be shocked if he sees me sitting on your bed."

"You told Cole?" She closed her eyes, choking on the shame.

"I told him everything," he said heavily. His big hand rested on her belly over the quilt. "My child," he whispered roughly. "That's twice, Katy. Twice!" His voice broke.

His wife had died pregnant. Now Katy had lost a child of his. She could feel his pain.

"I'm sorry, Turk," she said gently, hurting for him.

"You're the one who needs comforting, not me," he said with a harsh breath. "I don't need pity."

"Yes, you do." She held out her arms to him.

He wasn't going to show her any silly weakness, he told himself. But it would be nice to let her hold him, just for a few seconds. With a long, shuddering sigh, he lay his head on her breasts, and she cradled him there, smoothing his thick blond hair, gently caressing him. He felt the wetness in his eyes, but of course, it wasn't tears. He closed them, aware of the chill against his cheek as the wetness dampened them.

Katy felt them against her breast and she held him closer, giving way to her own grief. All she'd ever wanted in her life was in her arms right now, but it gave

her no pleasure to know that he was only in them out of
grief and guilt. He'd sent her away. He hadn't wanted
her.

"I wanted the baby," she whispered involuntarily. "I
wanted him so! When I lost him, I thought I'd never be
able to bear it. I hated Danny!"

His arms slid under her, drawing her closer, and he lay
there, home at last, at peace at last, until his breathing
regulated and there was no longer any wetness in his eyes
or Katy's.

Katy swallowed her anguish at last and stiffened, so
that Turk would get up.

He did, feeling her rejection, seeing pride make her
face rigid, her eyes evasive as she dabbed at tears.

"Your friend Wardell has muzzled the newspapers,"
Turk said quietly, watching the shock on her face. "He
told Cole he'd go to the chair before he'd involve you in
his trial."

"Oh, thank God," she said. "At least Mother's been
spared any more shame on my account." She saw the
anger in Turk's face and grimaced. "He tried to protect
me," Katy said defensively. "He . . . loves me," she
added. She didn't add that it hurt her that she'd taken so
much from Wardell and given back so little.

"You slept with him," he ground out. "You could be
pregnant . . ."

"There was only one time." She stared up at him
bravely. "And he's sterile," she whispered. "He told
me when I lost the baby and couldn't stop crying. He
knew how it felt, he said, not to have a child. He can't
have any, you see."

"And your . . . husband?"

It was difficult to talk about it, but he wasn't quite
sober and he wasn't going to let go until he had it all. She

stared at her pale hands on the colorful quilt. It was a
memory quilt, one Marion Whitehall had made just for
her out of scraps of leftover cloth from dresses she'd
worn, dresses even her grandmother had worn, so that
she looked at the fabric and remembered all the clothing
that went into its creation.

"Danny . . . couldn't, Turk," she said finally. "Only
once or twice, when we were first married. Then he
started using drugs and he wasn't . . . able to. I think that
was why he beat me." She shivered as the fear came
back.

He took her hand in his and held it tight. "I had no
right to ask," he said unsteadily. "God knows, I've been
a rounder." His eyes were solemn as they met hers.
"Since you, I haven't been with any other woman,
Katy," he said slowly, averting his eyes.

She didn't know what to say. Probably the guilt over
what he'd done caused him to become a Puritan. "You
don't have to go that far," she said. "Nobody blames
you for what happened. It was my fault . . ."

"No!" he said softly, frowning. "It isn't because I
felt guilty." His fingers lifted hers to his chest. "Katy,
don't you understand? I don't *want* anyone else."

She colored and her eyes dropped like coals.

"Which could have been better put," he said, with a
heavy sigh. "I'm tipsy, darling."

"I've noticed."

He nibbled on her fingertips. "It's all sordid and
distasteful to you now, because of what happened. But
you'll get over it," he said. "All you need is a little
time."

"Of course I'll get over it." She drew her fingers
away from that disturbing caress. "I think I'll join a
convent."

"No, I can't let you do that. I'd look pretty stupid in a habit."

Her eyebrows lifted curiously.

"Where you go, I go," he said, with quiet determination. "I let you get away once. Never again."

She bit her lower lip. "I can't be intimate with you," she whispered. "I know what Danny made me into, but . . ."

He drew in his breath sharply. "You think because of what he forced you to do that I see you only as a means to satisfy my lust, is that it?" he asked roughly. "My God! Do you really think I'm that low, Katy?"

"You're just a normal man," she said, hedging. "But I'm not a normal woman anymore. What happened in Chicago . . . changed me."

She shivered. He turned her face toward his, made her look at him.

"You wanted the baby."

"Yes," she said uneasily.

His fingertips touched her mouth. "I would have wanted it, too."

"I know."

He hesitated. "I'm thirty years old," he said slowly. "Even older than Cole." He pushed back wisps of hair from her cheek, oddly hesitant. "I would . . . like to have a child." He lifted his eyes to hers and held them. "Wouldn't you?"

Her body stiffened as she read what he was asking. But she couldn't speak.

"I'm fertile," he said quietly. "I must be, to have made you pregnant so easily before." He took a strand of her hair in his big fingers and stared at it. "I think a child would be good for both of us, Katy. It would help to heal the scars."

"I've disgraced the family enough," she began slowly.

His eyes came up. "We'd be married first, naturally," he said quickly. "I wouldn't ask you to give me a child out of wedlock."

Her face went white. Her eyes, in their ghostly oval, shimmered like wet moss. "I can't!"

"Why not?"

Her head rolled sideways on the pillow so that she couldn't see him. "I don't want to have sex."

His eyes closed. "Oh, my God," he groaned.

"I'm sorry." She felt the tears start again. "I'm sorry, sorry! I can't bear it!"

It was because of the trauma of what she'd been through. He knew it. But he didn't know how to cope with it, what to do. The mind was such a complex thing. She might never be able to face intimacy again after the sordid shock of her last experience.

The only thing that gave him hope was that she'd loved him. Love didn't die, even if it had the stuffing pummeled out of it. Love never died. If he were patient, and gentle, and kind, he might kindle it in her slim body again. He might win her.

"It's only been two days," he said softly. "Hardly enough time to recover, to face the future. I'm not asking anything of you now. I'm only making sure you know my intentions. I'll make sure Cole knows them, too," he added grimly. "And he can kick and rave all he likes. This time, he'll not keep me away from you. Not even if he fires me or beats me bloody, I swear it."

She turned back to him slowly, still uncertain and afraid.

"You've loved me so long that it's a way of life for you," he said slowly, and without conceit. "You've buried it, because I said I didn't want it. But I'll find where you've put it, and I'll dig it right back up. Because I do want it, now,'' he added very softly. "I want it with all my heart.''

"I'm dead . . . in here," she whispered, putting her hand over her heart.

"No, you aren't. You're just numb from all the hurt.'' His big hand covered hers, warm and strong, moving it so that he could feel the warm softness of her, the quick beat of her heart. His thumb slowly traced the soft nipple and made it hard. Then he slid his palm over it and cradled it. His eyes met Katy's shocked ones. "Your mind doesn't want that. But your body does. Eventually you'll heal, little one. I can wait until you do. Even for a lifetime."

He put his hand on her cheek and smiled as he bent and touched his lips to her forehead. "It's all right. Your scarlet past doesn't put me off, you know," he said. "I've never told you about mine."

Her eyes searched his curiously.

"You don't know why Cole and I are friends," he said, answering the unasked question. "Why I owe him so much. I'll tell you one day." He got to his feet and stretched hugely, his bloodshot eyes calmer. "I guess Cole's right. I'd better give him the rest of the vodka."

"Why were you drinking?"

His big shoulders lifted and fell. "It hurt me, knowing about the baby," he said simply, no longer hiding his feelings. "I've caused a lot of damage, haven't I, Katy?"

"*I've* caused a lot of damage," she replied. "I have to take the responsibility for what I did, Turk. You can't share it." She took a slow breath. "I broke all the rules. I deserve a little misery."

"I don't think so. Neither does Wardell," he added coldly.

"He loved me," she said sadly. "I felt so guilty." She didn't add that most of her guilt was because the poor man had loved her so desperately—and even at the height of her pleasure she was pretending that he was Turk! She couldn't admit that, though. Not even to Turk.

Turk, on the other hand, could hardly bear the thought of her in another man's arms. He could imagine how Wardell had felt, but did Katy love the mobster? Had she wanted him?

"You were drinking that night, you said . . ." he began, wanting her to tell him that it was the alcohol that had put her in Wardell's arms.

She couldn't look at him. Her face was scarlet. "Yes. And I was so scared of Danny. Wardell was caught in the middle. He wanted nothing to do with Danny, but he was afraid for me."

"I should have married you," he said harshly. "None of this would ever have happened if I'd asked you to stay."

"I didn't have to marry Danny," she said stubbornly. Her eyes glistened. "I deserve what I got," she said huskily, averting her face. "When you break the rules, you pay the price."

"My God," he said heavily. "What a price it is!"

He turned and went to open the door. He didn't look back. Jealousy was eating him alive. "Do you love Wardell?"

She couldn't say that without admitting what she felt for Turk. She kept silent.

He closed the door behind him, and Katy lay staring at it. She gave in to the tears one last time and finally slept.

Lacy cleared away the clean supper things, her mind

on all that had happened. She glanced at Faye, who was pale and quiet. The two of them had done dishes while Cole and Turk checked the livestock.

"Are you all right?" she asked gently.

"Oh, sure!" Faye said, and managed a smile. "I got all the washing done. Good thing it didn't rain!"

"Indeed." Lacy put away her apron. "Have you heard from your father?"

"He came by long enough to see how I was. He doesn't mind about the kid," she said, with a grin. "I guess I'm the scarlet girl, but I don't mind, either."

"Someday people will be less judgmental and more compassionate," Lacy said. "If we ever have a society where there are no hypocrites," she added ruefully. "Meanwhile, you can stay with us."

"Just tonight," Faye said firmly. "Lacy, I want to go to San Antonio," she said quickly. "I can get a job. I can tell people I'm separated or something."

"Are you sure?"

"I'm sure," Faye said. "I can't go on taking care of Papa and pining over Ben. I want to do something with my life."

"Then I'll help you," Lacy said quietly. "I have cousins there. One of them has a shop. Perhaps you could help him."

Faye brightened. "You mean it?"

"I mean it. We'll see later in the week. Right now," she murmured, "we've got enough problems to take care of."

"I know what you mean. Poor Mrs. Whitehall. And poor Katy. I guess she's sad about her husband getting killed."

"I'm sure she is," Lacy lied.

But later, when the house was locked and everyone

else had gone to sleep, Lacy sat quietly by the fire in her bedroom in her long white gown and worried. The soft knock on the door distracted her. She smiled as Cole came in.

"I'm sorry. Did I keep you awake pacing?" she asked.

He shook his head. He was wearing dark pajamas and a thick robe, his hair still a little damp from his bath. "You were too quiet at supper. What's wrong?"

The ways things had changed between them, she felt confident and possessive, especially when she saw the way he was looking at her, with such quiet tenderness. "I think I need loving," she whispered, lifting her arms to him.

He smiled as he bent and lifted her, his lips whispering over hers, as he carried her to bed.

"I think I can oblige you," he whispered back. He put her under the covers and paused just long enough to remove his robe before he joined her on the cold sheets. "God, it's freezing in here!" he burst out.

She curled close to him. "I only laid the fire a few minutes ago. It's just now catching up. Don't you worry, Mr. Whitehall. I'll keep you warm until it's burning properly."

"So that's what wives are for," he teased, searching for her mouth.

She clung to him, smiling under his cool mouth, enjoying the clean smell of his body. Cole was fastidious, unlike some of the men who never seemed to bathe. He deplored untidy personal habits—even his nails were pristine when he wasn't working out on the ranch.

He eased one long, powerful leg between both of hers and rolled her gently onto her back. "You'll freeze if I take your gown off," he whispered.

"I don't care."

"Don't you?" he asked, smiling. He eased it up and slowly touched her body with his lips, loving her immediate response, the tiny sounds she made as he explored her.

"Oh, Cole . . ." she moaned, arching her back to draw his mouth even closer against her breasts as he suckled them.

"You're so soft," he whispered hungrily. "It's like touching my mouth to silk. Do you like this, Lacy?"

"Yes!"

"And this?" He nibbled softly at a hard nipple and felt her go rigid and gasp for breath. But her clinging hands told him what her choked voice couldn't—that it aroused her feverishly.

He found her mouth with his as he moved, one hand opening the buttons on his pajama top and the one on his trousers, pushing away the last barriers between them. But he didn't remove them completely.

"Please," she whispered as he eased between her thighs, and her hands hesitated at his rib cage, wanting so desperately to go around him, under the fabric.

"Lacy . . ." he began, tormented.

"I love you," she said. Her hands trembled as they eased down very slowly to his lean hips, against the scarred flesh with its ridges and taut smoothness. "Please let me," she breathed. Her teeth nibbled at his lips. He was rigid all over, his body helplessly probing as he felt the touch of a woman's hands for the first time in his life on the hard muscles of his buttocks. He cried out, not because she hurt him, but because the pleasure was like a thousand volts of electricity as he felt those soft fingers caressing him.

"You see? It's sweet, isn't it?" she whispered, lifting her hips obediently to the insistent thrust of his. She enveloped him, warmed him, smiling under his hungry mouth as the springs made harsh noises under the fierce motion of his hips, grinding her into the mattress.

She gasped as the sudden stab of pleasure lifted her rhythmically to him. His hands gripped her slender hips and jerked them upward while he pushed feverishly against her, his voice breaking on her name as he drove helplessly for fulfillment. It was too soon . . . he knew it was too soon, but the feel of her hands . . . was killing him!

Lacy loved him this way, out of control and all hers. She drew her hands upward over the front of his thighs, against the secret core of him, and heard him suddenly cry out with anguished pleasure.

The heat and power of his body almost satisfied her at the last, but even then, she didn't mind that it wasn't quite enough. She held him, collapsed on her, his weight precious and dear, while he struggled to breathe.

Her hands smoothed down his long back, uncaring of the scars and burned places that had healed over and now felt oddly like satin. She touched him with wonder at being allowed such a forbidden intimacy.

"I never thought . . . you could bear it," he said unsteadily. "So many scars, Lacy. So terrible!"

"Silly man." She sighed, kissing his throat, his chest. "When I love you so much?"

"Lacy," he whispered, her name almost a prayer.

"Shh." She nudged him onto his side; her hands slowly removed his jacket, then the pajama trousers. He protested at first, but she whispered softly to him, coaxed, until he gave in to her. When he was totally nude, as she was—her gown long since having been tossed to the floor by his impatient hands—she began to pull the covers back in the soft light from the fire.

"No," he protested huskily. "Lacy! God, no!"

His eyes were frightened. It touched her that a man of his courage, his will, could fear just the eyes of the woman he loved.

"You're beautiful, Cole," she whispered. "Let me look at you."

"Lacy!"

She drew her mouth softly over his while her foot finished what her hands had started and edged the covers off onto the end of the bed. "Let me, darling," she whispered into his lips. "Let me see."

His hands clenched fiercely on her arms. He was terrified of how she was going to react. She was a gentle woman. She had no conception of what a burned body looked like, and he desperately didn't want her to see his.

But she was already looking. She pulled free of his protesting hands and slowly sat up, her eyes shy on the blatant maleness of him. His own attention was caught by the firm, soft thrust of her pale breasts with their fiery red crowns, still hard-tipped from his mouth. He let his attention waver as his eyes ran down to her taut waist and flat stomach and the shadow of her womanhood between creamy, soft thighs. He flushed, because the nudity of her body was still new and fascinating.

While he looked, so did she. There were patches where his normally rough, dark skin was white, and ridges from healed wounds. There were places that were red and raw-looking, and missing spots in among the thick hair that shadowed his thighs and stomach and chest. But he wasn't nightmarish. He was very well built

and extremely sexy, and Lacy groaned inwardly only at
the pain he must have felt.

"Roll over," she whispered, lifting her eyes to his. "I
want to see it all."

"My God, Lacy!"

She bent and put her lips boldly against his waist, the
thick hair tickling her nose. She felt him gasp and stiffen,
and when she lifted her head, she saw another helpless
reaction that pleased her shy femininity.

"Please?" she asked softly.

He couldn't refuse her. He rolled over, his eyes closed
in anguish, and let her look.

His back was the worst, she knew. She bent and
slowly began to put her lips against the most obvious
places.

He caught his breath.

"I'm sorry," she said gently. She rested against him,
her soft breasts warm heaven against his cool back. "Did
I hurt you?"

"It doesn't hurt," he managed through his teeth. "It's
just viciously arousing."

"Is it?" She smiled wickedly and did it again, letting
just the tip of her tongue come out as she drew her lips
against the center of his back.

He roared with sweet anguish and rolled over, catching
her hips with strong hands that were bruising in his need.

"Libertine," she whispered, slowly straddling his
hips. She laughed softly at the look on his face. "What's
the matter, cowboy?" she teased. "Are you too old-
fashioned to do it like this?"

"Yes, I'm too old-fashioned to do it like this," he
agreed, and abruptly caught her by the thighs and turned
her under him in one smooth motion. He lowered himself
down, impaling her almost at once, and then poised

above her to watch her expression. "Fairy," he breathed, his eyes moving from her white body to her face in its frame of disheveled dark hair. "You're so beautiful you take my breath away. How can you bear to look at me?"

"I love you," she said, and it was in her voice, in her eyes, her face. She moved slowly, holding his gaze as she lifted her hips to gently advance his possession and gasped at the sudden surge of increased pressure that heralded his response.

"Surprised?" he asked softly. "You don't know much about men even now." He eased down, shifting slowly from side to side. She made a sound he'd never drawn from her before, and he nodded even through his own raging excitement. "Now it begins," he whispered, bending to stay her mouth with his. His teeth caught her lower lip as he continued the movement of his hips and felt her begin to convulse. "Now it begins, Lacy," he whispered. "Now. Now. Oh . . . God, now!" He felt her completion, felt it in every cell of his body, heard the pitiful cries that tore out of her throat and came into his mouth with her jerking breaths. But he didn't stop, even when she relaxed suddenly and gasped for breath. Turk had told him once that a woman's body was capable of endless pleasure. It must be so, because it only took a minute before his slow movements kindled her again, before her legs entwined with his and her hips began to lift to meet him.

In the long, exquisite minutes that followed, it delighted him that he could give her such pleasure. He kept on until he was all but exhausted, finally giving in to his body's need in one rough thrust that, incredibly, sent Lacy convulsing again as well. The harsh slam of one of the wide wooden slats falling out from under the box springs made them both jump, and then laugh.

Later, when he could breathe, he lay with her cheek pillowed on his chest. He wondered at the newness of lying naked in her arms, his body open and vulnerable in the keen orange light echoing from the fireplace.

"Even Turk hasn't seen you like this, has he?" she asked drowsily, smiling as her hand lay flat and possessively just below his waist.

He stirred, aroused even after the long interlude at just the touch of her fingers. He chuckled. "No, he hasn't. Stop. You're much too fragile for another loving like the one we just shared."

"I know," she moaned. Her lips pressed against him through the thick hair. "Did you ever used to think it would be like this if we made love?" she asked.

"Before the war I did," he confessed. "After I crashed no. I couldn't allow myself to think about it. I had nightmares about your reaction."

She laughed wickedly. "I'll bet you won't have them again."

His arms contracted hungrily. "I worship the ground you walk on," he said. "My God, Lacy!"

She curled into him, snuggling even closer. "One of the slats fell out just at the last," she said shyly. "We were in too much of a hurry to move the mattress onto the floor. I hope we didn't wake anybody up."

He sighed. "I'm just glad it isn't summer," he said ruefully.

She flushed. "I'm noisy."

He bit at her mouth ardently. "I don't care. I meant the slats, not those exciting little sounds you make when we slide against each other."

Her mouth captured his and she moaned.

"We can't," he breathed into her lips. "It would hurt you now."

"I love you so," she managed. "Cole, I love you so!"

She trembled all over with the force of it. Gently, with quiet resignation, he drew her onto her side and, gazing into her eyes, slowly brought her against him in intimacy. She gasped as she felt the soft penetration and her body went rigid.

"Only this," he whispered. "We can sleep this way, if you like. But your body won't enjoy anything more."

She swallowed. This kind of intimacy was unexpected, and incredibly satisfying. She looked down, her eyes wide and curious. He looked, too, and drew back just a breath, to let her experience the total reality of how fully they were locked together.

She made a soft sound and her eyes lifted to meet his.

"This is a miracle, isn't it?" he asked gently. "Male and female, so perfectly made to fit together in pleasure. It awes me."

"And me," she agreed. She moved closer between his powerful legs, shivering as she felt the depth of his possession. Then she relaxed, her arms around him.

His chest rose and fell slowly. "Lacy," he said softly.

"Yes, Cole?"

His big, lean hands tenderly pushed against her back. "I love you," he said heavily.

Her body trembled. It was the first time he'd ever said it to her. It was probably, she realized, the first time he'd ever said it to anyone in his life outside his family.

"Don't cry," he whispered.

"Don't you know you've given me the world?" she asked brokenly. She clung to him. "You're my life."

"You're mine." His hands slid down to her hips and pulled, ever so gently.

And the contractions exploded at once, tenderly, racking them both in a hot sweetness that was unexpected and altogether impossible. Except that it wasn't.

When the spasms passed, they laughed.

"That couldn't have happened," he whispered deeply. "We imagined it."

"No, we didn't." She nuzzled her face into his throat. "No, don't pull away. I want to be part of you all night."

He shivered. "It's frightening," he said unsteadily, "to love like this."

"Oh, yes," she agreed, but when she closed her eyes, she was smiling.

By the time they woke, the bedroom was cold and they were lying in each other's arms with the bedclothes covering them.

"It's morning," Cole whispered, kissing her awake.

"Yes." She smiled, moving, and groaned. "Oh, Cole!" she said, grimacing.

"Sore?"

She flushed. "Yes!"

He laughed delightedly. "Stay in bed for a while. I'll have breakfast with the boys this morning."

"No, you won't," she teased. "I won't share you."

He smiled at her and started to get up. Then he hesitated. Her eyes were faintly chiding. He frowned, but he got out of bed without trying to grab for his pajamas first.

She sat up, her pretty breasts bare, and looked at him blatantly. There was no revulsion in her eyes, no hint of distaste. She could see him fully in daylight, see the damage that had been done to him. It wasn't half as bad as he thought, though, she decided. And they were honorable scars. But it wasn't the scars that were most noticeable, and she flushed a little.

"Is that because of me?" she asked, her eyes curious and a little shy.

He smiled ruefully. "Mostly. Although men usually wake up like this."

She lay back, stretching lazily. "I'll remember that when I'm back in shape again."

"There's nothing wrong with your shape," he said possessively, with bold, warm eyes. "God, I've got to get out of here!" he groaned.

"I'm sorry."

"Honey, I'm too uncomfortable to do anything about it myself, if it helps," he confessed while he pulled his pajamas and robe back on. He paused by the bed long enough to whip off the covers and stare down at her with hungry possession. "You're mine," he said huskily. "My own beautiful fairy."

She lifted her face for his kiss and smiled when his hands swept down to cup her breasts and he groaned.

"Go to work," she teased.

He laid her back down and threw the quilt over her. "Bent double and groaning," he agreed. "I'm sure I'll get a lot done."

"Cole?"

He paused at the door and smiled at her, looking rakish with his night's growth of beard and his thick dark hair over one eyebrow. "What?"

"It doesn't last, does it?" she said slowly.

He frowned slightly. "What doesn't honey?"

"I'm all used up, and I still want you," she explained. "And after last night . . ." She blushed in spite of herself.

He smiled gently. "Yes."

"I love you," she murmured.

"I love *you*," he replied, and it was in every syllable. "Want me to lay a fire before I go?"

"No, thank you. I'll get up and make you some breakfast. I . . . don't want to share you with the men this morning . . ." she began slowly.

He threw back the covers and lifted her in his arms to kiss her warmly, hungrily. "I don't want to leave you, either," he whispered roughly. He clasped her close. "I don't want you out of my sight!"

She clung to him, so happy that she didn't know how she was going to stand it all. Cole loved her. She knew she'd never want anything more than that. If only there could have been a child, she thought, promising herself that she'd never let him see her one glimmer of sadness in a perfect marriage. This, she told herself, would be enough. She couldn't ask for more when she had everything.

Chapter Seventeen

MARION WAS ALLOWED HOME FROM THE HOSPITAL A few days later, and she seemed stronger than she ever had. Knowledge of Katy's remarkable recovery had helped, she confessed, and having Katy come to see her had been the final balm.

Katy was slowly getting over the shock of her ordeal, and she was a different Katy now. She was quiet and not at all bubbly. She sat and crocheted and seemed sometimes a little disoriented.

Turk didn't press her. He stayed close to home. There were no more trips to town on Saturday night, and no more drinking. He didn't make passes at Katy or even touch her. He did occasionally sit and watch her crochet lace edgings for pillowcases, but his company was pleasant and nondemanding. She began to relax, especially when Lieutenant Higgins phoned Cole to tell him that all charges against Blake Wardell had been dropped, that the incident had been labeled self-defense, and that Katy would never have to become involved in its aftermath. Cole mentioned it. Katy was quietly pleased. Turk went out and drank himself senseless without a word, barely able to lift his head the next morning.

Cole watched his foreman's behavior with more concern than anger. He couldn't make Turk talk about what was worrying him, but he imagined it had a lot to do with Katy's involvement with Wardell. Whether it was jealousy or outraged morality, Cole didn't know. For the first time, his foreman refused to talk about his problems to his best friend.

Meanwhile Cole was finding himself at the end of some goodnatured teasing from family, cowhands, and friends over his helpless delight in his radiant wife. When he had to leave her to go to work, Taggart and Cherry wailed for him, bringing a reluctant grin to his hard face. He kissed Lacy coming and going, and their life together was complete and satisfying. It disturbed him that he wouldn't be able to make her pregnant, but she seemed to accept the fact with good grace.

The only cloud on their horizon was the worsening agricultural situation. Cattle prices were beginning a downward swing, and Cole was becoming more and more hard-pressed to find enough capital to keep things going. While the price of feeder steers had fallen over twenty dollars a head in the past three years, the cost of feeding them out was rising steadily. Cole had told her that he could expect—on his best day—to make a five-dollar profit from each steer he sold, if conditions didn't worsen. But conditions had. Farm equipment had to be replaced, seed and fertilizer had to be bought so that grain could be raised to feed the cattle over the winter. Calving sheds had to be built, fences had to be fixed, cowhands had to be paid. And all his expenses had to come out of the money he earned. A nearby ranch had already gone up for grabs at public auction. Lacy worried about their own situation. She could bail him out if worse came to worse. But she didn't like to think of the effect that would have on his pride. She prayed that he'd be able to find a way out on his own.

Faye went to work for Lacy's cousin and his wife at their dress shop in San Antonio. A letter had come from Ben before she'd left. He'd apologized for the things he'd said and done, and begged Faye's forgiveness. He would, he offered, come home and marry her if she wanted him to, so that his child would have a name.

But to everyone's astonishment, Faye had refused. She'd told Lacy to write him back that she was fine without him. Her eyes had twinkled as she thought about her new independence from her father's drunken binges, her poverty. As a shopgirl, she'd have a wage, and she was invited to live with her employers, who had a spare room. Her life was coming up bright and beautiful, and she wasn't going to spend it mourning Ben. She said so, patting her stomach. He could see the baby when it came, she'd conceded, but it belonged to her.

Lacy was proud of her. Faye had been a brick when they needed help during Marion's stay in the hospital and through Katy's ordeal. They'd never forget her. Lacy and Cole went with her to San Antonio the day she left and saw her installed in Mrs. Ruby Morrow's front bedroom. Miles Morrow was Lacy's first cousin. He and his wife were older people, and they were delighted to have Faye's help. They were good people, the kind who opened their doors to anyone in need or trouble. They promised they'd look after Faye, and the girl was radiant. They even promised to teach her to read and write.

Lacy paused just long enough to see her settled before she and Cole left.

He was silent and a little angry, because Ruby had mentioned seeing George. He remembered the man from Lacy's party the night he'd asked her to come back. They were almost to Spanish Flats before Lacy finally determined what was wrong with him.

"George is only a vague memory," she told Cole. "I only said he meant something to me to make you jealous. Heaven knows, you couldn't find a single reason to be jealous of him now." She leaned closer, laughing. "I wouldn't have the energy!"

He laughed, too, the anger forgotten as he clasped her close against his side and slowed the Model T long enough to bend and kiss her cool lips. "All right. I don't like remembering how it was when you left me, that's all. So much time wasted!" His expression was eloquent as he looked at her. It was late afternoon, cold as snow, and the dirt road was deserted when he paused in the middle of it. "If only I'd known more about women, you might never have gone."

"I'm very glad you don't know much about women," she assured him, her eyes adoring. "We were both innocent. That's precious to me, Cole. More precious perhaps than you realize."

He sighed. "For what it's worth, I'm glad, too," he said, searching her soft eyes. "Have I told you that I love you today?"

"Several times." She lifted her lips to his. "Have I told you today?"

"Say it again, anyway," he whispered as he covered her mouth with his and inhaled her husky whisper.

The sound of an approaching car didn't reach them until its horn sounded. They sprung apart to find Ira Cameron *putting* around them, a grin on his broad face.

"That's what I like to see, married people who act happy about being married," he called, raising his hand.

He asked about Faye, and they told him that she was

settled and happy, that everything was going to work out.

"I'll miss her," Ira said quietly. "But I'll never forget what you and Lacy have done for her, Cole."

"She'll be fine, Ira," Lacy assured him. "We're going to bring her home for Christmas. You can come, too. There's always plenty of Christmas dinner."

"Well, that's mighty kind of you," Ira said, "but I might go see my brother in Houston—and let Faye enjoy being on her own this year." He smiled, his eyes a little bloodshot. But amazingly he was sober. "She said she won't marry Ben."

"She may change her mind," Cole told him. "Ben's learned a hard lesson. He's growing up."

"He's lucky he can. War killed a lot of boys not much older than him."

"Amen," Cole said grimly.

Ira put the car back in gear. "I'll go along. Nice seeing you."

He threw up his hand and careened off down the road. Cole turned back to Lacy, hesitated, and with a laugh pulled her close to kiss her all over again.

Ben picked up the letter from home at the front desk of his Paris hotel. He sat down heavily on the bed in his small room. It creaked noisely, but he barely heard it. Lacy's letter was full of news, but foremost was the information that Faye didn't want to get married, thank you. She'd raise her child alone. Furthermore she had a job now and a life of her own, away from her alcoholic parent. She was radiant, Lacy said apologetically, and enjoying her freedom.

He let the letter slip from his hands. So it was going to be like that. He'd hurt her so badly that she no longer wanted him. Perhaps he deserved it, but he felt as if he'd been mule-kicked.

His head dropped into his hands. Poor little Faye, all alone and pregnant. He'd done her wrong. Really wrong.

The door opened without a knock, and he looked up to see the tenant next door with a bottle of wine and a tin of biscuits. She was redheaded and very Parisian. He liked her, but she didn't really fill the soft spot he had for Faye, even if she was very good in bed.

"Que voulez vous, chéri?" she asked, smiling wicked. "Vin, déjeuner, ou moi?"

He shrugged. "Je ne sais pas," he murmured weakly. "Cette lettre est très triste. C'est de ma famille."

"Pauvre garçon," she said, coming to sit beside him. "Venez, mon brave. Je tu console."

He drew back, his mind full of Faye. But the redhead slowly unbuttoned her blouse and tugged it off, smiling invitingly. She had big, firm breasts with enormous pink nipples. They were hard now, and Ben bent toward them with a long sigh. At his age, he told himself, consolation shouldn't be underrated. He opened his mouth and heard the redhead begin to moan. At least he hadn't lost his touch. He slid between her soft thighs and, moving aside only the necessary things, he plunged into her with sheer desperation. She accommodated him easily and without fuss, her body adjusting to his weight as the bedsprings began to protest noisily, drowning out her heated cries and his harsh groan. It was nothing like the tenderness he'd shared with Faye, and that was a good thing. He couldn't bear to think about her at all. On the floor, the letter lay as white as the snow drifting down on the Arc de Triomphe further along the street.

*   *   *

Christmas promised to be the best ever at the ranch. Despite the lack of money, Lacy and Katy made hand-crafted gifts for friends and neighbors and spent days in the kitchen cooking.

"You look so much better," Lacy told her sister-in-law affectionately.

"I suppose I'm not dwelling on it as much," Katy replied. She was wearing a very simple blue dress and no makeup; her hair was in a long ponytail. She seemed younger than ever, and less brittle. "I won't ever forget. I don't think I should. Danny's death taught me a tragic lesson."

"I'm glad you came home," the older woman said gently. "We missed you. Even Turk wasn't quite the same."

Katy sighed ruefully. "Turk feels guilty about the baby," she said quietly. She knew that Cole had told Lacy, although for Marion's sake, he'd made sure that none of the neighbors knew. He'd spared his mother and Katy the gossip and unpleasantness of public censure. And at home, too, there were no recriminations for Katy. Everyone felt that she'd suffered enough. "That's all it is. He's around quite a lot lately, but it's all very correct and formal."

"Because he knows you aren't ready for anything more," Lacy stressed. "He'll wait until you are."

"What if I never am?" Katy's green eyes were sad, stormy. "You don't know what happened, do you? Even as close as you are, Cole wouldn't have told you."

"It's no one's business but yours," Lacy said, smiling gently. "You know we love you."

"That's all that's kept me sane." Katy put down her drying cloth with a sigh as she finished the last bit of silverware. "It seems like a bad dream, sometimes, until

I remember. Danny's eyes were open, Lacy. Staring straight at me. So much blood . . .'' She shivered.

"He hurt you," Lacy said shortly. "A man who beats a woman deserves whatever he gets!''

Katy grimaced. "Maybe so. But I feel as if I caused it. I was with Wardell and Danny saw us, Lacy,'' she told her, her face shamed as she watched shock tauten the other woman's face. Lacy liked to think that she was modern, but she really wasn't.

"Oh . . . my,'' Lacy said hesitantly.

"There's never been anybody but Cole for you, has there?'' Katy asked, noticing the uncomfortable expression on Lacy's face. "That's the way it should be. But I couldn't have Turk, and Danny wanted to marry me. I took the coward's way out. It was terrible,'' she said, swallowing as she remembered. "I never knew men could be so violent, so cruel. If it hadn't been for Wardell, I think Danny might have actually killed me!''

"This man Wardell,'' Lacy said, absorbing the shock slowly, "he cared about you?''

"Oh, yes.'' She lowered her eyes. "Wardell loved me. I was drunk—and Danny'd made sure I knew that Wardell's business was more important than my prudishness, that I was to do whatever Wardell wanted or . . .'' She shuddered. "Wardell reminded me so much of Turk at first. I could have loved him, Lacy. He cared so much about me; he was good to me. It's easy to love someone like that. Wardell wanted to get me away from Danny, but I was afraid Danny might kill him.''

"That's why you wouldn't tell Cole, either, wasn't it?''

Katy nodded, her green eyes dull. "I didn't want anyone hurt because of me. I'm glad Blake won't go to prison. He was kind. He would have protected me if I'd left Danny, and asked for nothing. He didn't force me,'' she added, concerned that Lacy might think he had. ''I agreed. It wasn't all fear of Danny, though. You see, Wardell is . . . very special. Like . . . Turk,'' she said falteringly.

''You've never stopped loving our Turk, really, have you?'' Lacy asked, her eyes intent on Katy's pale face.

''I can't. He doesn't know,'' she added, averting her face. ''I've got just enough pride left to keep my distance from him. He's very upset about the baby—and about what happened to me—but that isn't love, Lacy. That's pity. I'd rather have nothing than that. And he's disgusted about Blake as well. I saw how he looked at me every time Blake's name was mentioned.'' She gnawed her lower lip. ''He holds me in contempt for that night. He probably thinks I've got Danny's death on my soul because of it.''

''Turk isn't like that,'' Lacy chided gently. ''He cares about you.''

''Not the way I want him to.'' Katy shifted restlessly. ''Oh, Lacy, my life is in pieces! Perhaps I should have gone to Blake. At least he loved me. He tried so hard to protect me.''

''I'm afraid he's still trying,'' Lacy murmured, peeking out the doorway to make sure no one was listening. ''He talks to Cole quite often, checking on you.''

Katy caught her breath. She knew the mobster had been acquitted, and she was fiercely glad. Despite the fact that her heart was forever Turk's, she was never going to be able to fully forget the pleasure she'd known in Wardell's arms that long night. A tiny part of her would always belong to him despite—her feelings for Turk.

''He's all right?'' Katy asked in spite of herself.

"Quite all right. He's opened a legitimate business and divested himself of his gambling interests," she said. "And he's made some very firm veiled threats about what he'll do to the 'blond ace' if he doesn't make you happy!"

Katy twisted her wedding ring nervously. She'd left it on her finger out of guilt and remorse over Danny's death.

"I'm glad he's going straight. He's a good man, in his way." She looked up. "He wouldn't really hurt Turk," she added. "He's not that kind of man."

Lacy had never seen a mobster except for Danny. She was curious. "What does Mr. Wardell look like?" she asked.

Katy smiled at the curiosity despite herself. "He's forty-one," she told Lacy. "Very big and dark and masculine, nice-mannered and kind. He's wealthy, too. But he's so alone, Lacy. He never seemed to belong anywhere. People respected him in Chicago, but they were afraid of him, too. He was always alone. Even his men kept their distance."

"That's sad."

"I might have died but for him," Katy said, staring out the window. "Danny had gone out after he hit me. He hardly even stopped long enough to make sure I wasn't dead. When I miscarried, he wasn't home. His mother was out; there was no one. Then Blake came by looking for me. He got me to the hospital, sat with me. He took me home when it was time, and brought roses with him to cheer up my room. Danny didn't come home for days. He didn't seem to understand about my losing the baby, or even to care. But Blake did."

Lacy was touched. "I'm glad he cared enough to look out for you."

"I wish I could have cared for him," Katy replied. "It's so hopeless, Lacy. I can't bear to be touched."

"Give yourself time."

"Perhaps I should go back to Chicago," Katy said, thinking aloud. "It would be better for Turk. It torments him to see me every day. He's changed so. . . Haven't you noticed? That's my fault, too. He isn't happy. He can hardly bear to look at me."

Lacy stared at her. "Do you love him, Katy?"

"With all my heart," she whispered. "But since Danny got killed I feel dead inside. I'm frozen up."

"I can understand that," the other woman said sympathetically. "But you aren't giving Turk credit for his own feelings. It isn't guilt that makes him sit and stare at you every evening, or pity that keeps him on the ranch when the other men go to town to carouse."

Katy flushed. "Isn't it?"

"I think I know how a man looks when he's in love," Lacy said, smiling wistfully.

Grateful for the change of subject, Katy smiled. "It's hard to miss, all right," she agreed. "If anyone had told me ten years ago that my big brother would lounge around like a lovesick bull over any woman, I'd have laughed. He's a case!"

"So am I." Lacy sighed. "I never dreamed of so much happiness!"

"I'm glad for both of you," Katy said. "I'll never forget how you looked the day Cole went off to war. You're lucky to be so happy in love. I seem doomed to the reverse."

Lacy took off her apron and moved away from the sink. "Christmas is just around the corner," she told Katy. "We have to finish making the decorations for the tree. That should keep you from feeling so morose."

"Turk wants to take me to a movie," Katy said, her green eyes troubled as she looked at Lacy. "I don't know if it's a good idea."

"Of course it is." She took Katy's hands in hers. "Try to remember how you felt about him before all this came up. I remember watching you sit and just look at him when he was working with your heart in your eyes. That much feeling can't be totally lost."

"Just buried," Katy murmured, and flushed, remembering what Turk had said about digging it back up again. But lately he hadn't said anything personal, which was why she felt so depressed. Perhaps he didn't want a deeper relationship, after all—now that he knew about Wardell. Perhaps he didn't want to soil his hands with her . . .

"Stop dwelling on it, dear," Lacy chided gently. "Come. Let's do some more decorations. You know, Marion gets better every day. I can't help but think the doctor may be wrong about her condition."

"And miracles happen," Katy said in agreement. She smiled. "I love the way she's rallying. I pray that she'll recover completely."

"That could happen," Lacy said. She smiled, too—because she knew all about miracles. That Cole loved her was her biggest one.

She went looking for him later that night and found him sitting in the study with ledgers spread out in front of him, his head in his hands.

"Are you all right?" she asked hesitantly.

He lifted his head. His eyes kindled with warmth—as they always did when he looked at her now. He smiled and leaned back, holding out his arm.

She went to him and allowed herself to be drawn down onto his lap. "Money troubles again?" she asked.

"Business as usual, I'm afraid," he replied. He drew her close and held her quietly for a long moment before he spoke. "I may have to default on the next mortgage payment," he said finally. "I don't think I can meet it."

"Oh, Cole," she said worriedly.

"Grain prices have gone right through the roof. I had to buy it this time for the first time in memory, because I overstocked when cattle prices were low. Now I've got to sell off cattle or feed them through the winter. Either way, I'm going in the hole."

"I'm not poor, you know." He started to speak very angrily, and she put her hand over his hard mouth to still the words. "No," she whispered. She bent and replaced her hand with her lips. A few seconds of that, and he forgot about being angry. In fact, he forgot everything in the heat of the sudden passion, his arms bruising and possessive, like the mouth that became instantly demanding on hers.

"Let's go to bed," she whispered softly, her eyes teasing and bright.

He glanced at the books and then back at her mouth. With a delighted laugh, he helped her up and followed her out of the room.

Two days before Christmas, Cole was forced to go to see Mr. Harkness at the bank. He explained his difficulties. The banker was sympathetic, but inflexible.

"You know I'd like to loan you the money, Cole," he said honestly. "But it just isn't good business to help you overextend even more."

"Damn it, man. I could lose the ranch!"

"I know that, too." Harkness leaned forward. "Can't you sell off some cattle, keep going that way?"

Cole grimaced. "Yes, I can. But I'll take a hell of a loss. You know what prices are. I overstocked earlier in the year because all the experts said that prices would go up. They didn't. Now I've got too many head and not enough feed."

"Everyone's having problems," the banker agreed. "It's the times we live in, Cole. War boosts the economy, but only temporarily. Then it plunges again. It's all going downhill now, like a runaway train. All this borrowing without adequate capital to back it up— I tell you, we're in for worse times than these. You can't live on credit."

"I'm finding that out," Cole said uncomfortably. He stood up. It had been a long time since he'd felt quite so desperate.

Harkness stood, too, looking very young and helpless. "I'm sorry. That sounds trite, I know. But I really am. My father lost his home in Houston this year because the bank foreclosed there," he added slowly. "I know how it feels, if it helps."

Cole lost a little of his bitterness. He managed a smile. "Thank you. It does, a bit."

They shook hands. "If you could manage anything for collateral . . ." the banker add.

"All that's left is the car," Cole said. "I can't mortgage that. We need it too badly."

The other man shifted uncomfortably and lifted his hands. "Times are hard."

"Getting harder daily." Cole nodded.

He left the bank and stood out on the street, his hands in his trouser pockets, his eyes wandering up and down the dirt road where a few cars were moving through town. Progress, he thought. In the old days, his father

would have held the banker at gunpoint until he got his
money. Civilization made it tough. Words, not bullets,
dominated the modern world.

He could hold up a train, he supposed. He laughed at
the thought. He could see Lacy's expression if she had to
bail him out of jail. No, he'd have to come up with
something . . .

His eyes narrowed as a thought occurred. He had a
banker, and he'd only just now realized it. He could
borrow, with interest, from someone he knew quite well
by now. Yes, he could!

═══ Chapter Eighteen ═══

FAYE SETTLED DOWN TO HER NEW JOB WITH A SENSE
of freedom that she'd never had in her young life. It
was like being in another world. She didn't have an
alcoholic father to worry over and look after. She didn't
have day-to-day poverty and the endless drudgery of
housework. Even the nausea of pregnancy didn't bother
her. She worked long hours in the dress shop with Lacy's
cousins, and she never complained about that or the
relatively low salary she got. Her wage included bed and
board, which was nothing to sneeze at. She had Sunday
off, and she went to church with the Morrows, who
treated her much more like a loved relative than like a
boarder.

Now and again she thought about Ben with real regret.
If she'd been older and less impressionable, perhaps the
experience might have been avoided. As it was, she still
cared deeply for him, but not enough to try and force him
into a relationship he didn't really want. She'd have her
baby all by herself and take care of it. At least Lacy and
Cole were proud of the new addition to the Whitehall
family, despite the fact that it would be illegitimate.

There were people who would ostracize her when they
knew about her circumstances. That was to be expected.
But there were also people who would be more open-

minded. In the city, attitudes weren't quite as rigid as
they were in small communities. Lacy herself had
allowed dancing and jazz in her home, while some
members of society considered both the devil's prov-
ince.

Since the one letter Ben had written to Cole, apolo-
gizing for the can of worms he'd opened, there had been
no communication at all. Faye wasn't surprised. She
imagined Ben was having the time of his life in Paris,
probably romancing every girl in sight and mingling with
the avant-garde of the literary world. He would be, Faye
decided, the perfect addition to the expatriated Americans overseas.

Meanwhile she was getting an education. Ruby Morrow had begun to teach her to read and write. An apt
pupil, Faye absorbed knowledge like a sponge, interested
in everything that was offered. In no time, she was
assured, she'd be as literate as anyone else in the city.
Faye wasn't sure of that, but it flattered her to think so.

Lacy wrote to her and invited her home for Christmas.
Faye decided not to go, though, since her father had
elected to visit his only brother in Houston for the
holidays.

"Faye isn't coming," Lacy told Cole, sitting down
beside him on the porch steps while he repaired a bridle.

"Why?" he asked absently.

She pulled her coat closer, nuzzling her face down into
the warm fur collar. "She says Ira is spending the
holidays with his brother, and my cousin has invited her
to Christmas dinner." She looked up, worried. "Do you
think she's all right?"

He smiled. "Lacy, she's enjoying her independence.
Let her alone. I imagine it's all exciting to her."

"I guess you're right." She folded the letter neatly

and put it back in the envelope. Her eyes went to the bare horizon, which was clouding up. "Will it rain?"

"Probably." He glanced at her. "I'll cut you a Christmas tree this afternoon."

She smiled and laid her head against his thick coat. "You're a nice man. I think that's why I married you."

"You married me because young Ben locked us in a line cabin together," he said wickedly, bending to nibble softly at her mouth. "Did we thank him?"

"You were much too busy calling him foul names, as I recall," she whispered, kissing him gently on the lips.

"I should have used that night to better advantage." He chuckled.

"You wicked man," she said accusingly. "We weren't married!"

He brushed a loose strand of hair away from her eyes. "We are now," he said. "Our first real Christmas together, Lacy," he added softly. "I hope you like what I got you."

"Oh, Cole. You didn't get anything expensive?" she asked. "Not when you're in such financial trouble!"

"It's something you'll like. Nothing extravagant, I promise," he said. He rubbed his nose against hers. "And I'll work out my finances. I've got something in mind."

"Have you?" she asked, excited. "What?"

"My secret, for now," he said, because he wasn't sure that she—or anyone else at Spanish Flats—would approve of what he planned to do. He was meeting a gentleman in town at the end of next week to discuss those plans. If they worked out, his financial woes were over. But he didn't dare tell Lacy what he was up to.

"You're very secretive," she accused.

He kissed her gently and got to his feet. "That's

nothing new," he replied, grinning. "Don't stay out here and get cold."

"I won't."

She watched him stride off toward the barn with warm, possessive eyes. Turk noticed as he came riding up, dismounting with lazy grace at the front steps.

"Still swooning over him, I see," he drawled, doffing his stained black Stetson as he came up the steps. He looked older these days, and leaner than ever. His batwing chaps flapped as he moved, his spurs jingled, but the only cheer was in those sounds. His pale eyes were haunted.

"I think it's mutual," she said, amused. "What are you doing home in the middle of the day? I thought you were helping mend fences."

"I was. I remembered that I'd promised Katy a movie today. It's Saturday."

"Yes, I know."

Turk waited until she got up from her seat on the steps before he spoke. He hesitated, his pale eyes narrow and curious. "That gambler in Chicago . . . Does she talk about him?"

She studied him intently. "It's natural that she would, Turk," she said quietly. "He was the only friend she had."

"I suppose so."

"She'll forget one day," she said helplessly. "It's just going to take time."

"She still has nightmares," he replied quietly.

"Considering how Danny died, it's not surprising. You used to have them, Cole said. Didn't yours go away eventually?" she asked daringly.

He drew in a heavy breath. "Eventually. It took a long time."

"Katy's will go away, too. A movie will do her good."

"I hope so." He went inside, his spurs jingling. He smiled at Marion and waited while Katy finished tying the ribbon in her long hair. She was wearing a sailor outfit with blue stripes and a pert little cap that matched.

"I need to get cleaned up," Turk told her, his eyes slow and bold on her face. "I won't be long."

"All right."

He left, and Katy sat down with Marion. "Are you sure you don't mind if I go, Mama?" Katy asked.

Marion smiled and patted her hand. "Dear, it delights me to see you taking an interest in life. Go with Turk. The entertainment will be good for you. Tell Turk I said take the runabout."

"Thank you, Mama."

The old eyes were loving. "I'm so glad that you're all right, my dear. Those first days at home were difficult ones for all of us. We worried about you so."

"I'm fine. I'm getting better all the time."

"I know. My prayers are being answered."

Katy wished she could say that her own were, but she was still much more upset and confused than the other members of her family realized. She kept it to herself, to spare them. The night with Wardell ate at her. Adultery, murder, drunkenness—she could barely believe she'd done so many wrong things. Of it all, the adultery made her saddest—not because she'd cheated on Danny, but because Wardell loved her. She thought of him often and worried about him. He was, she thought, so terribly alone. He'd never loved anyone until he'd loved her, and she hadn't been able to give him anything. Her body, sympathy, affection were all he'd had. She knew how it felt to possess an empty shell, because her one experience with Turk had been empty like that. He'd made love to her, but he hadn't cared for her, not really. It had been a physical response he'd given her, just as she'd given a physical response to Wardell. Without love, it was bitter and sad. Poor Blake. He'd only wanted her love, and she couldn't give it.

She wondered if she could ever feel it again. Her life had undergone such a radical change in a very short time. It was going to be hard getting back to normal, if she even could. Meanwhile there was Turk. She had no idea what he really wanted with her. He'd said he cared about her, but she didn't trust him. She remembered too well the things he'd told her before she'd left with Danny. Turk still loved his late wife, and he wanted no serious involvement with a woman. He'd said that and meant it, so he couldn't have changed his mind so quickly. He felt sorry for her, guilty about the baby she'd lost, but she'd better remember what he'd said the day she'd left the ranch. She'd better *never* forget it, or she could be in for as much heartache as poor Wardell.

Back in Chicago, Blake Wardell was trying to puzzle out a conundrum of his own. He'd had a letter from Cole Whitehall asking him to come down to San Antonio at the end of the week for a business meeting. He didn't know what Whitehall was up to, but he had a feeling he was about to be offered a partnership. He wasn't going to refuse it, if that was what the other man had in mind. He'd do anything for Katy. That feeling extended to her whole family. Over the weeks since Katy had left Chicago, his frequent conversations with her brother had given him a new knowledge of the man. It would be no hardship to invest in a ranching enterprise. Especially, he thought, with ironic humor, since he seemed to be going

the whole hog in his search for respectability. Katy
would be proud of him. She'd worked hard enough to
make him change his ways.

He put the letter down with a smile. The trip would
give him the opportunity to find out how she was. He
might even get a glimpse of her. The smile faded as he
realized how hungry he was for that small mercy. She
belonged to the blond ace. He'd never had any doubts
about her feeling for her brother's foreman. He couldn't
stop loving her, wanting her. But he had some precious
memories to carry into his old age; they were so good
that he hadn't even had the urge to tarnish them by going
to bed with some other woman. His eyes warmed as
he thought how it had been with Katy that night, how
she'd responded to him with such eager ardor, such
delight. Even if she'd spent the whole time thinking of
another man, it didn't seem to matter. That one memory
of her was all his, and he was going to treasure it until he
died.

The movie Turk took Katy to see was a Valentino one,
Blood and Sand, about a bullfighter's tragic rise and fall.
Katy sat stiffly at his side watching it, and he cursed his
own insensitivity in taking her to a picture that ended in
a bloodbath. To his credit he hadn't known about that
last scene, but now he wished he'd asked somebody
before he'd taken her to see it.

"Come on," he said gently, helping her out of the
theater before she realized what was happening.

Out in daylight again, she winced at the surge of bright
light. Turk walked beside her in silence, his dark suit
looking unfamiliar on his tall frame, the only recogniz-
able attire his boots and Stetson.

"I'm sorry," he said shortly as he took her arm and

led her back toward the runabout. "I never thought about the gore."

She searched for words. "It's all right," she said finally when they'd reached the car. "I didn't, either."

He helped her inside and went through the ritual of cranking the car while she sat uneasily inside.

They were outside town before he spoke again. "I mean it, Katy. I had no idea what the end of the film would be like."

"Could we get out and walk for a little bit?" she asked, glancing toward a path that led off into the trees, just before the dirt road crossed a little stream.

"Sure." He pulled off on the side of the road and cut the engine. Katy took off her hat and left it on the seat, lifting her skirts to keep them out of the grass as she wandered through the mesquite trees to the edge of the stream, then paused, listening to its cold burble as it ran over slick stones. In Chicago, she'd worn short skirts. But here in Spanish Flats, she was trying desperately to attain some measure of respectability again. The length of her dress—briefly in fashion this year—was armor.

Turk lit a cigarette and leaned against a mesquite's thick trunk, his wide-brimmed hat pushed back over his blond hair while he stared at the water.

Katy's eyes slid sideways, lingering on the way his slacks molded his powerful legs, the narrowness of his hips, the broadness of his chest and shoulders. He was perfectly built. For the first time since Danny's death, her mind wandered to the afternoon she'd known him in complete intimacy. Flushing she averted her eyes to the stream.

Turk caught the tail edge of that look and began to hope. So she wasn't completely indifferent to him. Thank God. He'd almost given up hope.

"You said you'd tell me one day," she said.

His heavy blond eyebrows arched. "About what?" he asked, and smiled.

"How you and my brother met."

He knocked an ash off his cigarette. Deep, soft laughter teased his throat. "That wasn't so much a meeting as a confrontation. I was having a hard time of it. I'd come straight from my wife's funeral into the army, been shipped overseas with no time to come to terms with the loss. I drank quite a lot," he said slowly. His eyes narrowed as he looked at the stream. "Cole and I were in the same outfit, both avid fliers. As we began to make names for ourselves, we started competing. Inevitably we got into a fight one day and almost landed each other in the hospital."

"What did you fight about?" Katy asked.

"Damned if I remember," he replied thoughtfully, his pale eyes twinkling with humor. "But it was enough to convince us both that we'd make better friends than enemies. I fought like a wild man in the sky, then drank until I couldn't stand up, remembering how my wife had died, blaming myself for leaving her there alone in her condition." He took a long draw from the cigarette. "One night, I tried to go up in my airplane while I was staggering drunk. I had some noble idea of crashing down on the German barracks at night, you see. Cole stopped me, put me to bed. I got a lecture the next morning about the reverence of life and how I was trying to waste mine. It worked. I pulled myself together."

"You did something similar for Cole, didn't you?" she asked. "Nobody tells me anything, you know—but Lacy sometimes says things without thinking. She said you saved Cole's life once."

"He was no more in control of his faculties than I'd

been," he said. "But what happened is between the two of us. Lacy may know, but only if he's told her. That's his secret, not mine."

She snapped a dead twig from a limb and turned it in her fingers. "He's lucky to have a friend like you."

"That works both ways."

She nodded. Her hair blew gently across her cheek as she lifted her face. "It's cold," she said after a minute, tugging her fur-lined coat closer.

He stared at her, the cigarette forgotten in his fingers. "You've changed," he said. "The light's gone out of you, Katy."

"I've had a rough time," she said, averting her eyes. "The memories won't go away overnight."

"Still mooning over the Chicago mobster?" he asked suddenly, his eyes dangerous.

She went white. With a tiny cry, she turned and started back toward the car, blinded by the sting of wounded tears. She should never have told him about Wardell. He'd never get over it. He'd never let her forget.

He cursed furiously under his breath and threw the cigarette in the stream, going after her with angry strides.

She felt his big hand on her arm before she reached the clearing. He whipped her around, close up against him. His size and strength had never been more evident as he scowled down at her, pale eyes blazing out of a face dark with anger and subdued passion.

"Why don't you go back to Illinois and marry him?" he asked curtly. "Maybe that would turn you back into the girl you were!"

She felt his grip even through the coat. It hadn't been long enough for the memory of Danny's white rages to pass. She felt the pain of his bruising hold and prepared herself subconsciously for the blow that always accompanied Danny's violent grip. She cringed and threw up a protective arm, shaking as she anticipated the beating Danny had accustomed her to.

Her posture brought Turk to his senses. He went very still, his grip relaxing as he realized what she was thinking.

"Oh, my God, Katy," he ground out, dropping her arm. "I'm not going to hit you! How could you think me capable of such a thing? I'm not Marlone!"

She had to fight for composure. It took more than a minute to regain it, and even then she could barely look at him.

His face had gone rigid. "I thought it was only the one time," he said, his voice rough. "When you lost the baby. But it wasn't, was it? He beat you more than once."

"For a while it was every day," she whispered huskily. She wiped at tears, but without looking at him. "The more dope he used, the worse it was. I have . . . marks . . ." She swallowed. "He didn't just use his hands. He used a belt." She lowered her face.

He didn't know what to say, what to do. He was more confused than he'd ever been in his life, about her feelings and his own.

"Wardell tried to stop him, you said," he muttered after a minute, his voice cold as he asked the question.

She lifted her wounded eyes to his. "You really hate it, don't you, Turk?" she asked huskily. "You hate the very thought of Blake Wardell."

His eyes flashed wildly. "I can't help it," he said harshly. "Marlone was your husband. But, Wardell . . ." He cursed, turning away. "It turns my stomach!"

Nothing had ever hurt Katy so much. Her face felt

drawn as the muscles in it went rigid. Turk wasn't going to get over what she'd done. He hated her and Wardell; she . . . repulsed him.

She turned away, moving slowly back to the car. She was soiled goods in his mind, something so low that he didn't want to touch her. That was just as well, because she wasn't sure if she could get past her fear of male strength to ever allow intimacy again. Her reaction to Turk just now had shown her that.

He smoked a cigarette before he went back to the car. He shouldn't have been so violent with her. He'd frightened her all over again, just when she was getting over her experience. He shouldn't have made that crack about Wardell, either, he realized belatedly. His jealousy of the man was getting completely out of hand. It wasn't Katy's fault if she loved the lousy gambler, was it? He had no right to punish her for what she felt. She'd loved him once, and he'd thrown her right out of his life. What did he expect, he wondered with self-loathing, that she'd moon over him as long as she lived and never let any other man touch her?

Katy, unaware of what he was thinking, had taken his contempt at face value and accepted it. Her eyes were staring straight ahead; she was deadly quiet when he came back and cranked the car.

"I'm sorry if I upset you," he said. "Are you all right?"

"I'm perfectly fine, thank you," she said, with eerie calm.

He hesitated, but she wouldn't look at him. He pulled back onto the road and drove home. When she got out at the front steps, she still hadn't spoken.

Two hours later, they found her in the bathroom between her bedroom and Marion's, lying unconscious on the floor, a bottle of sleeping pills spilled beside her disheveled hair.

They were just in time, Cole realized when the doctor came out to speak to them. He felt as sick as Lacy looked. Turk was another matter. The man had gone crazy when he saw Katy lying on the floor. Cole had finally had to hit him to make him turn her loose so they could get her to the doctor. He'd sent Lacy out of the room, in fact, to spare Turk the embarrassment of being seen in that condition, sobbing brokenly over Katy's limp body.

He'd explained it to her while they were waiting at the small clinic to see if Katy was going to survive at all.

"Poor man," she sighed, pressing close to Cole as they waited with cold fear to see what was going to happen. "Cole, if she dies, he'll kill himself," she said huskily.

"I know." His voice was bitter. He could barely speak at all for the lump in his throat. He loved Katy. They all did. He felt somehow responsible, as if he'd put her here by refusing to give in to her obsession with Turk.

Lacy caught his hand and held tight when the doctor came out. But he didn't look solemn. He was smiling wearily.

"She'll be all right. She'll sleep the clock around, of course. She didn't take enough to kill her. You got her here in time."

"Oh, thank God," Cole ground out. "And thank you!"

"It's a pleasure to bring good news to someone for a change. How's Marion?"

"Bearing up," Cole said heavily. "She's seeing her doctor, now—for something to calm her down. Turk's with her."

"We were in school together. She's a fine woman. Your father was a lucky man. Let Katy stay overnight. You can take her home in the morning if she's improved. Good night, now."

"Good night."

"Thank God." Lacy sighed, leaning against his chest. "It was a stroke of genius on your part, making Turk go with Marion."

I don't doubt he'll knock my brains out for it later," he said, "but I couldn't risk Mother as well as Katy."

"I understand. . ."

Booted feet echoed down the hall. They turned to find Turk coming along the narrow corridor with a face like tissue paper.

"Marion's in the car, resting comfortably. Doc says she'll be okay. How is Katy?" he asked, his eyes desperate.

"She's going to sleep the clock around, then we can take her home," Cole said quietly. "She'll be all right."

Turk tried to speak and couldn't. He turned away, not wanting them to see his face. He was shaking so hard with fear, that he could barely stand by himself. He'd never known such terror. He swallowed, and swallowed again, before he leaned against the wall and began to roll a cigarette with fingers that spilled half the tobacco in the process.

"What I don't understand is why she did it," Cole said heavily. "I thought she was getting better."

"It's because of him, that's why she did it," Turk said jerkily. "She loves him."

"She hated Danny," Lacy protested.

"Not Danny." He turned, his eyes blazing out of a white face. "Him! Wardell!"

Lacy stared at him uncomprehendingly. Katy had told her that she still loved Turk. Why did he have the idea that Wardell was responsible for her suicide attempt?

"What did she say to you today?" Cole asked Turk. "She must have said something."

"She said he was kind to her," he replied wearily. "I brought it all back. I lost my temper. I was so damned jealous of Wardell I could hardly see straight—thinking about how she'd known him . . . how *well* she'd known him. I was rough with her, and she cringed. Danny beat her often. She was scared to death of me. She actually expected me to hit her!" He shook his head to clear the glaze in his eyes. "My God, as if I could ever hurt her! *Her*, of all people!"

"Why do you think she loves Wardell?" Lacy asked gently.

"She's unhappy. He was good to her when nobody else gave a damn; of course she loves him." He glared at Cole. "I know you talk to him now and again. Tell him she needs him. Maybe he can keep her from doing . . . *that* . . . again."

He stared toward where the doctor had gone, his face agonized, before he turned and went back down the corridor.

Lacy turned to Cole. "But she doesn't love Wardell," she said. "She loves Turk. She said she'd never stopped, never would. Where did he get the idea that it was Wardell?"

"Maybe she gave it to him," Cole said thoughtfully. "I can't understand why she took the pills, though. Turk cares about her. I've never seen him so torn up."

"Perhaps," Lacy began thoughtfully, "she mistook his jealousy for contempt. She's very sensitive about what happened. Turk might have inadvertently given her the impression that her intimacy with Wardell disgusted him.''

He sucked in a harsh breath. ''Lacy, if that's true, with her self-image so low already, we might not be able to stop her next time. We've got to do something.''

''Could you ask Mr. Wardell to come and see her?'' Lacy asked. ''I don't like hurting Turk or Katy, but he might be the catalyst to bring both of them out in the open about what they really feel.''

He lifted an eyebrow. ''Well, little one . . . as it happens, I think I might just have a way to get Wardell here.''

He didn't add how. But as he began to recover from the trauma of the day, he realized that everything was working to his advantage right now. Even poor Katy's predicament. With luck, he could solve her problem and his own at the same time, and perhaps save her life

══ Chapter Nineteen ══

B EN HAD PRODUCED, PAINSTAKINGLY, THE FIRST chapters of his book. He was amazed at his own skill, at the way the words danced to life on the thick paper in his typewriter. He didn't type well, and it was slow going, but he was making progress.

He ran a hand though his hair and felt the beard on his chin. He'd all but gone without sleep and food during the creative process. Now, finally, he felt he had something to show a publisher. He knew one was in town, visiting Gertrude Stein. He wasn't as avant-garde as the other expatriated American novelists who lived in Paris. In fact, he was rather shockingly conservative in his outlook. But because of President Coolidge, the whole country was turning that way after the wild living and excesses of the postwar years. His book wasn't about breaking the rules. It was about the nobility of living up to them. He smiled excitedly as he thought about the trend toward that sort of thinking, and that he might be riding the very crest of the wave. If he were right, and the pendulum of morality was swinging back again, he could find himself at the top of the literary heap with a very old-line point of view.

His journalistic style had been polished during his brief stint with the Bradleys. He'd suffered—and had also witnessed the suffering—of others because of himself. All that had gone into the book; all his heart and soul had gone into it. It was the best thing he'd ever done. Now all he had to do was convince someone to publish it.

He talked his way into a cocktail party that night and followed Reb Garnett around like a puppy until the publisher finally got tired of ducking him and sat down with resigned irritation to listen to Ben's plot. But the irritation began to mellow into interest, and by the time Ben finished, the man was actually interested.

"You say you worked as a journalist?" Garnett asked.

"That's right."

"You're very young."

"It's a young country right now," Ben argued. "But don't you see everyone's getting sick of permissive living? All for me, nothing for the other man, is a philosophy that has seen its peak. President Coolidge is turning it all around. His fascination with the enduring values upon which society should and could be based has sparked much interest at home." He leaned forward intently. "The least you can do is give me a chance. I'll do anything you ask to help arouse interest in it."

Garnett eyed him for an entire minute while wheels turned in his mind. Hemmingway was making a name for himself, like several others, with characters whose decadent behavior heralded the boredom and alienation of an entire generation. Ben's book was different, dwelling on what was positive about morality. Five years ago, it would have been laughable. Now, it was another form of avant-garde literature.

"All right," he said after a minute. "Let me read the manuscript. I'll consider it."

Ben let out a whoop that temporarily interrupted the flow of conversation. ''Thank you!''

''Wait until you hear the verdict,'' Garnett said warily. ''You may change your mind.''

''Not a chance!''

That night, he sat down and wrote a long letter to Cole, telling about his potential success. He cursed the length of time it would take to get to the ranch even as he sealed it. He'd asked about the others, especially about Faye. Lacy had written that the girl was doing well and that she was in good health. Ben wondered about the child, about how Faye would manage. If he could get a good price for his novel, he could send her some money. Lacy would help her, but it wasn't Lacy's responsibility, it was his. He shouldn't allow a child to suffer for his lapse of control.

He leaned back in his chair, remembering how tenderly he and Faye had loved that long-ago afternoon. He'd never been with any woman the way he'd been with her. He missed her. She probably didn't miss him, he realized. But his life was never going to be complete without her in it.

Impulsively he pulled another sheet of paper toward him and began to write to Faye. Perhaps by now she'd have forgiven him enough to listen to his side of things.

Christmas Day was only a few days off when Cole met a nattily dressed Blake Wardell at the railroad station in San Antonio. He'd told no one where he was going or why; he'd simply taken the old black runabout and driven to the city.

He'd wondered if he was going to recognize Wardell, since he'd never seen the man. Lacy had given him

Katy's description, which helped. But the very posture and dress of the man set him apart. He was wearing a beaver-trimmed overcoat, with an expensive wide-brimmed hat pulled low over his forehead. Uncannily, for a split second he reminded Cole of Turk in his posture and size and the way he held that cigar. Turk smoked cigarettes now, but he'd been fond of cigars when they were in France.

Wardell was older than he'd realized, but still fit-looking, and even out of his element he was vaguely intimidating to passengers disembarking around him.

Cole had worn his best dark suit to the station, with matching boots and Stetson. He didn't want to give the impression of poverty—even if he *was* facing foreclosure.

He moved closer to the stranger and stopped, just staring at him.

Wardell turned. He had large, dark brown eyes, deep set in a face as dark and formidable as Cole's own. He returned the quiet scrutiny, his wide mouth finally cracking in a faint smile.

"You're Whitehall." He nodded.

"Which makes you Wardell."

The older man chuckled. "Aren't you afraid to be seen in public with a hood like me?" he asked, his eyes narrow and challenging. "I'm a bad man."

"That makes two of us," Cole said. "Coffee or booze?" he offered, because he knew where to get both, Prohibition or not.

"Coffee, if I get a choice. I've pretty much given up booze. It's starting to taste of soapsuds."

Cole laughed. "Coffee it is, then."

He led the way to a small cafe nearby and slid into a

booth, waiting to speak until the waitress took their order
and went to fill it.

"How is she?" Wardell asked. He'd taken off his hat,
and he had thick, dark hair sprinkled with gray. He
looked more like a banker than a mobster.

"She's fine . . ." Cole grimaced and ran a hand
through his own dark hair. "Oh, hell! She's not fine. She
took an overdose of pills earlier in the week and damned
near killed herself. All of us are watching her like
hawks."

Wardell went pale. "I was afraid of that," he said. "A
girl like Katy isn't meant for experiences like the one she
had. I'll bet she'd never seen a dead body in her
life—and I put that one in her way. She blames me,
doesn't she?"

"She hasn't said one word against you since she's
been home," Cole said firmly. "She said you were the
only person in Chicago who even tried to help her.
Katy's like me. She never forgets a favor."

Wardell took a deep breath. "Marlone was a dirty
little rat," he muttered. "My God, I hated him!" He
looked up as the young waitress brought coffee, and he
gave her a smile that made her flush. He chuckled,
watching her walk away. "You don't see many girls who
blush where I come from," he told Cole. "That's what
I liked about Katy. I could make her blush without
trying." He fingered his coffee cup. "What are we going
to do about her, Whitehall?"

"Turk isn't lucid," Cole began. "But, he
thinks . . ."

"He's the ace?" Wardell asked, his expression as
belligerent as Turk's was when Wardell's name was
mentioned.

Cole had to smother a grin at the irony. "Turk thinks Katy's missing you," he said. "And that's why she tried to take her life."

Wardell's dark eyes glowed with hunger for a moment before he shrugged his broad shoulders and looked down at his coffee. "No," he said, shaking his head. "I'd give anything to believe it. But I know how Katy feels about me. It's that blond mule she wants. She'd walk through hell to get to him. How can he not know it?"

"He hasn't been himself since she left. He's even worse since she came home. When we took her to the hospital, I had to knock him down to make him let go of her. He hasn't said two words since the doctor released her, but he's terrified to let her out of his sight. She won't even talk to him."

Wardell stared at him quietly. "He loves her that much, does he?" He took a sip of his coffee and leaned back to relight the cigar he'd laid in the ashtray. He studied it for a moment before he spoke. "Katy would have died for him." He looked directly into Cole's eyes. "Love like that doesn't wear out. So what did he say to her that made her think he didn't want her?"

"Nobody knows. Katy won't talk and neither will he. I gather that it had something to do with you. My wife thinks that Lacy's convinced herself that she's too soiled to appeal to him anymore."

"And is that the way *he* thinks?" Wardell asked curtly.

"He's not a hypocrite," Cole said simply. "He's been around."

He drank his coffee in silence. "Was Katy what you wanted to see me about," he asked, "or did you have something else in mind?"

Cole smiled to himself. "You're shrewd."

"That's why I'm rich." His eyes narrowed. "If you're offering me a partnership, I'll bite," he added, anticipating Cole's next question and grinning at the younger man's shock. "I told you I'd gone legit. I own an interest in a grocery wholesale house in Chicago. Part interest in a ranch fits right into my plans. Not that I want to be a working partner," he said firmly. "I'd rather eat a horse than have to ride one."

The younger man chuckled at the thought of this dignified city man on one of his broncs. "Point taken."

"Then let's talk business. Tell me what you're offering."

The discussion took the better part of an hour. At the end of it, Wardell had a working knowledge of the cattle industry and a good idea of what partnership would entail.

"Katy can't ever know," he told Cole quietly.

"Katy never will," he was assured.

What neither of them knew was that Katy had overheard Cole talking to Wardell on the telephone the night before. She'd caught Turk with his back turned and caged a ride into town with one of the neighbors. And although it took her a little while to locate the two men, she did it.

She pulled her fur-collared coat closer around her thin body, opened the door of the cafe, and walked in. It was very sparsely occupied at this time of day, and Wardell would have stood out anywhere. Katy had taken all she could of Turk's judgmental contempt. She might not love Wardell, but he loved her. She could go away with him—and she wouldn't have to suffer Turk's distaste for her anymore.

"Blake," she said softly, pausing by the table.

He looked up. His eyes widened. "Katy!" he whispered roughly. He got to his feet, and Katy ran into his arms, to be swallowed up like the most priceless treasure.

She held on for all she was worth, feeling safe now, warm and safe. She closed her eyes, trembling.

Wardell looked like a man clinging by his fingernails to heaven while fires beckoned underneath. He glanced over her shoulder at Cole with helpless anguish.

"Katy, what are you doing here?" Cole asked gently.

"I heard you talking," she said happily into Wardell's coat. "I had to come. Blake, take me back to Chicago. I don't want to stay here."

Wardell's eyes closed on a wave of agony. How could he refuse her? But if he let her go with him, he'd always know that he was only second best, that she was eating her heart out for the man she really loved.

"You can't run away, sweetheart," he whispered into her ear. "Don't you know that?"

"He doesn't want me," she said desperately. She lifted her face. "Tell him, Cole! Turk doesn't want me! He thinks I'm too low to even touch. He looks at me as if I disgust him!"

Cole searched for the right words. "Katy, you've got it all wrong," he said. "Turk doesn't think you're low. He cares about you."

"No, he doesn't," she said tearfully. "He asked me why I didn't go back to Blake, to Chicago. Don't you see he wanted me to leave?"

"Shouldn't you let him tell you that?" Cole asked gently.

"It's too late," she whispered miserably. She dabbed at tears and looked up at Wardell, who was fighting his better judgment tooth and nail. "Can't I go with you?" she asked.

His jaw tautened. He couldn't refuse her. But if he didn't, her life was going to go from bad to worse. She wasn't rational enough to make such an important decision. His eyes went to Cole's, finding the same impotence there.

A loud voice calling Katy's name caught their attention. A tall cowboy was striding up and down the street, his batwing chaps swinging with his terse strides, his hat pulled low and dangerous over his pale eyes, his blond hair peeking out from under the brim. He paused and looked toward the cafe, through the window. He threw down his cigarette and stormed in at once, his face as hard as Cole's.

"So that's why you came to town," he said shortly. He stopped a few feet away and looked at Wardell with pure hatred. "If you want her, you'll have to beat me to death to get her," he challenged, his light eyes glittering with anger. "If she goes, I've got no reason left to live anyway."

Wardell watched Katy's face color. She looked at Turk with shocked green eyes, not sure that she'd heard him right.

"You—you don't want me," she stammered. "You think I'm low. You can hardly even bear to look at me; you're forever throwing that night up to me. You asked me why I didn't go back to Chicago. All right, I'm going." Her voice broke and she rested her head on Wardell's broad chest, clinging to his coat. "Now, leave me alone!"

"I don't think you're low," Turk said hesitantly, scowling. "Where in hell did you get an idea like that?"

"From you." She felt Wardell's big arm contract around her comfortingly. She glanced across his chest at Turk. "I disgust you."

Turk grimaced. His eyelids actually flinched as he held his hands out in a helpless gesture. "Katy, that's not true. I swear to God it's not!"

She closed her eyes. She couldn't bear to see the pain in his eyes. "You don't want me," she said dully.

"Want you?" His big fists clenched at his side. He glared at her, his tall form almost trembling with rage. "You stubborn, blind little fool! How can you be so dim?"

"You said to go away!"

"I thought you loved him!" he raged, barely aware of the attention he was drawing to them. "I even asked if you did, and you wouldn't answer me!" He glared at Wardell and then back at her. "Can't you recognize blind jealousy? I thought you wanted him instead of me!"

She cringed back against Wardell, staring at Turk. "He doesn't yell at me!"

"He should," Wardell said thoughtfully. He looked down at her with pure tenderness, a little sad as he realized how completely she belonged to the furious blond man facing them. "You don't look, do you, honey?" he asked gently. "Look at him." He turned her chin. "Go on, look."

She did. And suddenly she realized why Turk was so furious, why he was practically vibrating with rage. He was jealous. Murderously jealous. He could barely contain it. Could a man feel like that out of desire, or pity, or even guilt?

"She's dim, all right." Wardell nodded. "You're a textbook case, birdman. You should never have let her go in the first place."

"Don't you think I know that?" Turk asked the older man, his eyes fiercely possessive as they glanced off him and back to Katy's pale face. "Come home, Katy," he said.

She didn't move or speak. Her eyes were wide, wounded, as she stared at him.

"I think you should," Wardell told her, his face serious. "Chicago is a raw, young place—full of bad men like me. You're a little orchid who needs a hothouse, not an icebox. You'd wither all over again if I took you back there."

She nibbled on her lower lip, her expression eloquent. She looked at Cole for help.

"It's your decision, Katy," he told her. "I can't make it for you."

Wardell tugged on a lock of her hair under her pert cap. His eyes softened as he looked at her. "This time, kid, you'd better follow your heart."

She sighed. "I want to love you," she whispered, so that only he could hear.

His jaw tautened. "We don't love according to plan, though, do we?"

She smiled tearfully. "No."

He looked over her head. "She'll be along in a minute."

Turk hesitated, but Cole maneuvered him away from them, persuading him not to make matters worse.

Wardell waited until they were out of earshot. He traced Katy's nose with a big finger. "He loves you. He can't quite bring himself to say it, but it shows."

She drew in a soft breath. "I'm so confused."

"All the more reason for you not to make a sudden decision on something this important. I'll be around, pretty girl," he assured her. "I'm as close as the post office or the telephone. I'll always be somewhere nearby . . . That's a promise.''

Her green eyes searched his dark ones and she flushed, remembering the night they'd been lovers. He looked so torn. She had to do something for him, make that horrible emptiness leave his eyes. The truth might just do it. She owed him that.

"That night," she whispered, "I told myself I was pretending you were Turk. But I wasn't." Her cheeks flooded with color as she heard his sharply indrawn breath. "That night, it—it was only you. I wasn't thinking of anyone else."

He made a rough sound and turned his head. He felt the sting of moisture in his eyes as the poignant bitter-sweetness of the admission stabbed at his heart.

"Thank you for that," he said jerkily.

She paused to get herself in control again. She stared at his chest. "I'll never forget you, even when I'm old."

"But it's the blond ace you can't live without," he added for her.

She nodded. "I'm sorry."

"Don't be." He tilted her face up to his quiet eyes and he looked at her, imprinting her on his memory. "I won't be taking anything away from him if I cherish the time we had. He'll have his own memories."

"Yes."

His hand touched her face very gently. Then, smiling, "You'd better go. Your brother is losing his grip on him."

"I'll miss you, Blake."

"I'll want to see a photograph of the kids when they come along," he said. He glared over her head at a scowling Turk. "I hope they take after you, poor little kids."

"Aren't you finished yet?" Turk asked curtly.

Wardell stuck both his hands in his coat pockets and pursed his lips as he studied Katy. "Go home."

She searched his eyes. "Good-bye."

"So long."

She hesitated, but Turk had had enough. He moved forward, catching her possessively by the hand.

"Don't expect a Christmas card," he told Wardell.

"You're breaking my heart."

Turk pulled her out of the cafe, his hard face unyielding, leaving Cole behind with Wardell.

"Will you stop dragging me?" Katy gasped, protesting his firm hold.

"Stop lagging back," countered. He didn't look at her. "What was that hushed conversation all about?"

"We were talking about the good times we had!" she raged, lashing out.

He stopped and looked down at her with furious eyes, almost shaking with rage.

She shivered at the look, pulled her coat closer. He was at the outer edge of his control, so she decided not to tempt fate. Turk in a temper was dangerous. She dropped her eyes to his broad chest. "You followed me," she said accusingly.

"I wasn't going to let you go out alone—not after what you'd already tried to do," he said doggedly.

She didn't like remembering what she'd tried to do. But she hadn't known that Turk cared that much. She'd thought he was trying to make her go away again. She still wasn't quite sure of him, despite what he'd said to Wardell. And he looked more murderous than amorous at the moment.

"How did you get into town?" she asked nervously.

"I hitched a ride, same as you did. Now we'll both

have to wait for Cole before we can go home." He dropped her hand and stared at her. "Do you know where he left the car?"

She looked around the square until she found it, parked in front of towering oak tree. "It's over there."

He walked with her to it and drew her down on a bench that faced the car and the street, near the statue of a Confederate soldier who stood guard over Spanish Flats. Lacy's people had settled here from Georgia, most notably her great-uncle Horace, who'd made his fortune in nearby San Antonio.

Katy clutched her purse, snapping and unsnapping the catch while Turk rolled and lit a cigarette, crossing his long legs as he glared down at her.

"You don't love Wardell?" he asked.

"I suppose I do, in a way," she said sadly. "But not enough to go away with him, and not in the way he wants me to. If I did go with him, I'd be cheating him. It's a very empty thing, desire without love. I learned that from you."

"From me?" he asked, frowning.

"Wardell had no more from me than I had from you," she said, with resignation. "It was only desire."

"I considered it safer to let you think that," he said enigmatically, watching her closely. He lifted the cigarette to his mouth and stared out at the sparse traffic. "I loved my wife," he said absently. "We'd known each other all our lives. I knew that snows came quick and deep, but we needed the money badly. I left her because I had to. It didn't help my conscience when I got home and found her dead. It took years to get over it, to stop blaming myself. I didn't think I could ever love anybody else."

Neither did Katy. She realized what he was telling her,

and it hurt. "You don't have to explain anything," she said.

He glanced down at her. "How in God's name could you think you disgusted me?" he asked abruptly.

"Every time I mentioned Blake, you got upset."

"I was jealous," he said simply.

"That was a waste of energy," she replied dully. "It's like being jealous of yourself."

"I don't understand."

"He's very like you," she said hesitantly. "The way he smiles, certain mannerisms . . ."

His eyes were piercing. "You pretended Wardell was me?"

"Not—not consciously," she stammered, averting her eyes.

The anger was draining out of him. He'd noticed a faint similarity himself. So *that* was why she'd been so fond of the other man. Not that he liked what she'd done, but it was more bearable now. He could certainly live with it, if his only other choices were to let her go to Wardell or kill herself. His own past wasn't lily-white.

He tilted her face up to his and studied her boldly. "Katy, were you only leaving because you thought I was disgusted with what happened in Chicago?"

She nodded.

"It wasn't disgust," he said firmly. "I felt sorry for you, but I don't think less of you because you had a lover. Did I really behave so badly over Wardell?"

"When you weren't raising the roof every time I mentioned Blake, you were withdrawn and very distant," she said helplessly.

"I thought that was what you wanted," he replied. He tossed the cigarette down and ground it out under the heel of his spurred boot. He turned back to her, framing her face in his cold hands, and he bent to her mouth. "Since it isn't, however . . ."

The words went past her shocked lips. He couldn't be doing this in broad daylight, in the middle of town!

But he was! She felt the cool insistence of his lips, parting hers, while his arms gathered her up against him. She stiffened, but he wore her down.

"Give in, Katy," he whispered mischievously, nipping her lower lip with gentle affection. "You know you love kissing me."

"We're in town—" she began.

"So we are. Open your mouth," he whispered outrageously, nudging it with his parted lips. "Remember how it felt the first time?"

She did. She moaned softy and gave him what he wanted, drowning all too quickly in the fires he kindled.

"I was your first man," he breathed roughly. "And I'll be your last man. The children you bear will be mine. The rest of it doesn't matter. I'm sorry for Wardell, but he can live without you. I can't." He lifted his head; his eyes were tortured as they searched hers. "I can't live without you, Katy. I wouldn't want too . . . Come here, little one!"

His mouth crushed hers, and she yielded without a struggle. The scars seemed to have gone, or at least settled, because she felt the first pangs of desire still in her body as he kissed her. She wasn't quite dead inside, she thought dizzily. Not if she could still feel like this!

Back at the cafe, Cole and Wardell had finalized their arrangement. Wardell was getting ready to board the train for the return trip to Chicago.

As they left the cafe, en route to the train depot across

the street, they spotted Katy and Turk in each others' arms, oblivious to the whole world.

Wardell shrugged, then he smiled. "She'll be happy," he said. "I can't regret leaving her here. It's hell loving someone who can't love you back."

Cole nodded. "It was like that with my wife when we first married. I thought I'd killed what she felt for me." He smiled slowly. "Life is full of surprises."

"Some of them are good ones," the older man agreed. The train had just pulled into the station when they reached it. Wardell turned to shake hands with Cole.

"You'll never know how much I appreciate this," Cole told him. "Heritage is important. I won't ever have kids, but somebody will inherit this ranch one day."

Wardell frowned. "What do you mean you won't have kids? Don't you like them?"

Cole told him why.

The older man grimaced. "You and me both," he said, shaking his head sadly. "Hell of a shame, isn't it? Two handsome devils like us! Think what beautiful kids we'd have produced." He clapped Cole heavily on the shoulder. "I guess we'll have to settle for being handsome and rich. Make me a lot of money. I've always had a yen to be a cattle king."

"Thank you," Cole added, "for what you did for Katy."

"Oh, that." He smiled wistfully. "I just opened her eyes, that's all. Sometimes people have to be told what they want, instead of asked. I'll be in touch. And remember, not a word to Katy. That gray-eyed fire eater she's going to marry would have a screaming fit."

"What he doesn't know won't hurt him," Cole said.

"Just what I thought."

Cole watched him off before he went back to the car.

Katy was wide-eyed and shaken, her lips swollen. Turk
wasn't in much better shape, and he was as irritable as a
teased rattlesnake.

"I thought you two had patched up your differences,"
Cole remarked.

"Let's go home," Turk said, jerking his hat low over
his eyes.

He put Katy in the front seat and he sat in the back,
crossing his arms and legs and looking gloomy.

"What's wrong?" Cole asked Katy.

"He wants to get married right away," she said dully.
"I don't."

"She's still mooning over her gangster!" Turk raged.

"I am not!" She glared over the seat at him. "I just
want you to be sure, that's all. You can argue until
the cows come home, but you never even thought about
marrying me until I came home hurt! I'm not some poor
hurt little calf who needs tending. I'm a woman, and
I may have thrown my heart at your feet in the past,
but I'm older and wiser now. I don't want a man who
isn't sure himself how he feels about me. And you
aren't, Turk," she said when he tried to speak. "You
think you've saved me from hell by keeping me from
going back to Chicago. But that's a far cry from loving
me."

Turk's pale eyes glittered at her from under the wide
brim of his hat. "You won't listen, will you?" he asked
furiously.

She turned back around, unaware of Cole's efforts to
stifle amused laughter at their expense. "No, I won't
listen," she said stiffly. "I do have a little pride and
dignity left. At least enough to keep me from marrying a
man who only sees me as a charity project."

Turk started to reply heatedly, but Cole cut him off.

"You two can hash this out when we're home," he said firmly. "This isn't the time or the place."

Katy had to agree. Then a thought occurred to her. She looked at her brother with open curiosity. "Why did Blake Wardell come here?" she asked suddenly.

Chapter Twenty

COLE STARED STRAIGHT AHEAD, TRYING TO THINK fast enough to field Katy's unexpected question. Well, he had to admit she was a Whitehall through and through, and much too sharp to be put off with lies. He had to come close to the truth.

"I asked him to come," he said, which was gospel. "Because I was worried about what you might do. And Turk had mentioned that you might be missing him. We were all afraid you might take your life."

Katy gnawed her lower lip. "I see."

"He cares about you," Cole said. "He was more than willing to take you away if you wanted to go."

"You had no right!" Turk said furiously.

"I had *every* right," Cole replied. "She's my sister."

"All the same, this is our business, not Wardell's!"

"He saved Katy once before," Cole reminded him. "Or have you forgotten?"

Turk calmed down. "All right." He sighed roughly. "I suppose he did, at that. But she's not going off with him!"

"That was her decision to make."

"Well, she'll marry me just the same, decision or not," Turk said, his eyes glaring hotly at Katy. "I'll talk to the minister and make the arrangements. And she'll go to the altar hog-tied and gagged if that's what it takes!''

Katy caught her breath. "You wouldn't dare!" she raged, showing more spirit than she'd exhibited since her return from Chicago.

"Stand back and watch me," he said smugly. "Your running days are over. You'll marry me, and you'll like it.''

She turned back around in the seat, facing front, crossed her arms, and glared through the windshield without answering.

Cole didn't say a word. But he had a feeling that Katy was going to find herself wed before she had time to think about it. He approved, too. Turk would settle down nicely with Katy, and there would be children at Spanish Flats; Katy's as well as Faye's.

Lacy and Marion laughed merrily when Cole told them later, in private, what had happened in town.

"Poor Katy!" Lacy said breathlessly. "She'll never live it down.''

"I'm delighted," Marion added, with a smile. "She'll be happy with Turk. But what about the mortgage, Cole?" she added worriedly. "How will we manage, now that the bank won't loan us the money?"

"I found a bank that would," Cole replied, and smiled.

Lacy lifted an eyebrow and gave him a knowing look, but she didn't interrupt Marion's excited monologue about her certainty that Cole would be able to cope.

Later, though, she asked if Wardell was his banker.

"You can't tell Katy," he cautioned.

She linked her arms around his neck and reached up to

kiss him. "I never will. But I'm very glad to have a friend like Mr. Wardell. We'll have to make sure he doesn't ever regret his decision."

"Oh, I intend to," Cole agreed. Then he bent again to Lacy's mouth and forgot about Wardell entirely. Cole had managed to pull the ranch out without having to rely on Lacy's inheritance, which saved his pride. Lacy didn't mind. If they were playing even a small part in the rehabilitation of a notorious racketeer like Blake Wardell, she was delighted. It was a shame that Katy couldn't love him. Maybe someday he'd get over her and find a woman who could.

Katy was pacing the floor at midnight, still overwhelmed by the events of the day. Her mind was clear for the first time since Danny's death, but she wasn't sure how she was going to manage Turk's proposal. Marriage was serious business. What if they were through with it and he discovered too late that he didn't want to stay married? That could happen, since he was doing it under duress. He'd sworn that he couldn't live without Katy, but he was overwrought himself. It probably all stemmed from the loss of the baby triggering old wounds.

The sound at the window distracted her and she went slowly to the curtains to look out. She hadn't changed for bed, which was a good thing. Turk was standing under her window throwing pebbles at it. He was wearing his work clothes, except for his chaps; his hat tilted back over a face that looked younger than it had in years. He was smiling as well.

"Come out," he invited.

She opened the window. "Turk, do you have any idea what time it is?" she gasped. "And it's freezing!" He had a thick denim jacket on, but Katy was in her sleeves, and the wind was cold.

"I'll keep you warm, baby doll," he said. His smile was possessive. "Come on."

She kept telling herself all the way to the back door why she should ignore him and go to bed. But nothing worked. Turk was so much a part of her that she couldn't refuse him.

Careful not to wake the household, Katy eased down the back steps, her coat hastily thrown around her.

Turk was waiting at the bottom of the steps. Without a word, he looped his arm around her shoulders and walked her toward the corral, where a single white mare pranced in the cold moonlight.

"I'd like a church service," he said. "Wouldn't you?"

She stared straight ahead, her face stony. "I'm not fit to walk into a church anymore."

He turned toward her, big and comforting. His hand tilted her face up to his soft gray eyes. "What do you think church is for?" he asked. "Perfect people? There aren't any churchgoers who have never done anything wrong, Katy. The whole purpose of it is to reform sinners." He tugged gently at a long lock of brown hair near her ear. "I've got more on my conscience than you have on yours, I expect. We'll start going to services once we're married. It will be good for the kids."

She flushed and averted her eyes.

"It hurts you to talk about children, doesn't it?" he asked perceptively. "But you won't lose the next one," he added quietly. "Nobody and nothing will hurt you again."

Her eyes landed on his big boots, dusty and stained from hard work. He wasn't a slacker, whatever else he was. He worked as hard as Cole did. He was a good man. He'd take care of her, even if he didn't love her the way she loved him. But, she wondered, wasn't she doing the same thing Blake had refused to do—marrying without being loved?

"I can't marry you," she said, her voice barely carrying even in the stillness. "If I'd pleaded enough, Blake might have taken me away, knowing I didn't love him. But I don't want to do that to you any more than he wanted to do it to me. Love on one side isn't enough."

"You don't love Wardell," he said curtly.

"I wasn't talking about me. I was talking about you. You still belong to your wife." Her chest rose and fell heavily. "You always will. I'd never be anything more than a poor second choice."

"That isn't true. It might have been, the first year I was here. But not for a long time now, Katy." He propped a booted foot on the lowest rail of the corral and studied her wan, sad face. "I told you in town: You mean everything to me. If I lost you, nothing would matter."

"You'll always resent my marriage, and what happened with Blake . . ."

He put a big thumb over her lips to stay the words. His pale eyes glittered in the moonlight. "I'm jealous of Wardell because I know he'd lay down his life for you. That's hard to swallow. But I'm not going to throw it up to you, not ever."

"You did," she accused.

"That was before I realized how you felt about me. You see, I'd convinced myself that you were in love with Wardell. I thought you'd taken those damned pills because you didn't want to live without him."

She hated remembering what she'd done. Her lips

trembled as they formed words. "It was because of the way you talked about what happened with him. I was certain that you thought me too low and soiled to ever want me again. I . . . couldn't have stayed here any longer, and it wasn't fair to Blake to ask him to rescue me. I thought I was sparing us all any more heartache."

"By killing yourself?" he asked, his voice husky with anguish. "My God!"

"I love you," she said miserably, averting her eyes. "And when you said what you did that day, I thought it meant you couldn't bear what I'd become. It hurt."

Her voice broke on the words, and his jaw tautened with feeling. His arms enfolded her with exquisite tenderness, cradling her against his tall, strong body while the wind blew violently around them, wafting her hair up near his face, drowning him in its flower scent.

"You won't believe I can love you back. Why?"

"Because . . ." She shrugged.

His hand smoothed her hair. "That part of my life is over. But I'm still alive, and I can't climb into the grave with her. I want children," he whispered into her ear. "Sons and daughters to spoil. Most of all, I want you. Nothing was the same after you left. I lost my taste for living without you."

She smiled wistfully, because she didn't believe a word of it. She'd spent too many years breaking her heart over him to think he'd changed his mind so drastically in such a short time. Perhaps he felt he owed it to Cole to save her reputation. She had, after all, been carrying his child.

He saw her expression and his chest lifted and fell with resignation. "I don't know why I expect you to believe me," he said abruptly. "I've spent years avoiding you or criticizing you, anything to keep you at arm's length. The day you left, even after I seduced you, I told you there could never be a future for us. I suppose you remember every word of it, all the hurtful things."

"You were kind to me when I came home from Chicago," she recalled. "Even though you must have thought I deserved everything I got."

"Deserved it?" He lifted his head, scowling. "Why?"

She shifted. "I'd already been intimate with you, almost wanton," she murmured, with flaming embarrassment. "Then, in Chicago, I ran wild."

"Out of hurt." His broad shoulders lifted and fell. "Katy, I'm sorry," he said huskily. "I didn't really know how I felt until it was too late. I don't hold you responsible for anything. When I think about how that rat Marlone treated you, I get sick all over. If it hadn't been for Wardell, as much as I hate to say it, he might very well have killed you."

Her attention settled on the horse in the corral. "At that time, I don't guess it would have made any difference to me. I'd given up. Life seemed to be one endless agony, especially after I lost the baby."

"We can have another baby," he said curtly. "Only this one will be wanted, planned, hoped for."

She twisted a tuft of fur in her nervous fingers. "You don't want someone like me," she protested.

"What are you saying?" He framed her face in his hands. "Damn it, Katy. I love you!"

Time seemed to stop dead. She stared at him. "You don't mean that," she whispered.

"Oh, but I do," he said, bending. His mouth brushed

hers roughly. "I mean it with all my heart," he ground
out as his lips covered hers.

She shivered at the depth of feeling his kiss aroused.
She wanted to protest, to draw back, to tell him that he
didn't have to pretend. But, oh, it didn't feel as if he
were pretending! His arms had a faint tremor, and his
mouth was devouring, passionate. He kissed her as poor
Wardell had—with so much helpless need that his body
shuddered.

That he loved her enough to be desperate for her was
more than she could bear. She made a tiny sound against
his mouth and then melted into him willingly, sliding her
arms under his and around him, moving close, into an
intimate embrace. It was the first time since Danny's death
that she'd really felt whole. Turk was her world, as he
always had been. It was incredible that he should love her.

Tears ran hotly down her cheeks, into the corners of
his mouth. He tasted their salty warmth and drew back to
look at her.

"Why?" he asked gently, wiping them with his
fingers.

"I never dreamed you could love me," she sobbed.

He smiled tenderly. "You're as blind as I was, aren't
you, little one?" he whispered.

"I must be. Turk, am I dreaming?" she asked.

He bent his head. "Let's see."

Seconds later, he could barely breathe at all. He
groaned against her mouth and pulled her even closer,
his hands low on her waist, possessive as he fought the
need that aroused him to fever pitch.

"We . . . mustn't," she whispered unsteadily.

He wasn't listening. His mind was on Katy, on
feeding the hunger that gnawed at his insides.

A sudden, sharp noise echoed from the house, and

Turk's head jerked up. He glanced toward the darkened windows as the sound came again. He began to chuckle.

"What is it?" Katy asked dazedly.

"Just a little reassurance that we don't have to worry about interruptions," he said enigmatically. He caught his breath, watching her possessively while she flushed with the memory of her headlong response. "No more looking behind us, Katy," he said softly. "Only ahead. All right?"

She nodded. "If you're sure . . ."

"Oh, I'm sure," he whispered, bending again toward her mouth. He kissed her gently, so that things didn't get out of hand again, and released her. "Go back inside. We'll talk some more tomorrow. But we're getting married Friday, just the same."

"You arrogant cowboy," she said, with exasperation.

He tipped his hat. "Yes, ma'am." He took her arm and propelled her toward the back door and into the kitchen. "Now, you go to bed . . ."

His voice trailed off at the sight of Cole in a long, thick robe heating up chocolate on the stove.

"What the hell are you two doing outside at this hour?" Cole demanded.

Turk pursed his lips. "Nothing anymore," he said. "Too much noise out there."

Cole actually flushed. Katy looked from one man to the other incomprehensibly. Masculine secrets, she supposed.

"Good night, then," she said softly, smiling at Turk before she went out and closed the door.

Both men said good night, but Cole waited until the door was closed and footsteps were dying away before he jumped down Turk's throat.

"I only meant we heard the slats falling," Turk

assured him in midtirade, "and Katy didn't even know what it was. So save your vocabulary for the cowboys, if you please. I'm shocked by such language."

"Shocked by it? My God! You invented half of it in France!"

"I'm reformed. I'm going to marry your sister and have kids."

Cole relented. "I guess you want my blessing," he said, taking the hot chocolate off the stove and filling two mugs with it.

"Not especially," Turk said with maddening imperturbability. "I'm going to marry Katy. You can try to stop me if you feel lucky."

The other man chuckled. "Good for you."

"I'll take good care of her," Turk said solemnly. "And I love her, if that matters."

"I knew that when you braced Wardell in the cafe," Cole replied dryly. "Takes some kind of guts to confront a man like that."

"He's not so tough. Not when it comes to Katy. I don't like him," he added firmly. "But I guess I'm grateful for what he did for her."

"I felt rather sorry for him," Cole said quietly. "What we have, he'll never know."

Turk was silent for a long moment. "I want to buy that land on the bottoms from you and build on it. Katy will want her own house."

"You can have the land," Cole said. "I'll make you a wedding present of it."

"I'm overwhelmed," Turk replied, and meant it. "But how can you afford to do that when you're in over your head already?"

"I got a loan." Cole grinned. "I'll make it now . . . You wait and see."

"Oh, I know how you are when you set your mind to something." Turk nodded. "I won't bet against you." He glanced at the hot chocolate and lifted an eyebrow. "Midnight snack?"

"Something of that kind. Aren't you leaving?" Cole asked as he picked up the mugs.

"I guess so." Turk sighed. "Well, good night."

"Sleep well."

"I don't think it would do much good to return the sentiment," Turk answered as he opened the back door. "You need to bolt those damned slats down."

Cole's eyes flashed, but before he could get the words out, Turk was safely out of range, still chuckling.

Christmas morning dawned cold and fair, and just after the regular worship service in the small church in Spanish Flats, Katy was married to Turk with the whole congregation beaming approvingly at them. In her long white dress with its high lace collar and satin train, a white Spanish mantilla covering her face that Turk lifted reverently to kiss her, she was beautiful. Turk told her so, several times, when they danced at the house where a small reception was held.

Marion Whitehall was blossoming in the affectionate atmosphere around her, and with the emotional turmoil reduced to a bare minimum, she was settling physically into a much less strained routine. Her health had improved to the point that her doctor even dared extend his fatal prognosis to a stretch of years, if Marion were careful. Indeed she would be, and now she had grandchildren to look forward to.

Faye hadn't come to celebrate with them, but Christmas was special all the same. They ate a hearty dinner of turkey and ham, and exchanged presents. Lacy's, from

Cole, was a new wedding band, with a raised relief of roses, that touched her heart. Hers to him had been a new watch, and a new chain to hang it on.

Late in the afternoon, Turk and Katy caught the train at Spanish Flats to San Antonio for a brief honeymoon, and they promised to see Faye while they were in town.

She'd pretended that she was supremely calm, but Katy had butterflies in her stomach when she and Turk were shown into their elegant room with their luggage.

It would be her first intimacy since the night Danny had died, and Katy had misgivings. She wasn't at all sure if she was going to be able to go through with it. If she couldn't, how would her marriage survive?

In San Antonio, Faye was still half in shock after having Lacy's cousin Ruby read Ben's letter to her. It was postmarked Paris, France, and in it Ben recounted his small successes, including the forthcoming publication of a book he'd written. He was doing very well, he wrote, but he still felt unhappy about the way he'd treated Faye. She was very special to him. He wanted to take care of her and the baby, if she'd let him.

Faye was touched, but there was plenty of water under the bridge now. She had her independence and a life of her own. She didn't have to be dependent on anybody. Besides, she was learning how to read and write. Who could tell what opportunities might present themselves once she was literate!

She couldn't write back. It had obviously escaped Ben's mind that she couldn't even read, that she would have to have somebody read his letter to her. He'd always been thoughtless. It wasn't malicious, but it was

an indication of how insensitive he was to other people.
She might like to see him again, but not until she was on
equal intellectual footing.

Later that day, she went to Ruby and asked her to write
to Ben for her. She thanked him for his interest, but told
him that she was enjoying her independence and could
do without his help. It was a cool, polite little note that
would say much more than words. She smiled to herself
as she went to bed that night. She did wish she could be
a fly on the wall when arrogant Ben Whitehall discovered
that the silly little country girl he'd left behind didn't
want him. She didn't doubt that it would come as a
shock.

In fact, it did. Ben read it three times before he
realized that the handwriting couldn't be Faye's, because
Faye couldn't even read. He groaned as he got up from
his desk and paced the room. Why hadn't he remembered
that? It must have been one more strike against him
where Faye was concerned.

He'd done an excellent job of messing up his life, he
thought. Not only had he ruined his relationship with his
family, he'd alienated the one woman who'd ever really
loved him . . . the woman who was going to have his
child.

His twenty-first birthday had come earlier in the
week, without a word from home. It was Christmas,
and he had no one to share it with except the pert
mademoiselle who lived down the hall. That wasn't the
appetizing proposition it would have been just a week
ago. He was homesick. He missed Texas. He wondered
if his mother was still alive, because no one at Spanish Flats had answered his letter. Cole was probably
still mad at him. His elder brother wasn't a forgiving
man.

He grabbed his jacket from the back of his chair and stopped to check his wallet for the advance he'd been given on his book contract. He had enough for a small celebration, he decided. God knew, anything was better than sitting here brooding about his mistakes.

══ Chapter Twenty-one ══

In a hotel room in San Antonio, Turk was standing by the window, wearing nothing at all. His face was harder than ever, his eyes full of anguish. Katy lay under the covers, still shivering as she tried to come to grips with her fear of letting go in a man's arms. All his skill hadn't managed to ease her trepidation, loosen her locked muscles. She was in tears, and Turk was furious. It didn't bode well for their future.

Katy dreaded the outburst that was sure to come as she stared toward Turk. She could feel his anger in the way he'd left her, the tautness of his nude body a threat in itself. But he hadn't lashed out at her, and that was puzzling.

"I know you're angry . . ." she began hesitantly.

"No," he replied, his voice very gentle, although he kept his back to her. "I'm not angry, Katy. I knew it wasn't going to be easy." He had a smoking cigarette in one hand and he was peering down at the streetlamps with eyes that barely saw, his heart still shuddering from frustrated desire.

Katy sat up against the pillows with her knees under her chin, swallowing tears. "I've done so many bad things . . ." she began brokenly.

"Oh, Katy," he said softly, turning to look at her with

356

eyes that were quiet and loving. "You've done nothing but be a victim, sweetheart. Your mind won't let go of the way Danny died. That's all."

She lowered her eyes to he nervous hands. "I can't help that," she said in a subdued tone. "I wish I could!"

He moved back to the bed and sat down beside her, his body warm against her hip. He was nude, and completely unselfconscious about it, but Katy's eyes kept darting away as she struggled between embarrassment and shy fascination. He was still blatantly aroused, which didn't help, either.

"We're married," he reminded her, smiling. "It's all right if you look at me, Katy."

"I'm not as uninhibited as I used to think I was." She looked up at him worriedly. "I loved you, that first time," she blurted out. "Loved you, wanted you—until there was nothing else in the world except you. Leaving was the hardest thing I'd ever done. It isn't what happened to Danny—Well," she confessed, "maybe a little. But mostly it's that I can't quite believe we're married." Her face was pale with her fears. "Turk, you never wanted to marry me before. What changed?"

"The way Wardell looked in that cafe," he said shortly. He averted his face. He hated acknowledging the other man, but it was unavoidable. "He'd have taken you blind, limping, and mindless—any way he could get you. And then I saw what I'd done to you, and I was scared to death that you might feel sorry enough for him to accept what he offered you."

"Nothing . . . scares you," she said falteringly, with a shaky smile.

He looked at her, his eyes like gray smoke in autumn. "Losing you does," he said simply. "Something inside me died when you left here. I didn't even miss it until you came back and all the colors were there again, all the vividness I'd lost. I ran all the way to the house, expecting to see you the way you were, all laughter and mischievousness.'' He flinched. ''And instead, I found an empty shell, without life or sparkle. I knew that I was responsible for that. You loved me. I knew it, but I wasn't ready. Rather, I thought I wasn't.'' He smoothed back her dark, tangled hair and searched her wide green eyes quietly. ''You don't trust me not to walk out again, isn't that the real fear, Katy? You don't think I'm committed—that we're married because of guilt or pity on my part.''

She couldn't deny it. Her face gave her away.

He smiled ruefully and belatedly noticed that his ashes were falling on the old Persian rug that covered the floor near the bed. He reached for an ashtray and put it out. ''Listen,'' he said when he'd finished, holding her gaze, ''we've got the rest of our lives. All the time there is. So don't feel that you have to force yourself to sleep with me, or that you need to feel guilty because you don't want me yet. I'm in no hurry, and there'll be no pressure, no matter how long it takes. I love you, Katy,'' he said softly, smiling. ''And I'm not going anywhere.''

The first tear caught her unaware. She felt it escape her eye, make a warm trail down her cheek that quickly cooled. It was followed by another and another. Turk held her close and rocked her, pillowing her wet face against his hair-roughened chest.

''Watering pot,'' he said accusingly, with a deep chuckle. ''What is it now?''

''You have to be sure,'' she choked. ''Because I can't leave you again—not even if it's the best thing for you. I think I might die without you now . . .''

His arms contracted involuntarily. ''You little fool!

Didn't you hear what I told Wardell? That if I lost you, I might as well be dead, because there was no life without you? It wasn't just words, Katy. I meant it. Oh, God, I meant it!'' He searched for her mouth and kissed it through the salty tears, groaning as the fever began to burn in him all over again. He had to pull back while he still could. Katy didn't want this . . .

''No!'' she protested when his head started to lift. She caught his full lower lip in her small teeth and trapped it. ''Not now.''

The sensations he felt made him shudder. He'd wanted her before, but never so desperately. He'd been in control the last time, but he knew instinctively that he couldn't hold back long enough to please her now. It would be quick and rough, and that was the last thing he could do to her under the circumstances.

He caught the clinging arms around his neck and gently pulled them loose. His hands were trembling, like his body. ''No,'' he said huskily. ''Katy, you don't understand. I can't hold anything back . . .''

She rubbed her face against his chest hungrily while her hands felt for the hem of her gown and suddenly wrenched it from her body. She sat up proudly, inviting his eyes to look at the firm thrust of her breasts, the taut dusky peaks blatantly signaling her hunger.

''Yes, look at me,'' she whispered, shivering. ''I used to lie awake at night and remember how it felt the first time you saw me like this.''

His lips parted on a shattered breath. His big hands cupped her gently and his thumbs rubbed tenderly at the distended nipples. He heard her gasp, watched her back arch like a cat inviting a stroking hand.

''Katy,'' he whispered in torment.

She kicked away the covers. The room was cool, but

she was burning, her skin almost feverish as she lay back, trembling helplessly.

"Whatever you do will be all right," she said in a voice that was too strained to be hers. She moved gently, so that her body positioned itself to receive him. Her lips lifted in sensual invitation.

He groaned, his body sliding down over hers in helpless response, his feverish mouth finding hers even as his hands slid under her thighs and lifted her to the involuntary downward thrust of his body.

"Katy . . . forgive me!" he ground out against her lips as he went into her with one quick, fierce thrust.

She made a sound he'd never heard, and her body stiffened and went very still.

He paused, shuddering above her, his eyes on her face. "Is it hurting?" he began urgently.

But even as the words escaped his tight throat, her body began to convulse. She clutched at his hips, sobbing.

"Help me," she whimpered. "Turk, please, please, help me!"

He realized belatedly what was happening to her. He smoothed back her damp hair and his hips began to move with quick, measured smoothness that brought her to completion in a matter of seconds. She was still clinging to him and crying as the first wave hit him and turned the world to a throbbing red blur.

A few seconds later, the room came back into blinding focus. He'd all but lost consciousness in the fullness of his pleasure. His heart was pounding and he was trembling, sweating in the aftermath. Under him, Katy's soft body was fluid, warm, clinging to his with tenderness.

He nuzzled his face into her throat and finally found enough strength to lift his head. Her eyes were misty, half-closed, her mouth swollen. She reached up and touched his face with fingers that adored it.

"It was too quick," he said huskily.

Her head moved sideways on the pillow. "Not really." She wrapped her soft legs around his when he started to lift away from her, and her arms slid over his broad shoulders. "No," she whispered. She held his eyes and her hips lifted.

"I can't," he said softly. "Not yet."

"Can't you?" She rubbed her lips tenderly over his and suddenly slid her hand down the center of his body to its core and touched him.

He groaned harshly and his body jerked, going sharply rigid. He looked into her eyes with stark shock.

"I love you," she said. Her face was radiant with it, like her supple body in his arms as she began to lift up to him. "Let me show you . . . how much!"

His hands stabbed into her thick hair and arched her head up to his. He held it while he moved, lazily this time, ardently, with techniques he'd never shown her before. Some of the things he did shocked her. All of them aroused her to a pitch she'd never achieved. When he finally gave her the satisfaction she was reduced to begging for, she cried out and fainted.

"Did you think you could match me?" he asked later, smiling lazily into her drowsy eyes while he smoked a cigarette. "You're just a babe in the woods, child."

She smoothed the thick hair on his chest with an idle hand while she studied him. "Were there a lot of women?"

"Yes," he said, without guilt or embarrassment. "Before I married, and after I was widowed. It never meant more than satisfying an ache. Except with my wife." He looked down at her. "And with you. I won't cheat on you, if you're worried about it. I don't take vows lightly.''

"I know." She gnawed her lower lip.

"What's wrong?"

Her shoulders lifted and fell nervously. "What happened that last time . . . It was frightening.''

"Something that profound should be," he said quietly. "Making love is an act of creation," he added, his eyes soft and possessive on her body. "A joining of bodies and souls in utter reverence. I've made light of it all these years, but when I do it with you, I feel as if I've touched heaven.''

She moved involuntarily. "I didn't think about a baby.''

He kissed her eyes, his tongue softly stroking her thick lashes. "I did.''

She smiled. "Will you mind?''

He chuckled. "No." He pressed a hard kiss on her lips. "If you're pregnant, you can't leave me.''

"I won't, anyway.''

He was satisfied about that, and about her devotion to him. He spared a faint thought of sympathy for Wardell, who would never have Katy's love or her children. He could afford to be generous. All the same, he was glad Chicago was so far away. He drew Katy close and put out his cigarette.

═══ Chapter Twenty-two ═══

BEN WAITED IMPATIENTLY AT GRAND CENTRAL STA-
tion for his train to Texas. It had been six months
since he'd finished his book, and it was already on the
book stands. He'd been living in New York while he
read and corrected galleys, so excited about the idea of
actually having a book in print that he didn't even mind
the sweeping revisions his editor had suggested. It was a
dream come true. Even if he wasn't a literary lion yet, he
was at least a published author. He had time on his side.
If it took years to build a reputation, he had them.

With his advance against royalties in his pocket, he
was finally secure enough to go home and face his
family. He'd written over the long months, and Cole had
finally taken pity on him after Christmas. Marion Whitehall had surprised everyone by rallying against the
doctor's prognosis. She grew stronger by the day. Katy
and Turk had married, a bit of news that Ben still had
trouble digesting. They were certainly an odd match.
But, then, love was strange. What puzzled him was the
postscript saying that Cole had raised a loan to save the
ranch from foreclosure. He felt guilty, because it had
never occurred to him that Cole was having financial
trouble. He'd been much too wrapped up in his own
problems to think about Cole's; disquieting, when Cole

was responsible for so many people, including his mother. Well, he was back now, and he was going to help. Cole was speaking to him, at least, so perhaps he wouldn't be thrown off the porch when he arrived.

Spanish Flats was prospering. Ben noticed the new paint on the house and the new fences with barbed wire strung neatly between them to keep Cole's huge herds of cattle in. The car he'd hitched a ride in was an old open-cabbed one, like Marion's runabout without the top, and he was getting his expensive light suit dusty, but he didn't really mind. Summer had come, and the landscape was green and lush this year, since adequate rainfall had given it a boost.

Marion was not only still alive, despite the dire predictions of the year before, she was more alive than Ben had seen her in years.

She ran onto the porch to hug him, tears in her eyes as she held him before her and looked at him with pride.

"You've grown up, haven't you, my dear?" she asked.

"It was inevitable, although I'm sure you wondered if it would ever happen," Ben said gently. He looked around. "Is Cole home?"

"He and Lacy are out at the barn, looking at Cole's new Santa Gertrudis bull. Why don't you go out and surprise them while I lay the table? You must be starved!"

"I am, indeed. I'll catch you up on all the news when we come in. Are you all right?" he added worriedly.

"I'm doing unexpectedly well, and keeping the doctor in knots," she said smugly. "My heart is stronger than ever. He calls me a walking miracle."

"You always were, though," he replied, bending to kiss her cheek.

He found Cole and Lacy staring over the gate into a large stall in the barn, where a huge red-coated bull was stuffing himself on corn and oats and molasses.

"Hail the conquering hero!" Lacy laughed, then opened her arms.

Ben hugged her, savoring her warm scent for seconds before he forced himself to let her go. Lacy was the only dream he wouldn't realize, he reminded himself. Fame and fortune would surely come his way with hard work, but Lacy was forever Cole's.

He shook hands with his brother. "How goes it?"

Cole smiled. "Very well, as you see. The latest addition to my breeding herd. Handsome brute, isn't he?"

"For something with four legs, I suppose so. How are you both?" he asked, because something was very different here. They were standing close together, and when they looked at each other, Ben felt like an intruder into their private world. Whatever they'd felt for each other when they married, it was love now. A blind man couldn't have mistaken it for anything else.

"We're fine," Cole said, smiling down at Lacy. "Better by the day."

"Oh, yes." she said, grinning. She slid her arm around Cole's slim waist and sighed as she snuggled against his chest. He drew her close, kissing her dark hair.

Yes, Ben thought, this was a marriage he'd envy until he died. And to think he'd brought it about!

"You said that Katy and Turk had married?" he asked, diverting his mind from Lacy.

"It's much more serious than that." Lacy laughed. "Katy is pregnant! Turk is driving us all up the walls worrying about her. Last week she mentioned that she wanted some ice cream, and he drove all the way to San

Antonio and brought it back in an old ice chest. She said she doesn't dare say she wants dates; Turk would probably fly to Arabia to get her some!"

"I suppose she's over that mobster she married?" Ben asked probingly.

"Well over," Cole replied. "He was on drugs. His death was tragic, but he was beating Katy. I didn't mourn him."

Ben grimaced. "Poor Katy."

She's fine, now. You can see for yourself when she and Turk get back from her doctor's appointment."

"And Faye?" Ben asked, looking at the bull as he asked the question, trying not to sound too concerned.

"Faye is due any day," Lacy told him. "She only works a few hours a day now."

Ben's hands tightened on the gate. "She won't answer my letters. I know she can't read and write, but she could get someone."

"Yes, she can read and write, Ben," Lacy said, correcting him. "Cousin Ruby taught her. She's quite a different girl these days. She's even being tutored in English."

Ben was shocked. "Our Faye?"

"Our Faye. You'd be very proud of the strides she's made," Cole replied. "She's quite sought after in San Antonio, despite her condition," he added, with only a bare concession to the truth, to draw Ben out. Sure enough, the younger man looked suddenly thunderous.

"I thought I might try to see her tomorrow."

"Good idea," Cole agreed.

"You said in your last letter that you'd sold your book," Lacy said. "Congratulations!"

"I've had to do a lot of revisions, but that's something a writer expects." Ben replied, smiling with helpless pride. He glanced at Cole. "I wasn't certain of my welcome, after what happened. I do regret it, Cole. I suppose I had my nose too far in the clouds to realize how callous I'd become."

"It was more your publisher's daughter than you," Lacy said. "And I was worried that you might not forgive me for closing him down, but I was furious at the way Jessica treated poor little Faye."

"Yes," Ben said. "You don't need to apologize for anything to me, Lacy. I was so infatuated with Jessica that it took that night to open my eyes. She was ice cold and calculating. I didn't even suspect that I was being used. I should have known when old man Bradley refused to talk about hiring additional staff. He didn't need it, did he, when I was doing everything from writing the stories to selling advertising!"

"Your name was his most valuable tool," Lacy said quietly. "Perhaps you didn't realize that San Antonio is only a small town that grew. My great-uncle was well known, and most people knew my background. When I married Cole, that was common knowledge, too. The Whitehall name carries a great deal of weight in San Antonio as well, and not because of me." She looked up at Cole adoringly. "Cole's word is his bond. The strength of it would have opened any doors you cared to try."

Cole knew that wasn't quite true, but Lacy's adoring eyes made his knees weak. He bent and kissed her forehead with aching possession. "Of course, your talent helped, too," Cole added, glancing at his brother. "You use words the way Cherry and Taggart gentle horses."

"That's high praise," Ben said.

"You're my brother."

Ben grinned. "Glad you noticed. Does that mean

you'll give me the loan of the runabout to drive in to San Antonio tomorrow?''

Cole groaned. ''I walked right into that one!''

''With your eyes closed,'' the younger man agreed. ''Thanks, Cole! You're a prince!''

It was a long drive. Ben had spent a wonderful night at home in the security of his family. It had strengthened the old ties and made him realize finally what he wanted most. He wanted what Cole and Lacy had. What Turk and Katy had. He wanted a wife and a home of his own, and a family. If he could convince Faye to give in and marry him, he'd have the family ready-made, he thought amusedly.

She was at the dress shop. He stood at the window and just stared inside at first, fascinated by the change in her. No more wild, flighty clothes, no more impish youth. Faye was a woman and looked it, from her neat gray maternity suit to the stylish short haircut that was neatly trimmed. She wasn't made up at all, and she didn't need to be. She had a flawless complexion and fine bone structure.

Ben opened the door, setting a small bell ajingle. Faye looked toward the door smiling.

''Yes, may I help you . . . ?'' Her soft voice trailed off as she stared at Ben. She went very pale and still, wondering if she was daydreaming again. So often, she'd thought how it would feel if he ever came to see her. Now she was struck dumb by the impact of it.

Ben took off his hat and swept back his hair, smiling quietly as he looked at her across the counter. ''Yes, you may,'' he replied. ''I'm on my way to the bookstore to buy a book on how to grovel. I've never done it before,

you see, but I think I've reached the age of enlighten-
ment. I'd like something to do with sackcloth and ashes
as well, if they have it, so that I can do the thing
properly.''

Faye put down the book she was slowly learning to
read—Tennyson, in fact—and just stared at him.

He moved a little closer so that he could lean against
the counter. His eyes went to her small, soft hand resting
there. No rings of any kind graced their whiteness. "You
look blooming, Faye," he said after a minute. "Are you
well?''

"Yes." The word sounded more like a squeak than a
syllable.

"You didn't answer my letters," he said, with soft
accusation.

"There seemed little point," she managed slowly. "I
do very well by myself. And you have your career."

"My career will do just as well with a family as
without one," he said simply. "You see, I've discovered
that I was searching for myself in all the wrong places. I
wasn't in Paris at all, Faye. I was right here," and he
touched his fingers very gently to the gray fabric over her
heart.

She jerked back, flushing. "Ben, you mustn't!" she
exclaimed, looking quickly around to make sure no one
had been looking in the window.

He smiled. "You're not my old Faye at all, are you,
darling?" he said softly. "You're very proper these
days. You don't even sound the same."

"I've been improving myself," she explained.

"You never needed improving," he said, watching
her. "You were always generous and giving and over-
flowing with love. I was the one who needed improve-

ment. I won't say I've achieved it, but I think I'm somewhat better than I was when I left. Take a chance on me, Faye?'' he added, his face somber.

''Be—because of the baby?'' she asked.

He shook his head. ''Because I need you,'' he replied. ''I didn't know it, but I do.''

''You don't love me.''

''Don't I?'' He took her soft hand in his and lifted it to his mouth. ''I've never been with any woman the way I was that day with you—when we loved each other so tenderly. If that wasn't love, I'll never know it at all.''

She hesitated. He'd hurt her very badly, and she wasn't sure that she wanted to risk her heart again.

''I don't know.'' She touched her swollen belly and suddenly jerked.

''Are you all right?'' Ben asked quickly, his face a study in horror. ''Faye!''

''She . . . kicks,'' Faye said hesitantly, and blushed.

''What?''

She reached for his hand uncertainly and, glancing around quickly to make sure they were alone, she laid his fingers against the hard mound of her stomach and let him feel the baby's feet pushing against them.

He gasped. He blushed and then he paled, and his eyes were full of astonishment, wonder. His fingers moved. ''Faye, I can feel . . . a foot!''

''Yes, of course,'' she said, laughing involuntarily at his absorption. ''Ben, they move. Didn't you know?''

''No!'' His hand flattened over his child and he lifted his eyes to hers. ''Oh, Faye. You've got to marry me now!''

''I can't go to Paris—''

''I'm going to buy a house here in town,'' he

interrupted. "You can go ahead with your job, if you like, while I write."

"The baby will interfere with your solitude . . ."

"I'll watch the baby while you're away," he said, with grinning practicality.

"That would be scandalous!" she gasped.

"So what? Don't you like shocking people? You must, to be working in that blatant condition." He leaned over the counter. "Marry me. I'll keep you in fashionable poverty and drive you mad with lovemaking."

She laughed. It was the first time she had in months. "Oh, Ben," she said, exasperated.

"One little word. It's very easy to say. Just, yes."

She hesitated. But the baby kicked, and Ben's smile widened, and she caved in. "All right, then. Just . . . yes."

His eyes twinkled. "I knew you would."

She hadn't, until now. But when he took her in his arms, as close as the baby would allow, it all came right. He kissed her warmly, hungrily, and then again.

"Wait a minute," he said abruptly, lifting his head and frowning. "You said—*she*—kicks!"

"I want a little girl," she said simply.

"But you don't know . . ."

"Well, Ruby says I'm carrying very much behind and I'm very wide, so it must be a girl. Boys are high up and very rounded in front."

"Old wives' tales," he scoffed.

"Just you go ahead and laugh," she said. "It will so be a girl. You'll see."

Teresa Margaret Whitehall was born three hectic weeks later. Ben and Faye had been quietly married two days after he'd arrived home, and he'd moved them into a small but neat house near the dress shop. As he'd promised, he kept the baby while Faye went out to work. The neighbors just shook their heads and smiled when he pushed the baby down the sidewalk in her pram. But they were kind smiles, just the same.

Turk unexpectedly inherited a piece of land near Victoria, Texas, and after much deliberation he and Katy moved there after their daughter, Mary Elizabeth, was born. Cole gave Turk a seed herd of his best Santa Gertrudis cattle to start with, and Turk grinningly promised that he'd parlay them into an empire. He was already on the way. He'd renovated the old Spanish house that sat on the property and named it Casa Verde. It was one of a kind, like the ex-flier himself. Katy was supremely happy, content with her loving husband and her little girl. There were frequent unsigned cards from Chicago. They came on Katy's birthday and Mary's. They came at Easter, Christmas, and sometimes on Valentine's Day. As Mary grew older, presents accompanied the cards. Turk snarled at first but as time went by and he grew secure in the love of his family, he unbent enough to overlook the attention from his old rival.

It did disturb him that he had no son to leave his holdings to. But Mary was a delightful child who'd inherited his blond hair and Katy's green eyes, and was as open and loving as her mother. She'd have sons, he supposed. Anyway, he had the moon. At least he had a child. Cole didn't. That had to be the one bare spot in his friend's plain of happiness.

The family had all come together for a Fourth of July celebration. It was early 1926, and the country was temporarily prospering as stock prices kept going up and up. Cole had actually made some investments through his business partner in Chicago, and had made enough to pay off Wardell and put a huge chunk of money in the bank as well. He'd invested in still more stocks and was on his way to wealth.

Lacy hadn't invested her money in stocks, despite all his coaxing. She'd put it in land, instead, even buying into Turk's enterprise over near Victoria. Land, she said, was safer than banks; he'd see one day. He only laughed.

She was walking with Mary Elizabeth, picking wild-flowers in the field near the house, when her head began to spin and she fainted. She came to with Cole's white face above her, his arm cradling her head.

"I'm so sick," she managed.

"Here, dear," Katy said, placing a cold, wet cloth on her head. "I didn't tell Marion. She's not doing at all well today herself."

"Good thing you didn't," Cole muttered. "Her heart is giving out. Lacy, sweetheart. Can you get up?"

"I don't think so." She groaned. "It must have been something I ate."

Katy grinned. "Really? You haven't kept breakfast down one day this week."

"I know." Lacy sighed. She looked worriedly up at Cole. "I didn't want to tell you. It's enough that Marion's so poorly without your having to worry about me. I can't imagine what's wrong."

Katy was laughing. She laughed until tears ran down her cheeks.

Cole glared at her. "Illness amuses you?" he demanded angrily.

Katy sat down on the ground. "Oh, Cole! Are you both blind? Don't you really know what's wrong with her?"

Lacy lay very still. Her monthly hadn't come. She'd thought it was because of all the upset over Marion's deteriorating health, but no emotional upset had ever made her late before. She wasn't just late, either. She counted mentally and blushed. There had been a very long night about six weeks ago that had left her exhausted and Cole strutting.

Cole's arm under her head was rigid. "But, it . . . can't happen," he said falteringly. "I'm not able to father a child."

Tears were blinding Lacy. Sheer joy shot through her slender body like lightning. "They didn't say you couldn't," she whispered, oblivious to Katy's shock, because she'd never been told the extent of Cole's injuries. "They said it was *unlikely*." Her voice broke. "Cole . . . I'm pregnant!"

He clasped her close, his tall body shaking. He buried his face in her throat and seconds later she felt the wetness, heard the throb in his voice as he whispered how desperately he loved her.

Katy had discreetly left them alone, but from the barn, Turk spotted Lacy apparently lying in the road with a shattered Cole supporting her, and he ran across the field to get to them.

"My God, what's happened?" he asked urgently, dropping to one knee beside them. "Is she dead?" he added, because Cole's face was wet.

"She's . . . pregnant!" Cole choked.

Turk's face relaxed, and then seemed to glow with wonder. He looked down at Lacy's pale face, her blue eyes almost too big for it, drenched with tears and blinding joy. "Well, my God," he said, chuckling. "Bolting down the slats worked, didn't it?"

"You son of a—"

Turk guffawed with delight, jumping out of range of Cole's furious blow. "And you said you couldn't! You'll strut for a month, now, I guess—and be so smug you won't get a lick of work done!"

Cole gave up and laughed. "I'll beat your head in later."

"I'll keep it ready for you," Turk said complacently. "Lacy, are you all right?"

"I'm fine," she whispered tearfully. "Oh, Turk. I'm just fine!"

Cole got up and lifted her, tenderly, into his arms. He couldn't take his eyes from her face. "Lacy," he whispered, and bent to kiss her with reverence and wonder.

She kissed him back, aware somewhere in the back of her mind that Turk had gone off grinning to share the news with the rest of the world. Lacy didn't mind. She could hardly contain her own joy. And Cole's was overwhelming.

Their son was born seven months later. Marion's death had been the only shadow on their delight, but the birth of the child took some of the edge off their keen mourning. They named him Jude Everett Whitehall. Two years later, another son was born, and he was called James. Two miracles, their mother and father related when they were old enough to understand. Their joy was complete.

James never married. He became a doctor and opened a practice in San Antonio. Jude married a young debutante named Marguerite and produced two sons, Jason Everett Whitehall and Duncan Whitehall. Turk's daughter Mary married a Texas rancher with a huge property of his own. Casa Verde passed eventually to Turk's nephew and namesake, Jude Whitehall. The younger man moved there with his family and lived very happily for many years. Ben became a bestselling novelist and made a mint. He and Faye bought property in San Antonio and treated their daughter Teresa, whom everyone called Tess, to the Grand Tour when she came of age. The Great Depression wiped out Cole's investments, but Lacy had kept out of the market, so the ranch prospered even then and grew to enormous size and fame.

Turk and Katy had a long and happy life together. When she was eventually widowed, a wealthy financier named Blake Wardell from Chicago appeared out of nowhere to comfort Katy and Mary Elizabeth and tie up all the loose ends. The community around Victoria was scandalized when less than six months later, Katy married the Chicago philanthropist—with no protest whatsoever from her radiant daughter Mary—and went off to live in Chicago. Mary surprised everyone by studying medicine and following in her cousin James's footsteps. She became the first woman doctor in Spanish Flats and eventually married a neighboring rancher with her doting stepfather to give her away.

All that, however, lay far in the future as Cole carried Lacy back toward the ranch house. He had yet to hold his first child in his arms.

"So long ago," Lacy said softly.

He searched her eyes. "What was?" he asked, smiling tenderly.

She smiled back. "I was thinking of the first time I saw you, sitting on horseback when the car drove up at the steps. I think I loved you then, you know. You were every dream I ever had." The smile faded. "You still are. You're everything!"

He had to catch his breath and get rid of the lump in his throat before he could speak. "No, little one," he whispered. "You are." He bent and kissed her softly. "You're the world and everything in it. I'll love you until I die, Lacy. And forever after."

She snuggled closer and closed her eyes as his long strides took them to the house. The sun was just going down in the afternoon sky. Lacy watched the lazy red patterns in the clouds before Cole stepped up onto the porch. Another day past. But now every new one would be complete in itself, every minute would take on new meaning, new joy. She clung to Cole with her heart in her eyes.

"It's only begun!" she whispered. "Cole, we've got all the tomorrows there are!"

He nodded. "All the tomorrows there are, my darling."

He carried her into the house, to the uproarious congratulations and laughter of the rest of the family. Love filled the very walls that day—and all the days that came after.

About the Author

Diana Palmer lives in the north Georgia mountains with her husband, James, and their son Blayne Edward. She spent sixteen years as a newspaper reporter and columnist before "retiring" to write novels full-time. Since 1979 she has written over forty books, won numerous awards, including four national Waldenbook Bestseller Awards, two Reviewer's Choice awards from *Romantic Times*, and a regional "Maggie" RWA Award. In 1985 and 1988 she was named one of the top ten romance writers in America by the *Affaire de Coeur* reader's poll. She is also known to romance fans as Diana Blayne and Susan Kyle.